SURVIVORS

SURVIVORS

Martin Tillmanns

Matador
9 Priory Business Park,
Wistow Road, Kibworth Beauchamp,
Leicestershire. LE8 0RX
Tel: 0116 279 2299
Email: books@troubador.co.uk
Web: www.troubador.co.uk/matador
Twitter: @matadorbooks

ISBN 978 1788032 926

British Library Cataloguing in Publication Data.
A catalogue record for this book is available from the British Library.

Printed and bound by CPI Group (UK) Ltd, Croydon, CR0 4YY
Typeset in 11pt Minion Pro by Troubador Publishing Ltd, Leicester, UK

Matador is an imprint of Troubador Publishing Ltd

For Jill

PROLOGUE

It was perhaps inevitable that mankind would be the architect of its own downfall, just four short weeks for thousands of years of civilisation to unravel, perhaps for millions of years of human evolution to draw to a close. What at first seemed a freak and terrifying chain of events, unforeseen, deeply unfortunate and to some an "act of God", could equally be viewed as mankind reaping the fruits of its own labour, having sowed the seeds of its own destruction.

Evolution selected man as the planet's dominant species, supplanting hundreds of millions of years of lower lifeforms but it was only over the last ten or twelve thousand years that the species demonstrated the advantages of its intelligence through the development of agriculture, the formation of communities and, in due course, the construction of great cities and ancient marvels of engineering. Man subjugated lower species for his own benefit and began to make his mark on the planet which was surely there for the greater good of mankind. Achievements in mathematics, writing and philosophy confirmed his pre-eminent position in the world.

Yet modern science would trace its origins to a little over four hundred years, a mere blink of an eye in the evolutionary timescale. The pace of development increased exponentially with the Scientific Revolution and the Renaissance paving the way for the industrial transformation of the eighteenth and nineteenth centuries, the rise and fall of empires and ever more effective ways of killing one's enemy. Science became the new religion. Man could conquer diseases, traverse the globe in a matter of hours, harness the energy stored in the Earth for millennia, explore the Solar System and even attempt to understand the Universe. Surely mankind could create the most glorious future both on this planet and even beyond? If a species could achieve so much in a few centuries, what could it do in a thousand years, ten thousand, a hundred thousand?

But surely this has happened elsewhere? Our galaxy alone contains billions of stars and from recent observations most are likely to have planets, some of which will fall within the "Goldilocks zone" to facilitate life. The building blocks of life do not appear to be uncommon and once it arises, evolution will eventually produce higher lifeforms with large enough brains to develop intelligence. Given sufficient time and favourable conditions the same scientific discoveries could be seen as inevitable. Even if the odds were stacked against the genesis of technologically advanced civilisations, the sheer weight of numbers of stars in the galaxy would still ensure the presence of thousands of such civilisations with the technology such as radio to contact one another. So where are they? The absence of alien visitations to Earth is hardly surprising given the extreme challenge of interstellar distances, even between neighbouring stars, but how do we explain the absence of radio contact and the complete failure to date of the CETI project to locate intelligent alien lifeforms. Some will conclude that the development of intelligent life on Earth was such a freak occurrence that it was unlikely to be replicated elsewhere, that man is probably alone in the galaxy, perhaps even the universe.

There is however a more logical alternative deduction. The conditions for life and course of evolution have within the vast scale of the cosmos created thousands of technologically advanced civilisations but they have each endured for a relatively short period of time in astronomical terms, such that they have little chance to co-exist and communicate. Even if an alien species that had reached the technological level of generating radio transmissions endured for a further thousand years, it would have existed in such an advanced state for an infinitesimally tiny fraction of the universe's timespan of over thirteen billion years. We could conclude that civilisations have risen and fallen throughout the history of the universe but have not survived long enough to make contact. If so, is it inherent in any advanced civilisation that they will eventually destroy themselves? Some could be extinguished by natural disaster, such as a massive asteroid strike, but any intelligent species with more than a few centuries of technological development would surely be capable of tracking asteroids on a collision path in sufficient time to engineer the required adjustment in the asteroid's trajectory. The far more probable scenario is that they were the cause of their own destruction, possibly through advanced forms of warfare, whether nuclear, biological, chemical or some horror as yet undiscovered by mankind, possibly through disturbing the ecological balance of the planet or maybe through the creation of artificial intelligence, a race of robots that outgrew their programming. The method may vary but the result is the same, another civilisation disappears and the celestial silence continues.

The tragedy for mankind is that the terminal event happened so early in the human story, no time for the eradication of poverty and disease, global harmony and the end of war, harnessing of nuclear fusion for cheap energy, hotels on the moon, or colonies on Mars. Just so many pipedreams. Mankind's vanity was finally exposed as foolishness and the frantic pace of technological change was brought to a sudden halt.

At first nobody appreciated the full significance of what was unfolding as it was a natural disaster which set in motion a chain of events both terrifying and unstoppable. People followed the developing story through the media, especially television, first with interest, then shock and anger, finally in despair.

PART ONE

CHAPTER ONE

PANDORA'S BOX

It was a pretty ordinary day, much like any other, or so it seemed at least, perhaps a little warmer than one might expect for October and yet the world would never be the same again. Like billions of others around the planet we pursued our routines with our ordinary little families in our ordinary little towns, others in teeming cities enjoying opulent wealth or perhaps just scratching out a living, blissfully unaware that we were at a turning point in human history with all questions of inequality, race, or religion subsumed to the simple distinction of victim or survivor.

Sue caught the news first, around 6.30 in the evening, hoping to find the weather forecast on channel 130. I was just bringing our dinners into the sitting room so we could eat in front of the TV. It was only the two of us that evening as Lucy had a sleepover with her best friend Emily and Jo was still at school at choir practise. I would be driving over from Buxton to pick her up from school in Macclesfield after dinner.

"Look at this Tom, another earthquake in China."

A global news agency was reporting breaking news of a "major earthquake" in China, recorded at 8.1 on the Richter scale.

"Wow, that's a big one! Anything over 7.0 is serious but 8.1, that's really exceptional."

The reports were only just coming in and were very sketchy.

The quake apparently struck in the Heilongjiang Province in north-east China and the usual statements were being issued on the lines of "extensive structural damage and fatalities are expected." The news reporters were desperately seeking somebody knowledgeable to interview and repeating endlessly the few facts to hand.

"God! Channel 130 is like watching paint dry. We can catch the proper news tonight," I suggested, switching to the usual Channel Four offerings of holiday property searches. After all, it was China. They were always having earthquakes and I had no idea where Heilongjiang was. This wasn't going to affect us. It was a fair conclusion to make at the time, however misguided.

*

Sue and I settled down to watch the BBC news at ten. Lucy had phoned in to say goodnight and Jo was tucked up in bed, a little tired after her late finish at school. The earthquake was serious enough to dominate the news schedules and the media were now sufficiently organised to draft in various academics to fill the information vacuum.

George Aliboah was the BBC anchor man and confirmed the sketchy details. The quake had struck at 2.15am local time (18.15 GMT) in the Heilongjiang Province in north-east China near the Russian border. The epicentre was close to the provincial capital of Harbin City, the location of which was displayed on screen for the benefit of over 99% of viewers who had never heard of the place. Henceforth, they would never forget it.

The media had been unable to contact local news agencies or obtain any eye-witness accounts, so reports were generally comprised of talking heads, most notably Professor Karl Steiner from the European-Mediterranean Seismological Centre. The professor confirmed that this was indeed one of the most powerful earthquakes anywhere in the world in recent years.

Asked whether such events could be expected in the region, he helpfully replied "well, yes and no." Yes, there was a long history of earthquakes in China, recorded since 1831 BC and, incredibly, over 800 Chinese quakes in excess of magnitude 6.0 had occurred in the last century alone, killing over half a million people, but one on this scale was unusual in the north-east of the country. The good professor explained the configuration of tectonic plates and seismic belts, accompanied by some impressive on-screen graphics but was a little less convincing in attempting to explain why none of the seismologists had predicted the quake.

Questioned on the likely impact, the professor was again hedging his bets. Whilst the magnitude was a major factor, the depth of the hypocentre – where the displacement actually occurred – could be significant in determining the intensity of the shaking on the surface at the epicentre, whilst casualties would depend upon the proximity of population centres such as Harbin.

"Have you ever heard of Harbin?" I asked. Sue looked blank and shook her head. We prided ourselves on being pretty well informed on world affairs but had to admit that China was a bit of a gap. Not only had neither of us ever travelled to China but we didn't even know anybody else who had done so.

"We'll get more detail in the Telegraph tomorrow," I said, conscious that that was my response to most events.

*

The following day was just as routine. It seems tragic looking back that we were all ignorant of the disaster unfolding but how could we be otherwise? Earthquakes happened and this was on the other side of the world. The front page of the Telegraph focussed on domestic politics with just a brief note of the earthquake, though a double-page spread inside contained similar graphics to the previous night's TV, lots of expert analysis and the history of Chinese earthquakes. I perused this sitting at a table seat on the train to Manchester, my regular commute, recognising many of my fellow travellers doing the same things they always did, reading novels or newspapers, knitting, a young girl carefully applying her make-up and many just catching up on sleep.

Arriving at the tax office and chatting in the kitchen amidst sundry late breakfasts, the conversation centred on the previous night's football with barely a passing reference to the earthquake. Just another ordinary day.

*

That evening after dinner we packed off Lucy and Jo to complete their homework whilst Sue and I settled down in time for Channel Four News, fronted by Jon Frost, which devoted the bulk of their broadcast to the unfolding disaster. Some of the international news agencies had obtained access to the area, if only by air, and Channel Four's correspondent on the scene was Stephen McDougall from Australian ABC News who was asked to describe what he had seen:

"Well Jon, I've covered many disasters for ABC but I have never before seen the like of this. The city has simply been levelled. We flew over the scene at 11.00 this morning in a light aircraft with the Chinese authorities and I can only describe it as total devastation. We made a number of crossings of what is, or rather was, a very large city – it's the provincial capital – and I couldn't see a single building left intact. The city centre is just a heap of rubble. There are many high-rise buildings, as you might expect of a modern Chinese city, but there's nothing left more than a few storeys. I am familiar with Harbin but it was difficult to distinguish streets or landmarks, just endless rubble. I did spot Saint Sophia Cathedral, the fabulous old Russian Orthodox church, revered by the thousands of Russian immigrants in pre-revolutionary China – a few walls were standing but the spire and roof had collapsed. We flew over the amusement park where the famous Harbin Ferris wheel, once the tallest in China, lay on its side, a mass of twisted metal. The suburbs of the city, where most of the population would have been sleeping when the quake struck, are literally flattened, buildings collapsed like a pack of cards."

Attention turned to the potential rescue efforts on the assumption that many thousands of people would be trapped in the rubble. McDougall reported that compared to the more remote locations of previous disasters such as Sichuan, the local infrastructure was favourable with good air, sea, rail and road links but the problem was the extreme level of devastation. Harbin had a modern international airport but the buildings had collapsed with reports of huge fissures in the runways. The city was also an inland port but the harbour was wrecked and all major bridges over the Songhua River were down. Reports on the state of the railways and roads were awaited but not expected to be any more favourable. The assumption was that the authorities would need to rely on helicopters and air-drops of relief supplies but the major concern was the high probability of significant after-shocks which would inevitably impede the relief efforts.

Frost introduced a studio guest, Professor David Marshall from Bedford College, University of London, introduced as an expert in the management of earthquakes and recovery efforts. There must be an expert for everything, I supposed. The professor suggested that although Harbin was outside the main earthquake zone, the experience of such events in China was such that the authorities would be well prepared and capable of responding quickly and effectively. He drew comparisons with the Tangshan quake of 1976 with over 242,000 fatalities. Tangshan had also been outside the most active zones but nevertheless experienced a 7.8 quake with the impact exacerbated by a 7.1 after-shock. The

7

city had fared badly as the buildings had not been constructed to a standard to resist quakes. Lessons however had been learned and following the International Decade for Natural Disaster Reduction, sponsored by the United Nations in 1989, the Chinese government had launched programmes to mitigate and prevent disasters, with all major cities having their own designated earthquake disaster management system. Professor Marshall went on to detail the institutional controls and infrastructure plans that should be in place. Frost pointed out that none of the plans appeared to have made much difference to the devastation described by their correspondent. The professor conceded that although in theory the modern building codes in China were up to international standards, enforcement remained a problem with contractors cutting corners to meet deadlines, substituting cheaper materials to cut costs and operating in a culture of bribery and corruption, concluding that, once again, the local population appeared to have paid the price.

There followed a video link with another academic, a Doctor Liu Chin from Edinburgh University, but her contribution was more personal in that she had grown up in Harbin and spent ten years in teaching and research at the Harbin Institute of Technology, apparently a well-respected Chinese university. The doctor was understandably distressed but managed to outline some of the key points in the history and development of Harbin from the earliest identified settlement on the banks of the Songhua River some 4000 years ago to the founding of a modern town in 1898 during the construction of the Trans-Manchurian Railway, it's growth under the influx of Russian immigrants and the building of the magnificent Russian Orthodox cathedral of Saint Sophia, in communist times used as a museum but now lying in ruins. Doctor Chin became quite animated in describing the cultural diversity, not simply the Russian heritage but as the fashion capital of China prior to the Second World War with a pronounced French influence. The city had been known as both "Oriental Moscow" and "Oriental Paris" and Doctor Chin recalled many walks along the central Zhongyang Street, almost a museum of European architectural styles with Baroque and Byzantine facades, little Russian bakeries and French fashion houses but also modern American fast-food outlets and Japanese restaurants, not perhaps what viewers might expect in a Chinese communist city. Doctor Chin was moved to tears by this point and Frost filled in with some statistics provided to him. Harbin was the capital and by far the largest city in Heilongjiang with six million inhabitants in the urban area.

We turned off the TV at that point, somewhat overwhelmed by the information and images.

"This has got to be one of the biggest earthquake disasters ever," I suggested. "I can't believe I'd never heard of Harbin. It must be virtually the size of Manchester. Imagine the whole of Manchester destroyed overnight. Incredible!"

"It sounds like a lovely city," added Sue. "That poor lady was so distressed. Perhaps we should send something to the relief fund. We might have a collection at school." Sue was head of the local primary school and organised collections frequently.

"Well, I feel sorry for all the people involved but I'm sure China can cope without our money. Half the stuff in our shops comes from China."

It was already clear that people were witnessing one of the greatest humanitarian disasters of modern times but nobody could possibly envisage just how great a disaster this would prove to be, not just for Harbin but for the entire human race.

*

The following day being Saturday and a welcome relief from the tedium of the Manchester commute provided a chance to study the Telegraph in depth over a leisurely breakfast. There was no debate now over the main news story. The whole of the front page and the first six inside pages were devoted to the Harbin earthquake and not just graphics and statistics but dramatic pictures to illustrate the human tragedy. However there were no Telegraph reporters on the scene. Most of the reports and all the photographs were supplied by the Chinese news agencies and those based in Beijing rather than locally. No foreign journalists had been allowed anywhere near Harbin but, in any event, the only way in was by helicopter. The airport was out of action and expected to remain so for some time. Rail connections were also severed owing to collapsed bridges and the situation was unlikely to change. The best prospect for large-scale relief efforts would apparently be the roads, all currently blocked but with teams working day and night to provide access. A number of relief teams were already in place, having been dropped by helicopter with essential supplies, some basic medical equipment and tents for temporary shelter. Pictures from state TV showed rescuers with helmet torches searching through the debris at night but the general consensus of reporters was that the authorities were overwhelmed by the scale of the operation, particularly as the structural damage had worsened considerably with two small aftershocks during the night. The main hospital in Harbin was out of use with most of the casualties being treated on site in makeshift camps and just a handful evacuated so far to specialist hospitals in Beijing. The Chinese government had welcomed the many offers of international assistance and gratefully acknowledged the disaster relief funds already established but had to date made no specific requests for outside intervention and emphasised that people should not attempt to reach the area. It was believed that the local authorities had the necessary equipment and technology, the problem being access and logistics, simply getting the resources to where it was needed and removing the severely injured which would inevitably take some time. Meanwhile, the world's TV audiences were gripped by the unfolding drama and pledged their support to the many financial appeals. Sue was right there but there was no way I would be sending money. If China could afford to pay exorbitant wages and fees for the best footballers or to dump excess steel production in the West, undermining our own industries, they could jolly well divert funds to supporting their own people. Anyway, we were already sending them money under the banner of international development.

I put down the Telegraph to chase up Jo as I was dropping her off for her riding lesson in half an hour. Sure enough, she was ready and eager to set off, definitely the highlight of her week. She had a real passion for horses and was desperate to have her own horse but it just wasn't practical, as I had to convince her every week. As I drove her the couple miles to Buxton riding stables she was clearly in high spirits.

"We're doing jumps today! Meg says I might be able to enter competitions next spring."

"That's great Jo but just be careful on the jumps. We don't want you breaking an arm or worse."

"Oh Dad, I'll be fine. Look, there's Amy Watson. She's getting her own horse." I suppose it was more subtle than the usual pleading.

"Yes well, Amy Watson lives on a farm. You haven't got the time to look after a horse, to say nothing of stables and paddocks and what have you. There's no way we're paying livery costs on top of your school fees."

"Right, got to go," and Jo was racing to the gate to meet the other kids, mainly girls of her age. It was good that she had active interests though Sue and I would both have liked to see her apply more commitment to her schoolwork. She was doing okay but nowhere near the level of Lucy, two years older but quite outstanding in her age group. She hadn't even taken a GCSE yet but was already talked of in terms of Oxbridge.

I tuned in to Radio Four on the way back and once again the Chinese earthquake dominated the news. Day Four of the emergency they called it and recovery efforts were well underway. It was announced that the main highway into Harbin had been re-opened earlier in the day with rescue workers pouring in, an estimated three thousand soldiers, over five hundred police and in excess of one hundred medical staff reported to be on the scene. That should make an impact. I wondered how long it would be before the rest of the world's media lost interest and returned to domestic issues, another couple days.

When I returned home Sue was watching channel 130, school books on her knee as usual. There were pictures from Chinese state TV as foreign journalists were still excluded from the Harbin area. The pictures showed huge expanses of rubble, teams of rescuers in orange overalls pouring over the ruins, aided by sniffer dogs, working through the piles of brick, concrete and wood in the effort to reach survivors. Now and then a survivor was pulled from the rubble to great jubilation but mainly it was dead bodies. Nobody was attempting to put numbers on the likely casualties but the general consensus was that the scale of the disaster was unprecedented. In the studio Professor Marshall from Bedford College was being asked to assess progress in the relief efforts.

"They've been working round the clock to clear a way into Harbin and broke through earlier today. In the last two days they've been relying on rescue crews and emergency supplies dropped by helicopter, workers tackling the rubble with shovels and even bare hands to reach survivors. Now they have vehicular access, the heavy equipment is arriving and rubble is being cleared more effectively. They will still need to work very carefully as many buildings could collapse further and there remains the danger of more after-quakes. People are still being pulled out alive after being trapped for three days."

The professor was asked to outline the problems the authorities would face in dealing with the disaster.

"Well, several major problems can be anticipated. The first

issue is that power has yet to be restored. We understand that work is ongoing to repair the lines and restore power, which they hope to achieve today. The second major issue is the water supply. Not surprisingly, given the extent of the devastation, the water pumping stations are badly damaged and pipes are fractured throughout the city. This will not be sorted quickly but emergency water supplies can be taken from the Songhua River and initially, a huge volume of bottled water has been trucked in today. The third crucial factor is shelter. Thousands of tents have been supplied and large areas on the edge of the city are being turned into makeshift encampments. The Chinese authorities have promised over a million sets of transitional houses but this is likely to take a few months to complete and, of course, winter is approaching. It is already bitterly cold at night to be sleeping in tents and it is certain to get much colder in the coming weeks. Truckloads of blankets and sleeping bags are being delivered but life will be very difficult for the survivors. There could be hundreds of thousands living in tents for some weeks."

Food supplies did not appear to be a problem. Once the main routes had been re-opened, supplies were flowing readily and the Chinese Red Cross were heavily involved deploying teams with food, water, medicines and rescue equipment. In addition, many Chinese citizens had spontaneously packed their cars with supplies and headed towards Harbin only to be turned back by the military. The State Council had issued a directive asking volunteers, tourists and anybody not trained as rescuers to stay out of the disaster area and this was being strictly enforced.

The medical teams were also better equipped with many military medical trucks providing x-rays for people with minor injuries and military doctors administering first aid. The local hospitals were beyond use but patients with minor ailments were being accommodated in tents outside the hospitals. Some of the severely injured were being evacuated to Beijing but these were the exceptions. The state news agency had estimated fatalities in excess of four hundred thousand and likely to rise much higher as bodies were recovered. It was officially recognised as one of the worst earthquake disasters of all time.

I left the TV to pick up the shopping list and head to Morrisons to do the weekly shop. Earthquake or not, we still needed to eat. Sue agreed to collect Jo from her riding lesson. I warned her of the pressure exerted by the example of Amy Watson but could see that this would be given short shrift. I knew Sue felt that Jo should be spending more time on her homework and a little less time riding horses, swimming, cycling and socialising.

*

The following day brought more warm, sunny weather, probably the last according to the forecasts. After breakfast I thought a little fresh air and exercise would be beneficial.

"It's a gorgeous day. Who's coming to the Goyt for a walk?" The Goyt Valley was the local beauty spot, just over the brow of the hill.

"Oh, I'd love to Tom but I need to finish a finance report for the governor's meeting on Tuesday. Take the girls," was Sue's predictable response. As a head teacher, Sue's weekends were not her own.

"I can't. I've got a history essay and maths to finish." Lucy was quick to produce her excuses where walks were concerned. However, I knew how conscientious she was in her schoolwork; her top grades were not simply the result of effortless brilliance.

"I'll come" said Jo. "Can we go round the reservoir?"

"Yeah, of course." I didn't need to ask why. The track around Fernilee Reservoir was a favourite for all the local dog owners. On a sunny Sunday morning it would be full of dogs and Jo's love of dogs was second only to horses.

It was busy alright. We managed to park only by driving half way up a grassy bank but as we had taken the Jimny I was confident it wouldn't get stuck in the mud. The reservoir was stunning, a deep blue reflecting the clear sky above and the sun catching the surface like a sparkle of diamonds. As expected there were dogs everywhere, most of them off the lead and determined to enjoy themselves. Stout Labradors were plunging into the water to retrieve balls, Spaniels were sniffing in the undergrowth and little terriers were barking at everything that moved. Jo was loving it.

"If we had a dog, we could bring it here every weekend."

"Jo! Give it a rest. I love dogs as much as you do but we're all out during the day. It just wouldn't be fair on a dog."

"Leanne's got a dog and they're all out. They have a dog-walker." Why was there always a friend to undermine my argument?

"You shouldn't have a dog if you're not prepared to exercise it. I'll be retiring at sixty, that's only nine years. We'll get one then."

"Nine years! I'll be twenty-one! I can't wait that long."

"I'm pretty sure you'll have other priorities by the time you're twenty-one Jo."

"Yeah, horses! I could start my own riding school."

Further down the track there was something of a commotion as a huge black Great Dane had taken exception to a yapping terrier. A somewhat frail and elderly man was attempting with some difficulty to rein in the Dane which was clearly in the mood to sort out the upstart terrier. Its owners finally succeeded in picking up the terrier, possibly a Jack Russell, and moved on looking rather aggrieved at the elderly man. The Dane then turned on me and Jo with a booming bark and almost pulling over its owner, who was shouting at it angrily. I crouched down and put forward a closed fist towards the Dane.

"Hey, hey, now then. You're alright. Come on then." The Dane stopped barking and sniffed my fist, suspiciously at first, then allowed me to stroke under his chin. Before long, we were the best of chums and Jo joined in the petting. The old man explained that he was eighty-two and had always kept Danes but this one had been attacked as a puppy, since when it was unpredictable. He was really soft but other dogs or strangers could set it off. We continued on our way but I had to think the fellow was far too old to control such a big dog.

"How did you know he was friendly Dad?"

"I find it's not so much whether the dog's friendly but how people approach them Jo. If you're confident and relaxed with them, the dog can smell that you're okay but if you're nervous, they'll sense it immediately and you're more likely to get bitten. Just don't make the mistake of putting out your fingers. A balled fist is very difficult to bite. Anyway, you're far more likely to get bitten by a small, snappy dog like a Jack Russell."

I told Jo the story, probably not for the first time, of when I was a toddler visiting my aunt with Gran and Grampy, now long deceased. My aunt and uncle kept a small mixed farm and had an Alsatian bitch that had just produced puppies. My aunt had warned that the Alsatian was very protective of her pups and shouldn't be approached. The dog was chained up in an enclosure at the back of the farmhouse. At some point my folks were having a drink and realised I was missing. Fearing the worst, they dashed round to the enclosure only to find me happily sitting with one arm around a puppy and the other around its mother. Jo loved the story, always keen to hear about Gran and Grampy, who had both died before Jo had started school. Her other grandparents were still alive but had retired to Cornwall and we didn't see them as often as we should.

On the short drive back from the Goyt Valley I caught the radio news. The situation in China was no longer top of the schedules but a brief update was provided of the recovery efforts, the only new factor being reports of a flu-like infection said to be ripping through the temporary encampments resulting in some fatalities, which I found a little surprising.

The following day I was doing a spot of gardening, the start of the autumn clear-up when Sue called me in to see the TV news. The flu infections had now become the main story with the astonishing development that an emergency quarantine had been placed on the ruined city of Harbin. The BBC obtained a report from Jane Li, its correspondent in Beijing:

"People will be aware of yesterday's reports of the flu outbreak in the temporary encampments. This has spread rapidly through the camps and most people are now infected. The illness is exceptionally severe and people are dying in their hundreds. The medics have been attempting to identify the strain and source in order to supply the most effective drugs and specialist epidemiologists have been brought in. They have not given a firm conclusion but believe the most likely source of the outbreak is apparently some experimental virus from a research facility which had maximum security until the earthquake intervened. The virus is considered to be so dangerous that the quarantine has been imposed while further investigations are carried out. All movement of people in or out of the Harbin area has been suspended until further notice, the only exception being medical specialists investigating the outbreak. They are being brought in by helicopter and have special protective suits."

"That's incredible!" I exclaimed, perhaps stating the obvious. "A huge city in quarantine? Protective suits? What the hell's going on?"

"I suppose they can do that sort of thing in China without our pre-occupation with human rights", observed Sue.

"Sure, but 'experimental virus', 'specialist epidemiologists', there's more here than they're telling us. People don't die in their hundreds from flu in a matter of days, surely?"

We followed the news all day, switching channels to get the best coverage. Every news studio seemed to be hosting a fierce debate, interspersed by web-cam reports from China and around the world. Many were suggesting an over-reaction by the Chinese authorities. Although specialists had arrived equipped with bio-hazard suits, large numbers of unprotected relief workers already in Harbin, the army, police and non-specialist medics were effectively trapped in the centre of infection. Considerable doubts were expressed over the official explanation of a flu outbreak given the number of fatalities so quickly. However, Channel Four News was contacted on-air by a Doctor Mark Lipton, a specialist in epidemiology at the Harvard School of Public Health and he appeared on screen via a web-cam in Boston. After some initial exchanges with Jon Frost, Doctor Lipton outlined the basis of his concerns:

"I sincerely hope that I'm wrong, that this is simply a precaution on the part of the Chinese, but I fear this is the disaster of which I have warned for years but my pleas have fallen on deaf ears. This almost certainly involves the Harbin Veterinary Research Institute, a biological research facility under the Chinese Academy of Agricultural Sciences. It is the oldest such research institute in China and they've been at the cutting edge of epidemiology and specifically control of the Avian flu virus. In fact there are lots of such viruses, commonly referred to as bird flu and classified H5N1. There have been a number of bird flu epidemics caused by people coming into contact with infected birds. It's a serious form of flu but doesn't spread rapidly. There are also many varieties of human flu virus which spread easily from person to person and can be fatal in exceptional cases but humans have built up a lot of resistance and we can develop vaccines. The problem with flu viruses is that they constantly mutate and become drug resistant. The great fear of epidemiologists such as me is that one day a new bird flu virus for example could combine with a human flu virus and spread rapidly from person to person. This would be a recipe for a global pandemic. To see how we might tackle such a situation, the Harbin institute have been seeking to create such a virus. This work was originally banned but the moratorium was lifted in 2013 after consultations with the health organisations. A number of us argued at the time that this was irresponsible and dangerous but we were overruled. The speed with which this infection has taken hold and the number of early fatalities, which we can expect to increase very rapidly, indicates a high probability that one or more of these mutated viruses has escaped from the research facility in the earthquake damage. I hoped I would never see this day but it's fair to say that mankind has just opened Pandora's Box. God help us all."

"What's Pandora's box?" said Jo.

CHAPTER TWO

CONTAGION

For the first time I resorted to Google to find out what was already known about these issues. Harbin, which I had never heard of before the earthquake, produced an extraordinary number of hits, as did the Harbin Veterinary Research Institute. It was quite astounding. It was all there, the research, the mutated viruses, the ethical debate, WHO deliberations. How could I not be aware of this? I relied on the Telegraph to keep me informed. Why was nobody warning us that this could happen? Delving into the sources of information, it was almost exclusively confined to technical and scientific journals, reports from such places as the Pasteur Institute in Paris and the Erasmus Medical Centre in Rotterdam as well as some of the well-known universities. It was more like reading an academic debate. The moratorium on the mutated virus research had been lifted in 2013 and some criticism from scientists was reported but not in the mass media. Would this have been regarded as unprofessional scaremongering? The more I read, the more I began to accept the wisdom of the Chinese authorities to impose quarantine so quickly.

I passed on the results of my searches to the rest of the family, as even Jo was now taking an interest. Lucy had been using Twitter or something as an alternative source of information and found an explosion of conspiracy theories mainly centred around weapons research and biological warfare, though admittedly somewhat low on evidence. However, the situation was so extraordinary that we felt anything was possible.

Monday morning and the commute to Manchester was an unusual experience. The train passengers were either buried in their newspapers, some of which carried the most alarmist headlines, or engaged in animated conversation with apparent strangers, which was simply unheard of on the 07.24 to Piccadilly. There was no sleeping, no knitting, just total engagement in the one story that had gripped the world. Okay, the same young lady was still applying her make-up but some things never change.

At the early morning office kitchen debate, for once the weekend's football was forgotten in favour of the events in Harbin. As I entered, Clive was holding forth as usual to several concerned-looking colleagues.

"It's obvious, its biological warfare agents, anthrax or something equally deadly. You're not going to get so many dead in a few days with normal illnesses."

"But what about this flu vaccine research," I interjected. "I checked it out on the internet and it was well documented in academic circles."

"An obvious cover story. This is China you know. They can drip feed whatever they want to the media without being challenged. Any biological weapons research has got to be top secret. I mean, they might have done some flu research as well, as a front like, but you don't get people dropping like flies with the flu."

"I must admit, that was troubling me," I conceded, "but they're not talking about normal flu, are they? This is some hybrid created in the laboratory. If people haven't got any resistance, they could die quickly."

"Nah!" Clive wasn't buying it.

Rebecca, one of our young trainees, piped up. "Actually, I did a project at Uni on the social effects of the First World War, including the flu epidemic which followed, the worst pandemic in recent history. A lot of apparently healthy people, young adults and so on, caught the flu and were dead by the following day."

"Maybe, but they didn't have much in the way of drugs in those days." Clive was having none of it. "It's weapons mark my words."

"Anyway, never mind that." It was Greg. "What about City's result on Saturday, eh?"

*

The media stuck to the issue of virus research as the cause but was no less enraged. Questions were being asked in Parliament on the theme of who knew what and why this research had been permitted. The official line was to exercise caution until the virus had been fully analysed but academics and politicians across the globe demanded an authoritative statement from the Chinese. This was finally released at 19.20 GMT on 16 October; six days after the earthquake had struck:

"The People's Republic of China acknowledges the legitimate concerns across the world over the recent events in Harbin City and wishes to assure all people of the top priority the Chinese state applies to the serious situation and the actions being taken to contain and address this emergency.

"For a number of years the People's Republic of China has pioneered research in tackling the influenza virus. A highly specialist team led by Professor Hualan Chen, the director of China's National Avian Influenza Reference Laboratory at the Harbin Veterinary Research Institute, has been at the forefront of this research. Part of this work involved mixing the H5N1 bird flu virus with a recent strain of H1N1 human flu virus in order to counter the risk of facing a highly contagious and deadly form of virus. The work succeeded in creating a number of mutated viruses which were passed by airborne transmission between laboratory guinea pigs. These viruses are of course extremely dangerous and a very high level of security was maintained at the research facility. We must stress that the research has been approved by the World Health Organisation and the results have been reported in the appropriate international publications. This is not secret research and the fruits were to be shared with the whole world. The ultimate objective was to develop a generic vaccine which could eliminate all forms of influenza as it mutates.

"We have to report that this work is in its early stages and no such vaccine has yet been developed. Unfortunately, on 10 October the Harbin area experienced an earthquake of magnitude 8.1 which is almost unprecedented in this region of China. The research facility was designed to withstand all forms of natural disaster but the intensity of the quake was totally unexpected and major sections of the facility have been destroyed. As the earthquake struck in the early hours of the morning, only a handful of staff was present. Some are known to have died and three are unaccounted for. It is thought likely that they are under the rubble but these bodies have not yet been located.

"It has been reported that an influenza outbreak has spread rapidly through the temporary encampments set up for the survivors of the earthquake. This outbreak is showing a very high mortality rate. We have just over 15,000 confirmed fatalities and around 300,000 infected patients. In the last 24 hours specialist epidemiologists brought in for this purpose have confirmed that the nature of the infection is the mutated viruses, though several different strains have been identified. The vaccines we have currently available are not effective and fatalities are expected to increase to much higher levels.

"Faced with this serious situation, the city of Harbin has been placed in quarantine. There will be no movement in or out of the city. Medical specialists and military personnel are already in place and will remain for the duration of this emergency. A small number of casualties of the earthquake were removed to hospitals in Beijing before the quarantine was applied. These number 36 and have all been re-located and placed in an isolation ward with top security. They are being monitored for any signs of infection. The absolute priority is that the infection does not spread any further. Meanwhile several other research institutes are being prepared to develop an effective vaccine.

"The People's Republic of China greatly regrets the unfortunate situation which has occurred and gives total assurance that whatever is necessary will be done to contain and eradicate the problem".

Channel 4 News followed the announcement with a video link to Professor Day at Oxford University, formerly Government Chief Scientist and Past President of the Royal Society. He gave his reaction to the statement:

"Well, this just confirms our worst fears. Epidemiologists have always warned of the nightmare scenario of this type of mutation which in theory could have occurred naturally but was extremely improbable. To create such a dangerous mutation in the laboratory and allow it to escape is just beyond belief and now 15,000 innocent victims have paid the price. I have gone on record in warning against such dangerous research and relying upon laboratory containment. It's appallingly irresponsible. Natural disasters are obviously unpredictable but you simply can't take a chance with such a potentially deadly virus. What we essentially have here is a totally new virus, or rather several, never experienced before, against which people have no natural immunity and no effective drugs. On top of that, you have a closed environment in those encampments that will enable infection to spread rapidly"

Professor Day speculated that the mortality rate could easily exceed twenty or thirty per cent, possibly much higher. With fifteen thousand fatalities within a few days, the prognosis was dire. The viruses could continue to mutate outside the laboratory and had the perfect environment to multiply. Frost pointed out that the World Health Organisation had apparently approved the research. Did they not share responsibility?

"To some extent. This research has been reported for some time. You can check the articles in the journal "Science" amongst others. The Harbin research originally used a 2009 strain of human flu virus, combining it with bird flu to produce 127 different viral hybrids and five of these were shown to pass by airborne transmission between laboratory guinea pigs. Two separate studies in 2011 caused alarm. Ron Foudrinier of Erasmus Medical Centre in Rotterdam and Yoshihiro Hashiko of the University of Wisconsin in Madison succeeded in creating airborne versions of the H5N1 bird flu that passed between ferrets. A number of us expressed strong concerns and for a while we had a voluntary moratorium of the H5N1 research, banning transmission studies using ferrets. However, the moratorium was lifted in 2013 after consultation with the health organisations, so there was nothing to stop the Harbin institute continuing with these experiments.

The professor dismissed the prospect of an early vaccine as this would require a great deal of research and development and even longer to manufacture on a commercial basis to produce the sort of quantities that may be required. However, he endorsed entirely the Chinese decision to place Harbin in quarantine as the only effective solution was one of containment.

We were all glued to the TV screen and Sue was becoming very anxious. "What if they can't contain it? It could spread to Britain and there's nothing we can do."

The girls were starting to look worried. I decided to put a brave face on it. "There's no point getting worked up. They now know what's happened and what they need to do. It's probably the easiest containment site you could have, a ruined city with broken transport links and all the survivors herded together into camps. I wouldn't want to be one of them but I can't see them allowing it to spread." I probably sounded more confident than I felt but nobody looked too convinced.

I was conscious of Sue tossing and turning that night and hoped for better news in the morning.

*

The following day brought a continued escalation in the crisis. Indeed, the developments in China had sparked a sudden resurgence of interest in epidemiology, albeit from a rather low base. BBC Radio Four addressed the demand by commissioning a special report examining the science behind the flu outbreak. Sue chose to escape the depressing news by watching "Housewives from New York" or San Francisco or somewhere, basically an exercise in conspicuous expenditure, whilst Jo was at a late swimming lesson, so Lucy and I decided to spend the evening catching up with the Radio Four feature. Biology was one of Lucy's best subjects at school and she intended to take science 'A' levels.

Presenter Hugh Morris was joined in the studio by Doctor Paul Spencer introduced as a specialist epidemiologist from Nottingham University. The discussion was prefaced by the news that fatalities in Harbin attributed to the virus had exceeded eighty-five thousand and that seven of those evacuated to Beijing hospitals were confirmed to be infected and were held in an isolation unit.

Doctor Spencer was asked to explain to the listeners why the Harbin outbreak was proving to be so deadly.

"Let me first explain what flu is. Influenza is what we class as an RNA virus. RNA stands for ribonucleic acid. The virus itself may exist in any shape from round balls to long spaghetti – like filaments, which is what we would see in a sample of the virus under a powerful microscope. The genome of this virus is associated with five different viral proteins and is surrounded by a liquid membrane. This means that flu belongs to what we call in the trade the "enveloped" group of viruses. Eight separate pieces of ribonucleic acid or RNA make up the flu virus genome and each piece of RNA specifies the amino acid sequence of one or sometimes two of the virus's proteins. This may sound very technical but the essential point is that the segmented nature of the RNA allows different flu viruses to easily "mate" with each other to form hybrid progeny viruses with bits of RNA from each parent virus. This is a natural process which is happening all the time, so the flu you may catch this year is not the same virus that you may have caught the previous year or say ten years ago. This is why we talk of seasonal flu and different strains of flu and need to customise specific vaccines to protect people. It is impossible, at least with our current medical knowledge, to immunise a person with life-long protection against flu, such as you might with say smallpox, measles, mumps etc. This constantly changing nature makes the flu virus a very successful organism.

"So how do you get the flu? Most people will be aware that such infections generally spread by coughing and sneezing. This is because tiny droplets of fluid are carried through the air, generally up to around a metre. It can also spread by touching if we get these drops of fluid on our hands. Once these drops of fluid containing the virus gets into our nose or throat, the virus invades living cells and grows inside them. This is the only way that any virus can replicate. It goes on to make thousands of new virus particles from the cellular machinery and moves on to infect other cells.

"You asked why it is deadly. For the common types of flu passed between humans, it generally isn't unless there are underlying weaknesses in the victim caused by age or other conditions, particularly breathing difficulties such as asthma. To give you some stats from recent American research, around thirty-six thousand people will die from flu in the USA in a typical year. That's bad enough but when you consider that between thirty and sixty million Americans catch flu each year, you can see that the mortality rate is tiny."

Morris pointed out that far more than thirty-six thousand had died in Harbin within a few days.

"That's because it's not a human flu virus that we're dealing with, but a hybrid mutation created in the laboratory. Their starting point was a strain of avian flu or bird flu as it's commonly called. The avian flu viruses far outnumber the human flu viruses. We classify them as H5N1 and under the microscope we see two proteins that stud its surface like spikes on a mace. This virus can pass from birds to people but doesn't tend to do so readily, so outbreaks of bird flu tend to be limited in their extent but can certainly be fatal. It most commonly breaks out in countries where it is normal for people to live in close contact with birds, typically in Asia. Once people are infected with bird flu, it doesn't spread easily from person to person. The difference in Harbin is that they've mixed the avian flu virus with a strain of human flu virus, which is less dangerous but very infectious. If the two flu viruses come together by infecting the same cell, they can swap genetic material and produce hybrids by the re-assortment of genes. A number of studies have shown that the H5N1 class of viruses have the potential to acquire mammalian transmissibility by re-assortment with human flu viruses. Previously published research from Harbin demonstrated the creation of a hundred and twenty-seven different viral hybrids between H5N1 and H1N1 and five of these could pass by airborne transmission between guinea pigs. Any of those five hybrids in an uncontrolled environment would be capable of causing a global pandemic not seen since 1919 when over twenty million people died. We're dealing with highly dangerous, highly infectious viruses against which people have no natural immunity and no available vaccines. The seriousness of this situation cannot be underestimated."

So did Doctor Spencer feel that the situation justified the extreme measures taken in placing an entire city in quarantine?

"I think it does. Of course we're not talking about a normally functioning city which would be extremely difficult to quarantine. Harbin City was all but destroyed by the earthquake. In effect, the quarantine applies to the tented encampments on the outskirts of the city where the survivors were being kept pending a more permanent solution, still hundreds of thousands of people but very little movement. For those people of course there is very little chance of escaping the virus, or viruses rather as it appears that a number of hybrids have escaped the laboratory. Most of these will not spread easily and if they cannot find hosts to infect, will die out within weeks. It's the airborne hybrids that are the problem, passing rapidly from person to person. One cannot imagine what the conditions are like in Harbin. With eighty-five thousand already dead, there will be many more infected, by now probably the bulk of the population, including the many soldiers, police, medical staff, Red Cross personnel and other relief workers who were brought in before the outbreak was identified. None of them are allowed to leave and no further personnel will be brought in to assist. No doubt many of them are already included in the mortalities. They've been handed a death sentence but realistically, what is the alternative? It would be impossible to bring out all those at risk and keep them in isolation. The risk of these viruses spreading further is just too great. The epidemic has to run its course and can only be tackled by absolute containment. The only way the virus will die is if it runs out of living organisms to infect. That will have to be the ultimate objective of the quarantine."

Doctor Spencer considered that the quarantine would be necessary for at least two weeks after any fresh cases had arisen, possibly longer to err on the safe side. But what of the infected removed to Beijing?

"Obviously it was not known that these people were infected

when they were moved and it is not clear when they started to show symptoms. Had the medics known what virus they were carrying, it is very unlikely that they would have been brought into Beijing. They are being monitored in isolation wards but if the virus escapes into the community it would be unstoppable. We just have to hope that all those infected are held in isolation. It's still possible that others among the thirty-five rescued could develop symptoms, or even worse have already infected others in which they came into contact before the severity of the situation was appreciated."

Morris invited Doctor Spencer to speculate on the worst case scenario if further cases arose outside the quarantined areas.

"It depends on the numbers involved and geographical spread. It may be possible to tackle isolated pockets if they are identified early enough but it is almost impossible to contain something like this once it gets loose. We are talking about at least several mutated hybrids and possibly more. These are completely new viruses against which we have no immunity. If they spread through the general population, they will continue to mutate as they spread. It's like a number of epidemics coinciding. It's even possible that an individual could survive one virus and then catch another. The situation would be unprecedented."

Morris suggested that in such a scenario the young and the elderly would be most at risk?

"Not necessarily. The flu always kills a lot of elderly people because they are otherwise frail or infirm. People of any age with breathing difficulties would be at risk. However, relatively healthy young adults can also be at risk simply because their body's immune system is generally strong but not experienced in resisting these viruses. The body goes into overdrive defending itself and people can drown in their own fluids. If you look at the global pandemic of 1918-19, a high proportion of the victims were young adults, not just children and the elderly. In short, nobody would be safe in such a pandemic."

It was sobering stuff. I found myself almost wishing we had joined Sue for 'housewives'.

"Do you think it'll reach Britain Dad?"

"Well it seems to me as long as the problem is confined to Harbin and the hospital in Beijing, they can keep a lid on it until it's finished. If it gets loose in Beijing, it could end up anywhere. We should know within days, then, if necessary, we start taking precautions but they'd have to act fast. One thing for sure, it would be a long time before it reached little old Buxton." I hoped this was reassuring. "Anyway, I need to get Jo in a minute."

As I drove to the Pavillion Gardens swimming pool and waited with the other parents for the swimmers to emerge, the air of normality was comforting as we seemed so far away from the events in China. As the children left the building in little groups, I was pleased to see Jo in animated conversation with a taller girl. She was very often on her own as most of the kids were older, Jo being a very strong swimmer for her age, and most of them attended the local Buxton school whereas Jo was at a fee-paying school in Macclesfield, which didn't go down too well.

"Hi Dad!" Jo came bounding up. "That was so much fun. We started on life-saving tonight."

"Wow, that's impressive. Who was that tall girl with you?"

"Oh, that's Heather. We were paired up. I had to save her and then she had to save me. It was hard work though."

"Brilliant! It's such a good skill to have, especially at your age. There are not many twelve year olds who can do life-saving, I'm sure."

Jo looked pleased with herself, then noticed the sky, crystal clear with a magnificent display of stars. I decided to test her. "Okay then, where's north?"

Jo turned round and studied the shapes of the constellations until she spotted the Great Bear. "There! The one that looks like a saucepan. Right, the last two stars, continue the line up, there it is, Polaris!"

I had taught her well. "Well done Jo. You'll never get lost at night."

*

The following day it was fairly late before the most dramatic news broke. The girls were already in bed when Sue and I settled down for the specially extended BBC ten o'clock news. Anchorman George Aliboah reported that the first cases of infection within the general population had been detected in Beijing but first they covered the even more sensational story of a firefight outside Harbin City. Coverage switched to their regular correspondent in Beijing, Stephen McDougall of Australian ABC News.

"Good morning George or good evening rather. Its 6.00 am here in Beijing but the news agencies are abuzz with the events of the night. Reports are somewhat patchy but it appears that a small convoy of military trucks, maybe three or four, left Harbin sometime after midnight. This movement was not apparently authorised and it would appear to have been some form of breakout from the quarantined city. It's the military of course who are enforcing the quarantine but it's not known whether military personnel were manning the trucks or whether this was some form of civilian action. The alarm was raised and fighter aircraft were dispatched from a military base somewhere near Beijing. The convoy was intercepted heading towards Beijing on the main highway some one hundred miles from Harbin. A rocket attack ensued and the convoy was destroyed in a massive fireball. That's pretty much all we know but we are expecting an official statement in the next hour or two.

"It certainly demonstrates how seriously the Chinese are treating any risk of this virus spreading from Harbin. Equally, one can only imagine how desperate these individuals were to attempt to escape in this way. No official mortality figures from the Harbin encampments were issued yesterday but there are credible rumours that deaths exceed fifty per cent of the population. People trapped in Harbin are clearly viewing this as a death sentence."

McDougall was asked to confirm reports of the infection spreading within Beijing.

"Yes. We believe there are six suspected cases which have been placed in isolation. They have severe flu symptoms but the source has not yet been confirmed as part of the Harbin outbreak. In a place the size of Beijing, you'll always find people with flu but the fact that these six have been placed in isolation does indicate a concern. It may be nothing more than a cautious approach which people would agree is justified given the dreadful mortality rate in Harbin. The authorities know this has to be contained and will do whatever is necessary."

Within forty-five minutes a statement was released via Chinese state television:

"At 1.20 am today an illegal attempt to break the Harbin quarantine was terminated by the intervention of attack aircraft. A convoy of four military trucks was destroyed by rocket fire. There were no survivors. Any further attempts to break quarantine will be dealt with in a similar manner. The viruses causing the Harbin quarantine are known to be particularly dangerous with an extremely high level of pathogenicity. The only effective response is total containment.

"The People's Republic of China regrets the heavy loss of life in Harbin but the viruses released cannot be allowed to spread further. Three cases of infection from these viruses have been identified in Beijing. Investigations are continuing to establish how these infections were contracted and whether any further cases are likely. These individuals are being treated in an isolation ward at the Peking Union Medical College Hospital in Dongcheng District. People known to have been in contact with these individuals in recent days are being held in quarantine and monitored for signs of illness. The health authorities will do everything possible to contain this outbreak and there is no need for people to panic. Any people experiencing flu-like symptoms are required to report to the nearest clinic for testing. A list of the clinics with the appropriate facilities will follow this statement."

There was something about the "required to report" that was more threatening than re-assuring but international support was forthcoming for extreme measures. The mood in Beijing was reported to be one of shock rather than panic and compliance with instructions was anticipated. The listed clinics were located all over the city and were said to be well organised and equipped to deal with the situation.

Coverage continued on the news channel but at 11.00pm and with work the next day, we decided to turn in.

"It's not looking good, is it?" said Sue as she switched off the TV. "It's only a matter of time before it spreads here. We'll need to make plans."

"Well, that'll be for the Government and local authorities. It'll have to be contained."

"I mean *we* need to make plans. We have to keep the girls safe."

"Of course, but this is still a problem for China. Let's not start panicking, just carry on and monitor developments."

"I'll tell you what. If this reaches Britain, or rather *when* it reaches Britain, there'll be no question of carrying on. We'll look after ourselves."

"Okay, just wait and see. We might be worrying over nothing." Deep down, I think I already knew I'd regret those words.

*

By the following day the mood in Beijing had changed markedly. The initial shock at the presence of the virus in the capital and the ruthless rocket attack on the attempted escape from Harbin was supplanted by escalating panic as the clinics were overwhelmed by people wanting to be tested either because they may have flu symptoms or simply to be given the all clear. Much of the demand was created by a government directive earlier in the day that any person attempting to leave the city by purchasing an air, train, bus or boat ticket must present a certificate from one of the designated clinics to prove they were free of the virus. People were advised not to travel unless their need was essential but after events at Harbin, that simply added to the panic. The authorities had set up check-points on all routes out of Beijing and were turning back any cars without certificates for all passengers, the many check-points manned by armed police and soldiers, with unconfirmed reports of shots having been fired.

Panic was further inflamed by rumours that the official count of confirmed Beijing cases exceeded eighty-five but the numbers changed by the hour. What was very clear was that infections were no longer confined to the isolation wards and further that it seemed extremely unlikely that even eighty-five cases could all be linked to contact with the original Harbin evacuees. New cases were springing up all over the city and many commentators were suggesting that the use of the clinics was merely exacerbating the situation by bringing infected people into contact with crowds. The general feeling on the street was that the authorities were losing control of the situation and had no coherent strategy. The increased presence of the military on the streets did nothing to ease the panic.

I had meetings out of Manchester and spent much of the day in the car keeping abreast of developments on BBC Radio Five which had shelved much of its usual sports coverage to focus on the unfolding crisis. A Doctor Spencer, an epidemiologist at Nottingham University was giving his reaction to events:

"There is no wish to spread panic but we have to be very concerned. This is no ordinary virus we're dealing with here. In fact we're informed that seven separate strains of these mutated viruses have now been identified. There may yet be other strains or they may be continuing to mutate. It's very clear that the viruses are highly contagious and exceptionally lethal. It will be a long time before we are able to develop effective vaccines and at present people have no defence. The situation in Harbin was dreadful but at least it was contained. With cases spreading rapidly through Beijing, it's going to be extremely difficult, if not impossible, to contain this."

Doctor Spencer concluded that the only feasible treatment was palliative care within strict isolation conditions. The Peking Union Medical College Hospital had been cleared of all other patients and reserved exclusively to deal with the outbreak, all staff equipped with bio-hazard suits. The principal problem was admitting patients before they had infected other people. With eighty-five or more confirmed cases, many of them were likely to have been in contact with a number of other people, possibly in crowded railway stations, buses, shops and offices. Those contacts could easily pass on the virus by coughing and sneezing without realising that they were seriously ill. The numbers affected were likely to increase exponentially.

The BBC had requested a response from the Department of Health and a spokesman confirmed that the situation in Beijing was being carefully monitored but with no reported cases in the UK, there was no need for panic measures. However, people were advised not to travel to China until the position had been fully assessed.

*

Every day brought a marked escalation in the crisis and the media devoted all their resources to just one story, now dubbed by the tabloids as the "Harbin Flu". On 22 October, just ten days since the earthquake struck, came the news that all of Britain had dreaded, the first confirmed cases in the UK. The whole population was glued to televisions in mounting panic. Jon Frost at Channel 4 News was joined in the studio by Doctor Colin Marshall from University College, London, "an acknowledged expert in epidemiology", and Linda Travis, Minister of State for Health. First he invited a summary of the day's developments from Chris Murphy.

"Thank you Jon. The Harbin Flu, which has all but wiped out the city where it originated and is now devastating Beijing, has officially reached Britain. A businessman was taken ill in High Wycombe, Bucks earlier today and was diagnosed in the local hospital as a suspected case. He was airlifted to St Bart's Hospital in London where an emergency isolation wing has been opened and it has been confirmed as a case of Harbin Flu. The businessman, who has not been named, is in intensive care and said to be in a poor condition. Later this afternoon a taxi driver in London's West End collapsed at the wheel, causing a minor accident. He has also been moved to Bart's. The businessman is known to have visited China in the last few days and returned to the UK on 20 October. He flew from Beijing Capital International Airport to London Heathrow by Virgin Atlantic Airways flight number VS 7937 leaving Beijing at 1.05 pm local time – that's 5.05 am GMT. Metropolitan police are tracing all other passengers on that flight for emergency check-ups. It is considered most likely that the businessman contracted the virus either at or on route to Beijing Airport. The taxi driver, who has not been named, had not left the UK in recent weeks and the strong possibility arises that he has come into contact with an infected passenger. He was not on contract hire and there is no way of tracing his passengers.

"Meanwhile, several cases have been reported in the USA, two in San Francisco and one in Chicago. They are all reported to be seriously ill. The fatalities are climbing rapidly in Beijing with in excess of 3000 confirmed cases in hospital and over

800 deaths. Many thousands more are attending local clinics to await diagnosis. The World Health Organisation has advised any person who has travelled to Beijing since 12 Oct or has been in close contact with such a person to report for a check-up. Jon."

Frost turned to Marshall. Could we expect London to go the way of Beijing?

"Well, people are entitled to be concerned as this is a very serious situation. We already know that this is one of the most deadly viruses ever encountered, or should I say groups of viruses, as the Chinese have already identified at least seven separate strains of these mutations, which will make it all the more difficult to develop vaccines. Currently, there is no effective defence and there's not likely to be for some time. Added to this is the speed with which this is spreading. The Harbin situation was exceptional and tragic in that one couldn't have created better conditions for a virus to spread, but just look at the situation in Beijing. On the first day of reported cases we had six confirmed, yesterday it was eighty-five and today over three thousand. Despite the best efforts of the Beijing authorities, that situation is out of control and we can expect the virus to spread throughout the city. We already have eight hundred deaths effectively two days into an epidemic, indicating an almost unprecedented level of pathogenicity. When we hear of London taxi drivers being infected, I'm not sure our attempts at containment are going to be any more successful that the Chinese. We are on the cusp of a global pandemic here and one of unprecedented severity."

Just how bad could this be, probed Frost. Didn't twenty million die in 1919?

Doctor Marshall continued to respond in measured terms.

"Generally, we'd say we're much better equipped to fight flu today than in 1919. However, we need to know what we're fighting. Very little work has been done yet on these new hybrids, simply to identify them, let alone develop effective drugs. We know we're faced with at least seven viruses which spread easily and kill rapidly, so the dangers cannot be overstated. It would be reckless and irresponsible to start putting numbers on it."

So how will people know if they've got this? Should people start panicking at the first sniffle?

"Initially it could be mild but from the Chinese experience, it would not stay mild for long. Flu can typically take four or five days to incubate after infection. In other words, you could be in contact with an infected person and not show any symptoms for several days. Once it takes hold, typical symptoms would be a very sore throat, quickly developing into a chesty cough which is increasingly difficult to clear. You are also likely to experience headaches, general weakness and aching joints, high temperature leading to a raging fever. You'll know it's not a normal cold but it could still be a conventional strain of flu. We would need to test it with a saliva swab or preferably, a blood test."

Frost turned to the Minister, Linda Travis, who was looking distinctly uncomfortable. What exactly had she put in place to deal with this?

"Well, let's not start panicking at this stage. The situation in China is very serious but we have two cases in the UK. It's far too early to start talking about pandemics. I want to assure the public we're taking this very seriously and all appropriate precautions will be taken. Our first priority is to trace if possible how these two men became infected. We know one travelled to Beijing for a business meeting on 19 October and returned to Heathrow the following day. Apparently he felt unwell on 21st and was admitted to hospital earlier today. It would appear that he contracted the virus on the 19th or 20th, so whilst travelling back to London it is unlikely that he was infectious. However it's possible that other passengers on that flight were exposed to the same source of infection, especially if it was at a crowded airport terminal. We have the flight manifest and are in the process of tracing all the passengers who embarked at Heathrow. We've also identified a few foreign nationals who flew on to other destinations and have alerted the relevant authorities. Fortunately, that was the only direct flight from Beijing to the UK on 20 October, so we think we have a lid on this. It is possible that people took other flights out of Beijing with subsequent connections to other UK airports but in practice, that is unlikely. People would normally transfer from Heathrow. We are also tracing contacts of the individual since his return and no further cases have been found to date. We have not been able to establish how the taxi driver became infected. We understand he was picking up trade from taxi ranks or simply being flagged down, so we cannot trace his passengers. Again, his known contacts since he became ill, also on 21st, have been tested with no confirmed cases."

Frost turned again to Marshall who had informed them that incubation of the flu virus typically took four or five days but if this businessman was in Beijing on 19th and 20th and yet two days later was seriously ill in hospital, would that not suggest a much quicker process?

"It does. The four or five days is only a norm and from our experience of conventional flu. This is a completely new virus and we have no experience yet of dealing with it. The rapid increase in reported cases in Beijing does suggest that people are passing on this virus quite quickly. The symptoms are also developing very quickly with people becoming seriously ill within a day or so of presenting any symptoms. That's not so unusual but it does confirm the potency of this virus."

The Health Minister was asked what advice could be given to viewers.

"There's no need to panic but we do need to take sensible precautions. If you have any flu–like symptoms, get it checked out immediately. If you've been in recent contact with anybody you know has travelled to Beijing and you haven't been contacted by the local health authorities, make yourself known to them. A helpline will follow and that will be manned 24 hours a day. Follow the news for further updates."

Coverage then turned to the USA where Frost reported that three cases had been confirmed. He spoke to Don Lipsey, the Washington correspondent for an update.

"Jon, that's just been updated to five confirmed cases and a further eleven suspected. This morning we had two confirmed cases in San Francisco and one in Chicago. We now have a second confirmed case in Chicago and one in New York. Other suspected cases are also in New York and additionally in Los Angeles and Seattle. There's a very clear link with flights out of Beijing. The Chicago gentleman left Beijing on October 20 at 10.00 am local time on an American Airlines flight and one of the San Francisco victims was on an Air China flight leaving Beijing also October 20 at 1.36 pm. His wife, who did not travel to China, is also infected. Other passengers on these flights are being traced as a priority. The suspected cases in New York, Los Angeles and Seattle have not yet been linked with travel to Beijing but there were flights direct to all three cities on October 20. A United Airlines flight to New York left Beijing at 1.18 pm local time, a United Airlines flight to Los Angeles left at 1.46 pm and finally, a Hainan Airlines flight to Seattle left at 4.35 pm. As a precaution, passengers on all these flights are being traced. Those were the only direct flights from Beijing to US airports on that date. Health authorities are working on the assumption that the virus was most likely spread within the airport terminal on October 20. In the meantime isolation facilities have been established in all five cities where the confirmed and suspected cases are being held. In San Francisco, patients are held at the Saint Francis Memorial Hospital. In Chicago they're using the Vanguard Weiss Memorial Hospital. In New York it's the New York Community Hospital in Brooklyn. Los Angeles are using the UCLA Medical Centre and Seattle the Harbourview Medical Centre. All medical centres throughout the USA are reviewing their facilities as a precaution. A major constraint is the supply of bio-security suits to protect hospital staff treating their patients.

Suits are being dispatched to all major city hospitals and suspected flu victims will only be admitted once full isolation protocols can be applied."

The mood in the TV studio was increasingly sombre as every report served to escalate concerns with no available straws of optimism to clutch. No reports of infection outside China, UK and USA had yet reached the news media but this seemed to be only a matter of time. A consensus had emerged that Beijing Airport was a hotbed of infection, with reporters checking the flight schedules since 20 October but as one of the busiest airports in the world with around seventy-five flights an hour at peak times, the task was hopeless.

Frost contacted Li Chang from Chinese State TV for the latest casualty figures in Beijing.

"Eight hundred and sixty dead but this number is climbing every hour. There are now three thousand four hundred confirmed cases admitted to hospital. Three hospitals are being used exclusively to treat the infected, the Peking Union Medical College Hospital, the Beijing number 1 Hospital, which is part of the Beijing Medical University and the Beijing Emergency Medical Centre at Qianman West Street. Isolation facilities have also been set up at the 301 and 302 Military Hospitals. There is scope to handle considerably larger numbers if the outbreak does not diminish. In the last half hour two major announcements have been made. The Beijing Capital International Airport has been closed until further notice and the quarantine of Harbin has been ended. At first light, in around four hours' time, survivors will be airlifted out of the encampments but will continue to be kept in isolation for further tests. I don't have the number of survivors. The medics are keen to test the blood of people who have contracted one of the viruses but pulled through."

Frost suggested that shutting the airport at this stage was a case of slamming the door after the virus had bolted?

"Perhaps", replied Chang, "but this was a huge decision to

take. This is one of the busiest airports in the world and nobody is aware that it's ever been closed before. It was so crowded with people trying to get out of Beijing that it had become a breeding ground for infection and it doesn't have the medical facilities to deal with this. Everybody is being told to go home and stay there."

Inevitably, residents were taking to the roads but the military had formed a ring of road-blocks around the city with orders to shoot any person attempting to pass. It seemed to most observers that Beijing was beyond salvation but the more terrifying thought was how many other major cities around the world would follow the same path.

"It's not going to stop, is it?" Sue was ashen-faced. "What are we going to do?"

Jo had escaped to her room, ostensibly to finish her homework but more probably to avoid any more depressing news. Lucy was chatting excitedly to her friend Emily on her mobile telephone. I felt I ought to say something vaguely reassuring on the lines of "there's only a handful of cases in the UK, let's not panic, we've seen it all before with SARS, swine flu, Ebola, it's never as bad as predicted" but had to admit I was coming round to Sue's view of impending disaster. To see one of the world's great cities reduced to chaos was really quite humbling. I was saved from making an immediate response by the telephone, Sue's mother on the landline. Now Sue had to adopt the more composed stance.

"Yes, we've been watching it on Channel Four News, its dreadful, isn't it? – Well, perhaps they'll be able to contain it better over here; they were caught on the hop in Beijing, weren't they? – I wouldn't panic at this stage, I'm sure it'll be a long time before anything reaches Plymouth – I'll talk to Tom but I don't think we can come down this weekend."

I was shaking my head vigorously as I departed to the kitchen to put the kettle on.

"Mum's really worried. She thought we might want to bring

the girls down. I've put her off for now as I don't think we want to be travelling. We'd have to go past Birmingham and Bristol, maybe use the services, anybody could be infected."

"I agree. It's not the time to be travelling long distances while events are moving so quickly. We'll stay put over the weekend and follow the news – see what we want to do on Monday. If it spreads to Manchester, I don't think I'll be going into work. It's just not worth the risk."

"I don't think you should go in anyway. It's only a matter of time, isn't it? They fly to China from Manchester, don't they? I bet somebody's already brought it back, then they'll be on those trains infecting everybody. It'll be in Buxton soon. I'll have to think about closing the school. Of course we've had no advice from County, typical!"

"I think everybody's struggling to keep pace with it. Let's see what the weekend brings and then we'll make some decisions. We'll not take any risks."

CHAPTER THREE

ISOLATION

The decision was effectively taken for us the following morning with the dreaded headline across the media, "Harbin Flu goes global" as reports of infection flooded in from around the world. The news in the Telegraph was bad enough with virtually the entire edition given over to the crisis but was already surpassed by the breakfast TV news with reports and numbers of victims constantly updated. There was an air of panic in the studios as the news teams struggled to keep up to date. Major outbreaks had been declared in Leeds, Birmingham and, as we had feared, Manchester in addition to the anticipated escalation in London. The Government had responded by calling an immediate meeting of Cobra and the world financial markets were in meltdown. There was no escaping the severity of the situation and no dissenting voices from the predictions of catastrophe.

Lucy and Jo were still in bed thankfully and spared the distressing scenes on TV whereas Sue and I watched in shocked silence. The crisis was described as a 'serious escalation' as the outbreak spread remorselessly beyond London. In the capital itself, confirmed cases were reported as 126 with 15 fatalities, including the businessman and taxi driver that had formed the focus of the previous day's news. However, all the commentators suspected that many more cases were not being reported as people could see little evidence of any effective treatment. Over

30 infected patients were held in Leeds Royal Infirmary, 25 admitted to St Mary's Hospital, Manchester and 19 to Queen Elizabeth Hospital, Birmingham. Other smaller pockets of infection were arising up and down the country, including Edinburgh, Newcastle, Liverpool, Derby, Nottingham, Bristol and Southampton.

"Shit! Derby as well as Manchester. We've got it on both sides!" It wasn't like Sue to use such language but understandable.

'Experts' concluded that earlier attempts to identify how the outbreak had spread and tracing contacts of the infected appeared to have been pretty much abandoned.

"It's totally out of control, isn't it," I said, stating the obvious. "We'd better ride this out in Buxton, keep the girls off school."

"I'll have to close the school on Monday, whether County like it or not."

The telephone rang. "Yes, I know, we're watching it. I'll put Sue on." " It's your Mum again."

Sue left the room to speak to her mother while I caught the rest of the report. The emergency Cobra committee were meeting in half an hour at 9.00am. That'll make a fat lot of difference, I thought. The military had already been put on standby to deal with any civil unrest which seemed a little premature for the current situation but was surely prompted by the horrific scenes in Beijing and Harbin. The news studio switched to a video link to Beijing for an update from Li Chang of Chinese State TV to comment on the declaration of a state of emergency:

"The state of emergency is confined to Beijing. Attempts to contain the spread of the epidemic have been abandoned as it is completely out of control. The nominated hospitals have been overwhelmed and people are now being advised to stay at home, whether they have the infection or not. It is impossible to know how many are infected but it is estimated to be over twenty thousand. The numbers multiply every day. There is a heavy military presence on the streets to maintain order and prevent looting. No travel is permitted except for emergency services and a curfew is in place. People are very frightened."

Chang further reported the extreme shock at the news that only twenty-seven survivors were rescued from Harbin out of more than three hundred thousand held in the encampments. It was thought that the only survivors were those that arrived with protective equipment, mainly medical personnel. The authorities had decided it was impossible and perhaps dangerous to remove bodies or organise burials, instead a large number of incendiary bombs were dropped to destroy the encampments, distressing to any relatives of the deceased but considered to be unavoidable. Elsewhere, outbreaks were reported in many Chinese cities, all with air links to Beijing. All airports throughout China had been closed in a belated attempt to slow the spread.

Other reports were received of major outbreaks in over twenty US cities, most of the European capitals, the Middle East, Sydney, Rio de Janeiro, Cape Town and many other locations. Some countries were still attempting to contain the outbreaks but with little success. The World Health Organisation had declared a global health emergency and the Harbin Flu was now officially designated as a global pandemic.

*

I had heard enough and switched off the TV as Sue re-entered the room, having finished her call.

"Only twenty-seven survivors from Harbin. They've firebombed the place. Can you believe it?"

"My God! That's dreadful. It's going to reach everywhere, isn't it? We're just going to have to stay in the house. We surely can't catch it if we don't go out."

"True but a pandemic is going to last many weeks, if not months. We'd need to stock up on food at least."

"Okay Tom, we'll get straight to Morrisons and fill the car with as much as possible, then lock the doors and stay put."

It seemed an extreme solution but I had to admit I couldn't think of anything better. Even then, we had to hope the infection had not yet reached Buxton but we had to get food or we'd run out within a week and emerge into an even worse position.

"Quick, get ready. I'll wake the girls but they can stay here." Now Sue was on a mission.

Ten minutes later we were on the road. We tried not to panic the girls. We were just getting the shopping in early and then we'd be spending the day at home. Jo took some convincing that she'd have to cancel her riding lesson, the highlight of her week. I promised her that when this little problem was resolved, we'd look into the possibility of getting her a horse, although Sue was less than impressed.

We drove across town easily enough but as we approached the roundabout at Morrisons entrance we found ourselves at the back of a long queue, which was most unusual. We didn't move for several minutes, then edged forward a couple car lengths.

"This is ridiculous! What the hell's going on?" I didn't enjoy queueing at the best of times. "Perhaps I could double back to London Road and loop round Duke's Drive?"

"Oh Tom, what's the point? You'll only get to the same roundabout and we're in the queue now. We'll just have to wait and keep the windows shut."

While we waited we listened to more doom and gloom on the radio including a Government spokesman who advised against panic buying, assuring listeners that there were no supply problems at the shops. That made me feel a little guilty as I'd always been critical of panic buying but we had no choice if we were to isolate ourselves at home.

"One thing for sure," said Sue. "As soon as the Government advises against panic buying, people will do exactly that. We'll be lucky if there's anything left."

It took around twenty minutes to get to the roundabout but seemed a lot longer. The main problem turned out to be people turning left, then waiting in a short filter lane to turn right across the road into the petrol station. The queue from the other direction was as far as we could see and the result at the roundabout was virtual gridlock.

"Perhaps we ought to get petrol as well while we're here," suggested Sue.

"Why, if we're not going anywhere? We could be here for hours. Anyway, we've got half a tank and the Punto's reasonably full. I can't see why everybody suddenly needs petrol. Where are they all going?"

"I suppose people are worried it's going to run out."

"Well, it will now with a queue like that. Idiots!"

Eventually we squeezed across the roundabout out of the petrol queue and into Morrisons car park, knowing it would be even worse trying to get out again. Never mind, we were there now and we wanted food. We had to drive round the car park several times to find a space. I had never seen it so congested, even on Christmas Eve, which I usually tried to avoid.

"Okay" said Sue. "We'll take a trolley each. Get plenty of bread and fresh meat for the freezer, vegetables we can keep fresh in the garage and as much tinned and dry stuff as we can carry. Rice and pasta would be good."

The strategy was fine but achieving it something else. The bread racks provided the first shock, just stripped clean. The in-store bakery was located behind the racks and a lady assured us that plenty more bread was coming out. I stayed by the racks with a number of other determined looking shoppers while Sue went in search of fruit and vegetables. After a few minutes the lady that had spoken to us began to wheel a large trolley of bread and rolls to begin re-stacking the shelves. As soon as she emerged from the back she was pounced upon by the hordes, grabbing anything available. I'm ashamed to say that I joined them, spreading my elbows to gain space and securing the prize of a large wholemeal, a large granary and a pack of six rolls. Within seconds the trolley was empty and nothing reached the shelves, the lady assistant retreating into the back, somewhat shocked.

Sue re-joined me, her trolley containing two bags of potatoes, a pack of onions, some small bags of green veg and some apples. She was pleased to see the bread in my trolley. "My God," she said. "I didn't think it would be this bad. It's a good job we came early."

We fared a little better with the tins and dried goods, collecting a decent stack of tinned vegetables, soups, fruit and fish, even some tinned meat which we hadn't bought for many years. The fresh meat counter was little better than the bread. Overall, Sue and I were reasonably pleased with our purchases given the circumstances which were much worse than we had envisaged. The worst scare was in the toiletries aisle, which was quieter than most, when a burly man emitted a loud, explosive sneeze. The aisle emptied in seconds with shoppers scurrying away with alarmed faces despite the man's protestations that he was fine. It was still possible to sneeze without having contracted the Harbin flu and we all felt a little embarrassed. Nevertheless, Sue and I were relieved finally to return home, unload our groceries, store the Jimny alongside the Punto in the garage and lock the doors for the duration, however long that may be. It was an extraordinary feeling. Although at first I couldn't help thinking our strategy was an over-reaction or at least a little premature, our experience at the supermarket had convinced me otherwise. With sensible management, we had enough food for three or four weeks at least, while we could watch events unfold on TV and maintain our isolation in safety. It was hard to envisage where this would all end but at least we had the security of being locked in our home. We would open the door for no-one.

ONE WEEK LATER

It had seemed a simple enough objective, sit at home, keep ourselves safe and await developments but after one week we were climbing the walls. I must admit, I was restless after two days but I don't think in my entire life I had spent so long indoors. After a week I could hardly bear it. Just getting into the garden would have made a difference but we had ruled that out as we didn't have enough information on how the virus could spread. Obviously we needed to avoid contact with other people but what if it could be carried by birds landing in the garden or maybe the squirrels which were frequent visitors. Despite following every report on TV there was still no definitive guidance on the subject. It was generally accepted that the original mutations included bird flu, so it seemed possible that birds could carry it and yet we hadn't seen any dead birds. As for squirrels, they didn't seem far removed from the guinea pigs in the Harbin laboratories. Our isolation had to be total.

I think Sue and the girls took the incarceration better than I did, although there were complaints over missed riding and swimming lessons (which I suspected were not taking place anyway) and particularly being unable to see friends. At least they could keep in touch by telephone and compare notes. At first there were accusations that we had sought isolation earlier than anyone else. The girls' friends were still visiting each other and even offered to call on Lucy and Jo, offers which were politely refused. We also noticed for most of the week that our neighbours in the close were still coming and going in their cars, though less frequently as the week progressed. We felt we had made the right decision however as the flu reached Buxton soon after Manchester and reports of deaths increased rapidly.

Our isolation even extended to nailing a block of wood across the inside of the letter box. Initially I'm sure some items had been left on the step but after the first couple days we had seen no postmen in the close. I spent a lot of time in the study reading which afforded me a view of the neighbourhood and shouted alerts to the others, though by the end of the week the most significant sitings were cats and the occasional unaccompanied dog, which was unusual in itself.

We spent many hours in front of the TV but the regular schedules had been abandoned with most content clearly pre-recorded. The news media attempted to maintain a service but by the end of the week it was withering on the vine. Without any advertising and with diminishing staff, virtually none in the field, paper copies of newspapers had ceased (not that I would be venturing out to buy one in any event) with a few on-line versions struggling on as bulletins. Commercial TV and radio had ceased broadcasting, leaving the BBC as the last resort for public information and the final outlet for government communications, although the girls found plenty of alternative views on social media with conspiracy theories abounding. Stories of biological weapons continued to circulate but even more prevalent were suggestions that vaccines had been produced in small quantities but reserved for the establishment. Constant denials from government sources were treated with derision.

The BBC carried a public information broadcast on 30 October, some of which appeared to have been dug from the government archives of pre-prepared material:

"The group of viruses, commonly referred to as "Harbin Flu", are now endemic throughout the UK. Eight days after the first reported cases, there is no part of the country free from infection and efforts to contain the epidemic have been unsuccessful. There is no effective medication which can be supplied and in the vast majority of cases the infection proves to be fatal. There is little point attending medical facilities as this only increases the risk of spreading the infection.

There are a few basic precautions which can be taken to reduce the chances of infection:

Keep your contact with people to an essential minimum. All schools are closed until further notice and no public transport is operating. Contact your employer to find out what is expected. Many employers will have a Business Pandemic Influenza Planning Checklist or a Risk Management Plan. You are advised to stay at home wherever possible.

If you have to leave your home, wear a facemask, which have been supplied in sufficient quantity to every household, or a respirator if available.

Cover your mouth and nose when you cough or sneeze. Use a disposable tissue and flush it down the toilet immediately, then wash your hands.

Keep your hands clean. Wash your hands throughout the day, especially after touching other people or any surface that others have touched. Carry an alcohol-based sanitizer with you.

Stay healthy to boost your immune system. Get plenty of sleep, be physically active, drink plenty of fluids and eat nutritious foods.

Stock up with non-perishable foods, bottled water, over-the-counter drugs, health supplies and other necessities. A two-week supply is recommended. Have basic medical supplies to hand such as a thermometer, facemasks, tissues, soap and hand sanitizers.

If you or a member of the family is sick, plan to stay at home for at least 10 days.

Stay updated. Details will follow of the relevant websites and hotline numbers. Local government websites are also available. Consult local and national radio, TV news and newspapers.

That is the end of the public information broadcast."

The same day the BBC broadcast what would prove to be one of the last ever news bulletins from its Salford studio, the only remaining one still operative. The sole presenter was Jeremy Clarke, all the regular personnel having succumbed to the flu. The BBC promised to continue a service as long as a skeleton staff was available at Salford. There were no remaining TV crews in the field, the only pictures being provided by mobile telephones and webcams. Clarke reported the headlines:

"The Harbin Flu spreads relentlessly with every community in the country reporting extensive casualties. There is no sign of any effective vaccine and the advice to the infected is now to stay at home. The mortality rate is extremely high but no current data on the number of deaths is available. Towns and cities are progressively closing down. All sports fixtures have been cancelled, all schools closed and all public transport has been suspended. The supply network to food stores is patchy and there are reports of panic buying. Some stores are operating informal rationing. Some petrol stations are closed and others have long queues of motorists. Soldiers have been deployed in city centres to maintain order and deter looting, though many reports of looting are still reaching us. Abroad the situation appears to be similarly dire and several US cities have experienced extensive riots. The stock markets continue to plummet around the world with expectations that all trading will soon be suspended. Parliament has today been suspended but the Cobra committee continue to meet daily to coordinate efforts to deal with the emergency."

Clarke then introduced reports from the regions via webcams starting with Brian Greenhalgh in Manchester:

"Hello Jeremy. It's been unnaturally quiet here in Manchester today. There are no buses or trains running and very few stores are trading. Food shops have managed to stay open and are still being re-stocked but shortages are apparent and customers are being restricted in the amounts they can buy. All local and central government offices are closed. There is a heavy military presence throughout the city centre with soldiers and riot police visible on just about every street. They are heavily armed, in full riot gear and respirators, looking for all the world like Darth Vader out of Star Wars. It looks menacing but is also reassuring that the streets will not be surrendered to anarchy. As I say, it's been very quiet during daylight hours but since darkness has fallen there are groups of youths moving around but keeping a good distance from the security forces. I've spoken to some of the soldiers and they are prepared for a repeat of last night's violence which peaked in the early hours of the morning. There was some looting but generally just destruction of property with many windows broken and some stores set alight. Molotov cocktails were thrown at the troops with a number injured. Much of the violence centred on the Chinatown area of the city with several restaurants on Princess Street torched in an apparent attribution of blame for the pandemic. The restaurants were empty at the times, as you might expect. No loss of life has been reported but the army say they are authorised to fire at civilians if necessary to maintain order. It just feels like a tinderbox here and one expects the worst tonight."

The next report was curtesy of Paul Gray in Leeds:

"It's just kicking off here as it has for the last two nights. There are plenty of riot police and soldiers on the streets but they're heavily outnumbered by youngsters, many of them not even bothering to wear face masks. I'm standing in The Headrow in the city centre and there have been running battles between the gangs and the security forces for the last hour or more. No shots have been fired but missiles have been thrown and every so often there's a baton charge. The police are using loud-speakers to warn the gangs to disperse and the situation is looking ugly. A number of arson attacks were reported at stores in the Merrion Centre."

To complete the gloomy picture, Clarke brought in Kevin Fletcher in Bristol:

"A major escalation in the violence tonight after two nights of sporadic disturbances. The first shots were fired. A large group of youths had gathered in the Broadmead area of the city centre with random acts of arson, looting and vandalism. They were faced by massed riot police and troops and ordered to disperse but responded by throwing missiles and Molotov cocktails, ignoring warning shorts into the air. Some of the troops opened fire on the mob and I can see at least six lying on the ground in Merchant Street with apparent gunshot wounds. The mob have now split into neighbouring streets but show no sign of giving up. It looks like it's going to be a long night."

Finally, Clarke reported that the situation appeared to be even worse in the USA and was joined on the line by Harold Kent of CNN:

"Thank you Jeremy. The crisis has escalated for several days with widespread riots across many cities including New York, Chicago, Detroit and San Francisco. The President has declared a national state of emergency with martial law imposed across the nation. A curfew will be applied from 7 pm this evening, after which anybody found on the streets will be arrested. Any person resisting arrest, found looting or engaging in riots is liable to be shot. This follows pitched battles between the rioters and the security forces over the last two nights. Baton rounds and water cannon have been deployed in a number of cities but the use of live ammunition has been authorised to maintain order. There are many gangs on the streets and it seems unlikely that the curfew will be effective. Meanwhile, the body count of Harbin Flu victims rises exponentially. The hospitals have all but given up and local authorities cannot keep up with the number of burials and cremations required. Most communities have begun to dig mass graves to inter thousands of corpses every day. Nobody knows where this will end. People have flocked to churches of all denominations to pray for deliverance but in doing so increase their chances of contracting the virus. There is still no sign of any vaccine. It seems that mankind has sown the seeds of its own destruction and is powerless to interfere in the process."

There was no studio discussion to follow the reports simply

because there was nobody else in the studio, all the usual "experts" either dead or keeping their heads down. A very sombre Clarke wished his remaining viewers good luck and promised an update at the same time the next day, a promise he was unfortunately unable to fulfil.

This was sobering stuff. Looking back, I think we must have realised by this stage that nothing would ever be the same again. We had thought our isolation might keep us safe while the crisis passed, the authorities prevailed with the eventual return of normality. However, it was now becoming increasingly clear that from the comfort of our home we were witnessing something much bigger, nothing less than the breakdown of civilisation. When we finally emerged from our hibernation we would be faced with a battle of survival, a battle for which our little family seemed ill-equipped.

ONE WEEK LATER

The whole world seemed to be grinding to a halt. We continued to keep watch from the house but very little was moving, the passing traffic diminishing by the day and no neighbours spotted for several days. Whether they had succumbed to the virus, moved on perhaps to join family or, like us, were waiting it out, monitoring developments, we had no way of knowing. Even worse, Sue could get no response from her parents' telephones, mobile or landline, and as they didn't use email, had no way of contacting them. There could only be one explanation but I couldn't bring myself to voice it. Conventional news coverage on TV and radio had effectively ceased with a single presenter reading a bulletin, repeated regularly and occasionally updated. Most of the content seemed to be provided by the Government. There were no reporters as such. However, social media continued to peddle conspiracy theories. The very last broadcast we heard was on 6 November, made by a Government spokesperson:

"Good evening. This is Linda Hodgson speaking to you on BBC 1 TV and Radio 4 on behalf of the emergency coalition government. All regular TV and radio broadcasts are suspended but these frequencies have been reserved for government information updates.

"Following the death yesterday of the Prime Minister, most of the Cobra Committee are now dead or incapacitated. The acting party leaders have come together to form an emergency coalition government and, in the absence of Parliament, have assumed temporary power. Fifteen MPs, drawn from all the major parties comprise the new government which meets in a secure location outside London assisted by a similar number of officials. TV / radio broadcasts are relayed from this temporary seat of government and communications are in place to maintain complete control of the military and police. A state of emergency has been declared and martial law applied throughout the country. A 6.00 pm curfew has been invoked and will be enforced rigorously. There will be zero tolerance of any further disturbances and troops are authorised to use lethal fire if necessary to maintain order. All citizens are advised to stay at home for your own safety. Everybody will be aware that this virus is highly infectious and is usually fatal. The only realistic prospect of surviving this disaster is to shut yourself in and avoid any contact with other people or animals. The casualty rate is so high, it is impossible to provide any medical assistance and, in any event, there are no effective drugs.

"The government's priorities are to maintain power supplies and water, to deliver emergency food to the designated collection points and to maintain order. Communication with the rest of the world is becoming progressively difficult but we believe the situation is equally serious in all countries. The pandemic is worldwide and no breakthroughs have materialised on the development of a vaccine. The speed with which this pandemic has spread, the unprecedented mortality rate and the consequent collapse of social, economic and political structures have rendered all attempts to contain the situation ineffective.

"All we can do now is ride this out and hope sufficient people survive to pick up the threads and maintain our civilisation in some form in what is likely to be a very different world."

ONE WEEK LATER

Our situation had deteriorated to the point of being unsustainable. We had no contact whatsoever with the outside world. First to go were the TV and radio. We followed the updates from the new emergency government for three days, then just static. The same day the landline telephone went dead and the mobiles had already given up the ghost. The internet went down with the telephones, since when we had no further contact. Anything could have been happening out there but it seemed incredibly quiet. The odd car went past but we hadn't seen a soul for three days.

The girls were going stir crazy because we wouldn't let them out of the house but at least they were still able to play DVDs and CDs on the TV to provide a little illusion of normal life. Then the power went down. No gas, no electricity, no TV. It seemed so unnaturally quiet. The old board games had a new lease of life. Cluedo and Monopoly had often been played but I couldn't recall the last time Risk had been fought to a conclusion. Sue was not really a board game person but even she was getting addicted to Rummikub. It was a pity the girls had never taken to chess but it wasn't too late to learn. We could have had some music from the piano but nobody was really in the mood to play. Even more serious after the loss of power, the water was cut off. I suppose they needed power for the pumping stations or something. We were on our own. It was like stepping back into the nineteenth century except that our house relied on twenty-first century services. I didn't think we could live there much longer but the alternative of venturing outside was terrifying.

What made our situation even worse was that the loss of power coincided with a marked deterioration in the weather. After a prolonged mild spell, temperatures had plummeted in the last two days with the first frost of the autumn that morning. Other than wearing our warmest clothes, there wasn't a lot we could do about it. If only we had lived in an old traditional property with open fires or log-burning stoves, even better an electricity generator. All we had that was working was an old camping gaz retrieved from the attic with no spare gas canister. I had no idea how long it would last. The loss of water wasn't critical as there was plenty left in the tanks but I had to think our house had outlived its usefulness even if the original strategy of staying put had probably saved our lives.

It was late and the girls had gone to bed with two duvets each. At least we were not short of bedding. We had agreed to hold a family conference the next morning to settle on a strategy. All sounds very enlightened but these were life and death decisions and the girls were old enough to have a say. I knew it was Sue who would resist moving on but I could see little alternative.

The following day was again bitterly cold with a hard frost. After several days of cold weather and no heating, the house was like a refrigerator. We actually had ice on the inside of the windows. A strip wash and shave in freezing cold water was more than bracing and I wondered when I might next have a hot shower. Nevertheless, two pair of thick socks and my thickist winter jumper and I was ready to face the day. A bowl of muesli with cold water constituted breakfast, the milk having run out a week earlier, but at least it was followed by a piping hot cup of coffee.

Sue was up next, complaining bitterly. She had always felt

the cold and would usually put the central heating on full blast in such cold weather. Sue suggested using the camping gaz to warm some water for washing until I convinced her that if she did that, she may not get a hot drink with her breakfast. Eventually she emerged looking rather bulky, wearing goodness knows how many layers of clothing.

We left the girls for a while, tucked up in a heap of bedding, but they at least appeared to be warm. It was after ten o'clock by the time the family conference was ready to start and I opened by taking stock of our current position, using notes I had prepared the previous night.

"Okay. As I see it, there are some clear positives and negatives in our situation…"

"Positives! This I've got to hear!" I was losing Sue already.

"Well, firstly, we all appear to be free of the virus which puts us in a tiny minority. That's the biggest positive possible." This was met with a grudging nodding of heads.

"Secondly, the house is reasonably secure." No real points scored for that one, probably in the 'stating the bleeding obvious' box.

"Thirdly, we're not about to run out of food or water, even if the meals available are somewhat limited without any power. There's no fresh food left and the eggs and bread are just about finished but we have enough tins to last possibly another week, a little cheese and butter, crackers and biscuits, some dried fruit and plenty more breakfast cereal."

"Cereal's disgusting without milk!" interjected Jo.

"I think we can all agree on that," I continued, "but we're talking about things to keep us alive."

"Alright. Let's hear Dad out first or we'll get nowhere." Sue was moving into constructive mode. "Go on, Tom."

"Thank you. We also have lots of rice and pasta but no real means of cooking it. I'm afraid it's going to be cold meals from now on but we're not about to starve. Now the negatives. We have no means of heating the house and the weather is only likely to get colder." Lucy was nodding vigorously at this point. She couldn't bear to be cold.

"Secondly, the camping gaz must be on its last legs. I'm surprised its lasted this long. So no more hot food and after today, probably no hot drinks either. Even with an abundant supply of warm clothes, the icy temperatures and no hot food or drink has to create a risk of hypothermia.

"Thirdly, although we have some food or water, it won't last forever. Even if we raid old Cynthia's water butt, it may not be safe to drink without boiling and we will clearly need more food." No arguments there.

"Fourthly, stuck in here we have no idea what is happening outside our own close, the only clue being the absence of passing people or traffic. It's fair to assume that any riots and looting have long since desisted – it's been so quiet – but there may be rescue efforts underway. The government and the military must have taken protective measures and may be organising survivors. There could be soup kitchens or something set up or maybe some of the locals have organised into groups."

"Surely if there was anything official happening we'd have seen military trucks or helicopters or something" said Sue. "They would have driven around with loudspeakers to announce meeting places and so on."

"You're probably right but my point is we just don't know what's happening and until we leave the house, we're not going to. There may be lots of families like us waiting for a sign that it's safe to go out."

"But that's just it, isn't it," Sue came back. "It's not safe to go out. People were dropping like flies and now there's nobody to be seen. We've only survived by staying in here."

" I know but we have to go out at some time, which brings me on to my fifth and last negative. We don't really know enough about the virus. I followed all the TV and newspaper reports, as you know, but nobody had definitive answers. Everybody assumes that its spread from person to person and it did appear to move out from Beijing with the international flights, but could it be contracted from birds, given that it was created partly from bird flu? Could other animals be carrying the virus, like the laboratory guinea pigs that were mentioned. Are other species dying from this virus or just humans? How long is the virus likely to stay in the environment and will it come back once the pandemic has run its course? If we come across dead bodies, will they still be infectious? I'm pretty sure they won't be as viruses invade other living cells but do they die immediately when an infected person dies? I'm not sure. We just don't know when it is safe to emerge and the only protection we have is facemasks, which I'm not even sure is any protection at all. Sorry about that, but that's my negatives. What do you think?"

Lucy had been weighing things up carefully. "Well, we've got to go, haven't we. It's freezing here and all we've got is that silly camping gaz. We can't sit here doing nothing and freeze to death."

"What about keeping ourselves holed up, like we planned, but in another house where we can keep warm," said Jo.

"Look I know we can't stay here forever – we'll have to get food and so on – but why go before we have to?" Sue was very agitated. "God knows, I hate the cold as much as anybody but this is a matter of life and death. Let's give it a few days to settle down, at least until the food runs out. If we wear lots of jumpers and maybe we could run up and down stairs to keep warm?"

That had Lucy rolling her eyes, her preference being hot food over exercise. "We have to find out what's happening. I haven't even been able to contact Emily for over two weeks. Even when the phones were working she didn't reply to my texts." I felt we had to assume the worst but Lucy wasn't ready to accept that.

"Look, I'll take one of the cars and check around Buxton to

see what's happening," I suggested. "Then we can make a final decision."

"But then you'll just bring the virus back and we'll all catch it," countered Sue.

We went round in circles for over half an hour before Sue relented and agreed to move on to somewhere we could heat but only if it was isolated and well out of Buxton. I pointed out that we'd still need to forage for food but we could probably put that off for a few days. We had a decision in principle.

"Right, we're going to need an older property with open fires or maybe a wood-burning stove. We'll also need ready access to fresh water, somewhere next to a stream perhaps. What about trying the Goyt Valley? We can get there without touching Buxton and there are plenty of isolated farmhouses. Most of them are probably near streams."

This was well received. We all knew and loved the Goyt Valley from many family walks and it was literally ten minutes away.

The next step was to draw up an itinerary of what we should take. That provoked even more debate. No question over the food. All the tins, bottles and dried stuff. That would fit into a couple boxes. The bottles would have to include my little collection of malt whiskies. There was no way I was leaving behind my cask strength Glenfarclas – essential survival rations. There was a bottle of gin for Sue and plenty of tonic but no ice – if it got any colder we could probably make some. Sue wanted to take all the cleaning stuff and the medical kit, such as it was. That was fair enough. Sue also wanted all the bedding and towels – that's sheets, blankets, pillows, quilts, the lot – that would be virtually a car load on its own. The girls also felt strongly that they didn't want to use other people's bedding, so I went along with it. For clothing and footwear, we agreed to take everything appropriate for winter but no summer stuff. We didn't know how long this arrangement was going to last but the priorities needed to be short term. Survive the winter and we'd take it from there. The girls were packing their cosmetics, which seemed a bit pointless but if it helped to maintain morale, so be it. Sue was for taking our pots and pans but I drew the line at that – we would use what we find. Finding something to cook on was more of an issue. Everybody was choosing a few books to take and apart from the obvious candles, torches, matches etc. that was about it.

We would come back for stuff. I would want to get the photo albums at some point – it was a lifetime of memories. We were not taking tools as we only had basic stuff and any other place would have the same. I'd not told the others but I slipped in a couple of decent kitchen knives to be handy in the car. I didn't know what we'd find out there but we ought to have some means of defence.

So where were we going to go? I got out the OS map for the White Peak which included the Goyt Valley. What we were looking for needed to be secluded with fresh water. There were quite a few possibilities on the map and Jo and I drew up a short list of six. We figured that to get around to these remote locations and check them out thoroughly, we would struggle to cover more than six in a day. We came up with two farms on Mill Clough, a small stream running into the River Goyt on the opposite side of the valley from Fernilee, a village on the way to Whaley Bridge. Madscar Farm and Oaken End Farm were both by the stream. We included two more farmhouses over the tops above the village of Kettleshulme : Tunstead Knoll Farm, which wasn't on a stream but was marked with a blue 'W' on the OS map, meaning well or spring, and Dunge Farm which was on Hodgel Brook. The next one was Saltersford Hall which was all on its own just off one of the single – track lanes through the Goyt Valley. That was on Todd Brook. Finally, moving over in the direction of Rainow, we added Round Knoll Farm, on Moss Brook.

We debated all going in the Suzuki Jimny, which would cope well with the farm tracks but would leave virtually no space for luggage, or taking both cars and packing everything in to do one trip. Initially Sue and the girls favoured sticking together in the Jimny and coming back for provisions when we'd found somewhere but what if we had a problem with the car or got stuck? We'd be stranded. We settled on taking both cars, me leading in the Jimny with Jo, while Sue and Lucy would follow in the Punto. We reckoned we could pack in everything essential and would set off the following morning at first light, around 9.00 am.

It was a very successful little conference. Everyone had their say and, with a few compromises, all the key decisions were made without any major fallings out. I think the difficulty of the current situation served to concentrate all our minds. It might have seemed like choosing a holiday home, but we were really talking survival here. Any mistakes and we could all end up dead. I think the extreme cold of the last couple days had also convinced everyone that we had to be pro-active. We'd been sitting there watching events unfold on the TV or lately, simply wondering what was happening. Now we could actually do something. Everyone just seemed more positive. Even the sun had come out and at its low winter elevation, was flooding through the south-facing windows at the rear of the house, generating an appreciable amount of warmth.

The conference had taken a couple of hours and we celebrated with a lunch of corned beef and the last of our bread, followed by tinned peaches. Sue and I got stuck into a bottle of Shiraz and the girls had some J$_2$Os. We were feeling pleased with ourselves. We had a plan. The rest of the day was spent packing and preparing for the move.

As darkness descended we all settled into bed, partly to economise on candles, though we still had a good supply, but mainly because it was simply the warmest place to be. The stars visible in the night sky signified the probability of another hard frost. I reflected how our needs and priorities had changed in a few short weeks. The most important things in our lives were those we had always taken for granted, the basic essentials since the dawn of mankind: food, water and warmth. I had considerable anxiety over what the next day would bring and whether our family had the skills and fortitude to cope with unknown challenges. I felt it was primarily my responsibility to provide for the family and keep them safe but harboured reservations over whether I possessed the right experience, practical skills or even the courage to take this on. In my professional life I had always been willing to take on new challenges and had generally been successful in meeting them but this seemed irrelevant to what was now required of me. I tried to hide these doubts from Sue and the girls as they were obviously frightened and looked to me to be strong but I had serious doubts as to whether I could meet their expectations. Only time would tell.

PART TWO

CHAPTER FOUR

REFUGE

17 November

The first day of my journal. It seemed appropriate for a fresh start in the world and I felt more positive about rising to the challenge. In effect we were taking part in probably the greatest challenge in history and as Sue and I were both history graduates, I felt there ought to be some contemporary account of what people went through, how they coped or maybe didn't. It may have been no more than foolish vanity but it made me feel I was doing something useful even if nobody ever read it.

As expected we were faced with another hard frost, the condensation frozen to form incredible patterns on the inside of the windows, something commonplace in earlier generations but unfamiliar in the age of central heating. Despite the cold everyone was up early in anticipation of the adventure, the temperature simply vindicating our decision to move on.

As expected, the camping gaz had finally given out, so it was cold drinks for breakfast. I suppose we should have been grateful it lasted as long as it did – it had been a real life saver. By 9.00 am we were all wrapped up and ready to leave. There was no alternative but it was still sad – we'd been there twenty years and it was the only home the girls had known. I think Sue felt the loss more than anyone. It was our third home since we married twenty-six years ago but the previous houses were just rungs on the ladder. We were very well settled there and probably would have stayed put until retirement. However, sentiment would get us nowhere – we needed a more practical base, at least to get through the winter.

I was first out to get the cars from the garage – uniquely in this neighbourhood, we'd always kept both cars in the garage, for security and to avoid scraping off ice in winter. We had recently had a very useful automatic door fitted but of course we couldn't use it as there was no power for the control mechanism. I used the mortice key to open the side door and pulled the manual override cord to open the automatic door. Both cars started first time – not bad after nearly three weeks, but they'd always been reliable starters. It took a little while to pack everything in, which we only managed by collapsing the back seats and removing the parcel shelves. We said goodbye to the house and Sue had a final lock-up and checked the doors several times, but then she always did that – a bit of OCD, I think. And then the Morton family were finally on the move, Jo and I leading the way in the Jimny.

I gave Jo the OS map so she could navigate, partly to give her something to do but also because she was damned good at it. Roadmaps, street maps, OS maps – you name it, she was absolutely brilliant. Our first objective was Madscar Farm near Fernilee. That meant heading towards Whaley Bridge, so we took the main road out of Buxton, known as Long Hill, which was just round the corner from where we lived. There was no sign of any activity in the neighbourhood. Lots of properties had the curtains drawn and I half expected to see some curtain-twitching at the sound of our cars, but nothing. It was like driving out at 4.00 am to catch a holiday flight from Manchester Airport, but quieter. There was nothing on the road at all – no abandoned cars and thankfully no bodies. At least people had been able to get home before they died.

As we neared the top of Long Hill the car heater was kicking in and we turned it up to max to luxuriate in the first proper warmth for several days. Five minutes later we were passing through Fernilee – just a few houses and a roadside pub – but still no signs of life. Another mile and Jo identified a lane which headed steeply down the side of the valley, crossed the river Goyt and up the other side to the village of Taxal. We then turned back on ourselves, heading back upstream on an even narrower track called Whiteleas Road, part of the Midshires Way. We passed Overton Hall Farm, took a sharp left, and then right down a steep farm track towards Madscar Farm. Well, we wanted remote – the only people likely to pass here were dog-walkers and I didn't see any of those around. I don't know why I thought of dogs but we no sooner reached the farm that all hell broke loose. Five or six dogs came racing out, barking excitedly. We stopped the car and waited for Sue and Lucy to catch up – they were taking the farm track very steadily – the Punto wasn't really built for that sort of thing. By the time they reached the farm, we were surrounded by the dogs which were jumping up at the windows and a couple of them – a German Shepherd and something big like a Rhodesian Ridgeback – were showing their teeth in a rather aggressive manner.

"Oh God, I don't fancy this," was Jo's verdict.

"Well, farm dogs do tend to be rather territorial and make a lot of noise but, I must admit, these look like they could be dangerous. In any event, there's no way Mum and Lucy will get out of the car with these around. We need to move on."

Despite all the commotion, there was no sign of any people coming to investigate. It looked like the dogs were fending for themselves. Clearly the virus was not a problem for them and it seemed probable that we'd be meeting plenty more dogs.

I signalled to Sue to back up and turn round and she was nodding vigorously, clearly in approval of my executive decision. The dogs followed us up the track for a while, then dropped off and headed back to the farm. That was clearly their territory. I supposed it was possible the farmhouse was still in use and the owners were out foraging for food, in the knowledge that the dogs would protect the property. There surely must be other survivors somewhere. One of our other possibilities was close by, on the same stream in fact. Jo plotted a route to Oaken End Farm. We backtracked to Overton Hall Farm, headed up a steep rough track, across the side of the hill for 100 yards or so, then plunged down another steep track back to Mill Clough, but well upstream from our canine neighbours. Oaken End Farm was a small farmhouse next to the stream, a main house with a number of outbuildings that looked like they had seen better days. There were no dogs, no people or any other signs of life with no smoke from the chimneys and all the curtains closed. It appeared to merit closer inspection and we parked outside the farmhouse to wait for Sue and Lucy. After a few minutes they came bumping along, nursing the Punto along the rough track and parking behind us.

"Looks empty, let's check it out," I said as the others emerged.

"We can't be sure it's empty," said Sue. "At least knock on the door."

I duly obliged with no result. I shouted through the letter box. Still nothing. We moved round to a side door, also locked.

"It'll have to be a window," I said, picking up a large stone. "Stand well back."

"Tom, be careful!" Sue was a little shocked at the prospect of breaking and entering.

I hurled the stone through one of the windows at the side of the farmhouse with an ear-splitting crash.

"If anybody's asleep in there, that should wake 'em."

The house was obviously unoccupied but it occurred to me that the owners could be out foraging for food, probably in Whaley Bridge, but why would they leave all the curtains closed? It seemed odd.

Removing the shards of glass, I reached in and opened the window latch – not exactly burglar proof.

"Right. I'll climb in and let you in through the front, providing the keys are around."

I managed to climb in without cutting myself and entered the kitchen. The first thing I noticed was an electric cooker – not a good start. The smell in there was pretty strong – some pans on the side were covered in fungus. There was certainly nobody using the place. Off the kitchen was some sort of utility room with a back door. There was a mortice lock with a key in it. I could let the others in here if I couldn't open the front door. Back through the kitchen, a corridor lead to the front door. Another mortice lock with a key in place. The door was also bolted. A dreadful thought – everything locked from the inside – the owners had to be dead somewhere. I let the others in through the front door and suggested they explore downstairs while I checked upstairs, knowing what I expected to find. At the top of the stairs was a bathroom, empty. Then a back bedroom, also empty. As I opened the next door, which turned out to be the main bedroom at the front of the house, the overwhelming smell told me I'd found what I expected. I got a quick glimpse of what looked like an elderly woman in bed and an elderly man in an armchair, both clearly in an advanced state of decomposition. I closed the door again quickly, hoping my assumption of viruses dying with their hosts was correct. In any event, I'd not got close – it surely couldn't travel on a smell. Lucy was just coming up the stairs.

"You don't want to go in there," I told her. She looked a little shocked as she guessed my meaning. I was thinking, we've got to get used to this and toughen up if we're going to find somewhere to live.

We regrouped in the entrance hall.

"There's two bodies in the bedroom, an old couple. I thought there had to be, given the keys in both doors. They've been dead quite a while. I'm sure they're no longer infectious," I said, trying to sound like I knew what I was talking about.

"Oh God, let's go somewhere else," said Jo.

"Don't be too hasty. We're going to have to get used to dead bodies. Most people will have died at home after the hospitals gave up the fight. We've at least got open fires in the two main rooms. We could soon get the place warm. The rest of the heating appears to be electric storage heaters but we could probably get hold of some paraffin stoves or something. We could bury the old couple in the garden and burn the bedding."

"Tom, I am not staying in a house with dead bodies!" Sue had spoken and that was the end of it. I must say, the prospect of clearing out that bedroom was turning my stomach but what would we find elsewhere? It was time to hit the road again. Before leaving, we raided the kitchen and managed to find several packets of breakfast cereal, a large box of tea bags, a jar of instant coffee, a large bag of rice, some unopened biscuits, even a pack of individual cakes and assorted tins of soup, vegetables, fish and fruit. There was also a half – full sack of potatoes in the utility room. We quickly searched the cupboards for torches, batteries, matches and candles.

Quite a haul. We found some old supermarket bags and filled three before hauling these and the sack of potatoes back to the cars, which were now seriously full. The girls were complaining that they were hungry but Sue didn't want to stop at the house any longer, so we agreed to picnic at one of the car parks in the Goyt.

Back to the map. Our next objective was Tunstead Knoll Farm, which should have a well or spring. That was towards the village of Kettleshulme, which by road meant going via Whaley Bridge but Jo identified a possible short-cut over the top of Taxal Edge. We retraced our steps to Overton Hall Farm, back on the Midshires Way towards Taxal. At the start of Whiteleas Road we took a track to the left over Crowhill, rather bumpy but not too steep. Then we hit Taxal Moor Road, still no more than a farm track but quite navigable. When we reached the main Whaley

Bridge to Kettleshulme road, we doubled back into the Goyt Valley, high up above Kettleshulme, down below us on the right. It was a beautiful day and the views were absolutely stunning from the top but we were too focused on our task to take much notice. Sue and Lucy were close behind. From there it was plain sailing, through a cross-roads at Five Lane Ends until the road finished and became another farm track. Just off to the right, about 30 yards, was Tunstead Knoll Farm. As we approached I could see that the curtains were not closed, so maybe no dead bodies this time. Otherwise, no signs of life – no parked cars, no barking dogs. I drove into the farmyard with Sue close behind. I was about to park up when something disturbed my peripheral vision – a movement near the top of the house. Before I even noticed an open window on the top floor, a loud crack rang out and the headlight smashed. "Christ, we're being shot at!" I could see a figure at the window holding a rifle and taking aim again.

"Enough of this. We're out of here!"

I swung the car round and accelerated out of the gate scattering loose stones. Sue was already reversing as fast as she could. A second shot but this one hit the track, bringing up dust. Reaching the main lane, Sue reversed round and I sped past, turning left the way we came, with Sue following. We were driving far too fast for the lane but were soon out of range. There were no more shots. Jo looked absolutely terrified, understandably.

"I can't believe it! They tried to kill us Dad!"

"Don't worry, we're safe now. They were probably warning shots but a bit close for comfort. We're going to have to be more careful."

The property search was turning into a nightmare.

"I think it's time for a break. We can forget Dunge Farm. I don't fancy having a psycho for a neighbour." We back-tracked to the crossroads at Five Lane Ends and turned right up along the ridge to the highest point at Pym Chair. I was familiar with this spot, having parked here for walks on the ridge and I knew there was a handy car park. I didn't need Jo to navigate which was just as well as she'd gone very quiet since the shooting. We parked the cars at Pym Chair and got out to talk. Jo was shaking and after a hug with her mum, started to cry. Lucy was putting a brave face on it but the colour had gone from her face. None of us had faced gunfire before and the Goyt Valley, normally a haven of tranquillity, suddenly seemed a dangerous place.

"Bloody Hell! That's a bit much," was Sue's verdict. "Hasn't there been enough death without people trying to shoot each other."

"We'll just have to watch out," I suggested, somewhat needlessly. "With no rule of law, some people are clearly prepared to do whatever they deem necessary to avoid contact. A lot of these farmhouses will contain shotguns but that idiot was using a rifle. Maybe we're being a bit rash just driving up to farmhouses. Perhaps we should park up out of sight and approach cautiously on foot."

"That tactic would have worked well with the first place with the dogs," said Sue sarcastically. "Perhaps these farmhouses are not such a good idea."

"But you wanted us to get away from Buxton and be on our own," I reminded her. "Look. We've just been unlucky so far. Let's have a spot of lunch before we move on."

It was well past lunchtime but the shock of being shot at had taken the edge off our appetites. Nevertheless, we saw off the cheese and biscuits we'd left at the top of our food packs and, as a bit of a well–earned treat, followed this with the packet cakes liberated from Oaken End Farm. We ate in the cars and washed it down with our bottles of water. That raised the spirits a little and at least Jo had stopped shaking. I was thinking we needed to find somewhere soon as Sue and the girls wouldn't take many more set- backs.

We agreed to rule out Dunge Farm and headed straight for

Saltersford Hall, which was less than a mile down the valley. Jo was navigating again, although I knew the way, having driven past the place many times. We moved steeply downhill in the direction of Rainow, turning left at the old Jenkin Chapel, on downhill, round the bend to the left and the hall was in sight. The title sounds grand but it was no stately home, just a substantial country house with Todd Brook running alongside. We decided against approaching on foot on the basis that the cars provided protection, at least against dogs, so we parked in the wide driveway at the front of the property. I was already thinking this may not be as secluded as we had envisaged. Even though it was on a small, single-track lane, we did have one of the key strategic routes through the Goyt Valley passing just twenty yards from the front door. Furthermore, any smoke from the chimneys or even lights at the windows would be visible from quite some distance.

I put the reservations to the back of my mind and tried to remain positive. There was no smoke or any other sign of life. It was time to investigate. We all left the cars and headed as a group towards the front door, a datestone above it declaring the hall's construction in 1593, late Tudor.

"Right. I'll knock on the door. If somebody's in there, they must have heard the cars but I suppose they could be hiding. I don't want to provoke an extreme reaction by breaking more windows."

There was an impressive cast iron knocker in the shape of a lion and it made a resounding noise. We waited a while but there was no reaction from inside the house. I tried the handle and, as expected, found it was locked. The house was either empty or we had more dead bodies but I decided it was wise to keep my thoughts to myself.

"Okay. Move round the sides. Look for a way in." The windows were very substantial with thick hardwood frames and some window locks were visible. We'd have to demolish a whole window to get in and we'd need some serious tools to do it.

Lucy tried a side door, also locked, and constructed of solid hardwood with no glass panels. The house was looking pretty secure. Jo was peering up. "Is that window open?" We looked where she was pointing. It was a small window with opaque glass, presumably a bathroom or toilet, and sure enough the bottom edge of the window wasn't quite flush against the wall. There was possibly a half inch opening.

"You may be right. Well spotted Jo. The question is, is it fastened on some form of latch or just hinged at the top to swing open. I could easily fit through there. It's worth a try."

"It must be fifteen feet up," said Sue. "How are you going to get up to it? I don't see any ladder."

"There's bound to be one," I suggested. "The garage is the obvious place."

Separate from the house was a large double garage and it seemed probable that there would be a ladder in there as the other outbuildings were quite small. It had a sectional up-and-over automatic door with no external lock or handle, similar to the one at our own home and I knew it would be impossible to open from the outside. However, the garage had a side door with a large glass panel, which provided an obvious means of entry. As the door was locked, it was time for some more breaking and entering.

"Alright, stand well back," I said, picking up an ornamental garden brick from a stack beside the garage. I threw the brick as hard as I could from four feet back onto the centre of the glass panel with a very loud and effective result.

I reached inside and cursed as I found no key in the mortice lock and it was too dark to see much inside the garage with the door closed.

"Lucy. Can you get one of the torches from the car? I can't see a thing in there."

While she fetched a torch, I removed the remaining shards of glass from the frame, trying to avoid cutting my hands. Some heavy duty gloves would have been useful, which I had at home but hadn't thought to bring. Lucy returned with the torch and, shining it through the broken window, an aluminium extension ladder was clearly visible hanging on some brackets on the opposite wall.

"That's what I want. I'll have to climb through". The empty panel was too high to step through, so I arranged a little platform of the garden bricks to stand on.

"Now don't cut yourself. We haven't got much in a way of a medical kit", reminded Sue.

"It's okay. I've cleared the glass now," I said, stepping through the panel and dropping onto an internal step. I found the cord to activate the manual override for the garage door and swung it over as the others moved round to enter the garage. It was fairly empty apart from old pots of paint and car maintenance stuff, nothing useful apart from the ladder.

I opened up two sections of the three-section ladder and propped it up at the side of the bathroom window. Up the ladder and I could just get my fingers under the edge of the window. It easily swung out on its hinge, leaving a full open window, about two feet square. Perfect. Things were looking up. "Okay, I'm going in", I shouted.

"Be careful, there might still be somebody in there", called Sue. Only if they're dead, I was thinking, and I was not in favour of walking away from another property. I had Lucy's torch but it was reasonably light inside, so I kept it in my pocket. Clambering through the window, I was actually on top of a toilet and carefully lowered myself to the floor. The bathroom door was open leading to a long landing with four or five other doors, all ajar. Although it was a touch stuffy, there was no smell of decay, which was a good sign. Before moving downstairs to let the others in, I quickly checked out the bedrooms for bodies. There were five bedrooms and another bathroom, all thankfully unoccupied. Moving downstairs to the entrance hall, which was impressively half panelled in dark oak, I came to a massive studded oak front door with a heavy mortice lock but no sign of any key. I could hear the others outside the door.

"It's okay," I shouted, "just looking for a key to open up. I'll try the back."

I found the back door through the kitchen, which was a bit pungent – some rotting food somewhere. Another heavy door with a strong mortice lock. No key. I tried some of the windows but they were all securely locked – again no keys to hand. I was beginning to think they may have to follow me up the ladder, which could be a touch dangerous. Moving sideways from the ladder into the window required a little care. Surely there were some spare keys somewhere. If I could just find the key for the window locks, I could at least open a ground floor window. I tried the kitchen cupboards. It was a modern fitted kitchen with a couple of drawer stacks. Trying them I found tea towels, oven gloves, various brochures probably relating to the appliances and quite a lot of miscellaneous junk but no keys. I tried the entrance hall again. There was a wooden cabinet with a mirror next to the front door. A drawer in the cabinet was full of papers and mortice keys. Yes! I tried them in turn on the front door but neither of them worked.

Back through the kitchen I tried the back door and finally the second key worked. At last! "Round here, gang" I shouted. The girls came running round, followed by a relieved looking Sue. All the thanks I got was "you took your time".

"Welcome to your humble abode, I'll show you round. Actually, from what I've seen so far, not so humble". Sue looked impressed with the kitchen. "That's a wood-burning stove, isn't it?" In my haste to find keys, I'd not really assessed the appliances but Sue was right. In fact, not an ordinary stove but a La Nordia wood-burning cooker – a stove that will heat the room but with a hob on top for cooking. Exactly what we needed. It was a spacious kitchen with built in seating around a kitchen bar.

There was a fridge-freezer in the corner. I opened the fridge door to be met by an unpleasant smell.

"We'll see if there's anything to be salvaged later." We moved into the long entrance hall and the girls were visibly impressed with the oak panelling. The next door took us into the lounge which was quite breathtaking. The same dark oak panelling extended from floor to ceiling, supported by huge oak beams, leaded light windows on two of the walls and on the opposite side a magnificent inglenook fireplace surrounded by an elaborately carved oak mantelpiece. There were stone seats on each side within the inglenook and what looked like the door to a bread oven.

"My God, it's fantastic", Sue was impressed. "It's like stepping back into Elizabethan days. I think we'll put an offer in on this one, Tom."

"Awesome" was Lucy's verdict. "Fab" added Jo. Approval was unanimous.

"Do you think anyone's coming back? They've left it all locked up", said Sue with concern.

I examined the fireplace which contained a large heap of grey ashes. Stone cold.

"The fire's not been lit for a while", I said. "The stove in the kitchen was also cold and the smell in the fridge suggests the place has been empty for at least a few days. Either they've moved on or were perhaps taken ill when they were out. I can't see anybody coming back."

"Yeah, lets stay here. I love it! Can we explore?" Jo was getting excited now.

The other downstairs rooms were comprised of a large dining room, a study / library and a cloakroom. There was one other door which was locked, which seemed odd. I remembered the extra mortice key which fitted neither front or back and, sure enough, it did the job. The door turned out to be at the top of a stone staircase leading down into complete blackness.

Cellars. We could explore those later. A quick survey of the upstairs confirmed five bedrooms, two bathrooms and no dead bodies or other unpleasant surprises. It felt rather stuffy upstairs and the rooms were quite dusty. Sue thought the place had been empty for at least a week and I suspected she was right.

Everybody was suitably impressed with our find and spirits had risen noticeably since the unfortunate set-backs earlier in the day. It hardly needed debating but we all agreed unreservedly to make this our next home.

I decided it was time to focus. "Right, we probably have no more than an hour of daylight left. Top priority is to set up some heating and lighting, unpack the essentials from the cars and get the ladder put away. I'll sort the ladder. You girls can start bringing stuff in."

"I'll look for some candles", said Sue "but don't bring any bedding in until I've had a chance to sort the bedrooms."

We all pitched in, the girls so excited to be setting up a new home. The lighting was sorted quite easily with a good stock of candles in the kitchen cupboard. We found a stack of wine and spirits bottles in a recycling bin outside the back door. Sue selected suitably sized candles and whittled a few to shape with a sharp kitchen knife. We soon had eight bottle-mounted candles ready to light.

We needed logs for the stove. There was a large basket in the corner of the kitchen with a little kindling but just two logs. There had to be a store somewhere. The girls and I checked around the outside of the house and garage. Nothing. Behind the garage were two smaller stone outbuildings with no windows and padlocked doors. There could well be a wood store in there. We would need to find keys to the padlocks first or attack them with some heavy tools, which could take some time. The only other possibility was the cellar. I took a torch and ventured down the stairs. It was cold and dark. The torch was only capable of illuminating a small area at a time but I could see that there were several rooms and an awful lot of old junk. I spotted a few rough sacks in the corner. One contained potatoes which was excellent, though not what I was looking for. Another revealed a good supply of kindling and the third had logs. They probably wouldn't last long but they'd see us through for the next few days at any rate. Hauling up the sacks of kindling and logs, Jo and I set to getting the fires going while Sue and Lucy started to organise the bedrooms. Jo began cleaning out the ashes while I organised the fuel. We didn't have any firelighters but we did have a heap of Daily Telegraphs in the recycle bin. I started screwing them up into tight balls – that would work just as well. With the newspaper balls, kindling and logs, we soon had a blaze going in the stove and the inglenook. We decided that would have to suffice for heating, at least until we found a more plentiful supply of logs. I reckoned it would take quite a while to warm up the substantial lounge. The kitchen would be quicker but I didn't know how long we needed to wait before using the hob. Trial and error I supposed, but a hot drink would be welcome. We left all the internal doors open so the heat would circulate and at least take the edge off the cold upstairs.

Sue and Lucy had stripped all the bedding from two of the bedrooms and piled it into a third, implemented a quick clean up and brought in our own bedding. Lucy and Jo had elected to share a room, which was quite out of character. Jo in particular was fiercely protective of having her own space but I supposed they'd both found the move to a strange, albeit beautiful, house and the earlier events of the day rather unsettling. We'd not had a chance yet to discuss the ramifications of being shot at, but it was something we needed to consider, sooner rather than later.

For the moment, we just wanted to settle in and make ourselves comfortable by warming up and preparing some food. The stove was starting to throw out some heat, so we filled a pan with two large tins of vegetable soup and put it on the hob. It was dark enough by then to need the candles. Not wanting to waste them, we lit two in the kitchen which created a flickering light but very cosy atmosphere. We just needed some Venetian prints and an Italian flag and we could have been in a little bistro. We positioned some more bottles with candles in the entrance hall and lounge to be lit when we needed them.

While the soup was warming up, we investigated the smells from the fridge/freezer. The milk was identified as the obvious culprit. A four-pint plastic bottle was half-full and had separated into different coloured layers. Before throwing it out, I checked the "use by" date: 5 November. Given that the supermarket always allowed at least a week, I reckoned this milk was bought around three weeks ago and the house had most likely been abandoned for at least two weeks. It probably reflected a personal tragedy for the owners but it was lucky for us. It was extremely unlikely that anybody was coming back. The rest of the fridge contents had not fared much better. An opened packet of bacon covered in cling film had turned brown and reeked. There were several plastic punnets of fruit covered in fungus. The salad compartment was in a similar state. The only things worth salvaging were two unopened packs of butter, several cheeses, all past their dates but probably okay, a carton of eggs with ten left and various jars of marmalade, jam, mustard, and the like. Better than nothing. The freezer yielded quite a few packs of meat, which could be useable and one loaf of granary bread, which raised a cheer from the girls. The bread seemed to have been sweating a little in its wrapper but there was no sign of any mould.

We settled down in what was then a warm and cosy kitchen to a sumptuous meal of hot soup with bread and butter, followed by cheese and biscuits. Wonderful. A pan of water had finally come to the boil and I made a cafetière of fresh coffee, which we took into the lounge. The fire was really well established by then with half a dozen logs crackling, throwing out a surprising amount of heat and adding to the flickering light from the candles. It had been a tough day with a successful end and we congratulated ourselves in the implementation of our escape plan.

We celebrated by opening a bottle of Barolo which we found in the kitchen – somewhat better than our usual Australian Shiraz – and even allowed the girls a small glass. They'd worked hard with barely a complaint. We would need to pull together and plan our survival in this very different world. I didn't underestimate the size of the challenge ahead but for the moment we would enjoy our comfort and drank a toast to our new home.

CHAPTER FIVE

PROVISIONS

18 November

It was raining steadily but at least it wasn't as cold – frost free
that morning. Nevertheless, it was still a chilly start in the house.
We had let the fires die down before going to bed in view of the
fire risk. I was up first as a habitual early riser and the first job
was cleaning out the fireplace and stove and laying new fires.
Within ten minutes I had a blaze going and some pans of hot
water warming on the stove. When the water was hot, I woke
the others and we took it in turns to use the two bathrooms for
a good hot wash, a touch of luxury.

After a pot of coffee, cereals and the rest of the bread with
jam, we discussed how to spend the day.

"Can we stay here today and settle in properly", proposed
Lucy. "I don't fancy getting shot at again."

"I want this house scrubbed out from top to bottom before
anything else", declared Sue. Jo and Lucy were keen to help.

"Okay", I agreed, going with the flow. "We do need to
reconnoitre the area to see what's going on but it'll keep until
tomorrow. "I'll concentrate on exploring the rest of the house
and outbuildings to take stock of what we can use and what we
need to find."

First I continued the search for keys and found a row of hooks on the back of one of the kitchen cupboard doors with quite a few keys in place. How we had missed that, I couldn't imagine. There were two heavy mortice keys for the back door and the cellar but still nothing to fit the front door. The owners must have taken those with them, whenever they went. It mattered not. We could manage without the front door. There were a couple double sets of what looked like padlock keys which hopefully would get me into the outbuildings. I decided to check those first. The first one, stone built with a slate roof, about the size of a large garden shed, contained garden equipment and tools, lounger chairs and other outdoor stuff – nothing of immediate use to us. The second one was similar but slightly smaller and revealed a welcome stack of logs covering two of the walls, another sack of logs and a large axe. There would be enough there to last two or three months at least. I brought the sack of logs into the house and parked it in the corner of the kitchen. At least we'd be warm.

Next the water situation. The brook ran past the end of the garden and it would be a simple matter to fill buckets but first I wanted to check what was already in the system. That meant going into the loft. There was a hatch in the landing ceiling and, standing on a chair, I could just reach it. Pushing it released a catch and it swung open to reveal a sectional loft ladder which I could pull down. The first thing that hit me was the cold. If we thought the rest of the house was cold, it was close to freezing up there. I took up the most powerful torch and quickly identified the cold water tank. There was an awful lot of junk up there and I had to clamber over most of it to reach the tank. At least most of the loft was boarded over, so it was safe to move around. The water in the tank was only a few inches below the overflow pipe which again indicated that the owners departed before the water was cut off. If we were careful with the water, we would be able to use the taps for a week or so. I'd just need to fill some buckets from the brook for flushing the toilets. While I was up there I sifted through the junk to see if we could use anything. It was mainly decorating stuff, old toys, suitcases and several boxes which appeared to be full of books. There was an old electric fan heater but nothing that we could use. Okay, we could forget about the loft.

I was summoned to the kitchen for coffee and biscuits and found it transformed. Everything was sparkling and fresh smelling. Sue in her marigolds was getting stuck in with a bucket of Flash and bottle of Domestos, looking very satisfied.

"What do you think?" she said, beaming.

"Wow! Fantastic. That horrible smell's gone."

"That was the fridge. The fridge and freezer are completely cleared out now and scrubbed clean. We won't be needing them but at least they won't smell."

Jo had emptied out all the cupboards, cleaning and re-organising.

"I've made an inventory of what we've got and what we might need", she said.

"Brilliant. Perhaps we'll go shopping tomorrow."

Lucy was busy mixing flour, sugar, butter, eggs and fruit in a large bowl.

"We're going to have a fruitcake", she said.

The stove was throwing out a comforting warmth. It really was a picture of domestic bliss and extraordinary normality given the situation outside.

*

After coffee I checked out the library/study. Two walls were covered with floor to ceiling shelving, holding an impressive collection of books. One section was almost entirely medical books – one of them must have been a doctor. Against another wall was a large leather-topped partner's desk with a desk-top computer, monitor and keyboard – we were not likely to be using that. There were also two framed graduation photos, one boy and one girl. One showed the front of a building I recognised as Manchester University, where both Sue and I graduated many years ago. The other looked like an old Oxford or Cambridge college. This was a pleasure we would never experience with Lucy and Jo. However, at least our girls were alive. These people were almost certainly victims of the Harbin Flu.

I tried the desk drawers, none of which were locked. The top left had all the financial stuff, bank statements, chequebooks etc. The cheque book was in the name of Dr Hargreaves and there was another for Mrs Hargreaves. The second drawer had folders of various documents and the third was confined to stationary. It was all very well organised but nothing to assist survivors in a precarious world. The single middle drawer had Christmas wrapping paper, cards, tags, and the like, hardly a priority at this stage. The right-hand drawer contained mainly office equipment. The calculators would still work but I couldn't think that we'd need them. There was also a good supply of batteries, some of which were likely to fit the torches. There were no torches or candles in the desk but such an organised household were hardly likely to keep such things in the study.

I moved on to the dining room. Another impressive traditional room with half-panelling, a substantial solid oak dining table and chairs and an ornate, inlaid sideboard, which looked like it could be an antique. The first useful find in the sideboard was a large box of standard white candles, about 20 of them. There were also various ornamental and scented candles and quite a few candle holders. The second useful find was a well-stocked drinks cabinet. Some good malt whiskies, an Irish whiskey, Jack Daniels, some top-end French brandies, Gin, Vodka and several liquors. Not bad. The rest of it was comprised of the expected china, table-cloths and the like.

Time to explore the cellar. This time I took down a couple of lighted candles in addition to a torch. It was still quite creepy down there with a rather damp, earthy smell. It was divided into several rooms. One could best be described as an old washroom, of the sort people used before they had automatic washing machines. There was a huge Belfast sink with a mangle rigged up to the side of it. Numerous buckets, mops, brushes, all sorts of cleaning utensils and materials. We wouldn't go short there. The second room was fixed up with wine-racking and looked pretty well stocked – certainly over 100 bottles. I pulled out a few and wiped the dust off – French chateaux over ten years old – not labels I recognised but looked to be expensive stuff. We were certainly well placed for drinks on the dark winter evenings to come. The last room was a general repository for old junk. On a quick perusal I failed to find anything of immediate use.

*

After a light lunch of tomato soup we sampled Lucy's fruitcake.

"Oh wow, Lucy! You've surpassed yourself. This is excellent!" I enthused. Lucy had won prizes for her baking at school but in the context of our currently restricted diet, the cake was an exceptional treat.

"Well, make the most of it. That's half the butter gone and I don't suppose we'll get any more", replied Lucy.

"Certainly not in the shops", I agreed.

We continued with our cleaning and organising, generally settling into the house until it was time for a further little conference to assess our options. We sat around the fire in the lounge with some drinks and biscuits as Sue started the ball rolling.

"I was worried about moving on and yesterday was a day to forget but now we're here, I'm glad we came. This is ideal. We're warm and comfortable with fresh water and a cooker. I think we've been very lucky and now we should stay put."

The girls were nodding their approval. "I love it here. It's going to be fun," added Jo.

"Okay. I think we're all agreed on that," I said. "We needed somewhere safe and habitable to survive the winter and we've certainly found that. We can go back and clear out whatever we want from home and at the same time we ought to check out the state of Buxton and Whaley Bridge for that matter, then maybe Macclesfield. We need to know if there are pockets of survivors. So far, the only live person we've seen is the one who shot at us and I'm sure he's not typical."

"Just when I was starting to feel safe," said Sue. "Can't we just keep to ourselves?"

"Well we need to be careful but we're going to have to forage to top up our supplies, so it makes sense to find out what's happening. There could be organised groups or some advice from the government or military."

Sue looked sceptical "If there was anything like that, wouldn't they use the radio to broadcast messages?"

"Possibly" I conceded. "We can check out the emergency broadcast frequency on the car radio – it's what used to be BBC Radio 4, isn't it? However, I think at the very least I need to have a drive around the Goyt Valley just to assess our safety. We're not particularly hidden and our smoke is a giveaway."

It was agreed that I'd do this the following day, accompanied by Jo as navigator, while Lucy helped Sue with the house. We then took stock of our supplies, using Jo's inventory and adding the rations we brought with us from home and those acquired from the farmhouse on the way.

"That's not a bad stock," I suggested. "We're not about to starve."

"The tinned meat will be the first thing to run out as we haven't got any fresh," said Sue.

"We could always catch a sheep," I said. There's plenty in the fields. It can't be too difficult. The butchering might be a bit tricky though."

"Oh no! We can't do that." Both Jo and Lucy looked disgusted.

"Okay, but unless we're going to turn vegetarian, we'll have to face up to these things." I decided to leave it for now but when the tins started running out it would be a different matter.

We agreed to stock up on any tinned food we could find, meat, fish, soup, vegetables, fruit, whatever.

"In terms of equipment, we could do with some mobile heaters, perhaps paraffin and some oil lamps would be an improvement on the candles," I added. "They might not be easy to find, however. What about guns?"

This was met with shocked silence.

"You're surely not serious," said Sue eventually.

"Well I'm not keen on the idea either," I said "but we have to think about it. If we got shot at again, do we want the option of firing back?"

"No, we stay well clear. Anyway, you don't know the first thing about guns."

She was right but I didn't know the first thing about a lot of things that may turn out to be necessary. I decided not to pursue it.

We agreed that I would make a reconnaissance of the area the next morning with Jo navigating.

19 November

Soon after breakfast, Jo and I were packed up and ready to leave in the Jimny. We took some bottles of water, freshly topped up from the stream, a packet of biscuits, some cheese and a slice each of Lucy's superb fruitcake – enough to keep us going.

Sue insisted that we took no risks and turned back at the first sign of danger, as though I would do anything else with Jo in the car. We were buoyed by the prospect of returning to a beef casserole and baked potatoes. Lucy was intending to make a cherry crumble to accompany our solitary tin of ready-made custard. We'd be putting on weight at this rate.

There was no great strategy to our expedition. We just wanted to look for signs of life or at least some indication of whether we were surrounded by dead bodies or people waiting to shoot at us. If the opportunity presented, a little more foraging would be useful. The more useable food we had stacked up the better. I reckoned the empty farmhouses would be full of rats before long. We'd planned to head across the valley past Lamaload Reservoir, pick up the Macclesfield to Buxton road and see if anything was moving.

We could possibly go up as far as the Cat and Fiddle where we would get a panoramic view. I wish I'd brought my powerful binoculars from home but I hadn't thought of it at the time. Jo was following the OS map and located our nearest neighbour, a farm called Redmoor, which would certainly be close enough to see our smoke. We headed downhill to the bottom of Todd Brook, climbed a little way up the other side until we found a narrow farm track on the left with an old wooden sign announcing Redmoor.

"That's the one", confirmed Jo. "The farm's about a quarter of a mile up the track".

As we approached we could see that a white van was blocking the track just before the farm. With a dry stone wall on each side of the van, there was no room to pass.

"Just stay in the car a minute, I'll take a look," I said, bringing the Jimny up behind the van. It seemed odd to abandon a van in the middle of the track. As I began to edge around the van I caught a reflection in the wing mirror of the driver still inside and slumped over the steering wheel, clearly dead. I wasn't expecting this. Had his illness worsened so suddenly that he was unable to get out of the van? Had lots of people died in their vehicles? What would the main roads and motorways be like?

There was no need to expose Jo to this. I returned to the car.

"Okay. We'll give up on this one. We'll have to reverse back down the track."

"There's somebody in the van, isn't there? Dead bodies?"

There was no point trying to hide things from Jo.

"Yeah okay. The driver's in there. He must have died very suddenly, or passed out, whatever."

"Dad, you don't have to protect me. I know we're going to see bodies. We've just got to get used to it."

"Sorry Jo. You're right, of course."

I had underestimated her. Maybe she was tougher than I thought. She would need to be.

Back on the road, we climbed steeply up to a sharp bend at Nab End and turned onto Hooleyhey Lane, passing Lamaload Reservoir. Our next stop, right on the side of the road was Ankers Knowl Farm. Once again there was no sign of smoke, so we were assuming it was empty. It was just a small place with no livestock around, presumably a sheep farm. It had clearly seen better days. We were not intending to go to any lengths to get in but we could at least try the doors. The front door was locked but I knocked anyway without any expectation of a result. Round the back and another door was locked. "Do you know what," I said. "This place is so dilapidated, I think I could kick this door in."

"Go for it" said Jo, clearly keen to see what was inside.

With Jo standing well back, I took a short run up and planted my foot to the side of the lock with all my weight behind it. The lock held but the wood completely splintered leaving a gaping hole. I reached in to find a key on the inside and unlocked the door. As soon as I opened it, a tiny creature scuttled out and disappeared into the undergrowth. A rat! Jo gave a little scream and was immediately embarrassed.

"Don't panic," I advised. "Just leave a clear route to the door if there's any more rats. They'll only be interested in escaping."

Jo's face showed her disapproval but she entered the house nevertheless. We were in a tumbledown kitchen which was a total mess, half-chewed boxes and packets with dry food scattered all over. The rats had had a field day. We were wearing our face-masks but that did nothing to cover the horrendous smell, a mixture of rat droppings, rotting food and general decay. It didn't appear that we'd be acquiring much here in the way of provisions.

Moving from the kitchen into a dingy corridor, a further door opened onto the sitting room and the smell became even stronger. As we approached more scuttling sounds emerged and I signalled to Jo to hang back. As I entered the room several rats found cover in the corners of the room. In an armchair by the fireplace was an elderly man who had clearly been dead for some time. On one hand his fingers had been chewed down to stumps.

"Okay, we'll leave this room," I said, closing the door. The rats could finish their work.

"A dead body, not in a good state," I said in response to Jo's quizzical stare. "Let's get out. We'll just check the kitchen cupboards for tins or unopened jars and bottles.

The kitchen yielded some tinned tuna, baked beans, quite a lot of soup and some corned beef – worth the visit. We quickly filled a carrier bag and returned to the car.

The next stop would be the Cat and Fiddle pub. I knew they did lunches which meant the possibility of some catering supplies. We soon reached the main Macclesfield to Buxton road and headed up to the top of the moor, passing a few tracks to various farms but with no visible smoke or any other signs of life. As we ascended, a stunning view was afforded across the Cheshire plain but it wasn't clear enough to see any detail at such a distance without binoculars. Reaching the top, we turned into the large pub car park, empty apart from a Vauxhall Vivaro van in the corner. We left the Jimny next to the van and approached the main entrance to the bars, finding the door open and badly damaged. Somebody had been here before us but at least it meant we weren't the only ones foraging in the area. In such a prominent location the Cat and Fiddle was a fairly obvious target.

Jo and I entered the central bar which opened onto two rooms, a public bar and a more modern dining room. The bar seemed to have been stripped of bottles but our priority was food and we made our way through to the kitchen at the back.

There were some enormous fridges against the wall and, as expected, the contents had seen better days. However, we found a couple packets of unopened cheese and several packs of butter, which were well worth taking. I wondered why the raiders of the bar hadn't taken them. Maybe they were more concerned about drowning their sorrows. That was all the kitchen had to offer. At the back of the kitchen was some sort of storeroom, presumably for the food not requiring refrigeration. We found some boxes of rotting vegetables but amongst them was a bag of carrots, some onions and potatoes that were still salvageable. We filled an empty box with our finds.

Some stairs lead down to the cellar – even darker down there and our torches didn't provide a lot of light. There were a few barrels of ale connected up to the bar and some standing at the side, which from the weight of them were full – must have been too heavy for the bar raiders to get up the stairs. There were no crates of bottles – I assumed these had been taken. In a side room off the cellar some old furniture was piled up and some shelves held lots of dusty boxes and oddments. Investigating further, we were rewarded with a box of candles and then I spotted the star prize, some old oil lamps, six in total. I was hoping they might have something to cater for emergencies. Examining the lamps, they didn't appear to have a lot of oil in them. We searched the store until we located a large plastic bottle of oil – that would fill them all several times over. This was an excellent result. Last call was a small office at the back of the pub which yielded nothing of interest except a set of Vauxhall keys hanging on a hook.

"Let's see if these fit the van outside," I said. "It could be useful for us."

"Mum will be pleased with this food and the oil lamps," added Jo. "Its good fun this foraging, isn't it."

I could have pointed out it was really a matter of life and death but left her to enjoy the adventure.

Feeling rather pleased with our success, we loaded our haul into the Jimny and then I tried the keys to the van. Sure enough, the central locking responded with a reassuring clunk and flash of lights as I pressed the button on the key fob and another button opened the back. Apart from some old packaging, the van was empty and after a couple attempts the engine fired up, the fuel gauge registering half full. Perfect.

"We need to stick with the Jimny today. We'll need that anyway to cope with the winter roads but I think we'll come back for this when I've got Sue to drive." I locked it up again and pocketed the keys.

"We've done well there, Jo. Let's try another pub. We can call by the Stanley Arms on the way back."

*

Five minutes later we arrived at the Stanley Arms car park at the bottom of the old Macclesfield road.

"Look. The front's all smashed in. Somebody's doing all the pubs," observed Jo.

"It looks that way," I agreed. "Let's take a look round anyway. If it's the same people that raided the Cat and Fiddle, they didn't seem to bother with the food."

We stepped over the broken wood and glass to enter the main bar – it was much smaller than the Cat and Fiddle. Again the bar stock had been stripped out but the place was also badly smashed up – why would anybody want to do that? At the back of the pub was some living accommodation and in the sitting room the first thing we saw was two bodies on the floor.

"This looks odd," I said, taking in all the damage in the room and the position of the bodies. "Keep back while I turn them over." It was a middle-aged man, a horrible grey colour but not in any advanced state of decomposition, possibly only dead for a day or two. However, the cause of death was only too apparent and it wasn't the virus. There was a gaping wound in his chest and his clothes were covered in blood, stains extending a further foot across the carpet.

"Oh God," exclaimed Jo. "Why would anybody want to do that?"

Why indeed? The other body, a middle-aged woman, bore a similar wound. The pub had been attacked and the couple murdered.

"Look at the candles," I said, pointing to several saucers holding partly-used candles. "These people clearly survived long enough to be coping with the loss of power. I don't think they've been dead for long. There are clearly some dangerous people about."

"They must be sick!" was Jo's verdict.

We were still taking in the scene and the implications of the violence when we heard a soft whimpering coming from the next room – was there another victim still alive? Opening the door to the kitchen, we found the source of the whimpering, a young beagle, not much more than a pup, clearly in great distress. It was painfully thin with its tail tucked firmly between its legs – her legs, I should say, as it was a young bitch. She moved uncertainly towards us, not constrained as much by fear, I thought, as physical weakness. She must have been shut in there for days, as also evidenced by the volume of dog mess on the floor which was producing a stench sufficient to turn my stomach. Jo was smitten immediately and squatted down to comfort her, the dog still whimpering but managing to lick Jo's hand.

"Oh she's gorgeous, the poor little thing."

"Give her some water Jo. She must be dehydrated." Jo tried the kitchen tap and was rewarded with a flow of water, filled a bowl and placed it in front of the beagle, who frantically cleared the bowl in what seemed like a few seconds. Jo refilled the bowl and the dog lapped a little more before looking up at Jo expectantly. "She's hungry," cried Jo. A frantic search of the kitchen cupboards produced some tins of dog food. Jo emptied a whole tin into another bowl and the dog wolfed it down in seconds. That was one hungry dog. She was still distressed and started moving around the kitchen convulsing and retching before opening her mouth and bringing up the food in a neat pile on the floor. She looked relieved and then started eating her own sick. "Gross" said Jo.

"I think we are taking it too quickly" I suggested. "She's been starved for days and her stomach can't take the food. We need to get her to take a little bit at a time." We couldn't stop her consuming the sick and this time, it looked like she was going to retain it. We found a small tin of tuna in the cupboard and Jo gave her about a quarter of it, which she took gratefully followed by some more water. We then waited a few minutes before giving her another quarter. It was working and the dog was perking up.

Meanwhile, I was sorting suitable supplies from the cupboards: more tinned soup, tuna, baked beans and tinned fruit. There was also quite a few jars of cooking sauces, some rice and several types of pasta. No tinned meat but not a bad haul.

It was not long before the inevitable plea from Jo: "Can we keep her, Dad?" Well having rescued her from the brink of starvation we could hardly leave her. With all the stresses and problems of trying to set ourselves up to survive the winter, did we really want the extra responsibility of looking after a dog? On the other hand, Jo and Lucy had already been through a lot and it would raise their spirits. They both loved dogs.

"Okay, we'll take her with us but it'll be up to you and Lucy to look after her."

"Yes!" Jo gave the dog a big hug.

I hardly needed convincing but I wasn't sure that Sue would be as keen, especially as she was making the place so clean. Maybe we could pass her off as a guard dog? Looking at her, that seemed unlikely. It would be alright. Deep down, Sue was a dog-lover as well. We'd need to take the dog food – there was a dozen tins of Pedigree Chum in the cupboard, a sack of mixer biscuits, a bag of dried tripe and some dental sticks – that would get us started.

We loaded up the car and set off home, Jo in the back seat with the beagle, who was being very affectionate. She didn't seem the least bothered at leaving her home. I think dogs are always more attached to people than places and she'd taken to Jo from the start.

After less than ten minutes we were back at the hall, Sue and Lucy eager to see what we'd found. As soon as we opened the car door the beagle leapt out barking excitedly and jumping up at an astonished Lucy and Sue. Lucy was absolutely delighted and started playing with the dog, now joined by an equally excited Jo. Sue looked nonplussed: "a dog! I thought you were going for supplies!" I explained that I'd got it to cheer up the girls, especially after what Jo had seen today. I'm not sure Sue was convinced by that but with the girls so happy I could see that the beagle had won the day. The girls chased off to their room, hotly pursued by a barking beagle, while Sue and I sat down to a glass of wine to discuss the day's events. She recoiled at the story of the rats, was delighted at the acquisition of the oil-lamps but turned quite white when hearing of the murdered couple.

From the state of the dog and the fact that it was still alive, together with the apparent lack of decay in the bodies, though decomposition would have been slowed by the recent frosts, we figured the murders probably occurred around three days earlier. There was clearly an armed gang combing the area, possibly targeting pubs, though how much alcohol did they need? It was six days since we had lost power and water, so maybe that was when this gang had taken to the road, though it could have been earlier as from the TV and radio reports the civil disturbances were widespread and extremely violent. We could only hope that this gang had passed through and moved on. Both of the pubs were on a route between Buxton and Macclesfield, although the Stanley Arms was not on the A road. There was no reason to think they'd be trailing round the Goyt Valley farmhouses. From what we were finding, the pickings were thin. I was sure that our smoke would not be visible from any of the main through routes but if anybody chose to explore the valley, they would soon spot us. We couldn't think why they needed to shoot that couple – they could surely have taken what they wanted at gunpoint. Perhaps the couple were resisting and defending themselves. The alternative that the raiders just went on the rampage and shot them in some orgy of violence was too horrible to contemplate. I was acutely conscious that we had no weapons to defend ourselves but, even if we had, would we be capable of using them and possibly killing people? When we left home as a survival strategy, none of us expected it to be easy and it many ways, we were doing really well, but this took things to a whole new level. Rather than trying to survive on our own in isolation, maybe we needed to explore the possibility of joining a larger group. We certainly needed to find out what was happening beyond the Goyt Valley.

The girls re-emerged to announce that they were calling the beagle Poppy and had made a comfortable bed with some old quilts. Sue insisted that Poppy would sleep in the kitchen, not with the girls, and as she was curled up in front of the stove, I didn't think that would be a problem.

That evening, after a sumptuous meal of beef casserole with baked potatoes, followed by cherry crumble and custard, rounded off with a pot of coffee, we relaxed in the lounge, a crackling fire in the inglenook and a wonderful glow from two of the oil lamps creating a cosy ambience in the oak-panelled room. The girls were reading and the well-fed beagle was stretched out in front of the fire. It was a picture of domestic bliss and we could forget for a moment the dangers that lay outside the door. We'd already settled well, yet I had a foreboding that this was unlikely to last.

20 November

The next day we were making our return to Buxton to assess the situation and to pick up the rest of our stuff from home. We took a packed lunch and plenty of water and all piled into the Punto, Poppy included, which didn't leave much room for collecting supplies but I was planning to pick up the van we had found at the Cat and Fiddle on the way. It was a lovely crisp sunny day but with a very cold wind. Once again we were grateful for the car heater. The radio was producing static as usual, so I put on a CD of David Bowie's greatest hits, one of the few CDs acceptable to all the family. As we followed the same route as the previous day, wearing sunglasses as we drove towards the low morning sun and listening to "Life on Mars", even singing along, it seemed like we were setting off on holiday rather than another survival mission.

The Cat and Fiddle was exactly as we left it, the van in the corner of the car park. Jo and I transferred into the van and lead the way across the top of the moors towards Buxton, Sue, Lucy and Poppy following in the Punto. As we dropped down into the outskirts of Buxton, we approached Rock Bay petrol station and I had an idea. Signalling to alert Sue behind, I turned into the forecourt and parked next to the small shop.

"I'm just after something. Come and have a look round if you want." Jo followed me out of the van and we pointed to the shop to show Sue our intentions. Sue and Lucy stayed in the Punto, trying to restrain Poppy who clearly wanted to join us.

There was no access problem as both door and window were smashed. The shelves were pretty well stripped as I expected but at the back of the shop I spotted what I was after – empty jerry cans. There were six ten-litre plastic containers. Looters had clearly had other priorities, probably the cigarettes, but these could be invaluable as we would have to stock up on fuel. We couldn't access the service station tanks, which would probably be empty in any event, given the panic buying and supply problems but there would be plenty of petrol in the tanks of abandoned cars and we would need to syphon some off, plus diesel for the van. The jerry cans would hold 60 litres for a start and we could transfer it into larger containers later.

We emerged with the cans, grinning sheepishly, and threw them into the back of the van. Sue and Lucy looked a little puzzled but I could explain later. Next stop was our old home. A few dogs barked at us, setting off Poppy in response, but we saw no people. Parked on our drive, we surveyed the neighbourhood which looked exactly the same as we left it. The quiet was unnerving and we could only assume that all the neighbours were dead, possibly lying in their beds. I could see that Sue was thinking the same thoughts and was visibly distressed. The sooner we got away from here the better.

"Okay. Let's not waste time, there's lots to do," I said. "Gather together what you want to take, anything within reason but be sensible. I'll get some cases down from the loft, then we'll pack and be away."

There was no argument with that as we entered the house in a sombre atmosphere. Poppy however had other ideas as she dashed through the house excitedly, exploring each room, clearly pleased to be out of the car. It felt even colder than before, the contrast with the heated car and van quite shocking. I brought down several of the largest suitcases and we began packing our clothes. I took virtually everything apart from my work suits which belonged to another world. Sue collected a lot more bedding and towels. We filled a box with a selection of our favourite books which required uncomfortably quick decisions, some board games and all the photo albums, our family history. I also dug out my old binoculars and the girls pulled together a veritable mountain of cosmetics and toiletries.

Before leaving I unlocked the shed and removed the better of the manual tools and my solitary jerry can – that made seven. What I hadn't found yet was a flexible tube for syphoning petrol, until I remembered the washing machine – there were tubes at the back connecting the hot and cold water. I dragged out the machine from its space in the fitted utility room and cut off the maximum length available – about four feet off each tube – that would do nicely.

We left home, almost certainly for the last time, with more than a tinge of emotion. However, any regrets were tempered by the freezing temperature and the knowledge that we could return to blazing fires and hot food.

We agreed that our next stop would be the Morrisons superstore on the edge of town. It was bound to have been looted but it was worth checking what was left. With no signs of life around, there shouldn't be a queue of people foraging. We headed back down Carlisle Road and along Burlington Road, passing Pavilion Gardens. This gave me another idea. The gardens were always well stocked with ducks and geese and, although I wasn't keen on the idea of killing animals, it would be quite easy to throw a blanket over some and club them. I didn't think they'd be too difficult to prepare for cooking either. Fresh duck would be so much more palatable than bloody tinned stewing steak.

I signalled to stop on Burlington Road and got out to speak to Sue.

"I won't be a minute. I'm just going to check on the duck situation."

Sue was horrified. "Tom, you can't! I'm not eating ducks from the park!"

"Well, let's just take a look," I said. She would have to get used to it unless we were going to live out of tins all winter, assuming we could find enough anyway.

I needn't have bothered, not a live duck to be seen but a whole mess of feathers and carcasses, odd bones strewn all over the slopes down to the lake. I think the local dogs had had the same idea, except they wouldn't need a blanket. As I surveyed the scene I could hear a lot of excited barking, which appeared to be getting closer, and decided to beat a hasty retreat. I was no sooner back in the van when the dogs emerged, about seven or eight, various breeds. They surrounded our vehicles, particularly the Punto, jumping up and barking aggressively, Poppy responding in like manner. Normally I wouldn't worry about dogs but I had to think a determined pack of this size could be dangerous. It was unlikely they'd been loose for more than a week or two at the most and they would have been family pets but they'd clearly reverted to pack mentality. There was probably just one lead aggressive dog and the rest were following. In any event, whenever we left the cars we needed to be prepared to defend ourselves. The trouble was, Sue and the girls were likely to run which would make the situation worse and Poppy's barking could make the other dogs more aggressive. We had better not stray far from the cars.

The dogs moved on once we started up the cars and we headed down Dale Road to Morrisons. Apart from a few parked cars, all the roads we passed were deserted. Was there nobody left alive in Buxton? Morrison's car park was completely empty, which seemed the most surreal sight of all.

We parked by the front entrance, the sliding glass doors being smashed and all emerged wearing our face masks.

"Can we leave the dog in the car please," said Sue. "We don't want her running riot in there."

"Yeah, fine," I agreed. "There'll be a lot of broken glass anyway. We don't want her cutting a paw. Watch out for rats and let's see what we can use. Any edible food, obviously. Rice or pasta would be good. Virtually anything in tins or bottles but I doubt if there's much left."

"Can we get cosmetics?" suggested Lucy.

"Sure. Whatever you want. We'll all need torches. It looks very dark in there."

Sure enough, the only light came from the entrance and beyond the first ten yards it was very gloomy. The far side of the store was in complete darkness. An overpowering smell of rotting food assaulted us and as expected, there was plenty of scuttling to be heard. I advised the others to stamp their feet if they saw any rats and not to block their escape route to the exit but the rats were keeping themselves well hidden. Their droppings were everywhere contributing to the nauseating smell, which the facemasks did nothing to hide. We ignored the fresh food aisles and moved down the store to the tinned food section but with no luck. The shelves had been stripped bare. In fact, all the food aisles were much the same. The only shelves with any stock were things like gardening, greeting cards and cleaning products, anything edible had gone. This didn't look like the result of foraging but rather panic buying when the deliveries were drying up. There must have been some looting to account for the smashed door but otherwise the store was not particularly vandalised. Anything left that wasn't in tins or bottles had probably been finished by the rats.

We gradually made our way to the back to check the storeroom in case anything hadn't make it to the shelves. Past the in-store bakery, we entered quite a large storage area with substantial closed doors at the back for unloading deliveries.

A number of manual trolleys were parked at the sides laden with packaging and other boxes were stacked up against the wall. As we approached, several rats raced out from under the stacks of boxes and ran into the store. I assured the others that there wouldn't be any more rats but nobody looked convinced.

The girls kept their torches trained on the stacks of boxes while Sue and I tentatively moved the boxes to see what was there. There must surely be more than just packaging to attract the rats. It was nearly all rubbish but with a few full containers underneath. One contained biscuits of various types and the rats had had a real go at these – it wasn't worth attempting to salvage anything. Another contained Herbal Essence shampoo which pleased the girls, hardly a lifesaver but worth taking. A third contained tins of own brand vegetable soup – 48 tins in all and a good find. Apart from some cleaning materials, of which we had sufficient, the rest was just packaging. We removed our shopping and loaded up the van.

"Not bad," I suggested. "That soup's a real bonus. I thought we'd just find the odd tin, not a whole box full."

"Excellent", agreed Sue. "Far preferable to cutting up ducks from the park."

The girls were pleased to have lots of shampoo, a type they would often choose. We headed on for the town centre, along Ashwood Dale and turning into the main shopping street, Spring Gardens. Here was a totally different scene. Smashed shop fronts we expected but the pedestrianised area was a carnage of looted goods dumped in the street, heaps of rubbish, glass and bricks strewn around, several burnt out cars and blackened shop fronts, clearly the result of a major riot. From the TV coverage we had assumed serious riots were confined largely to the cities but this must have occurred since the broadcasts finished. We left the vehicles at the end of Spring Gardens and proceeded on foot to survey the damage and check for any salvageable supplies. The interiors of the shops were simply devastated, not just stripped of goods but systematically wrecked. The Marks and Spencer store was burnt out and the smaller shops in ruins. Any attempt at foraging would be a waste of time.

We looked at each other in shocked disbelief. "My God," I said. "This may have started as looting but clearly degenerated into wanton destruction and anarchy. I know there were riots in the cities but I didn't expect anything like this in Buxton."

"I think people became angry," replied Sue. "They felt abandoned by the authorities."

It still seemed extraordinary that social norms could break down so completely in a matter of a couple weeks. To see a community where we'd spent the last twenty years reduced to this was deeply depressing and not a little frightening. I think we had all simply assumed that any pockets of survivors would behave as normally as possible, help each other and perhaps form larger groups to rebuild. If all that was left was anarchy, was it a case of kill or be killed?

We abandoned any prospect of getting supplies in Spring Gardens and returned to the vehicles. Before leaving Buxton I wanted to check out the Town Hall which meant getting up to the Market Place. As Spring Gardens was impassable, we headed back to the town centre bypass, up past the railway station and up the hill to the Market Place, passing lots more smashed shop fronts. The Market Place was not quite as bad, pubs and restaurants with smashed doors but no burnt out shops or cars and no heaps of debris. The riots had clearly been concentrated on Spring Gardens.

Parking up and approaching the front of the Town Hall, which appeared to be undamaged, we could see immediately that some form of notice was attached to the solid wooden door. I dashed forward to find a plastic document wallet pinned to the door with a single sheet of plain A4 paper inside, on which a manuscript note had been neatly written in biro:

To any survivors of Buxton:
We, the Salt family (John, Helen and Christine) and the Fernyhoughs (Paul, Emma, Ian and William) are leaving together for Manchester, where we hear a survival group is established. We are all free of infection – either immune or just lucky.

We've seen some cars leave town but cannot find any more survivors. If you see this and are free of infection, please follow and join us – we need to be organised to survive. We'll leave more notes at Manchester Town Hall.

John Salt
18 Nov

Underneath, in another hand, had been added:

We're following – please come.
Lucas family from Chapel en le Frith
19 Nov

CHAPTER SIX

CONTACT

21 November

"Oh, I don't know, my head's spinning. I don't want to leave this lovely house and just end up catching this awful flu." Sue was exasperated. This family conference was turning into a marathon. We had to agree how to react to Salt's message. The decision to leave Buxton had been simple in comparison. We had resisted the initial temptation to add our names to the notice until we had decided what to do, realising that this was going to be the most significant decision in our survival strategy. At last there was cause for optimism amongst all the death and destruction. Here were other healthy survivors willing to cooperate and organise themselves to provide some possibility of a long-term strategy. Up to then our only concern had been surviving the winter – finding somewhere warm and sufficient food and water in a safe and secure environment. I think we always knew our set up at Saltersford Hall was not a long term option. Picking through the wreckage of the old order to forage for survival rations could only take us so far and would become increasingly difficult as the rats and dogs took over the towns. Fairly soon the only food remaining viable would be tins and bottles and to get at them would mean continually raiding individual houses full of rats and rotting corpses. It was even possible that rats were carrying the virus. The scientists had used guinea pigs to transmit the virus and they must be very similar to rats. We'd been fairly careful but maybe we'd also been lucky to avoid the virus so far. We could easily have been bitten by a rat. We also remained deeply shocked at society's rapid descent into violence and anarchy. We had seen reports of the riots in the cities but the destruction of Buxton had taken us aback. The vast majority of these rioters would since have died and maybe their violence and anger had been directed against property and authority rather than their fellow man but the recent evidence of cold-blooded shootings for little apparent gain showed the depths to which some survivors had sunk. The urge to join up with the families Salt, Fernyhough and Lucas – and whoever had joined up in Manchester ahead of them – was very tempting. Just a little normal social interaction with mutually supportive families would be such a relief from the surreal world we'd entered since leaving our home. On the other hand, we'd made a comfortable base here and could meet all our immediate survival needs.

It was early days yet and the virus may not yet have run its course. There was an argument for keeping our heads down and letting the dust settle rather than embarking on further adventures into the unknown. Some of the adventures so far had been rather traumatic, especially for young Jo.

On the other hand, if we didn't seize this opportunity, would the chance be lost? There were lots of factors to consider and no easy answers. We explored these at length over coffee and biscuits around the warm stove in the kitchen, Poppy curled up on a cushion on the floor after a good breakfast and a romp outside with Lucy and Jo.

We eventually concluded that we had three options:

1. We would pack up and follow immediately to Manchester.

2. I would travel alone to Manchester to assess the situation.

3. We would stay put until the spring and evaluate our options then.

We then prioritised the factors for and against each of the options:

For option one:

It was a definite opportunity to join a survival group. We didn't know what intelligence the families were acting upon and how it reached them, but we did know that at least three families were heading for Manchester and similar notices were likely to attract more, so a viable group appeared to be a realistic prospect.

The opportunity may be limited in time. A group may form and move on to a suitable location, which was highly unlikely to be in Manchester City Centre. In the short term it may be possible to follow but there was no guarantee that the opportunity would still exist in the spring.

Being part of a group would give us greater security and the means to defend ourselves. People would bring different skills and experience to such a group and some may have access to and experience of weapons.

A group would provide social interaction, particularly for the girls with others of their own age group.

It had the potential to create a long- term solution, which had to be a self-sufficient community to move on from foraging.

Against option one:

We were giving up a relatively safe and comfortable home, which we had been quite lucky to find, for a venture into the unknown. The intelligence may amount to an unfounded rumour or an intention which didn't achieve fruition.

The more we ventured out, the more we risked contracting the virus. We just didn't know how long it would be active in the environment, whether it could only be spread between people or cross species, such as rats or birds. The longer we could avoid any potentially dangerous contacts, the better the chance of the pandemic eventually dying out, if it hadn't already done so. There was no way of gaining this information.

We were exposing ourselves to violent attack. A working van with fuel and full of supplies may now be an attractive target.

If a survival group was successful, it should not be impossible to find some months later. This was of course an assumption and it was impossible to be confident.

For option two:

This in effect kept option one and three open. I would gain information which would allow us to make a more informed decision. If it was clear that a safe and viable group was being formed, we could take option one. If nothing had been organised or I could see that it was a shambles, we could revert to option three.

Sue and the girls would remain safe at home.

Going alone, I could probably minimise the risks and get out of danger more quickly.

Against option two:

This meant splitting up. If something happened to me, the others would hear nothing. Could Sue and the girls survive on their own?

Although Sue and the girls would be left behind, I would be exposing myself to danger from violent attack or contraction of the virus. I could be unaware that I had the virus and could bring it back to infect the others.

Would Sue and the girls remain safe if violent groups were on the move? Their presence would always be betrayed by the chimney smoke.

For option three:

We had a safe and relatively comfortable base for at least the winter and longer if we wished. Why give this up for an unknown quantity?

Our strategy to date had kept us free of infection. We should stick to our plan.

If viable survival groups were formed, we may be able to find them later.

Against option three:

We needed to think long-term with a viable survival strategy, not just short-term comfort.

If we didn't act now, we may lose the opportunity.

Staying put was not a guarantee of safety as we didn't yet have the means to defend ourselves. We would be safer in a large group.

We were agreed that these were the main factors. To some extent, options one and three were opposite sides of the same coin, whereas option two was something of a compromise. Each family member was then invited to express their preference with reasons, starting with Jo as the youngest.

"Well, I like it here at the house because it's warm and cosy, at least downstairs, and now we've got Poppy to play with. I don't mind staying here through the winter but going into other people's houses is scary with the rats and the dead bodies. I don't know what it would be like in Manchester or who we'd be living with, so that's a bit scary as well but I'd go as long as we can take Poppy. I don't want Dad to go on his own – maybe I could go with him to navigate?"

Lucy then offered her thoughts:

"I like this house as well but I don't see why we can't find another good one as they're nearly all empty. I hate the rats as well but I suppose they're going to be everywhere. I think we need to move on and join with other people – we shouldn't pass up this chance. It makes sense to check out the situation first before we move out of here but I don't like the idea of Dad leaving us and Jo must not go along. I vote that we go together and of course we take Poppy."

Sue and I were quite impressed with the rational manner in which the girls had addressed the problem.

Sue went next:

"I'm still very concerned that we need to avoid any contact that could expose us to the virus. We've been quite safe here and although Lucy's right, there are a lot of available empty houses, if you don't count the decaying bodies and rats; I think we'd go a long way before we find another that suits our needs as well as this one. In fact I'd definitely vote for option three apart from one factor, the violence we've seen around here and the fact that we can't defend ourselves. I would certainly feel safer in a larger group and it would be much better for the girls. The problem is we don't know what's there and I'm reluctant to give up this place for something unknown. I suppose that brings us to option two but I'm really nervous of Dad going on his own. If we go for that Tom you'd have to promise that you keep a low profile, take no risks, make contact if that's possible and get straight back. And there's no way that Jo's going. She's been exposed to too much already. I would hate to leave this place but the girls need something more – some sort of fresh start, not just day to day survival."

I get the chance to sum up:

"Okay, I think we're all thinking on similar lines. This place has been great but we need to move on and look for a longer-term solution, which means being part of a larger group. I think we would have reached that situation next spring or summer anyway but the opportunity is too good to pass up. But we need to make sure it's a credible venture, which means option two. Much as I enjoy having you navigate Jo, you need to stay here. And if we do move on, of course we'll take Poppy – she's one of the family now. I'll pack a couple day's rations in case I need to stay overnight and set off first thing tomorrow. And don't worry, no risks – I'll be ultra-careful."

It was settled: option two. I would go to Manchester, assess the situation and report back. No commitment. If we were not entirely happy, we'd stay put for the winter and continue our local foraging. There were reservations – it was the first time we'd split up and Sue was quite worried. I had to reassure her several times that there was really very little danger involved. I almost convinced myself.

I was feeling really positive then, having agreed action which could lead us to an improved situation. Being part of a survival group was an attractive proposition. That evening I decided it was my turn to attempt a proper meal. I offered to prepare a lasagne, one of my (admittedly very few) signature dishes, and the prospect was received enthusiastically. I'd need to use our last tin of mince, so had to make it worthwhile. Ordinarily, the idea of using tinned mince for a lasagne would be horrifying but it was the only way it was going to happen. I used generous amounts of onion, oregano and black pepper which disguised to some extent the taste of the mince and, if I say so myself, the result was pretty good for survival rations. It would have been better with a nice fresh side salad and some garlic bread but we had to make do with some crackers and butter. At least we could wash it down with some quality wine from the cellar – a really good Bordeaux Premier Cru – I didn't recognise the chateaux but I'd get it again. We would have to pack up these wines in the van if we moved on – it would be a crime to leave them behind.

Relaxing after dinner in front of the fire in the lounge with the mixture of light from the fire and oil lamps providing such a warm illumination of the oak panelling, one couldn't help having second thoughts on the merits of a further move.

22 November

A good early start and it was shaping up to be a fine day. After stoking up the fires and finishing a decent breakfast, including a rare treat of fried eggs – we were thinking they might not last much longer, although we kept them in the cold cellar – I prepared my rations for the trip: a two litre bottle of water, a packet of biscuits, chunk of cheese, a tin of tuna and some tinned pears. I syphoned some of the petrol from the Jimny to top up the Punto – we'd yet to fill the jerry cans – and I was ready to leave by 9.00 am. I could manage without lights by that time, which would avoid attracting attention from a distance, though the engine noise itself would be enough. It was agreed that the others would not leave the house, apart from exercising Poppy in the garden. Everywhere would be locked up and in the unlikely event of any attack, the plan was to lock themselves in the cellar and keep quiet, although the chances of keeping Poppy quiet were not great. For my part, I would drive straight to Manchester and make the earliest possible contact with any organised groups, returning as quickly as possible. After hugs all round, I was on my way.

As usual, the Goyt Valley was eerily quiet – it was still hard to get used to the empty roads. Back up the steep hill to Pym Chair – a peculiar little rocky outcrop with spectacular views – nobody seemed to know whether the Pym, from whom it was named, was a highwayman or a preacher. It was a very remote spot to be preaching but equally I couldn't imagine many coaches passing through. From there it was left to Kettleshulme, passing less than a mile from Tunstead Knoll Farm, where we were shot at on our first day in the Goyt , but it wasn't visible from the road. At the deserted village of Kettleshulme, I joined the main Macclesfield to Whaley Bridge road and headed right to Whaley in order to pick up the A6 route into Manchester. Turning left at the Horwich End crossroads I took the main road through the centre of Whaley Bridge which didn't appear to have escaped the general mayhem of the last few weeks – hardly an intact shop window to be seen, the road strewn with broken glass and rubbish but I drove through it with some difficulty, hoping I wouldn't pick up a puncture. I passed a small gun shop on the left – I must have driven past many times but barely registered it and I'd forgotten it was there. This could be very useful to us and I was tempted to stop and take a look around. It had obviously been looted but there could be something left. However, conscious of my promise to head straight to Manchester, I left it on my mental "to do" list and headed on through the centre. There were a few abandoned cars but nothing like the level of burnt out vehicles that we found in the centre of Buxton. As I left the town I passed the Tesco superstore on the right. That could also be worth checking out. It would have been looted and down near the canal, I was sure the rats hadn't wasted any time taking over, but it was a much bigger store than Buxton's Morrisons and we could get another lucky find – that box of soups was our best result to date. On the "to do" list.

Past Whaley Bridge I joined the A6 which was deserted. However, I could immediately see a blockage ahead. It was under the railway bridge at the turning for Chinley, where a huge articulated lorry had slewed almost sideways across the road, the cab at a 45 degree angle to the trailer, having apparently jack -knifed. Another smaller van had crashed into the bridge itself and several cars were at various angles on the other side of the lorry. No bodies were visible. It looked as if the drivers had walked away but had no way of recovering the vehicles. Nobody would be using the A6 in the foreseeable future. I turned around and headed back into Whaley Bridge. I'd have to try the short cut over the top to pick up the A6 at Disley – it was a narrow road which was likely to be blocked by any abandoned vehicles but worth a shot, otherwise I'd have to head back in Macclesfield direction. I turned right at Whaley Bridge station and up the steep track behind. It was a residential area with a few cars parked on the side of the road but no serious obstructions. Luckily it was also clear across the top where the road was at its narrowest and I was soon descending into Disley, arriving at the Ram's Head back on the A6. No sign of any riots there, just a few abandoned cars and a few dogs scavenging. I made better progress on a clear road past Lyme Park and through High Lane, down towards Hazel Grove. Once I reached the junction with Macclesfield road, I was met with further disruption and this time it was serious. Looking up the A6 in the direction of

Stockport and Manchester the view was one of total carnage. Vehicles everywhere, many of them overturned, shop fronts smashed or burnt out and much of the contents just dumped in the street. This was totally impassable. The row of shops must have acted as a magnet to looters. The housing was quite dense around Hazel Grove and the riots must have been well supported. I needed an alternative route as it was much too far to walk to Manchester from here, at least another fifteen miles. In any event, I needed to know that I could transport the family and our provisions to any meeting place.

I figured that if I could cut across to the west and reach the A34 it was a wider road with fewer concentrations of shops than the A6 – I could try Bramhall or Cheadle Hulme and see what the roads were like. From the junction I headed down Macclesfield road, then turned right onto Jacksons Lane towards Bramhall. This was fine, though Hazel Grove High School was nothing more than a burnt out shell, probably disaffected kids using the riots to extract retribution. At the end of the road I'd reached the roundabout next to the grounds of Bramhall Hall. It crossed my mind that a substantial hall with extensive grounds and a lake could be a good contender as a base for a large survival group and I should check it out but, conscious of my promise to Sue, and not knowing what blockages would like ahead, I pressed on, turning left onto Bramhall Lane South. Plenty of parked cars there but no obstructions. This would lead me right into the centre of Bramhall, which may not have been the best idea, so I took a right onto Carr Wood Road, skirting the grounds of Bramhall Hall. Beautiful properties up there, prime commuter belt for Manchester and no signs of damage, not which could be seen from the road anyway. It occurred to me that this would be a good area for a spot of foraging, all Waitrose shoppers up there, but no time at present. I reached the approach to Cheadle Hulme centre and again there were lots of vehicles across the road. It could be possible to pick a way through but I thought it would be easier to skirt round the centre through the residential area as I knew I was quite close to the A34. I cut down Ravenoak Road and Church Road, past Cheadle Hulme College – at least that one hadn't been burnt down – and headed down Gill Bent Road. No blockages there but I wasn't sure where I was going. This was a bit off the beaten track for me and I was cursing that I hadn't dug out a Manchester A to Z when we cleared out from home. I'm pretty good in south Manchester but I didn't know how many more detours might be required – I would just have to rely on sense of direction.

I came out onto Grove Lane and then I could see one of the main roundabouts for the A34 just a couple hundred yards down the road and with no obstructions. As I joined the A34 with some relief I congratulated myself on getting this far. This was a dual carriageway which would take me most of the way into Manchester. There were the usual abandoned cars and vans but nothing I couldn't get past and no signs of riots. Now I was making good progress and soon passed over the M60 orbital motorway – I could see some abandoned Lorries but it was clear enough, easily navigable, which was worth knowing should I need to move round to another arterial route into Manchester. I was sticking with the A34 for now, the Kingsway at that point heading through East Didsbury. I was getting into shopping areas again and the usual devastation was apparent but it was a very wide approach there and the fall out had only reached the edge of the road.

I reached the end of the dual carriageway and carried on up the A34 but there it was just an ordinary street heading towards Rusholme and the University sector. This wasn't too salubrious at the best of times and was usually one of the first areas to join any riots but most of the shops were concentrated on the A6, so it was nothing like as bad as Hazel Grove. What shops there were, which come in short runs, were smashed up and cars were left almost at random, but with a little careful manoeuvring, I could get through. I reached the University with mixed emotions. Some of the happiest years of my life had been spent there, straight from school in the Cotswolds to arrive in the big city, still a carefree existence in the days on a state grant, making new friends, lots of beer and football with a little study in between, finally meeting Sue, although it was a few years later that we married. Most people have a rosy view of their University town and I was no exception but seeing it then, amidst such devastation, my thoughts were soured by the potential future for my girls. What could they expect now? We took for granted our lifestyle and prosperity and now it was all thrown away.

The road widened into Upper Brook Street and I made good progress, reaching the Mancunion Way, the overhead urban motorway. I cut to the left to join the start of Oxford Street heading up towards St Peter's Square. Now it was seriously congested with abandoned cars, some evidently crashed and some burnt out, scattered across the road. I could see the dome of the Central Reference Library about 100 yards ahead in St Peter's Square and it seemed pointless trying to drive any further. It was time to walk. I quickly packed my provisions and water into a rucksack and left the Punto straddling the road like the rest of the abandoned cars, not wishing to draw attention to it.

Walking up Oxford Road was a little unnerving. I'd walked this many times, passing Oxford Road railway station, but today was very different. It was unnaturally quiet with no signs of life, human or otherwise, but I was surrounded by the results of the recent violence and on my own, very conscious that I had little protection other than a small knife in my pocket. If there were people around, they could be waiting, observing my every move. But then, what would they have to gain by killing me, the meagre provisions in my rucksack? And yet, it was impossible to escape this feeling of insecurity. I reached St Peter's Square, still quiet, not even a dog barking, had they abandoned the city centre? Round the back of the circular Central Reference Library brought me to Albert Square and the Town Hall. Hoping my mission had not been in vain, I searched for messages, finding nothing until the main entrance in the centre of Albert Square where various papers were pinned to the door. It appeared that a number of people had had the same idea for communication. They were all handwritten notes, some a little worse for wear as the rain had driven in against the door, and others better prepared had inserted their messages inside plastic wallets. Most of them were from families seeking to re-establish contact but one in particular attracted my attention:

> Mancunion Survivors.
> We are a small group of survivors free from infection seeking to establish a self-sufficient community. Please join us and help to make our venture a success. We will pick up recruits daily outside the Town Hall entrance until we have a viable group.
> 19 November
> Next pick up: 20 November 15.00

The date and time was then crossed out and re-entered as 21 Nov 14.00.

*

This was just what I was hoping for. None of the other messages offered anything like this. I checked my watch: 10.45. It had taken me almost two hours to get into Manchester, a journey of less than 25 miles. Just over three hours to wait for the pickup. I had to make contact first before returning home or we could miss the chance to join this group. I would use the three hours to see if I could find anything useful in the city centre. Just reading that message had boosted my spirits. The chance of being part of a large group and building a self-sufficient community, it could be the start on what was going to be a slow and painful process of re-building. It was some prospect of a future for the girls.

With no real plan in mind, I started wandering down Cross Street. There wasn't a lot of looting there as its virtually wall to wall banks and building societies but it was still the usual war-zone with barely a window intact. At least there was no sign of rats or dogs for that matter, probably because there was nothing to eat. I turned down St Ann Street into St Ann's Square, one of my favourite spots in Manchester. More broken windows, even the beautiful stained glass windows in St Ann's Church. I'm not in the least religious but such wanton destruction was enough to make one weep. Onto Deansgate and the first shop was Waterstones, which apart from one broken window, appeared to be untouched. I peered inside and it seemed to be much as it always was – lots of tables stacked up with "three for two" offers. This had always been my favourite shop in Manchester – in fact, one of the few I could tolerate, being something of a shopaphobe – but now, surrounded by destruction, it was a haven of tranquillity.

With so much time to spare, I couldn't resist going in and stepped gingerly through the broken window on to the window display, then jumped down to the shop floor. Once I moved away from the window, it was quite dark and I needed the torch from my rucksack. I was aware of a Costa Coffee concession on the second floor, which would be a relaxed and secure environment in which to eat my lunch. As I climbed the stairs and moved away from the ground floor windows, it became very dark indeed and the only light was from my torch but at least my presence didn't prompt any scuttling noises, so I concluded that the rats had decided that a bookshop didn't merit their attention. I suppose it was predictable that just about the only shop to escape being looted would be a bookshop. I reached the little coffee bar on the second floor and settled down on a leather sofa to unpack my lunch. It was tempting to get something to read while I was there but in practise a little difficult holding a torch and trying to eat. I sufficed with some biscuits and cheese, just to keep me going. It was tempting to stay for a nap in the comfortable surroundings but I decided to spend my time more productively checking out the shops for any useful supplies, not that I expected to find any food left. Before leaving the coffee bar I checked out the serving counter. Although the displays had all been cleared, behind the counter were several unopened packs of ground coffee and a small box containing cereal bars, the type the girls loved. I emptied the box out into my rucksack along with the packs of coffee, an unexpected bonus. In fact, it was so tempting; I rounded off my lunch with a blueberry cereal bar. I had always criticised these treats masquerading as health food but in the current situation, it was delicious and most welcome.

Across Deansgate was the House of Fraser store or Kendals as I thought of it. As expected, this had been heavily looted but at least it hadn't been set on fire. Once again it was very dark inside and I had to stumble around by the light of my torch – it was like finding my way through a maze. From what was left of the displays, it was clear that this was the cosmetics section of the store but the stock had been picked clean, no doubt of great assistance to the looters' bid for survival. Eventually I found the escalators. Down to the basement would take me to the menswear department but I wasn't desperate to acquire any clothes, most of it had probably been looted and if the rats had got in, they were likely to be down there. I decided to head up to the top of the store and work my way down. After six escalators I was decidedly leg-weary and as the furniture was located on the top floor, looked for somewhere to have a rest. There had clearly been some looting up there but nothing like as extensive. In fact, some of the displays appeared to be almost intact. I moved around slowly, illuminating about twenty feet or so with my torch. I would have to find some more powerful torches, preferably ones that could be worn on the head like cavers, though I doubted I'll find such things in this store. I was about a quarter of the way around the floor when I heard some scrabbling – maybe the rats had reached here, after all. Pointing my torch in the direction of the sound, I couldn't see any movement but some of the furniture was stacked up, almost forming a separate little enclosure and curious, I decided to take a look. Then I received the shock of my life as a figure jumped up and dashed further back into the store, crashing into tables and chairs in the dark. I tried to pick out the figure with my torch and was amazed to see a young girl, about Lucy's age, lying on the floor, holding her leg, clearly in pain.

"It's okay", I shouted, "I won't hurt you, let me help".

The girl looked at me warily but she probably couldn't see anything past the torch. "I'm sorry" she said, "I didn't mean any harm." Looking around her, she had a rough bed made up, there were water bottles and the remains of food.

"My God! Are you living here?"

"I had nowhere else to go."

"Look, don't worry. You're not in trouble. I didn't mean to shout. I was just surprised to find anybody here. Tell me what's happened to you and I'll try and help."

Belatedly, we made our introductions and she told her story. Her leg appeared to be fine.

It turned out she was called Lisa Grundy, 14 years old and had lived for the last year with her mother and older brother in a flat in the Northern Quarter. She'd never known her father and had moved around a lot. Her mother changed her job frequently and they often moved when they couldn't pay the rent. Her brother was 17 and frequently got into trouble with the police. He got involved in the riots in Manchester until he was infected. Then Lisa and her mother also caught it and nobody could help them. Lisa was very ill for a few days, then woke one morning and knew she was through it, though she was very weak. Finding her mother dead in bed and with no trace of her brother, she tried the neighbouring flats but everybody was ill or not responding. Too frightened to stay on her own because youths were riding around on motorbikes at night and firing guns, she put what food she could find in a bag and wandered the streets of Manchester looking for somewhere to hide. When she got into Kendals, she went straight to the top floor and made her little den. It was cold but she managed to wrap up in lots of bedding. She wasn't sure how long she'd been there but thought it might be six or seven days and the food she had brought with her had just about run out. She was refilling her water bottle from a tap in the store toilets. I was the first person she'd seen in the store but she still heard the bikes and shooting at night.

By this time she was a lot more comfortable in my company and seemed quite relieved to be telling her story to somebody. I fed her a couple blueberry cereal bars, which were well received, and told her about my girls and my reason for being in Manchester. I suggested that she should come with me to meet the survival group and she readily agreed. Lisa was the first person I'd spoken to since the epidemic became serious and it was quite a relief. I was glad that I may be able to help Lisa who'd clearly had a rough deal. She seemed a nice kid and, although she probably had some rough edges, could make a good friend for Lucy and Jo.

We made our way back to Albert Square at 1.45pm. I decided that we should stay hidden until we assessed the situation, given the rogue elements apparently still stalking the city and as the meeting time was displayed for all to see. We took cover in a derelict café on the corner of the square, opposite the front entrance to the Town Hall. A couple minutes after 2.00, two men emerged from the direction of the Central Reference Library and made their way to the Town Hall entrance. From a distance one looked about fifty and the other perhaps in his thirties. They were both wearing trainers, jeans and heavy anoraks. Most significantly, the older man was carrying a rifle over his shoulder – they'd come prepared for trouble. They stood outside the Town Hall entrance, looking around the square and checking their watches. Nothing else was moving. Time to announce our presence. We emerged from the café and started to cross the square as the older man raised his hand in welcome. I felt an extraordinary anticipation at the prospect of meeting fellow survivors after several weeks of no contact outside the immediate family.

"Hello. I take it you saw our notice", said the older fellow with a smile. "Brian Curtis", he announced, shaking my hand firmly, "chairman of the Mancunion Survivors Group. My deputy, Adam Griffin."

"How you doing", said Adam. "You and your daughter coming to join us?"

"Hi. Tom Morton. This is Lisa. She's not my daughter. We just met in Kendal's furniture department where Lisa's been camping out. My family's back in Buxton. We saw a note at the town hall and I've come to check it out."

"Alright, we've got a few from round there" said Brian. If you want to come round to our base, I'll introduce you to the others and explain our plans and then you can decide if you want to be part of it."

"Sounds good. Lead the way".

"We'll just give it another ten minutes to see if anybody else comes."

Brian began amending the notice to advertise another pick up the next day at 2.00 pm.

"That'll probably be the last pick up" he said. "We need to move on."

We walked back towards the Central Reference Library and I was intrigued to see where they were based. Adam was surprised that Lisa had been living in Kendals. "I've checked out that place twice in the last week to see what we could use, looked round every floor."

Lisa was still a little embarrassed to have been discovered. "I was hiding amongst the furniture. I heard someone rooting around, that must have been you. I couldn't find anywhere else to stay."

"That's alright love, you're safe now. We'll look after you."

Lisa still looked a little wary. I got the impression that her experience of adult males had not been entirely favourable.

Brian explained that he and Adam, who had both lost their families to the flu, had met in Manchester six days ago and decided to give it a week but progress was slow until a few families arrived from Derbyshire in the last few days. They now numbered fourteen, including a five year old girl and a 79 year old man, and were hoping to get a viable group of around twenty and look for a suitable location. At present they were in a "holding camp" as he called it in the city centre but needed to move on as it was still very dangerous at night. There remained plenty of people more intent of mayhem than any organised attempt at survival.

We followed Brian and Adam out of Albert Square, down Mount Street around the back of Central Reference Library to Peter Street. Across the street was the imposing façade of the old Midland Hotel, one of the great relics of Manchester's Victorian heyday. "Okay. This is home" said Brian.

"What! You're staying at the Midland! I thought you were keeping a low profile?"

"It's alright" said Adam. "We've taken some precautions." The front of the hotel was totally smashed up and we were led round the side to a bistro entrance, also smashed. Through the back of the bistro and a short corridor brought us to the entrance to a kitchen. It was clearly a swing door for the waiters with no lock but a heavy metal bracket had been added with an open padlock attached.

"That's Phil Lucas' handiwork" said Brian. "He used to be a joiner – useful fellow to have around."

I was thinking what skills I could offer to the group. I had never been a great one at DIY – painting and decorating fine but property improvements and maintenance usually meant the cheque book. It was as though Brian had read my mind "Don't worry. You don't need to be a tradesman to join our group. We can each contribute in our own way. Until a few weeks ago I was a solicitor. Not much call now for legal expertise. We take what we need and try to make sure we're strong enough to defend ourselves, but it is useful to have a mix of skills. Adam here's a plumbing and heating engineer. We've got a builder on the team, a haulage contractor who's a dab hand at vehicle maintenance, a school cook and a retired farmer. The idea is to set up a community where everybody works together and pitches in but with some specific areas of responsibility based on their experience."

I was beginning to get a positive feel that this had the makings of a well-organised group and got the impression that at this stage it was Brian that was doing most of the organising. We were invited into the kitchen to meet the others. Brian knocked three times, paused, then twice more. There was a scrabbling on the other side of the door before it swung open. I noticed another impressive padlock on the inside – no uninvited callers were going to get through here.

"This is our centre of operations" said Brian and introduced Emma Fernyhough and Christine Lucas who appeared to be in charge of the kitchen. An elderly fellow, sitting in a chair, was identified as Paul Naden, who was presumably the aforementioned retired farmer and on the floor with some books and crayons was a young girl, Anna Lucas. Lisa and I introduced ourselves. Brian explained that most of the others were out foraging and scouting for suitable bases. Three vehicles were searching within 30 miles or so of Manchester. The rest of the Fernyhoughs, Paul and sons Ian and William were in one, the Salt family, John, Helen and Christine were in another, with the third driven by Phil Lucas with Mo Nawaz. They would all be back before dark to report their findings. Brian was compiling a dossier of all possible bases, the pros and cons of each and what equipment or work would be required. A final decision would be made the next day before moving out the day after. The priorities were a suitable size to accommodate around 20-25 people, a supply of fresh water, some means of heating and cooking (although it may be possible to bring in suitable equipment), a secluded and defendable position and appropriate surrounding land to start some farming. The expectation was that the first winter would depend on foraged supplies but thereafter the group must become self-sufficient with crops, animals and food production. This was very much on the lines that I had envisaged and the reason why it was desirable to join a viable group rather than remain as an isolated family. I explained our current set-up in the Goyt Valley and our original intention to over-winter there. Brian and Adam were quite impressed with my description though felt we needed to consider defence. Adam specifically requested that, if we decided to join the group, we bring the logs with us as it seemed most likely that they would settle for a place with a wood-burning stove, or install their own if necessary. Adam suggested it would be simple enough to bring in a stove, subject to setting up adequate venting and I took his word for it. It might not be as easy to find a wood-burning cooker, though if necessary they could go over to Saltersford Hall and remove it. They had assumed that they'd probably go for calor gas and the caravan parks were a great source of spare canisters. It was a calor gas cooker they were using in the kitchen. This had already been in place and must have been kept for emergencies. Emma was already preparing an enormous pot of something interesting. A fair quantity of empty tins were on the side together with a pile of fresh carrots and potatoes.

"It's the Midland Casserole," explained Emma. "I trust you two are staying for tea. Chis is making some cherry pies for afters." Lisa's eyes lit up and we gratefully accepted.

I discussed in more detail the plans with Brian and Adam. They were quite determined to move on in two days as they felt they'd pushed their luck staying in the city centre. Apparently, it became seriously dangerous after dark and although they were very discreet, confining themselves to the kitchen at the back of the hotel, they couldn't completely hide their presence. "We have the means to defend ourselves": Brian opened a cupboard to reveal a couple rifles, several handguns and quite a few boxes of ammunition. That was addition to the weapons Brian and Adam had carried to the Town Hall and all three vehicles out scouting were carrying arms. "We could fight off an attack but our fear is that the place gets torched. An old building like this with so much wood would go up like a bonfire." They locked up the kitchen securely at night and climbed the back service stairs to use rooms on the top floor at the back of the hotel, hoping that the light from oil lamps was not too obvious with all the heavy curtains drawn. The main stairs from the front of the hotel they'd blocked by throwing down furniture from the floor above. Should anybody attempt to scramble past that lot they would find the access doors from the stairs padlocked. Apparently Phil Lucas removed the padlocks from an industrial estate, which explained their size.

I had forgotten to mention Poppy the beagle and enquired whether this would be a problem. "We can train her to catch rats" pipes up Paul from his chair in the corner. "Jack Russells are best or even German Shephards, but Beagles are quite fast as long as you keep 'em trim." That's settled then, though I had my doubts whether young Poppy would graduate from cuddly, if boisterous, pet to chief rat catcher.

We were just settling down to a pre-dinner glass of wine when a knock came at the rear entrance to the kitchen – three knocks, followed by two. "It's John", came the call. This was a big heavy door with a mortice lock, no padlocks on this one – it appeared to be where food deliveries had been made. Adam opened up and introduced John Salt, closely followed by his wife Helen and daughter Christine, all heavily laden with bags of supplies.

"More shopping," said John cheerily, "what's for tea?"

John was delighted to find that I'd come on the strength of his note at Buxton Town Hall, soon after the Lucas family. It turned out John was a building contractor based at Chelmorton, a village just outside Buxton. Helen worked as a secretary for the firm and Christine, who was only 19, was an English student at Sheffield University.

The shopping bags were unpacked, mainly tins which were stored in the already well stocked cupboards, some packets of rice and pasta, batteries of various sizes and packets of biscuits. John said he had acquired quite a few more tools which he had left in the back of the van at the rear of the hotel. I wondered how they managed to get vans to the hotel, given my experience on Oxford Street.

John explained the system.

"It's quite easy really. Instead of Oxford Street, we approach along Lower Mosley Street next to the old G-Mex Centre. There's no shops along there, so no looting and less debris in the streets. As you get to Windmill Street to reach the back of the hotel it's completely jammed with abandoned cars but, with pushing a few out of the way, we've cleared a winding track through the chaos which, hopefully is not too obvious. We've then blocked it again with a big white Transit van straddling the middle of the road. We've left the keys in it and just move it about ten feet to the side when we need to get in and out. Once through, we can park right up against the rear entrance for loading goods. Nobody passing would think there's a way through but we can be out and away in a couple of minutes."

I was impressed. They'd clearly thought through the problems and come up with workable solutions. It was already apparent that they were working as a team and a team which I'd be quite happy to join. I was pretty sure I could convince Sue and the girls to leave behind our comfortable abode in the Goyt to join this venture. It would however be useful to know where they intended to establish a permanent base.

Helen presented three sets of notes to Brian, more possible locations to throw into the pot. They said they'd checked out five properties but two were non-starters. They'd completed some sort of template showing the location of the property, even including a six digit OS map reference, then commenting on size and condition of property, defensive properties, availability of water, any existing cultivation or facilities for keeping animals, potential means of heating etc. Now I was even more impressed.

"Okay. That's fourteen we've got now," said Brian. "I'll sift them down to a shortlist of half a dozen, subject to anything the others bring back, and we'll talk them through tomorrow to reach a consensus. The best options are looking like the larger country house hotels."

The light was just starting to fade outside when another coded knock on the door was followed by a call of "Phil and Mo". They unloaded their bags, lots more tins and a couple oil lamps, and Phil said he could see Paul and his lads approaching down the road, so he'd left the way clear. A third van arrived in a matter of minutes and a strapping young man jumped out and ran back to re-position the Transit across the road. More supplies were unloaded and Lisa and I were introduced to all the new arrivals. Phil Lucas, king of the padlocks, was being hugged by young Anna, and was accompanied by a middle aged Asian man: "Mohammed Nawaz – people call me Mo." Paul Fernyhough was about my age and with his two sons, Ian, 21 and Will, 16. Now we'd met everybody and they were all keen to hear our stories. Just to talk to people again was such a relief after weeks of isolation. The group was an odd mixture of family units and bereaved individuals. Brian had lost his wife and probably his three children, though they had lost contact. He seemed to be coping by throwing himself into organising the group and forming a survival strategy. Adam had no children but had also lost his wife. Both Brian and Adam had caught the virus and been laid up for a week or so but pulled through. Mo had lost his whole family, a wife and four children. Paul Naden was already a widower and had lived alone on his farm.

As we chatted, Emma finalised preparation of the "Midland Casserole" and she and Christine served out piping hot helpings in large soup bowls. Despite the fact that most of the ingredients came out of tins, it was absolutely delicious, the blandness of the meat disguised by the generous addition of herbs. Lisa had finished hers before I was half way through and was ready for a top up. Emma had made a huge pot and we were all well satisfied by the time it was finished to universal acclamation. Emma took it in her stride and was already well used to coping with large numbers, having been a school cook for the last fifteen years. The casserole was followed by cherry pie and tinned custard, which was absolutely wonderful, then cheese and biscuits, finally filter coffee with After Eight mints. By this time I felt I was getting to know the group and I liked what I saw. There was a relaxed, supportive and positive atmosphere in spite of the personal tragedies which all had experienced. Lisa and I insisted on doing the pots in order to make some contribution.

Soon after 8.00 pm the disturbances commenced. At first it was the sound of a few motorbikes, then some gunshots and screaming. Everybody started clearing up and preparing to withdraw from the kitchen. Adam explained that it was like this every night after dark, nothing particularly organised or any discernible intent, just general mayhem for the sake of it. There appeared to be fewer people involved, perhaps because they'd succumbed to the virus, and there was far less shooting than a few nights ago, possibly also because their ammunition was running low, but the more serious development was the increasing use of Molotov cocktails, no doubt fuelled by the ready supply of petrol syphoned from the many abandoned vehicles. If our lights were spotted from the rear of the hotel, it was possible we could be targeted, so many buildings in the city centre having been torched already. The kitchen was locked up and all lights extinguished except a couple of oil lamps which we carried whilst trooping up the service stairs at the back of the hotel. As we ascended the floors I noted with approval the secure padlocks fitted at the top of each flight of stairs. On the top floor I followed the others turning left to reach a corridor of bedrooms at the rear of the hotel. At the end of the corridor was the fire escape just in case. John, Paul and Phil had the van keys ready if we needed to evacuate. The doors to the bedrooms were not locked as they had to be broken open, being designed for computer- programmed key cards but the corridor itself was considered to be secure. Each room had an oil lamp which was turned low and the thick dark curtains were drawn to minimise any light visible from the street below. They were all twin rooms. Chris Salt offered to take in Lisa and I shared with Mo. There was no heating in the rooms but Adam had rigged up several paraffin heaters in the corridor and it was enough to keep the chill off.

Mo explained the bathroom arrangements. Water was still flowing from the hot tap, though obviously cold, but they were using the minimum in order to conserve whatever was left in the tank. The toilet flush was empty but a jug of water had been drawn off and was standing next to the toilet, only to be used to flush solid waste. All very practical.

Before turning in, Mo opened up a little about his family and how they were all struck down in a matter of days. I could feel the depth of his loss but was struck by the dignity with which he bore it. As a Muslim, Mo felt that Allah had a purpose for his survival and it was his duty to carry on. I felt like asking what purpose his Allah had for wiping out most of humanity but decided this was not the time for a theological argument.

It had been a long day and I was just grateful for a comfortable bed in a secure environment and quite excited by the prospect of bringing my family over the next day to build a future.

23 November

Up with the first light I was eager to return home. Some quick coffee and biscuits and I took my farewell, assuring Brian that I would return that afternoon well before dark. I was thinking that it may take a few hours to organise everything before we could take our leave of Saltersford Hall. I thanked Mo for sharing his room and wished Lisa all the best with her new family. She said she was going to help Emma with the cooking and seemed very well settled. I set off in a most positive frame of mind.

Leaving the hotel through the rear entrance, I made my way round to Peter Square. I was relieved to find my car untouched, not even frosted up for once. To avoid the pleasures of the A6, this time I headed straight down the A34 and it was much easier, some abandoned vehicles but always a way through. After Handforth I cut through the country lanes skirting Mottram St Andrew and Prestbury until I reached the outskirts of Macclesfield, then cut across the Hurdsfield industrial estate and up on the Cat and Fiddle road. Ten minutes later I was back at Saltersford Hall, not much over an hour since leaving the Midland, a far superior route.

As I was parking up in front of the house, Poppy dashed round from the side door, barking excitedly and ran up to be petted. It was amazing how quickly she'd bonded with the family. I approached the side door and Sue was standing there. From the expression on her face it was obvious that something was terribly wrong.

"What's the matter? You look terrible."

"Oh Tom", her voice breaking, "the girls have got the flu."

CHAPTER SEVEN

INFECTION

23 November

It was the worst possible news, the thing we had dreaded from the start and half expected, and yet, since I had left for Manchester and made contact with Brian's group, I had almost put the danger out of my mind as though it had passed. I was so full of optimism at the prospect of joining an organised community and making a go of it, the last thing in my mind was the possibility of finally falling to the virus. I suppose it was complacency but I thought we had taken adequate precautions. We were in total isolation whilst the virus was sweeping the country and since we emerged we hadn't come directly into contact with any living victims though we had come across some dead bodies and quite a few rats that could be carrying the virus. How had this happened? I supposed it was too late to worry about that now. The girls were infected and we'd failed in our first duty to protect them. It was fairly inevitable that we'd all get it now and our chances of getting through it were pretty minimal.

Sue said that Lucy showed the first symptoms, a raging sore throat and headache not long after I'd left for Manchester. She had deteriorated rapidly and by lunchtime Sue had put her to bed. She was running a temperature and refusing to eat but Sue managed to get some water down her and some paracetamol, which seemed rather pathetic to fight the worse disease in the history of mankind. Jo developed the same symptoms in the afternoon and was now just as bad as Lucy. We went together to the girl's bedroom, accompanied by Poppy, though on entering the room the dog was immediately subdued, her excitement on greeting my arrival disappeared, her tail between her legs and emitting a soft whimpering, which was quite unnerving.

"She knows the girls are ill," said Sue. "She spent last night on Jo's bed, which I wouldn't have allowed but Jo took comfort from her. I don't think Lucy even knew she was there."

The girls were both asleep but breathing irregularly. They were both well covered up but Jo was shivering.

"Do you think they're warm enough? It's pretty cold in here. Should we move them downstairs?" I suggested.

"I didn't know what to do for the best. Lucy was sweating, then Jo was shivering. I feel so hopeless and there's nobody to turn to. I can't lose my girls. I wouldn't want to get through this without the girls. There's no point going on without them." Sue was in floods of tears and looked close to collapse.

"We'll set them up in the lounge and keep them cosy. It'll be easier to keep an eye on them. People do pull through this, you know. I've met some of them."

We pulled some mattresses off the spare beds and carried them down to the lounge. The fire was almost out and I threw on what logs were left in the basket. I could get some more when the girls were sorted. We pushed back the furniture and positioned the mattresses at a safe distance from the fireplace, thinking it would be as well to leave them there for half an hour to warm up. In the meantime, I opened all the curtains to let some sun in, it being quite a bright day. I checked the wood-burner in the kitchen – just ashes. Why didn't Sue keep it going? "We ran out of logs and I didn't want to leave the girls." Sue seemed to be on the point of giving up.

"Look, this is a dreadful situation but we've got to stay strong to look after the girls. What have you eaten today?"

"I haven't bothered yet. I wasn't really hungry. I don't feel that great anyway. I'm probably getting what the girls have got. Might as well – what's the point in fighting it."

This was even worse than I thought. I put Sue in the lounge to keep warm – the fire was already sparking into life, while I opened up the storeroom to bring in a good supply of logs. I then cleared the ashes out of the log-burner and quickly laid a new fire. While that was warming up I could have a go at moving the girls downstairs. Wrapping up Lucy in her bedding, I put her over my shoulder, carefully descending the stairs and depositing her on one of the mattresses in front of the fire. She still didn't wake up. I then repeated the exercise with Jo. When I returned, Sue was fast asleep in the armchair. I wondered if she'd slept at all the night before – probably not. Jo was half awake and mumbling, seeming to recognise me. Poppy immediately jumped onto her bed and snuggled into her. Jo half smiled and put her hand on Poppy. She didn't seem to be quite as far out of it as Lucy.

The stove was beginning to warm up and I opened a couple tins of vegetable soup and left them on the heat. While I was waiting I took one of the blueberry bars from my bag and finished it in a couple bites, feeling an immediate boost to my sugar level. When the soup was ready I first brought in a couple bowls for the girls. Having no success waking Lucy – she was in such a deep sleep and I didn't know whether that was good or bad – I tried Jo and at least she opened her eyes, realised what was on offer and managed a "no thanks". Sue managed a bowl with little enthusiasm and Poppy and I finished the rest. Sue confirmed my suspicions that she hadn't slept last night and I left her to take a nap on the sofa. She sounded quite hoarse and it seemed likely that she was also in the early stages of the virus.

There was little more I could do, so I left all three to sleep and took Poppy out for a run. It seemed unlikely that she'd had any exercise other than being let out of the back door and she at least was full of beans. It would give me time to think as I was totally shocked at what I had found on my return. I took a tennis ball to throw and headed down the lane, Poppy delighted to have some attention. As I walked and Poppy scampered after the ball I tried to think through the options. The girls were both seriously ill and I was particularly worried about Lucy, who was virtually comatose. I couldn't think of anything to do for them other than keeping them warm and trying to get some fluids in them but even that would be difficult. In normal circumstances they'd probably be in hospital and maybe on a saline drip but we didn't have any equipment like that. It looked like Sue would be in the same condition by tomorrow. I remembered the TV reports from the start of the crisis discussing how much quicker the symptoms developed than conventional flu, also how terrifyingly quickly the illness was concluded with most people dying within two to three days, often sooner. I'd rather not think about that. As for me, I felt absolutely fine but I had to assume that I'd catch it, presumably within a day or two. It was possible I would escape as I'd always been resistant to illness. Even when I used to catch the train to work in Manchester and sat in crowded carriages surrounded by commuters coughing and sneezing, I could literally go for several years without catching a cold and even if I felt one coming on, gargling with Listerine usually stopped it in its tracks. When we were tested at school during vaccination programmes, I was often found to have natural immunity. I must have had a very strong immune system. Pity that Lucy and Jo didn't inherit it. Was my fate to be like Brian and Mo, sole survivor of the family? Was it worth surviving in those circumstances? Mo took comfort from his religion but that wasn't for me. I decided that if I were to survive alone I would stay at Saltersford Hall with the graves of my family. There was no point trying to make a new life. It would be preferable if I got the virus as well.

I was suddenly consumed by anger at the waste and

stupidity of mankind. Okay, we'd seen a lot of benefits from science and specifically medical advances but deliberately to create mutated viruses – not just one apparently but seven or eight, perhaps more – against which we had no natural or manufactured defence, and then to allow the viruses to escape into the environment, just seemed so arrogant and culpable. It was no good blaming the Chinese. The scientists were just part of the international community, exchanging their learned papers and no doubt advancing their careers as their work was published. They just pushed the boundaries of science instead of stopping and asking "should we be doing this". If nobody else stopped them, it must be okay. What if something went wrong? Maybe major earthquakes in Harbin were rare but what if it happened? Or were the conspiracy theorists right after all? Was this biological weapons research that went wrong? We created the means to destroy mankind with nuclear weapons, now we had an even more effective method. An invisible enemy that spreads remorselessly and kills virtually everybody it meets. Was it inevitable that we would cause our own destruction sooner or later? These were idle thoughts that were not helping my situation.

I returned to find all three patients sleeping peacefully, which hopefully was a positive, certainly in Sue's case as I thought she was mentally and physically exhausted. I busied myself by taking stock of our supplies and getting essentials to hand in case I was also taken ill. Fresh water first. I filled several buckets with water from the stream, filled pans in the kitchen ready to boil and placed a full bucket next to each toilet. Next I filled two large sacks of logs and placed one in the kitchen to feed the stove, which was now radiating heat and one next to the fireplace in the lounge. The lounge was now quite cosy and I didn't want to make it too hot. I reckoned we wouldn't need any more fuel or water for two or three days.

As far as food was concerned, there seemed no point being

too adventurous as it was difficult to tempt anybody to eat. The vegetable soups were a good bet as I could prepare them quickly, we still had plenty in reserve and they were at least hot and nutritious. There was probably enough cheese left for one more round of cheese and crackers. There was also a lot of tinned fish but something hot would be preferable. That evening I persuaded Sue to take some more soup but the girls were still out of it. I stoked up the fires and settled down for the night, hoping for better developments tomorrow but fearing the worst.

24 November

Lucy died last night sometime between 2.00 and 3.00 am. I checked on everybody at 2.00 and Lucy was taking very shallow breaths. Something woke me around 3.00 and Lucy was already cold. She must have been dead for a while. I felt guilty that nobody was with her to hold her hand but she wouldn't have been aware and at least she passed peacefully. Neither Sue nor Jo woke and remained unaware of the loss. I carried Lucy back upstairs and put her on her bed with a quilt over her. Although I had realised that our deaths were virtually inevitable, losing Lucy still came as a crippling shock. It was almost as though I were in a dream and I was functioning as though I were on autopilot.

Jo was unchanged. Her breathing was stronger than Lucy's had been but I didn't know how long she could survive in this state. Unless she pulled through in the next day, I thought we'd lose both our daughters. Sue was in a similar state to Jo now. If she found out that Lucy was dead, it would finish her.

I was feeling pretty rough myself – just weak and fuzzy headed with an absolutely raw throat. I was sure I'd caught it. It was quite a relief really. I didn't want to be the sole survivor.

The only one unaffected was Poppy. She slept on Jo's bed and now she was awake, she wanted to play. She was still a puppy at heart. "I'm afraid you're out of luck today, girl." I let her out to roam around and do her business but I wasn't up to walks. I put some breakfast out for her, stocked up the fire and went back to bed.

At 10.00 that evening I found that Sue had died, just faded away like Lucy. Could the day get any worse? At least she hadn't seen the girls die. She wouldn't have wanted to live. I eventually managed to carry her upstairs and put her to bed. It was quite a struggle as I hadn't eaten all day and had very little strength left.

Looking at how the illness had progressed in the others and how I was feeling, I couldn't imagine that I'd be up and about the next day. I wondered whether I should leave Poppy outside rather than risk her stranded in another house of dead people but it was fearfully cold outside and she'd probably bark all night to get back in. Also, if Jo should wake, it would be some comfort to find her dog on her bed.

What if Jo pulled through and I didn't? How on earth would she cope on her own? I just couldn't plan for this. Before settling down for the night, I built up the fire and poured a large tumbler of cask-strength Glenfarclas. I would let this virus sample a 60% alcohol punch. If it did finish me off, I wouldn't be aware of it.

26 November

I woke up with a splitting headache, rasping dry throat and a pervasive weakness throughout my body, yet with the realisation that I had come through the illness, survived the most deadly virus in human history. I wasn't clear how I felt about that. Drifting off in front of the fire with my whisky had seemed a pleasant enough escape from this nightmare. Perhaps I should finish the bottle combined with a couple packets of painkillers. That ought to do it. Yet there was still a feeling of relief, the instinct for survival against overwhelming odds, even if I was sharing a house with the bodies of my family. The nightmare would continue.

It was very warm in the lounge and the fire was well stocked. I didn't recall getting up to tend to the fire, perhaps I was on automatic pilot. It was while I was mulling over these thoughts that Poppy dashed in, followed by Jo.

"Dad! You're awake. Are you okay?"

"Jo! Am I dreaming? I thought you were all dead. What's going on?"

"I came round yesterday but I couldn't wake you. You've been asleep for so long. But mum and Lucy are cold in their beds. I didn't know what to do and I thought I'd be all alone."

The tears were flowing now and I stood up to hold her but my head was spinning and my legs gave way as I sank back into my chair.

"Jo, I'm sorry you had to find them like that. They died yesterday – sorry it must be the day before, I seem to have lost a day. I carried them up to their beds. You'd been out of it for so long, I thought I'd lost you as well. When I went to sleep by the fire I thought that was the end. At least we've got each other."

I supposed my trusty immune system had kicked in once more. It couldn't stop me contracting the virus but it had fought it off. Jo must have inherited the same defence, though her body took a little longer. Poor Lucy was not so lucky. In the midst of my grief for Sue and Lucy, now I had something to live for. This would not be wasted. I would build a better life for Jo.

Eventually I managed to drag myself to the bathroom, used the toilet and had a thorough wash. I could shave later but I felt half human again. I went to the bedroom for fresh clothes to the faced with the unnerving sight of Sue motionless on the bed. She must have been dead for two days now. When I had some strength back I would have to think about burials, as long as the ground wasn't too hard. This would be another ordeal for poor Jo.

While I'd been unconscious the previous day, Jo had managed to keep the stove burning, had made herself some hot drinks and cooked a tin of soup. She'd also looked after Poppy, which was pretty good going if she'd felt as I did and after the shock of finding her mum and sister. I was proud of her but also so relieved that she wasn't left on her own.

Jo made a pot of coffee and we had a light breakfast. I should have been starving but hadn't recovered my appetite yet. I forced myself to eat in order to rebuild some strength and determined that we would sort our supplies and cook a huge meal that night just to recover our spirits, if that was at all possible.

Feeling a little revived after breakfast, Jo and I sat in the lounge for a long chat over a second pot of coffee and some biscuits. I related all the details of my trip to Manchester, the people in the survival group and the plans taking shape to form a self-sufficient community. Jo was understandably subdued but nevertheless showed some interest, particularly in Lisa and her attempt to camp out in Kendals. Although we had missed the intended departure of the group, I felt that Brian or Adam would have left a message for me to make a later rendezvous and Jo and I should seriously consider this. Jo became even more quiet and defensive.

"Can't we just stay here, you, me and Poppy? We've got everything we need."

"Everything we need for the next month or so but we need to think long term. We'll be secure with this group, able to defend ourselves, grow crops and keep animals so we've got fresh food. We might even set up some electricity – just think what that would mean. We could refrigerate food, have a hot water supply, all mod cons like hairdryers or playing DVDs on the TV. It would be something approaching normal life. Most importantly, we'd be part of a social group. Eventually, we could probably make contact with other groups and start to rebuild. You can't spend the rest of your life just with me and Poppy."

"What about mum and Lucy?"

"When I'm stronger we'll have to bury them in the garden. We'll give them a proper burial with headstones and stuff."

"Of course, but we'd have to leave them, wouldn't we. If we stay here, they'd still be close and I could look after the graves."

It was too much too soon for Jo, after all she'd been through. We agreed that we wouldn't make a decision yet. We'd give Sue and Lucy a proper burial and see how we felt after a few days. I knew what the decision had to be but I didn't want to force it on Jo. Finding her mother and sister was traumatic and she needed time to grieve. I was just concerned that the opportunity to join the Manchester group might be lost and what other options did we have? However, I had to give Jo some time. It was the worst week in both our lives.

Later in the day, as I felt a little more robust, Jo and I took Poppy for a walk on the ridge in the crisp winter sunshine. It was the sort of walk Sue loved with stunning views over the Goyt Valley in one direction and across the Cheshire plain in the other. I suspect Jo was feeling the same as she was very quiet, not once mentioning her mum or sister. Sooner or later I needed to get her to open up but Sue was always better at that sort of thing. I would need to develop a more sensitive side if I were to function as a lone parent.

27 November

We woke to heavy rain and much milder temperatures. I decided that we must make an attempt to bury Sue and Lucy while the ground was soft enough to dig. I had wrapped them both in sheets as a form of shroud and thought long and hard over whether to attempt some form of coffin. I didn't have the skills, tools or materials to construct anything from scratch but thought I could remove one of the units from the fitted wardrobes in Jo's bedroom. I would need to dig a very large rectangular grave to bury the wardrobe but felt this would be more dignified than placing the bodies directly into the soil. I ran the idea past Jo and she was surprisingly positive. I don't think she had envisaged a coffin and was pleased that we were doing things properly.

After half an hour or so of removing bolts and brackets I had the unit free but it was far too heavy to carry down the stairs. Most of the weight appeared to be in the solid doors as the carcass was just laminated pressboard. Once I had removed the door hinges I carried it downstairs in three pieces. I could re-assemble it once it was in the grave. Jo helped select a suitable site and I managed to push in a bamboo cane to a depth of well over a foot, so it looked like we were in business. I marked out a rectangle about six inches longer and wider than the wardrobe unit and started digging.

The first foot or so wasn't too much of a problem but I soon worked up a sweat. At least the rain had eased off. As I dug deeper it became more difficult with substantial rocks, which I had to lever out and some very deep tree roots which needed to be exposed and sawed. It took most of the day to complete but I had a regular grave seven feet by four and around three feet deep. Once the wardrobe was closed this would still leave around fifteen inches of soil on top which hopefully would be sufficient to stop any foxes or dogs investigating. It would in any event have been impossible to dig much deeper and water could start seeping in.

Declaring it finished, Jo and I lowered the wardrobe carcass into the hole. It was a good fit and rested quite flat. I then climbed down into the wardrobe and re-fastened the door hinges to attach the doors. I carefully carried out first Sue, then Lucy and laid them side by side in the wardrobe. Thankfully, I managed this without Jo's help as I don't think it would have helped her state of mind to handle the bodies. Finally I closed the doors and it was at this point that Jo broke down, possibly reacting to the finality that they would never be seen again. I held her against me and the tears flowed in great heaving sobs. It needed to happen.

When Jo had settled a little I invited her to throw some soil on the wardrobe coffin, which seemed to help a little, and then I filled in the grave. It was getting dark by this time and the rain was getting heavy again. The headstones would have to wait for the next day. We spent that evening in front of the roaring fire leafing through the old photograph albums, reminding ourselves of better times. A lot of them were holiday snaps, particularly of Sue with the girls as I tended to take the majority. There were so many Alpine peaks, the girls squinting against the sun and we had fun remembering which resorts and walks featured. One volume was confined to Lucy's baby and toddler photos and I found it difficult to distinguish between Lucy and Jo at the same age. The ones with Lucy and Jo together were the most poignant and set Jo crying again several times but the emotional release was palpable. We even perused our wedding album and laughed at some of the older generations, now long deceased. I felt that by the end of the evening an adjustment had been made and we were ready to move on, though life would never be the same again.

28 November

A better day today, at least in terms of the weather. The rain had stopped and a weak sun was filtering through the light cloud cover. We needed to complete the burial process, which was depressing but necessary both in respect for Sue and Lucy and to enable Jo and me to move on. I had had my eye on two large and fairly smooth stone blocks at the back of the out-houses, which would form acceptable headstones. I found some black paint in the cellar and a thin paintbrush with which I fashioned Lucy and Sue's names and dates.

There was no room for anything else but Jo and I both felt comfortable that a record was being left rather than just a mound of earth. We placed the two headstones side by side at the head of the mound of black soil. In front of the headstones I knocked in a sturdy wooden stake for a purpose agreed with Jo the previous evening. Jo had selected one of her favourite photos of her mum and sister together – it was from Lucy's last birthday – and we'd sealed it inside a quarter of a plastic document wallet. We then pinned it to the stake to personalise the grave. Some people might regard this as in poor taste but Jo and I were pleased with the result. On our visits to churchyards in Austrian villages, Sue had always been impressed with the meticulously maintained graves which nearly always included a photograph of the deceased, in contrast to the overgrown and neglected graveyards at home, often with headstones falling over. We had no flowers to place on the grave but dug up a young rose bush growing in the border and re-planted it on the grave. This would hopefully produce blooms for years even without maintenance. Given the circumstances, we were quite satisfied with our efforts and felt we had done Sue and Lucy proud. There would be very few victims of the Harbin flu that received such a dignified burial.

Later that day, as we were performing our routine household chores of bringing in fuel and water, re-laying fires and preparing food, Jo approached me with a look of resolution.

"Dad, I've been thinking about what you said, you know, joining the group of people you met. I don't think we can do any more for Mum and Lucy, so if you still want to go, I don't mind."

"Thanks Jo. We do need to go. I know it's difficult but I just want to give you a better chance of a reasonable life. Mum would want us to do that. One day – I don't know when – we'll come back here and see how Mum and Lucy's rose is doing."

"I'd like that" said Jo and gave me a hug.

For the rest of the day we made our preparations with a view to setting off first thing the next day. We didn't know how long it might take to catch up with the group, assuming we could find out where they were. I wanted to take everything useful which meant using the Vivaro van but not knowing how far we might be travelling, it seemed prudent to top up the diesel. I recalled the van abandoned on the drive of a neighbouring farm and this seemed the best option for supplementing the fuel. I had already filled some of the jerry cans but only with petrol to use in the Punto or Jimny and they were too small for what we needed.

I didn't want to take Jo with me as I knew there was a body in the driver's seat and she had suffered enough trauma, so I set her to packing her clothes. I suggested that she took everything and most of Lucy's, which would fit her within a year, as it would be difficult to find new clothes in good condition. The shops that hadn't been trashed or burned out would be very cold and damp, overrun with rats and insects. Any clothes left were likely to be mildewed or full of spider's webs, moth eggs and the like. It may even have been worth taking some of Sue's stuff but Jo didn't seem very comfortable with the idea. I left it up to her and gave her one of the largest suitcases to fill.

Meanwhile, I loaded four empty jerry cans into the Vivaro and set off down the lane, soon reaching the track to Redmoor Farm, parking behind the white van blocking the track. The driver's window was half open and I could see the driver slumped over the steering wheel. The smell was nauseating but at least there were no flies – wrong time of the year, I suppose. The keys were still in the ignition. Death must have been sudden, perhaps the virus had brought on a heart attack. Holding my nose to avoid the stench, I turned the key, trying not to look at the driver. There was at least some charge in the battery as the fuel gauge slowly moved up to between a quarter and a half. Not bad. If I could syphon it all out, the Vivaro's tank would be more or less full and good for maybe 250 miles.

However, with the short tube I was using, there was no way to position the van's fuel tanks close enough together. I would have to fill a jerry can at a time and empty it into the Vivaro. This increased the risk of receiving a mouthful of diesel but there was no alternative. It took the best part of 45 minutes to complete but I ended up with a full tank and two full jerry cans spare. An excellent result.

When I returned, Jo had finished packing all her and Lucy's clothes and was preparing some lunch for us, including the inevitable, but nonetheless welcome, vegetable soup. After lunch we started loading up the van, including the entire stock of logs as I was fairly sure Brian's team would be using log-burners or at least open fires. We took all the useful hand-tools, saws, axes and the like, the oil-lamps and spare oil, torches, batteries, matches, some of the better cooking utensils and packed up all the remaining food apart from what we needed for the evening and breakfast. We packed a separate rucksack with food and water for the next day. I decided it would be excessive to move the entire wine cellar as it should not be difficult to locate wine but I packed up what I judged to be the best couple dozen bottles, plus some spirits, including the Glenfarclas of course. We packed up the books we'd brought from home, all the photograph albums and a case of Jo's favourite CDs. She could play them in the van if nowhere else and I dare say we could find a CD player that ran on batteries. We also took a selection of warm bedding as we weren't sure how we might be spending the night once we hit the road. If necessary, we would sleep in the van.

By the time we had loaded everything it was getting dark and I set to making Jo a spaghetti Bolognese, one of her favourite meals, if you can still call it Bolognese with no suitable meat to use. We had plenty of dry spaghetti, a jar of sauce and some oregano for flavouring. It was quite acceptable, especially washed down with a bottle of Barolo. Even Jo had a glass, mixed 50/50 with water. We drank a toast to Sue and Lucy and promised to return. We slept in the lounge in front of the embers of the fire as we couldn't face going upstairs to the cold on our last night in Saltersford Hall.

29 November

We woke to a cold and dismal day, the steady rain turning to sleet, the hills shrouded in mist, not a bad day to be moving on. With the stove fired up, we breakfasted in the snug kitchen and packed our final items into the van, including a rucksack with enough food and water to last us for two days. I was determined to make every effort to meet up with the Mancunion Survivors within that period or we would need to find another base where we could keep warm and cook food, a scenario on which I preferred not to dwell.

Before leaving, we said our final goodbyes to Sue and Lucy, which once again reduced Jo to tears. I was pretty torn up myself – it was the thought of leaving them behind – but I tried not to show it as I needed to be strong for Jo. My principal mission in life was now to protect Jo and ensure she had some sort of worthwhile future in this messed up world. Nothing else mattered and to achieve that we both needed to be tough. I left the Hall unlocked with the keys inside the side door. We had never located any keys for the front door but there seemed to be no point locking up. Maybe another family like ourselves would chance upon the place and set up home. It didn't seem very likely given the extremely low number of local survivors but you never knew. For the same reason I left the keys to the Punto and Jimny. Personal possessions were irrelevant now. It was simply a case of take what you need and the Vivaro would suit us fine for the present. There were three seats in the front and predictably,

Poppy took ownership of the middle seat, resting her head contentedly on Jo's lap.

I decided the easiest route to Manchester was the way I had returned last time, via Macclesfield. Although I knew the roads well, Jo took the roadmap and the Manchester A-Z to navigate as that was her job and gave her something else to think about. The journey was uneventful and everywhere looked much the same. I didn't spot any more abandoned cars or vandalised shops. The nightly mayhem appeared to be coming to an end, the vandals either dead or engaged upon more constructive attempts to survive. As we approached the centre of Manchester I changed the route to avoid the blockages around Oxford Road. From the University I cut across on Moss Lane East to join Princess Road and headed to the centre. There was no shortage of abandoned vehicles but we moved through easily enough, reaching the Mancunion Way flyover, on through Medlock Street, Albion Street and across Whitworth Street to Lower Mosley Street. I knew this would take me to the back of the Midland Hotel and this is where the serious blockages began. Taking it slowly, I began to make out the convoluted passage through the jam that John Salt had explained to me at my evening in the Midland. It wasn't obvious and I had to back up once or twice, clipping a couple of the abandoned vehicles, but eventually I managed to slalom through the wreckage right up to the rear service entrance of the Midland. Jo was quite impressed with the grandeur of the place and emerged from the van with Poppy barking excitedly. There would be no quiet arrivals now. The back door was unlocked and accompanied by Jo and a very curious Poppy, I entered the kitchen which was cold and deserted. As expected, our party had moved on, presumably a week ago as planned. I was hoping a message would be left here as they would surely expect us to come here rather than the more public Albert Square where their first messages had been left.

It was Jo that spotted it first. In the middle of what looked like an old staff notice board, alongside rotas and health and safety advice was a small sheet of paper, folded in half, with "Tom" written on it. Yes! I knew Brian wouldn't let me down. Jo took down the note and read it:

Tom
Hope everything's OK. Sorry you missed the departure. If you're reading this, you must be following on – please join us with your family.
    We've settled on the Inn at W. (103-659469)
    See you soon.
    Brian.

"What's that supposed to mean? Is it a code?" Jo was exasperated.

"Oh that's Brian. He's very keen on security. He doesn't want anybody picking up that note and knowing where they are based." I must admit it seemed a little unnecessary. What were the chances of somebody having the means and inclination to track them down. However, I knew Brian was highly organised and left nothing to chance.

"But where's W? it could be anywhere!" Jo protested. "And what inn? What do these numbers mean? This is ridiculous!"

"I think I know where we can find out. When they wrote up their research notes on possible bases, they headed each sheet with a six figure OS reference. This will be the co-ordinates of W and it's probably a small place with just one inn. We just need to find the right OS map for these coordinates, which is probably what the 103 prefix relates to, and I know where we can get one. When I was here last week Waterstones on Deansgate was relatively intact and they always had a good map section. We'll need our torches though as its very dark in there."

We decided there was no alternative to leaving the van where it was and heading on foot. We took the rucksack and the note and headed across to Albert Square with Poppy on the lead as we couldn't take the risk of her running off. Passing the Town Hall I decided to take one last look at any notices on the door but found that Brian's note had been removed and no new ones had been put up. I was still amazed that there was so little activity. I thought many people would be trying to get together in this way and the Town Hall was the obvious place to attempt to make contact. Maybe people were afraid of venturing into the city centre? Down John Dalton Street and along Deansgate, we soon reached Waterstones and took our torches out of the rucksacks. Poppy wasn't too keen to enter the dark interior and had to be pulled on the lead. We found the store directory at the bottom of the stairs and noted that maps were housed on the second floor. We climbed the stairs and it became darker and darker as we ascended, relying totally on our torches. As we emerged onto the second floor we turned left into another section where I recalled the maps were located and found five or six shelves full of OS maps, still perfectly in order as though the shop was still open for business. I played the torch across the red Landranger series of maps and found number 103 which covered an area of Lancashire north of Preston. It was a bit further from Manchester than I had expected but they had been looking for a country house hotel in a secluded location, so this had to be it. We unfolded the map and spread it on the floor, Jo having to restrain Poppy from attacking it. The OS references took us west of Clitheroe and a touch further north. There were a few Ws on the map: West Bradford, Waddington, Walker Fold. We needed to be more precise. I opened another map and used the edge of it as a ruler running north to south, then another one running west to east. They intersected almost exactly at Whitewell, a small village well off the beaten track on the edge of the Forest of Bowland, which I was aware was not actually a forest but an area of moorland known for its natural beauty. That was it, we had found our W. There shouldn't be any problem locating the inn.

"Wow! That was fantastic – like using a treasure map." Jo had perked up a little.

While we had such access to maps I thought it prudent to help myself to those for all the bordering areas in addition to 103. I reckoned they could be useful when we needed to source supplies, which would be essential over the winter.

"Okay. Let's get going. We don't know how long it will take to get up there."

We gathered up our purchases and left, retracing our steps to the Midland where the van was safely parked.

We decided to have lunch while we had the comfort of the hotel kitchen – some plain biscuits with sardines, followed by tinned peaches and the last two blueberry bars left from my previous raid on Waterstones. Poppy helped finish off the sardines, then chased the tin around the floor. I gave the A-Z and the roadmap to Jo.

"Right Jo – we need a route to Whitewell." She studied the maps for a couple minutes and came up with Regent Road to get through Salford, M602, M60, M61, M6, then leave the motorway just past Preston on junction 31a to follow the country lanes to Whitewell. It sounded good to me so long as none of the motorways were blocked. We used the coffee bar toilets at the Midland and set off on the next leg of our adventure. Back into the Vivaro, Poppy taking up position of the middle seat again, her paws on the dashboard to get a better view. There was no way through to the front of the hotel on Peter Street, so we had to retrace our steps, weaving through the maze of vehicles onto Lower Mosley Street, then right onto Great Bridgwater Street and back down Deansgate but not a person, nor a dog, not even a rat to be seen. I powered down the windows but could hear absolutely nothing, the silence overwhelming. Even the sound of some dogs fighting would have been reassuring.

Manchester was just a ghost city and I wondered what would become of it. Any survivors would surely shun the cities now. I supposed nature would eventually take over, the weeds at first, then trees and bushes. That would bring in more insects, birds and small animals. The buildings and roads would break up in the frost and storms, rooves and walls collapsing into heaps of rubble. Eventually the roads might collapse into the sewers beneath and be buried under stone, soil and plants until the massive city ceased to exist. How long would it take? 500 years? 1000? If a new civilisation emerged, would future archaeologists uncover the ruins and research how people lived before the great death? With so few surviving, I found it hard to envisage any new civilisation developing. If so, it would surely take thousands of years. Would they reach the same heights of scientific discovery and technological development, a new era of super computers and space weapons of mass destruction? It was hard to envisage. I didn't convey these thoughts to Jo as it was so difficult to feel any optimism for the future and Jo was low enough already. We were alive and needed to continue doing what was necessary to stay alive.

We travelled in silence for a while down Liverpool Road with the Castlefield area to our left with its meagre Roman remains, an earlier lost civilisation, and to the right we passed the Museum of Science and Technology, which pretty much summed up the whole city now. We left the city centre behind, making good progress on Regent Road, wide enough to get round the many abandoned trucks, before joining the M602 motorway, or Eccles by-pass, which would take us out to the orbital M60. This was easy enough as the abandoned vehicles were on the hard shoulder, leaving the main carriageway free. It appeared that the motorway would be the easiest way to cover any distance. Passing Eccles, we still saw no signs of life. We cruised down the empty M60 before splitting onto the M61 towards Preston. This was easy and we made good time, approaching Preston less than 40 minutes from joining the motorway network, then disaster: almost at the junction with the M65, just a few miles south of Preston, a complete jam as far as we could see covering all three lanes and the hard shoulder. There was no sign of mayhem, just orderly rows of cars, vans and lorries, all empty as far as I could see. I could only assume that a major accident had occurred some miles ahead and a tailback built up at a time when the emergency services were breaking down and nobody was available to remove the blockage. Fed up of waiting, people must simply have left their vehicles and set off on foot. This motorway would never be used again. I wondered how many similar jams were left uncleared across the country. I had feared this could be the case although we had escaped the city quite efficiently.

Jo consulted the roadmap and worked out we needed to backtrack several miles to junction 8 just north of Chorley and pick up the A6. There was no way of getting across the central reservation, so we did a U-turn and headed back down the northbound carriageway – not much chance of meeting something coming the other way. Three miles back we came off on the entry slip road, with no signs of course, as we were headed the wrong way but on reaching the roundabout, found that it was indeed the exit to Chorley. Well done Jo. We headed in the opposite direction, northbound on the A6 towards Preston, passing a built up area of Whittle-le-Woods but didn't need to tackle the town centre. The A6 was quite passable and a couple of miles further on we joined junction 29 of the M6 at Bamber Bridge, on the outskirts of Preston. This motorway was reasonably free, barring the odd truck on the hard shoulder. As planned we left the motorway at the Fulwood area just north of Preston, taking the B6243 marked to Longridge. Passing through a small village called Grimsargh, no discernible damage to property or vehicles was apparent. Hopefully that was confined to the larger towns and cities. We approached Longridge past the lovely Old Oak Pub, navigated a few roundabouts and left this small town at the Alston Arms. Again the town did not appear to have experienced any riots and had a selection of small shops, probably well worth a visit to check for supplies. For today I just wanted to reach Whitewell as quickly as possible. It was already 2.30 and the weather was very gloomy, threatening snow. Darkness would fall by 4.00 at the latest and I wasn't confident of handling the van in snow. Jo was following the map very carefully now and we pressed on down a country lane towards a small village called Hesketh Lane. We turned right at a fork before entering the village, an old road sign indicating 3 miles to Walker Fold. A sign for Whitewell would have been more re-assuring but Jo was confident we were on the right track. After a mile or so we forked again to the left, the sign marked to Dunsop Bridge. After another right fork, a left, then another right and yet another left, the sign indicated not only Dunsop Bridge but also two miles to Whitewell. Brilliant! We reached a wooded area and after a mile or so arrived on the edge of a tiny village dominated by a large hotel with tall gables and chimneys, ivy growing up the wall and a magnificent old oak front door. Smoke was pouring from the chimneys and above the door, the hotel sign announced "The Inn at Whitewell". A more welcoming sight it was difficult to imagine. Our quest was at an end just as it began to snow.

By the time we had parked the van and opened the doors, two men emerged from the front of the hotel, not threatening but both carrying rifles. I was impressed by the speed of response and recognised one of the men as Adam Griffin, accompanied by a younger man I could not recall.

Adam recognised me immediately.

"Tom. Glad you could make it. Come on in. the bar's open."

"Hi Adam. I am so glad to find this place. This is my daughter Jo, all that's left of my family."

As we entered into the warmth of the inn and others came to greet us, I could feel myself relaxing already. I looked at Jo who hadn't spoken and was shocked to see her glazed eyes and face virtually devoid of colour. It was at that point Jo collapsed in a heap on the floor.

CHAPTER EIGHT

THE INNKEEPERS

20 December

It was three weeks since we arrived at the inn but it seemed a lot longer. It was a whole new way of life and I think it's probably fair to say that it was generally what we were looking for: a viable and mutually supportive group in a secure and comfortable environment. It was early days but the possibilities here were so much better than we could have envisaged as a family, even if we hadn't been struck down by the flu so tragically.

At first it appeared we were heading for disaster when Jo collapsed without warning. Nobody present had any medical expertise but Christine Lucas said she had once completed a first aid course and took charge. She made her comfortable and took her temperature, which was a little high but apparently not dangerously so. I feared the return of the virus, which would have been alarming not just for Jo but also for a number of the group who had survived so far by avoiding contact. With hindsight I think it was more the after-effects of suffering the illness, rather than the contagion itself. In fact we put it down to mental and physical exhaustion and to think what she'd been through since we first left our home, it could hardly be surprising. She was very poorly that night and pretty much out of it the next day but then slowly improved with a lot of care and attention from Christine and some wholesome food prepared by Emma Fernyhough, our head cook. Jo was weak for several days but was fully recovered and engaging with life at the inn, though understandably she felt acutely the loss of her mother and sister. I must admit I was really worried at first. After Sue and Lucy, I couldn't bear to lose Jo as well. It was my responsibility to protect her and provide her with a tolerable future. If I couldn't do that, there was no point in going on.

We survived the crisis but I just felt so helpless and I'd always felt the need to be in control of the situation. Despite the advantages of being part of a group, of which there were many, the incident highlighted a major weakness in our virtual absence of medical knowledge or resources. Christine did her best but she hadn't really got a clue and our stock of medicines didn't extend much beyond various painkillers and basic cold remedies. How were we going to cope with a genuine medical emergency? What would happen if we suffered burns or broken limbs? We were bound to experience some dental problems. I thought back to the last time I had an impacted wisdom tooth extracted, a burly dentist sweating with the effort of removing the wretched thing, the cracking sound as the root separated from the jawbone, the swabs to stem the bleeding. It was bad enough with a competent dentist and generous application of anaesthetic but what would we do now? There was no doubt about it, we had a serious gap in our skills base and it wasn't clear how this would be addressed.

On a more positive note, the choice of the Inn at Whitewell as a base was inspired. It was everything that Brian Curtis, the self-appointed leader of the group, had specified in the search requirements. First and foremost, it was located right next to an abundant supply of fresh water in the form of the river Hodder, which flowed alongside the lawns at the back of the hotel. I say hotel because this was much more than a local pub. It was a very extensive seventeenth century manor which had long since been converted into a traditional and very comfortable hotel. It had extensive lounges and dining rooms, no fewer than 23 bedrooms, many with four-poster beds, a superb wine cellar and even had a board room with flipchart and the like still in place, from which we deduced it must have hosted management conferences. The best feature of all was that every significant room contained a large open fireplace, including 14 of the bedrooms, presumably to retain a traditional atmosphere, which must have been quite a fire risk but was ideal for our purposes. As one would expect with a large hotel, it was serviced by an extensive well-equipped kitchen.

The only thing missing was a log-burning stove as had proved so useful to us at Saltersford Hall. Prior to our arrival, some of the lads had set up the kitchen with several calor gas cookers and a ready supply of replacement gas canisters which they had liberated from a local caravan site. It wasn't as cosy as a log-burning stove and left a persistent gas smell but worked well enough. As long as we could continue to source plenty of fuel for the fires and dried and tinned food for the kitchen, we could see out the winter in relative comfort. We had more ambitious plans for the future. Behind the hotel were extensive grounds, mainly lawn, leading onto a field by the river. The plan was to dig up the lawns to cultivate fruit and vegetables and use the field to graze livestock. A further building near the river had been used as a holiday cottage and was called The Piggeries, suggesting it's original function in the days of the manor house, and Adam reckoned it would be possible to re-convert the property for livestock, perhaps some beef cattle, pigs, goats and chickens. We would all be busy in the Spring.

Whitewell itself was certainly secluded, located on a country lane between Longridge and Dunsop Bridge. There was no reason for anybody to be passing through, not that there was any sign of people moving around. Whitewell could hardly be described as a village. Apart from the old manor, now the inn, there was a church alongside and that was about it. Brian had been very concerned about security, requiring somewhere out of the way and this certainly fitted the bill, although we produced so much smoke from the numerous chimneys, that this would be visible for miles around. If people wanted to find us, it would not be difficult. However, we were well defended with plenty of guns and ammunition, apparently derived from Brian and Adam's raid on a shooting club before they started recruiting people to the survivor group in Manchester. In any event, we shouldn't assume that visitors would be hostile and at some point we would have to make contact with other survivors. Yes, all in all, the Inn at Whitewell was a pretty good choice. I congratulated Brian and the team on finding the place but it turned out that inside knowledge was involved. Brian and his wife used to enjoy walking weekends in the Forest of Bowland and had sampled the occasional meal at the inn. Realising its potential, he had primed one of the search teams to include it on their itinerary. Brian consulted the others but, by all accounts, steered the decision to his preference, which was fairly typical of Brian's management style.

Thanks largely to Brian, we were extremely well organised. We all had designated responsibilities and made decisions through a management board with weekly meetings in the hotel boardroom. We'd even been known to make use of the flip-charts, which took me back to my previous life as a civil servant, and yet Brian was much more of a bureaucrat than I ever had been. My driver had always been getting things done and producing results but Brian was very keen on the correct process. Believe it or not, he even had minutes prepared, which seemed surreal in our circumstances. To be fair, he only recorded the key points agreed, individuals responsible for completing tasks and points to be reviewed at the next meeting, which had some merit though one couldn't but help noticing a little eye-rolling around the group. Brian enjoyed being in charge and became de-facto Chief Executive simply because he set things up. I think everybody was happy to let him get on with it and he did meet a need. He had suggested standing for re-election after a year but I couldn't see anybody challenging him.

Brian appointed Adam Griffin as his deputy. Brian and Adam knew each other before the Death and worked well together. The deputy role didn't amount to much but Adam was also the Estate Manager which meant he had overall charge of the inn and all aspects of its development for our needs. Adam was a lot younger than Brian and was more "hands-on" in getting the job done. He had been a heating engineer and had a lot of practical skills. Like Brian and myself, Adam lost his wife to the virus but they didn't have any kids. He was in his early thirties and I don't think he was married that long. Unless they volunteered the information, I found it rather difficult to ask these questions. The women in the group seemed to find out these things, which I suppose is what you'd expect. Anyway, Adam's Estate Team included Phil Lucas, who did most of the property maintenance. John Salt was in charge of security, Paul Fernyhough vehicles, Paul Naden farming, Christine Lucas housekeeping and Emma Fernyhough was head cook. Paul Naden was assisted by Jim Clarke and William Fernyhough, younger son of Paul and Emma. Jim was a young accounts clerk who joined the group after I left them in Manchester and was the only addition to the group. Of course the farming didn't generate much activity at that time of year but others would pitch in when required. Emma had a real challenge creating meals for 18 people with limited resources and was assisted by Christine Salt, Lisa Grundy, who I recruited in Kendals, and my own Jo. Lisa and Jo also helped Christine Lucas with the housekeeping.

My official title was Head of Resources which earned me a seat at board meetings. What that basically meant was I lead the foraging team, assisted full-time by Mo Narwaz and Ian Fernyhough but also Phil Lucas unless he was needed to work on the inn. We went out in pairs in the vans, so Mo and I were out virtually every day and Ian and Phil joined us when available. From a management point of view I needed to liaise with the others to prioritise resource needs then plan how we're going to source them, for example Adam would discuss what he needed for the estate and Emma or Christine for the food. The routine foraging was fairly obvious. We'd go into any property and raid the kitchen for tinned food and any dried food that was robustly packaged and still serviceable. Unless we saw smoke now, which we invariably didn't, we made a quick shout then smashed the door down with sledge hammers. We'd found a lot of dead bodies in an advanced state of decay but nothing shocked us anymore and we'd even got used to the nauseating smell. Although we had encountered a lot of rats, nobody had yet been bitten but we took the precaution of wearing boots and tucking our trousers firmly into our socks. If the rats ran too close to us, we just kicked them out of the way. We hadn't attempted to catch any as nobody had yet suggested eating them but that day could arrive. So far we'd managed to maintain an adequate supply of food, if a little lacking in variety. Any grocery shops or supermarkets were usually a waste of time as they'd long since been picked clean but the private houses were a good source as the panic buying had been so extensive once the virus spread and people began to appreciate the severity of the problem, that typical stocks were vastly greater than could be consumed in the time left to people. We'd often clear out around ten homes per van in a day and return to Whitewell loaded up with every sort of tin. We were running quite a big surplus which was stacked up in the cellar. Our other priority was fuel, which primarily meant wood. We had plenty of calor gas for cooking but all the fires consumed an enormous quantity of wood. We didn't use a huge amount in the bedrooms – just enough to take the chill off – but the fireplaces in the old lounges and bars needed to heat a very large area and were constantly replenished throughout the day. We came across the odd log store but not very often so we'd taken to removing any easily accessible wood, furniture, even solid doors. We then stored it all at the Piggeries and Adam had it chopped into firewood. We'd found the odd coal cellar and filled a few sacks but I was thinking of trying to locate a coal yard and see if we could remove a serious stock.

The other specialist role in the group was Christine Salt's as resident teacher, which she managed part-time in addition to assisting Emma with the cooking. Christine was only nineteen and had been a first year English student but was keen to take on the role. She had just three pupils, Lisa Grundy who was fifteen and not the most academic, my Jo at thirteen and little Anna Lucas, five. We had quite a debate over what should be taught. The emphasis was on practical skills which the girls would learn on the job. Lisa and Jo were already learning the housekeeping and cooking but as the opportunities arose, would also experience property maintenance and building skills, probably with John Salt or Phil Lucas. During the peak farming months they would learn horticulture and animal husbandry from Paul Naden along with his assistants Jim Clarke and William Fernyhough, who were also very much trainees. They could even get involved with vehicle maintenance by helping Paul Fernyhough. When they were older they would be taught how to maintain and fire weapons. These were the basic survival skills. Christine would be leading the more formal learning, which given the age differences would be largely one to one tuition. Maths and English would form the basics. We wanted some coverage of the sciences and I argued strongly for some English history. Not everybody was convinced on that one and I acknowledged that there was no survival advantage but felt it essential that we did something to preserve our heritage. It wasn't a priority at the time but I intended to argue the need to maintain a good library at the inn.

And what of young Poppy? She had probably settled down best of all. They say dogs relate to people rather than places and that was certainly the case. Just as she had settled at Saltersford Hall, she made herself at home at the inn. You'd think she'd lived here all her life. Her role in the group was to bolster morale by loving everybody and she had certainly become a great favourite. Her main motivation was food and she looked on all the group as potential suppliers but particularly those associated with the kitchen. She got into trouble with Emma occasionally for jumping onto surfaces, leading to temporary bans whilst meals were being prepared. Little Anna thought she was wonderful despite being knocked over more than once when she was at her most boisterous. Even Mo, who didn't really relate to dogs, was gradually coming round and had given her a tentative pat on the head. Above all else though, Poppy was absolutely devoted to Jo. Perhaps it was because she remembered Jo rescuing her from her prison when she was so weak, or the initial bonding in their short period together at Saltersford Hall, but they were now inseparable. In our early days at Whitewell I took Poppy in the van foraging but on the second occasion we encountered a pack of dogs in the neighbouring village of Newton. That set Poppy off barking and the pack went for the van. Mo scared them off with a warning shot but if Poppy had been outside then I think she'd have been torn to pieces. We'd seen several packs of dogs recently and since then I'd left Poppy at the inn. She was allowed to run in the grounds as she hadn't attempted to cross the river, which was quite fast –flowing but I wouldn't let Jo take her further afield in case she came across dogs. We couldn't provide her with an armed escort just to walk the dog. When she'd had a good run or a feed, which was generally scraps from our meals, Poppy would settle down as close to the fireplace as she could get and had often been heard snoring. She slept on Jo's bed for a couple nights when we first arrived, which gave Jo comfort while she was weak, but since then we'd put her bed in the main lounge near the embers of the fire and she wasn't complaining. It was also useful to have her downstairs as an early warning system if anybody tried to break in. She wouldn't attack an intruder but she would certainly make a lot of noise. That was Poppy's little contribution to our security.

*

That evening was our weekly management board meeting. We always met after our evening meal and took a pot of coffee and some biscuits in with us. It was well after dark and didn't disrupt anybody's work schedule. It also excused us from the washing up. There were six of us at the meetings. Brian Curtis was Chairman, Adam Griffin spoke on estate issues, John Salt on security, I covered resources and Paul Naden the food production, obviously still at the planning stage. Helen Salt, John's wife, covered the admin, particularly the note-taking. It seemed rather sexist that the only female present was the note-taker but that was just the way it panned out. Helen used to be secretary in John's building company, so the role came easily to her.

Brian called the meeting to order and thanked us for our prompt arrival. We all approved the minutes, which were just a single page of hand-written bullet points, mainly points agreed and issues to take forward. No doubt one day we'd be audited and the auditors would be most impressed with our record-keeping.

We each gave updates on our areas of responsibility and I waited until last so that the others could flag up resource needs. Adam took first turn: "Well, I think you'll all agree that the inn is meeting our needs very well. We have more than sufficient space for our numbers and could easily take another ten if we need to. The heating's okay once the fires have been going for an hour or so in the morning and the girls are coping very well with the kitchen facilities. We've got plenty of calor gas, though we'll need to ensure we've always got spare canisters ready –it's not an issue at the moment. The thing that would really improve our position is electricity. It would be a big exercise but it would be worth our while trying to install a generator. Of course we'll have to find one first."

Everybody agreed that having a power source would be fantastic but Brian queried whether the installation would be feasible.

"Absolutely. I've put in generators before. You can get little portable ones but we might need something a bit bigger, say 16 KW. We'll need some electrical supplies, cabling and the like but that should be easy enough to get hold of. The main problem will be sourcing the generator and shifting it manually but with three or four of us and the right sort of vehicles, I reckon we could do it."

"I could do much more on the security front with an electricity supply", added John.

"Okay, if we're all agreed, let's go for it", said Brian with enthusiasm. "Something to add to your shopping list, Tom."

"Fine, though I won't have a clue what we're looking for and I don't think the others on my team will either."

"I'll come out with you when you're ready," said Adam. "Once we've identified a suitable generator, we can find the right vehicle to move it. We might need to get to an industrial estate or something."

"Some of the farms round about might be using generators," offered Paul, "particularly the bigger ones, not the little sheep farms. They'll have had to cope with power cuts."

"Any local hospitals will have a generator but they'll probably be too big for our purposes" said Adam.

It's settled that the installation of a generator is a priority. Adam continued his report:

"Most of the work on the estate will be at the Piggeries and building a farm for Paul, rather than the inn itself, though I know John wants to commission some work on security. Over to you John."

"Right well, we wanted a place we could defend against attack, though so far we haven't seen a soul. We can't hide because we're producing so much bloody smoke, it must be visible for miles, so if anybody wanted to attack they could plan their approach undetected. If they come down the road from either direction they'll approach the inn from the front. As you know, we've blocked off two of the three doors and when that thick oak front door's bolted it'd take a battering ram to open it, so that's safe enough. The back of the inn is not as secure but we've got the protection of the river and the church to the side. You'd have to leave the road a few hundred yards to the south, move through the field and to the side of the church to get to the back of the inn by the Piggeries. This is where we could erect some security fencing, maybe some heavy duty stuff, ten feet or so. I'm thinking that we're going to need some good fencing anyway when the farm's working to keep the dogs and foxes away from the stock. Now, if we've got electricity, we could think about electrified fencing and a decent alarm system, perhaps some lighting as well."

I could sense my shopping list getting longer and longer.

"If dogs come round yer, I'll shoot buggers!" was Paul's observation.

"Okay Paul, but you can't be there 24 hours a day. They'll come at night time," responded Adam.

We resolved that security fencing was desirable but would be part of the plans for the development of the farm and we would attempt to integrate the grazing and horticulture areas with the inn and church all within one secure complex, electrified if possible. We were going to need an awful lot of fencing.

Paul's plans for the farm came next.

"Aye well, as we've no stock yet and nowt growing there aint much to do in actual farming like. The main thing is to get the Piggeries place ready. We've stripped out most of the ground floor for livestock and the first floor will be for storage. The garden at the back and right down to the river is going to be the growing area. The whole lot will need ploughing up first. We'll need a tractor and some tackle but there's no rush like as we can't do didly squat while grounds hard. If we're lucky with the weather, we might get going in February. We'll start off with root crops, you know, spuds, carrots, suedes, onions and some cabbage and caulis will be easy enough. The cooks want some fruit brushes – we'll have to find some young ones growing that we can transplant. Then there's that big greenhouse – that'll be for salad stuff, lettuces, cucumber, tomatoes, that sort of thing. We can easily grow all the fresh fruit and veg we need, then we just eat what's in season."

"Sounds great," says Brian. "What about the livestock, what's feasible, do you think?"

"Ah well, that's a bit trickier, isn't it. All the farms have been abandoned for two months now. From what I've seen most of the animals have either broken loose, been attacked by dogs and the like or are just dead in the barn, especially the dairy farms."

"I see plenty of sheep in the fields on my travels" I offered.

"Aye, they're quite hardy. A lot will survive the winter as long as they're not buried in snow, but if we want to breed from 'em and get some lambs to eat, you'll have to find mc a ram. Good luck with that."

"Would they not be ready to lamb in the springtime anyway?"

"Well, that all depends whether they were serviced before everything went belly up. It takes 145 days to produce a lamb, so if they were aiming for April, they'd take ram to ewes in November but that won't have happened. I doubt they'd be looking at February lambs round these parts – much too early. The only chance is if they planned for March and had ewes serviced in October. That's possible but you can't tell this early. Best wait til March and keep an eye out. If you see a field with a lot of fat ewes, leave 'em to give birth, then take 'em quick like – the ewe and her lambs – before the dogs and foxes move in. if we want to plan long term we could keep one or two males and use 'em to mate when they're ready. Other than finding a mature ram now, that's about the only way we're going to build our own flock for a regular supply of lambs."

We were all realising by now that getting a productive farm started was not going to be easy but we needed to do it. We couldn't live out of tins forever and the prospect of some roast lamb was absolutely mouth-watering.

It finally came to my turn to provide an update on the resources: "So far we've concentrated on the immediate needs of food and fuel. We've been working our way round the local villages, checking out all the houses. There's very little in Chipping, Dunsop Bridge and Newton – no shops, the odd pub and a small garage – but Waddington's a bit bigger. We're doing very well for tinned food as a lot of the houses are quite well stocked, a legacy of the panic buying when the virus spread. We're still finding some useable dried food, particularly rice and pasta. It all depends how it's been stored and whether it's in a high level cupboard because the rats have had a field day. We're planning to move onto Clitheroe now, which should keep us in supplies for a long time. We're basically picking up whatever we can but we are looking for some particulars as Emma keeps a shopping list updated – quite a lot of Christmas stuff – I think the girls are planning a good spread. Anyway, we're running a good surplus on the food front, so there's no urgency there. We're also bringing in wood for the fires wherever we find it but we get through a hell of a lot. We were thinking our next priority would be to locate a reliable source of coal and stock up for the rest of the winter. We'll track down some coal merchants and see what sort of stock they're holding. Apart from that, the message I would take from today's meeting is to check out all the farms in the area for generators, vehicles, equipment and even livestock. When we find any likely targets we'll bring in Adam and Paul to check out what we can use."

"Okay. Sounds a good plan. Any other business?"

Brian soon had the meeting wrapped up and I think we all had a better understanding of the challenges ahead.

21 December

"Right Mo, fancy being a coalman today?"

"Long as I don't get any jokes about a black face!"

"Wouldn't dream of it mate."

I had just informed Mo of our objective for the day. From a quick perusal of the telephone directory in the hotel office I had identified the nearest source, Pimlico Firewood and Coal Merchants at 88 Pimlico Road, Clitheroe.

We set off straight after breakfast in the same Vivaro that Jo and I had used for our arrival, empty apart from a jerry can of diesel and some tools in case of breakdown. We just took the one van as Ian and Phil were working with Adam on converting the Piggeries. I would drive and Mo ride shotgun, well a rifle to be more accurate, and we also had a hand-gun in the glove compartment. I still hadn't used any firearms but Mo had taken some lessons from John and knew the basics. John and Adam were the marksmen of the group and most of the others had taken some instruction. I had promised to do the same but felt little inclination. I just couldn't see myself shooting anybody, nor a dog for that matter and in any event, a warning shot from Mo was always sufficient to deter the dogs.

We followed our well established route north to Dunsop Bridge, across to Newton, then taking the B6478 through Waddington towards Clitheroe. Having consulted the OS map we knew we wouldn't need to hit the centre of Clitheroe to reach the coal merchants, so didn't anticipate any problems and were rewarded with an uneventful journey. We crossed the river Ribble and headed towards the centre. Once we had crossed the railway line we needed a left and after 100 yards or so, spotted Pimlico Road. So far, so good.

A couple hundred yards down the road and amongst a number of industrial enterprises a sign on the gate announced:

PIMLICO FIREWOOD AND COAL MERCHANTS

Our objective had been reached but now to gain access. The depot was surrounded by very high heavy duty security fencing probably twelve feet or so. There was no barbed or razor wire on top, so it was climbable but it would be little use getting in without being able to get coal out. The front gate itself was secured with a huge padlock. We had wine-cutters in the van but nothing that would break a padlock of that size. As a lock-up depot, there seemed little prospect of finding a key inside.

Mo and I parked the van and inspected the perimeter of the site, looking for an easier way in. The front gate was the only way in or out and the same standard of fencing surrounded the compound. This was not going to be easy. We debated the possibility of backing up the van and ramming the gates at speed but I reckoned there was more chance of wrecking the van than smashing the gate so we decided to try the wire-cutters at the side of the gates. The cutters were sharp but short-handled, only nine inches or so, insufficient to provide much in the way of torque. Tackling the thinnest wire and using both hands and all the strength I could muster eventually it split with a twang. We examined the rest of the fence on the basis that if one cuts, they'd all cut. The section of fencing was uniform up to around three feet from the ground where a line of much thicker wire was used. We would need much better tools to get through that. There were fifteen lines of thinner wire up to that level, so we concluded that with 45 cuts we could make a three foot square opening which would be big enough to remove sacks of coal. It was worth the attempt.

I left Mo to get on with the cutting while I climbed over the fence to see what was worth taking. Getting over the fence was easy enough, apart from ripping my trousers on the top, and I climbed half way down the other side before dropping to the ground. I looked for vehicles first, hoping they might be loaded up for delivery but no such luck. Three lorries were parked up, all empty. Moving on to the main building in the compound, there was a small office at the front, a toilet and some washrooms. Beyond the building was what looked like some sort of loading area but again there was no stock lined up. To the side was a big metal container with a narrow opening at the bottom, some form of hopper for filling bags and there were buttons on the wall to operate it. Even if there was stock in the hopper, without power this would be no use and I moved back out to investigate the rest of the compound. At the back was a JCB type digger and next to it was a large enclosure about one quarter full with loose coal. I was beginning to work out how the system operated. Delivery vehicles dumped the loose coal in the enclosure at the back, the digger lifted the coal into the top of the hopper as required and then controls were set to release a sack full at a time. These would be loaded manually onto the lorries to deliver to the customers. The lorry drivers would presumably bring back the empty sacks. So where were they? The logical place was underneath the hopper as that is where they would be needed. I went back to the hopper and in the open room underneath a heap of old sacks had been thrown into a corner. I reckoned there were at least a dozen and at a rough guess, there was enough coal left to fill about twenty sacks. Okay, we were in business but we'd have to fill the sacks by hand, then drag them to the fence and load up the Vivaro. This was going to be a slow job, heavy work and very dirty. Some gloves would be useful if we could find any.

I went back to check on Mo. He was struggling but had made some progress in cutting a vertical line up to the first intersection on the fence, about three feet from the ground. He was finding it hard work as the thickness of the wire was at the absolute limit of the capacity of the short-handled cutters. I made a mental note to prioritise the acquisition of some long-handled cutters before attempting any similar ventures. Mo passed the cutters through the fence and I took over while Mo nursed his right hand, looking decidedly unhappy.

"Cheer up mate, we'll get there. The bad news is we'll have to fill the sacks by hand. We could be here a long time."

As a devout Muslim, Mo was forbidden to swear but I could see that he was sorely tempted.

Between us we eventually removed a section of fence three feet square and I gave Mo a guided tour of the depot. I still hadn't found any gloves, so we checked out the contents of the office, if you could call it that, more of a shed really. We searched it thoroughly but no gloves. One more place to look, the cabs of the lorries. Two of them yielded nothing but the third had an extremely tatty pair of heavy duty gloves, thickly matted with coal dust. It was better than nothing. We picked up the old sacks from the hopper, counted fourteen and carried them over to the remains of the coal heap. Mo held open the first sack and I took the gloves, manhandling the lumps of coal until the first sack was filled. It took about twenty minutes which meant around five hours work plus breaks to fill the sacks, another hour or so to load the van and we'd already been here over an hour. It would most likely be dark before we finished. All we could do was press on. Mo and I took it in turns to hold the sack or handle the coal, swapping the gloves every fifteen or twenty minutes before our hands became completely numb. I cursed our lack of foresight in not bringing two pairs of gloves. Even standard gardening gloves would have helped as the temperature was close to freezing but at least there was no rain.

With six sacks filled, we decided to break for lunch and get warmed up. We had no means of tying the sacks closed, so we just dragged them across the compound to the hole in the fence, squeezed them through, taking care not to snag the sacks or indeed ourselves on the sharp edges of the cut wire, and paired up to load them into the back of the van. By now we were absolutely filthy and needed to clean up a little before we could eat, visiting the washrooms to see what was available and finding a large pot of Swarfega on a shelf. Taking a scoop each, we eased all the grime from our hands which was an unexpectedly comforting sensation.

I turned on the tap to rinse off the green jelly to be met with a dreadful gurgling noise and a few drops of thick brown liquid. We searched for any sort of towel or cloth to wipe our hands but without success, then an idea struck me. I lifted the toilet flush lid – believe me, that's not easy when your hands are covered in Swarfega – and found the cistern full of water. It had not been used since the water supply failed. We both plunged in our hands and rinsed off the jelly, trying not to touch the ballcock and other bits which were covered in something approaching black slime.

"Nadine would not be impressed with this, not a bit." Nadine was Mo's late wife and it was unusual for her to be mentioned as we were both rather private in our respective grief.

"Neither would Sue, now you mention it. That was pretty disgusting but needs must. Just think Mo, we've both survived the worst contagion ever to hit mankind. Our immune systems must be second to none. Why, any germs lurking in that cistern will be child's play to our antibodies."

"What we survived was a virus" pointed out Mo, "whereas that toilet will be full if bacteria, but never mind, it's not going to stop me eating my lunch."

"That's the spirit Mo."

We returned to the van, started the engine, turned on the heating and unpacked our lunches from the foil – fairly normal rations : a big chunk of corned beef, some digestive biscuits, a large Conference pear and to round it off, some comfort food for the cold weather, a Mars bar. The pears were a good find. Ian and Phil had come across a well laden tree of ripe pears in a garden at Dunsop Bridge soon after we settled at the inn. In fact the bulk of the crop was already on the ground but they took what was left on the tree and filled several boxes. They'd stored quite well, though some had to be thrown. It was such a treat to have fresh fruit instead of all the tinned stuff. Lunch was washed down with a thermos of piping hot black coffee which really warmed us through. All in all, quite a satisfying meal.

Refreshed and thawed out, we returned to work with a will, taking it in turns to bundle the coal into the sacks until they were all filled, a further eight to add to the six already loaded. By this time the rain was falling steadily and the light failing, even earlier than I expected. The sky was heavy and I feared the rain would turn to snow after dark. Our route back to Whitewell could be difficult in snow and I wasn't sure how the van would handle. The rain was mixing with the coal dust to create a dirty sludge and Mo and I were absolutely filthy and rather miserable.

"Come on, Mo. Let's get this lot loaded up and we can finish the coffee and get the heater going."

"Sounds good to me, boss. I think I'll pass on the Swarfega and toilet water this time."

"Agreed."

It was another 45 minutes before we were on the road, past four o'clock and totally dark. As expected, the rain had turned to snow with a thin covering already on the road. We agreed we needed to get back as quickly as possible and decided to take a more direct route. Instead of heading north back through Waddington and Newton, as we had come, we left Clitheroe going west on the B6243 in the direction of Longridge but after a mile or so, would need to cut across the country lanes through little hamlets like Bashall Eaves and Cow Ark, past Browsholme Hall. Mo and I hadn't driven this route before but we could see on the map that it was only half the distance of our outward journey and knew that Ian and Phil had checked out Browsholme Hall a couple weeks back with no problems on the road. Mo was navigating by using a torch on the OS map and was not having the easiest time finding the route. The imperative was to eat up the miles before the lanes disappeared under the snow. I cursed the decision to fill all fourteen available sacks. If we'd quit an hour ago, we'd have been back by now with no difficulty.

We left Clitheroe on the B road without incident, crossed the river Ribble again and then turned right onto a lane marked to Bashall Town and Bashall Eaves. At least the heating was working well by then and we were as warm as toast. The road however was a concern. A thin blanket of snow extended across the road, the verges and everything else with perfect evenness making it impossible to discern where the road started or finished. All I could do was judge the mid-point between the hedges and aim for that but the only light was from the van headlights. The snow was getting heavier which reduced visibility dramatically. The only positive was that the lane was reasonably level and almost straight. However, I was beginning to get worried now. I was not inexperienced at driving in the snow but being the only vehicle on the road was a completely different situation. There were no vehicles to clear the snow, no tracks to follow and no other lights. What light there was from the van was reflecting on the heavily falling snow. It wasn't exactly a whiteout but not far off. There seemed little point waiting for the snow to ease as it was building up on the road and I could only see it getting worse. We needed to get some miles covered. For the first time I envisaged the possibility of having to abandon the van but it was much too far to walk back to Whitewell and too dark to find our way with just small torches. It was dawning on me how badly prepared we were for this situation.

Mo was trying to follow where we were on the road and at

the same time use the torch to scrutinise the map. I was simply concentrating on keeping us on the road and we had now slowed to around fifteen mph. We must have covered a couple miles when we came to a fork in the road. An old style sign post on the other side was covered in snow but would have been impossible to read in what was now nothing short of a blizzard. I was about to volunteer Mo to get out and clear the signpost but he read my thoughts and stated confidently "It's okay. I see where we are. We turn right towards Bashall Town, then an immediate sharp left bend for Bashall Eaves. I am sure of this."

"I hope so. I don't want to get lost in this."

I slowly took the right turn and quickly spotted another fork about twenty yards on. To the right we could see the dim outline of a few houses which must be Barshall Town, only a small hamlet despite the name. For an instant I considered breaking in to one of the houses to stay the night but it would be freezing cold and may not be possible to make a fire. At least we were warm in the van and apparently moving towards our objective, albeit rather slowly. The roads could only get worse. We needed to press on. Mo reckoned that according to the map we had a reasonably straight and flat run to Bashall Eaves about two miles on.

We ploughed on through a tunnel of light into the blizzard but I could hardly see what was on the ground. We were literally crawling now. Every now and then the van bumped along which indicated we had left the road surface and I corrected to the left or right more on instinct than judgement.

"There should be another fork coming up soon", advised Mo. "We just bend a little to the right."

I finally spotted the fork through the blizzard but only when we were half way across it. I realised we were going to overshoot the road and saw a hedge looming up in front. Turning sharply to the right, I had to touch the brakes or we would be off the road. That was enough to do it. The rear end of the van whipped round and we left the road back-end first and dropped several feet. We were left with the rear of the van in a ditch and the front end looking up to the sky. The front wheels were still in contact with the road but spinning hopelessly.

"That's it. We're going nowhere in this. Sorry Mo. What a mess. I can't believe I've got you into this situation."

"Don't blame yourself Tom. It was just bad luck, you know."

"Nothing to do with luck. Bad planning, complacency. There are so many things we should have done differently."

"Well what are we going to do Tom? Stay here or walk?"

We considered the options for a while. There was no food left in the van but we had some water and enough fuel in the tank to keep the engine running and the heating on. The lads would soon realise that we were in trouble and may set off in the Landrovers to look for us. Our two Landrovers were great in snow but they'd have the same visibility problems and were unlikely to assume we'd be on this lane. They knew where we were going but would probably assume we back-tracked through Waddington, Newton and Dunsop Bridge. Had we done so, we'd probably have found somewhere in Waddington to spend the night. We were literally in the middle of nowhere and the chances of being found were not good. The other option was to walk out. Mo reckoned we were about a mile short of Bashall Eaves, another hamlet of half a dozen houses. Nobody had yet checked out the village so there was likely to be some tinned food available and if there were open fires we could at least break up some furniture to make a fire, a better prospect than spending the night in the van. Was it feasible to walk a mile in a snowstorm? We had good boots and decent coats, the snow was only a few inches deep and it should be possible to follow the road, however severe the blizzard. We decided it was worth a try.

With the van pitched up at twenty degrees or so, it was quite difficult exiting without falling into the ditch. Before closing the driver's door I gave a few long blasts on the horn just in case the Landrovers were in the vicinity. We listened for a response but all we could hear was some distant barking muffled by the snow.

"You'd better take the rifle Mo."

"Got it, boss."

"You sure you know how to use it?"

"Oh yes. John showed me what to do. It's not a problem."

Mo didn't sound very confident but he had more chance of firing it than I had. The main concern was the barking, the sound of which appeared to be moving around but it was impossible to say whether it was any closer, the volume dependent on the gusting of the wind. The snow was driving across the road horizontally with visibility almost down to zero. It would have been impossible to drive any further even if we hadn't hit the ditch. Using our torches we could just about see where the road was. Although the snow was several inches deep and drifting, it compacted evenly under our boots indicating a hard tarmac surface underneath. Could we manage a mile of this?

We pressed on as best as we could and very soon lost sight of the van, which was a little disconcerting, though I reckoned we could retrace our footsteps for quite a while before they filled in with snow. The barking was definitely getting closer and I wondered whether using the horn had alerted them. It sounded like quite a few dogs in a state of some excitement. Although I was comfortable with dogs, I realised that they could be dangerous in numbers as the pack mentality set in, but they were surely not tracking us as prey. These were family pets little more than two months ago. It was then I saw the first dog, a large German Shephard. It emerged from the snow out of what I assumed was a field to our right. As soon as it saw us it began barking more aggressively and snarled with bared teeth. This animal meant business. It was soon joined by several more dogs of disparate sizes and indeterminate breeds. Luckily they were separated from us by a wire fence. They were pushing the fence with their front paws and trying unsuccessfully to clamber over but it was too tall.

I could see Mo's face in the edge of my torchlight and he was clearly terrified.

"I think you'll have to use the rifle, Mo."

The German Shephard then withdrew and ran ahead alongside the fence, quickly followed by the others, disappearing into the blizzard. I had a bad feeling about this. We moved as quickly as we could, almost breaking into a run but after fifty yards or so the German Shephard appeared in the road, flanked by two others. To the right I saw two other dogs scrambling through a broken gate. As I feared, the dog pack knew the area and used this as their hunting territory. The German Shephard advanced slowly towards us with a crouched stance, the others following. They were preparing to attack.

"Mo, quick, fire at the Alsatian. He's the leader," I whispered.

Mo quickly raised the rifle and fired but he hadn't taken aim properly or adopted an appropriate stance. The shot went into the air and Mo landed on his back, unprepared for the recoil. The dogs froze at the shot but saw Mo on the ground and saw the chance to attack. I tried to help Mo to his feet but the German Shephard was on to him in a frenzy. Mo tried to fend him off with his hands but the dog caught him by the forearm, ripping his coat and sinking in his teeth. Mo screamed as I grabbed the rifle and swung it at the dog making a hard contact with the side of his head. The dog yelped and let go of Mo, retreating a few yards. Meanwhile, the other dogs were moving round and were approaching from three sides. In grabbing the rifle, I had dropped my torch and couldn't see where the dogs were moving. Our only chance was to shoot one of the dogs, preferably the German Shephard.

Suddenly the scene was bathed in light as a large vehicle approached from the rear. We turned but were blinded by the headlights. The driver sounded the horn and flashed the lights, causing the dogs to recoil. Some of them turned tail and ran away but the German Shephard and several of the larger dogs held their ground, barking aggressively. In the next instant a loud shot rang out and one of the dogs yelped as they scattered. The door of the vehicle opened and we were greeted by a cheery "What the fuck are you doing out here? Get in quick!" We didn't argue.

CHAPTER NINE

BILL and ALICE

21 December

"Bill Weston's the name. Got yourselves in a bit of a pickle back there, didn't ya?"

Bill was taking us back in the direction we'd come from in what looked like a big Range Rover. He was driving at twice the speed I'd attempted with complete confidence despite the appalling conditions. Reading my thoughts, he added: "It helps if you know the road. Couldn't believe it when I heard your horn blaring. First vehicle I've seen in well over a month. Saw yer van in ditch. Couldn't ya make bend?"

"No. I only saw it at the last minute as I was blinded by the snow. Tom Morton, by the way. Pleased to meet you. This is Mo Narwaz. We were trying to walk to Bashall Eaves and find somewhere for the night but we didn't reckon on the dogs. Lucky for us you were nearby. We were in trouble there."

"Reckon you were. That's the worst pack. That fucking Alsatian, he don't take fright. They're always trying to get at my bloody chickens. Did he get hold of ya then?"

He had seen the blood on Mo's arm.

"Yes. It hurts like hell. I thought he was going for my throat. It's my worst nightmare. I hate dogs."

"Don't worry. My lass Alice will fix you up when we get to the farm, then we'll have a bit to eat. She'll be surprised to see you."

It was then that Bill noticed the state of us.

"Christ, what you bin up to then?"

"Ah, just a bit of coal mining." I explained how we had spent the day in Clitheroe. "There's fourteen sacks of coal in the back of that van, if you need some."

"I stick to wood," said Bill. "If we're running short like, I just take chainsaw into woods. No shortage of trees."

After today's experience, I was beginning to wish we'd taken the same line. It had seemed like a good idea.

As the snow cleared a little, I could see our van sticking out of the ditch, just one more abandoned vehicle. At least it wasn't entirely blocking the road. Before we reached it, Bill turned right on a little track flanked by a row of short posts, less than a foot tall.

"If I can't see posts, it's too bloody deep," explained Bill.

The track turned to the left, rising slightly, until the farm buildings came into view, dim lights showing from two of the downstairs windows.

"Welcome to Horse Hey Farm, gents."

I couldn't see much of the farmhouse other than a glimpse as the headlights swung round as Bill parked the Range Rover in front of the main door but the impression gained was large and old. Bill led the way inside.

"Alice! Got you some visitors, there's a surprise. Two more for supper."

A pretty young girl in her mid-teens appeared from the back, wearing jeans, a thick jumper with an apron over the top.

"This ere's Tom and that's Mo. This is my Alice, all I've got left in the world since the flu took my missus and my lad Jack. Mo here's had a bit of a set–to with that bastard Alsatian that's bin sniffing round hens. I think I put some shot in 'im. Let's hope he's bleeding to death somewhere or maybe the rest of the pack have finished 'im off. Have a look at Mo's arm, there's a good girl."

"Okay Dad." Alice seemed a little embarrassed at meeting strangers, her shyness no doubt enhanced by enforced isolation for over two months. Her cheeks had reddened and she avoided eye contact. "Pleased to meet you", she said.

Mo managed to remove his coat with a little assistance and pushed back his shirt sleeve to reveal his wound, which looked rather unpleasant. It was more than a few tooth marks, rather a tear where the dog had caught hold of him. No wonder he screamed. Alice brought a bowl of hot water, a flannel, towel and bottle of TCP. She soon had it cleaned up and although Mo winced at the application of the TCP, it was clearly essential to prevent infection. An infected dog bite was not to be countenanced in the absence of a ready supply of antibiotics. There were no bandages available but Alice produced strips of clean cloth, possibly an old tea towel, and bound the wound. Mo was hugely relieved and extremely grateful.

"Now then," said Bill. "You'll not be going anywhere tonight, so you'll join us for supper. Omelettes, ain't it girl?"

"Yes. Omelette with bacon. Is that alright? I could get something out of the freezer but it would take a lot longer."

"Sounds wonderful," I said. "Most of our food has come out of tins for the last couple months. How are you running a freezer?"

I had seen no sign of any power. The farmhouse was lit by oil lamps and heated by log fires.

"We've got a little generator in the milking shed. We used to run the milking machine for a dozen cows but we've only kept Mavis now and she produces more milk than we can get through. We milk her by hand now. Anyway, since power went off, we moved the fridge and the freezer into the milking shed and run them from the generator."

"Could you not run your lights, heating and so on in the farmhouse from the generator?" I asked.

"I dunno. I don't know much about electric stuff. I stick to me animals, that all I know."

"We've got somebody who could probably fix that up for you, if the generator's big enough. We're looking for a powerful generator ourselves."

"It's no problem. We're alright as we are, ain't we girl."

"Yes Dad," said Alice but without conviction.

✳

In less than an hour we were sitting down at a huge oak table in the farmhouse kitchen in front of a roaring fire. Alice had prepared enormous omelettes with bacon, which Bill had cured himself from his own pigs. Mo politely requested an omelette without bacon as he wasn't permitted to eat it as a Muslim.

"You don't want to worry about that lad" said Bill. "It's all gone now, all these different religions. Just staying alive, that's all that counts." Nevertheless, Mo stuck to his principles.

The omelette was absolutely delicious. It was so long since I'd tasted anything prepared with fresh eggs. This was followed by coffee with fresh milk and accompanied by an enormous fruitcake. Apparently, they made their own butter as well and had stocked up a good quantity in the fridge.

The cake was as good as anything Lucy used to make and Mo and I complimented Alice on her baking skills. "Aye, lass is a good cook, learnt it all from her mum, bless her."

Alice smiled, embarrassed at the praise but happy to let her father speak for her. I felt sorry for Alice, living under the shadow of her father with no company of her own age. I was thinking this could have been me and Jo if we had chosen to stay at Saltersford when Sue and Lucy had died. Although Jo was a little more confident than Alice appeared, it would have been very easy to withdraw into her shell. She was so much better now and had become great friends with Lisa, Christine and little Anna, the "school group". It seemed to me that Alice would open up in their company and greatly benefit from joining our group.

I was also fairly certain that Bill would resist leaving his farm. The subject would need to be approached with some delicacy.

After supper we relaxed in front of the fire and Bill offered drinks.

"I've got a good selection of single malts. I used to stick to the cheaper blended stuff but I've bin collecting 'em since everything went ape-shit like. Seems a shame to waste 'em."

He pulled out a number of bottles from an old sideboard,

"What we got 'ere? Aberlour, Glenlivet, Macallan, Jura, Glenfarclas."

"Wow, my favourite – Glenfarclas. You knew I was coming!"

"Right. Glenfarclas all round then?"

Mo opted for a lemonade. He wouldn't touch alcohol.

During the evening, as Bill and I worked our way through the Glenfarclas, we exchanged survivor tales. Bill was surprised at the size of our group at Whitewell. He didn't frequent the hotel – "a bit pricey for the likes of us" – but had attended a cousin's wedding there a few years ago. He was particularly interested to hear of our plans for developing a farm and thought we may struggle to get the livestock established. Even Alice asked a few questions about Jo and Lisa.

It transpired that Bill had inherited the farm from his father nearly twenty years ago. He had learnt his farming on the job from a young age – "better than any ruddy college" – and his wife Doreen had also hailed from farming stock. His son Jack, who had recently turned eighteen, had helped with the farming and Alice had helped with the house. They had been largely self-sufficient with a small herd of dairy cattle, some goats, a dozen or so chickens and a few geese. They had grown all their own vegetables, made cheese, butter and bread and bartered some of their surplus produce with local farmers for the occasional leg of lamb or side of pork. Their main commercial income was from the milk and sale of calves, though Bill complained bitterly at the price he had received for his milk. Although it appeared that they had little money for luxuries and holidays were virtually unknown, he seemed quite contented with his lifestyle. Bill hadn't taken too much notice when the flu arrived, being used to health scares and assuming it would pass over in due course. Alice was attending school in Clitherow and used to catch the school bus. One day she came home poorly and developed a temperature overnight. Her mother had kept her in bed but within a day or two they had all come down with it. Bill said he had never experienced anything like it. He had never been seriously ill and had always refused to take medicines but this had "just knocked me for six". Within three days of Alice returning from school, her mother and brother were dead. She was devastated and blamed herself for bringing the virus home. I assured her that from what I had seen, it was almost impossible to avoid. To have two survivors in a family was incredibly fortuitous.

The similarity of Bill's experience with my own was striking. I too had always shunned medicines and was rarely ill. I reasoned that allowing my body to fight infection without artificial aid – I had never had cause to take anti-biotics, indeed in 51 years I hadn't even taken an aspirin – had strengthened the immune system and ensured my survival. Maybe I had passed this on genetically to Jo but unfortunately not to Lucy. Bill and Alice's survival reinforced the conviction. I could see no other reason for two people in the same family surviving when the general mortality rate was so catastrophically high. I put my view to Bill who had been thinking on similar lines. "I just wish I could have saved my lad. I'm grateful that Alice was spared. I couldn't have gone on by myself."

Since losing his wife and son, Bill had tried to carry on with his own model of self-sufficiency. The loss of power and water were minor set-backs. They collected their water from a stream at the back of the farm feeding into the river Hodder. The milking shed generator provided enough power to run the fridge and a big chest freezer, which was already well stocked with meat. Their main source of heating was already open fires but they had replaced their electric cooker with a calor gas aperatus similar to those in use at the inn. They'd had some oil lamps available and found others in the neighbouring farms. Bill had some harrowing tales around checking out the farms. Most of the farmers had died at home and Bill discovered the bodies of many friends and associates, some of whom he had known most of his life. He explained that after the first couple days he became hardened to what he found. At one farm he had rescued two starving pigs, ensuring a future supply of bacon. Now he reckoned he was set up with everything he needed.

We thanked Bill and Alice for their hospitality and they in turn assured us how much they had enjoyed having company for the evening. I expressed the hope that they would at least join us at Whitewell for Christmas Day and was somewhat shocked to realise that they had no idea that Christmas was four days away.

"We've not kept track of dates and stuff. When you've not got TV, you don't realise like. I mean, I can see that days are short but Christmas, no I hadn't thought of it. Don't seem much point with Doreen and Jack gone. Ain't much to celebrate, is there?"

"I can understand that. We'll all feel the loss of families and friends but life goes on. My daughter Jo and I regard the group at the inn as our family now. We'd love you to come, if only to thank you for your help and kindness but it will give you a chance to talk to other people. I'm sure old Paul would love to discuss our plans to set up a farm. I know our ladies are organising a good spread. There'll be a Christmas tree, decorations, some simple presents, music and games. I'm sure Alice would love it."

"I dunno. I ain't one for mixing and small talk. What you think, girl?"

"It sounds fun Dad. I think we should go. It'll be good to meet the others."

"Alright then, but we'll have to sort the animals first and get back to milk Mavis."

"Excellent. That's settled then."

22 December

We woke to brilliant sunshine streaming through the windows. Checking my watch, I was aghast to find that it was almost nine o'clock. I had slept so soundly, which I blamed on a surfeit of Glenfarclas, though I don't know what Mo's excuse was, perhaps the trauma of the dog attack. Bill came in with a blast of cold air, having fed the animals and milked the cow.

"'Ere we go. Fresh milk for breakfast. Sorry to wake you up like. We farming folk are up with the dawn."

Alice was busying herself in the kitchen.

"Anybody for porridge? We've got some other cereals: Branflakes, Shredded Wheat, Sugar Puffs."

Mo and I both opted for porridge and after a quick wash, we all sat down to a hearty breakfast of delicious porridge made with fresh milk, toasted home-made bread with marmalade and a huge pot of fresh coffee.

"Snow's melting fast in the sun. Give it an hour and I'll run you back to Whitewell. I don't think you'll get that van out of the ditch. You can take some milk, bacon and eggs with you. We've got more than we can use."

"Oh thanks Bill. That'll go down an absolute treat."

*

It was around 10.30 when we set off, Bill driving us in the Range Rover. The roads were still covered in snow but it was soft and slushy, quite easy to drive through. I was keen to get back as the lads could be out in the Landrovers looking for us. As we left the farm track and joined the road we had a quick look at the

Vivaro and decided it would be a waste of time trying to recover it. We had tow- ropes back at the inn but it was so far down in the ditch, there was no way the Landrovers would pull such a heavy vehicle out. The rear doors appeared to be accessible however, so it may be possible to remove the sacks of coal into a replacement van. It seemed a shame to waste it after all the trouble we had been to.

We were past Bashall Eaves in five minutes or so, just a few houses and an old pub at a fork in the road. This is what Mo and I had risked our lives for attempting to reach. The lane climbed a little cutting through snow-covered fields, dazzlingly bright in the low sun. I could see animal tracks in the snow but of yesterday's dog pack, there was no sign. We passed the entrance to Browsholme Hall and arrived at Cow Ark, another tiny hamlet. The direct route to Whitewell was on a narrow lane over the top of the ridge, which even though the snow was slushy, we thought would not be a good idea. Instead we turned south to join the main through route following the river Hodder until we reached Whitewell at nearly 11 o'clock.

There was activity in front of the inn with several people milling around, the driver of one of the Landrovers leaning out of the window in discussion. As we drove up I could see it was Phil Lucas in the car talking to Adam. Brian, John and Jim were also standing around but they all turned, open-mouthed, to stare at the Range Rover.

"What happened to you? We've been searching everywhere," asked Adam, as I emerged from the car.

"Sorry lads. We got into a spot of bother last night, came off the road in the snowstorm. Bill here came to our rescue and put us up for the night. If truth be told, I messed up badly but I'll fill you in later."

Then there was a scream of "Dad!" as Jo came running out of the inn and flung her arms around me. She was hotly pursued by Poppy, barking excitedly.

"I was so worried", said Jo, "I didn't sleep a wink last night. Thank God you're safe."

"I'm sorry love. I was an idiot. If it wasn't for Bill here, we'd have ended up as dog food."

We all went into the inn for some coffee as I introduced Bill to those present. Bill fetched the food from the car and we took it into the kitchen for Emma. When she saw a gallon container of milk, a dozen eggs and a large pack of bacon, her eyes were on stalks.

"Thought you could use these as I 'ear you ain't got fresh stuff on the go."

"Oh you lovely man. Just in time for Christmas too." Emma planted a big kiss on Bill's cheek.

"Eh. Give over, girl. It's no trouble like."

Emma was beside herself. "Fresh milk! We can make brandy sauce for the pudding. Real eggs to make cake. We might do some Yorkshire puds. Oh, I can't believe it."

"I've invited Bill and his daughter Alice over for Christmas Day, Emma."

"Oh, of course, yes. That'll be lovely."

After coffee and biscuits, Bill took his leave, eager to get back to Alice and his animals. Mo and I thanked him again and confirmed the arrangements for Christmas.

I then gave Brian and Adam a detailed account of our adventure.

"I'm sorry Brian, I've let the side down here with a lack of basic precautions."

"Don't be too hard on yourself. You had some bad luck but there's probably some lessons to be learned."

"I'll draw up a foraging protocol for the management board. This won't happen again," I promised. "The good thing that's come out of it was meeting Bill and Alice. They'd be a real asset to our group if we could persuade them to join us. I'm hoping that getting them here for Christmas Day might swing it. Bill's a bit of a loner but he'll be persuaded if he can see it's in Alice's interest."

Foraging Protocol.

1. All journeys to be undertaken with two vehicles.
2. If vehicles need to separate, fixed time and place of rendezvous to be arranged.
3. Both vehicles to carry emergency recovery kit, including tow ropes and jump leads.
4. Minimum of two people in each vehicle.
5. Each person to be armed and trained in the use of firearms.
6. Journeys to be planned to return to Whitewell before dark, allowing for adverse weather conditions.
7. Copy of journey plans to be left at the inn.
8. Each vehicle to carry emergency supplies, including food, water, blankets and first aid kits.

"Thanks Tom. That seems to cover it and should cover all eventualities. Common sense, really." Brian gave his immediate response to my draft for the management board. "I'm sure everyone will be happy with this."

"I should have done this earlier, then Mo and I wouldn't have been placed in danger yesterday. Of course, we'll be committing four people to every foraging trip which might be an issue, especially in the spring/summer when there's more work required on the farm. But we don't need to be out every day."

"Quite, but your safety comes first. You had a narrow escape with those dogs. How is Mo?"

"Christine Lucas has had a look at it. She thinks it would have needed stitches normally and a tetanus injection, but she's applied loads of anti-septic and replaced the dressing, so fingers-crossed, he'll soon be on the mend. As you say, a narrow escape. I've never known such aggressive dogs but I suppose we'll have to get used to it."

"Quite. I can see that Bill would be very useful for us. Do you think he can be persuaded to join?"

"From his own inclination, no. He's quite content in his farm and has really got everything he needs. He's far more self-sufficient than we are at this stage. I mean, they're making their own bread, butter and cheese. They've got a freezer full of fresh meat, more milk and eggs then they can get through. It's a very good set-up and pretty much what they're used to. He won't want to give it up. Alice is the key. She's all he's got left in the family and he thinks the world of her. It's Alice that will benefit the most from joining us. From what I've seen, she's retreated into her shell since losing her mother and brother. She needs company of her own age. If we can give her a good time at Christmas, Bill may be prepared to make the sacrifice."

"Let's hope so. We need somebody who knows what they're doing with a farm. Poor old Paul can't go on forever."

23 December

It was another fair day with no sign of any further snowstorms, which was just as well in view of the extensive foraging required. We needed a replacement van for the Vivaro and I was determined to recover our hard-won coal from the ditch. In addition, Emma was beginning to panic over the Christmas supplies, unnecessarily in my view but probably the stress of planning a lunch for twenty people, including Bill and Alice. I thought I'd better not find any more people to invite. The meat for the main course was already taken care of through Adam and John's little hunting expedition a few days ago. There were now about a dozen assorted wildfowl and several rabbits hanging from hooks in the kitchen. The unexpected eggs and milk had changed some of Emma's plans for the better. She still reckoned she needed another Christmas pudding, wrapping paper for presents and some Christmas crackers. Another jar of mincemeat was requested, as much tinned custard as we could find (which was a standard shopping item in any event) and the flour was becoming depleted. This was not an easy list to fill as most people's kitchens tended not to contain Christmas stock in October. I thought we would be lucky to find a Christmas pudding. There was plenty of flour but the packets were usually found to be damaged by pests. We thought Clitheroe would be our best bet.

In accordance with my draft protocol, we were to take both Landrovers and pick up a van en route. Phil Lucas and Ian Fernyhough took one and I drove the other, accompanied by Jim Clarke in place of Mo, who had been ordered to rest to avoid re-opening his wound, which was still quite painful.

We decided to try Dunsop Bridge for a van and if unsuccessful, move on to Newton, then Waddington. Once we had a van on the road, we would get across to the Vivaro and load up the coal before splitting up with one Landover escorting the van back to Whitewell and the other going ahead to the centre of Clitheroe, meeting up later at the entrance to the castle. We all had guns and emergency supplies, though we hadn't yet had time to implement any additional training. Ian was quite handy with a gun apparently and I decided not to ask him how he had acquired this expertise. Overall, I felt we were better prepared than our last trip. A copy of our proposed itinerary had been left with Adam.

We arrived at Dunsop Bridge looking out for any vans parked outside the houses but drew a blank. As we left in the direction of Newton we passed a small garage on the left with a Ford Transit van outside. Signalling to Phil and Ian in the car behind, we parked in front of the garage. This was easy enough as long as we could find the keys. The van was locked up and so was the garage. It was basically just a small repair bay with a little shop attached selling motor spares. Phil forced an entry into the shop and checked the area behind the cash register but still no luck. We reasoned that the proprietor most likely lived in one of the neighbouring houses and kept the van keys at home. We could waste too much time with no guarantee of success and decided to move on.

Newton was no better, not a van in sight. We decided to head straight to Waddington as a much better prospect, being a larger community. En route, Jim began to open up. I hadn't spent a lot of time with Jim since our arrival at Whitewell and hadn't really found out what made him tick. Understandably, Jim tended to associate with people closer to his own age such as Ian and Phil. He also hung around Christine Salt whenever possible, which may have indicated a budding romance. I knew that Jim was single and some sort of company accounts clerk. You tended to assume that young people without a family had not suffered the same level of bereavement as the rest of us but I discovered that Jim had watched his parents and younger sister die before succumbing to the virus himself.

When he recovered, all communications were down and he was unable to contact his long-standing girlfriend, Chantelle. They had been planning to move in together and start a new life. Chantelle was a nurse at Hope Hospital in Salford and Jim had been hoping to start training for an accountancy qualification. In desperation, he had driven to Chantelle's family home in Eccles only to find them all dead in their beds. Jim had felt angry and helpless, joining in some of the rioting in Manchester, looting and smashing shop fronts, generally just getting drunk to drown his sorrows, until he saw Brian's note at the Town Hall and jumped at the chance to join up. I worked out that it must have been the same day I had left the group at the Midland Hotel to return to Saltersford Hall. He didn't really have any useful survival skills, so he had agreed to help old Paul with the farming, though so far he had spent more time with John Salt and Phil Lucas working on the Piggeries. He had been very low at the start but felt a little more positive now that plans were beginning to take shape. He felt fortunate to have joined the group and wanted to make himself useful.

We had arrived at Waddington and moved down the main street looking for suitable vans. There was nothing obvious, so we turned right onto one of several side streets, then right again. It was just residential properties here but I soon spotted a small white van parked in a drive and pulled up outside, Ian and Phil parking behind. The van was a Citroen Dispatch, a little smaller than the Vivaro but big enough for our purposes. It had a roof rack fitted with ladders on top and on the side announced "C. Clarke & Sons : Decorators of Distinction." We checked the van: locked. The keys must surely be in the house. Phil soon forced a window, climbed in and opened the front door. We split up to search. The entrance hall seemed the obvious place but there were no hooks for keys and just a small telephone seat with a cupboard full of directories, papers and address books but no keys. The kitchen also failed to yield any keys other than the back door key still in the lock.

However, while we were there I had a quick raid of the cupboards and found a dozen or so useful tins, including a tin of custard. That was one off Emma's list. I was hoping we wouldn't need to go upstairs. As the house was locked from the inside, there would certainly be bodies up there and most likely dead for over two months. I had seen plenty of bodies but preferred to avoid them if possible.

A door to the side of the kitchen was unlocked and opened onto the garage. There was no light whatsoever in there. Jim ran back to the Landrover to get torches. Using these, we could see that the garage was full, mainly with decorating equipment and supplies. Phil trained the torch on the walls near the garage door and there they were, a set of keys hanging on a hook. We dashed back out to the van and opened it using the remote control on the key fob. The back of the van was full of paints, step-ladders and miscellaneous bits and pieces.

"If you want to get that lot cleared out, I'll get her started up." Phil set to organising jump leads and the like. He tried the ignition key at first but, as he anticipated, there was insufficient charge in the battery. Luckily the van have been reversed into the drive which meant Ian could drive his Landrover up to face it, bonnet to bonnet. They soon had the leads attached and at the third attempt, the van started up. They kept it running to start charging the battery. Meanwhile, Jim and I had emptied all the contents onto the drive and we were ready to go. The van had around a quarter of a tank of diesel, enough for the day's purpose.

We were driving in convoy to the site of the crashed Vivaro. I drove the first Landrover with Jim navigating, Ian followed in the Citroen with Phil bringing up the rear in the second Landrover. Phil warned Ian not to let the van stall before the battery was fully charged. We spotted a little lane on the map which cut across from Waddington to Bashall Town, close to the location of the abandoned Vivaro. The only place en route was Backridge Farm and as usual, there was no sign of life but we had agreed that we would not investigate any more properties until we reached Clitheroe in order to save time. Turning right at Bashall Town towards Bashall Eaves, we were soon alongside the Vivaro.

The others were surprised at how far it had tipped into the ditch and agreed it would not be feasible to pull it out. We opened the rear doors, which swung out from the centre, but each door could only move twelve to eighteen inches before catching the ditch. It created an opening of two to three feet which was just about wide enough to pull through a sack of coal. Jim crawled inside the Vivaro to hand out the sacks. I stood in the ditch to receive them, then handed them up to Phil, who in turn lifted them up to Ian in the back of the Citroen. A couple of the sacks had spilled in the crash and had to be re-filled, but otherwise the four of us made short work of it and the Citroen was soon loaded up. Although it was considerably smaller than the Vivaro, it held the fourteen sacks of coal comfortably. It was agreed that Ian would drive the van back to Whitewell with Phil following in the Landrover, unload the coal, then make their way to the centre of Clitheroe. Jim and I would go ahead and start looking for supplies, meeting up at the castle entrance at the top of the town by 2.00pm. That would leave us between an hour and an hour and a half before returning to Whitewell before dark. Before leaving the Vivaro, Ian and Phil syphoned the remaining diesel from the tank into a jerry can and filled up the Citroen.

With everything agreed, Jim and I set off for Clitheroe, retracing the route Mo and I had taken from the coal yard two days before, then straight up the hill to the centre, onto Castle Street and parking at the end alongside the grounds leading up to the castle walls. It occurred to me that the castle could form a useful base, easy to defend and with lots of supplies close to hand. However, it would only work if the well was still in use. From here we set off on foot, taking our food, water and torches in rucksacks. In addition, Jim brought his rifle, just in case. It was approaching 12 o'clock, giving us a full two hours before the rendezvous. In my experience of foraging, town centre shops were not generally productive as anything useful had more often than not, been looted, but given some of the specific requests from Emma, we could try some of the shops before moving out to the residential houses. The three things likely to prove most difficult were Christmas wrapping paper, flour in good condition and Christmas puddings. We were basically looking at early October stock, which was a little early for Christmas specialities. Given our circumstances, wrapping paper hardly seemed a priority but I was aware that Emma Fernyhough and Christine Lucas were planning a really special event for Christmas day and I didn't want to disappoint them. There was a real danger that the celebrations would be a damp squib as everyone was likely to have their minds on lost loved ones. At least Emma and Christine still had their immediate families and had not had to watch their children die. I think they were very conscious that a real effort would have to be made to encourage people to join in. Jo had been noticeably quiet in the last few days, which I attributed to the prospect of facing Christmas without her mother and sister. It was my responsibility to get her through this and if Christmas wrappings could make a small contribution, fair enough.

We walked back down Castle Street, examining the shops. There was nothing like the devastation of central Manchester but even here a number of shop fronts were smashed in and a few burnt out, no doubt copy-cat riots when the violence was being reported on TV or perhaps communicated via social media before everything closed down. The sides of the street were littered with abandoned vehicles but not enough to form blockages. Just 50 yards down on the left we arrived at a branch of WH Smith, the windows smashed but otherwise in a reasonable state. I decided to try for wrapping paper while Jim checked out the shops on the other side of the street. After five yards or so inside the shop I needed my torch. These deep shops with lots of display racking were incredibly dark once you left the entrance and this made it considerably more difficult to find anything. Some goods were scattered on the floor as a result of looting but much of it was still quite orderly on the shelves. Clearly books and stationery products had not attracted the looters. I found a section of greeting cards, which I noted did include some boxes of Christmas cards. At the end of the rack I found what I was looking for, rolls of wrapping paper. It was nearly all birthday paper, some for weddings and christenings but certainly nothing for Christmas. As I suspected, it had been too early in the season. However, I then found some rolls of foil wrap, some gold, silver and red. I figured this would be an acceptable substitute and took two rolls of each, stuffing them into my rucksack.

As I emerged back on the street, Jim was leaving a small electrical store clutching a box and looking please with himself.

"It's an old CD player and it takes batteries. I've not seen one of these for years. Just the job for the Christmas Eve party."

"What Christmas Eve party?"

"Me and Chris Salt, we're putting on a party after tea."

"Oh right, first I've heard. I'm sure that'll be fun. We'd best look out for some CD's then."

We turned left down the High Street, full of shops and cafes. After passing a few snack bars we found a local cake shop displaying a sign "Fresh bread and cakes – baked on the premises."

"Let's try in here," I suggested. "Emma needs flour." We passed the serving counter and shelves all of which were stripped clean, then a few tables and chairs for eating in, before reaching a door to the back, slightly open. It was completely dark in the back and we switched on our torches to reveal a chaotic scene of broken boxes and cartons strewn over the floor. A large rat scampered out of the boxes and shot past us into the shop. There was a smell of damp and rotting food and I thought this was likely to be a fool's errand before spotting some large plastic storage containers on a high shelf which appeared to have escaped the attention of the rats. We lifted them and prized open the lids. One contained white flour and another wholemeal flour, both around half full. They looked and smelled okay. There were two smaller containers of dried fruit and one of sugar. Other miscellaneous packets had not fared as well but we decided it was well worth taking the flour, fruit and sugar. We were well laden now and headed back to the Landrover to store our findings.

The weather was still fine with a clear sky but very cold. We started up the engine to keep warm and ate our lunch in the car. It had turned 1.30 by the time we had finished and we decided to wait for Ian and Phil. With this weather it shouldn't get dark until around 4.00 so I reckoned we had another two hours foraging time. We could move on to the residential area and stock up on tins, if nothing else. Within fifteen minutes we could hear an engine labouring up the hill and then the Landrover emerged with Ian and Phil.

"That was easy to find, "said Ian, "just keep going up hill."

"Yeah. That's the good thing about castles, difficult to miss," I agreed.

I briefed them on our plans and we agreed to tackle as many houses as possible in pairs and return to the Landrovers by 3.30 for the return journey. We stayed close to the castle to save time. At the first house Jim and I forcibly entered we encountered several rotting bodies and a number of rats, deciding to try our luck elsewhere. The stench was just unbearable and we didn't want to risk cornering a rat and getting bitten. God knows what diseases they were carrying. The second house appeared to be empty but so were the kitchen cupboards. One tin of tomato soup and an unopened pack of spaghetti was all that was worth taking. Not everybody had loaded up with food. The third house was more rewarding, no dead bodies or rats to contend with and a reasonable supply of food. We filled our rucksacks with an assortment of tins, coffee, tea, rice and even an unopened pack of mince pies. Full of preservative, they should be fine. I know Emma already has mince pies but you can't have too many. Still no sign however of Christmas puddings. While I was ransacking the kitchen, Jim was searching the lounge and managed to find a case of CDs. We didn't bother to check what they were, they'd have to do.

We met up with Ian and Phil at the Landrovers, each with bulging rucksacks. Phil was wearing a broad grin.

"You'll never guess what I've got in here. Marks and Spencer luxury Christmas pudding, a big 'un too. They must have kept it as surplus from last Christmas. I bet it'll be alright though. They can always pour a glass of brandy over it."

"Well done Phil", I said. "Emma will be pleased with that. I was thinking we were going to strike out on the pudding front. I think that's a pretty successful trip."

We set off back on the direct route passing the abandoned Vivaro once again and returned to the inn ahead of 4 o'clock to display our finds to a delighted Emma.

"Oh, that's wonderful. Our Christmas menu is really taking shape now."

I no sooner left the kitchen than Christine Lucas sought me out.

"Tom, I'm really worried about Mo's arm. It's still causing him pain and it looks angry and swollen. I'm pretty sure it's infected and there could be all sorts in there from a dog bite. All I can do is keep it clean but it's not doing any good. What if he gets blood poisoning? He ought to at least be on anti-biotics."

"That's bad news. I'll go and see him. We passed a pharmacy in Clitheroe today but it had been badly looted. We could try for some anti-biotics but I wouldn't have a clue what we're looking for."

"Well we've got to try something. We can't cut his arm off."

I found Mo slumped in an armchair near the fire in the main lounge. He certainly looked unwell.

"How you doing mate? I hear this dog bite's still acting up."

"Hi Tom. I thought I'd be okay by now. My arm's really tight and sensitive. I think my body must be fighting against the dog's germs. I hope I can win."

"I've just had a word with Christine. We're going to try for some anti-biotics tomorrow. Don't worry, we'll soon get you sorted."

I wished I'd felt as confident as I sounded.

CHAPTER TEN

CHRISTMAS AT THE INN

24 December

Another bright, crisp day for Christmas Eve, continuing a good run of weather since the snowstorm. There was a busy atmosphere around the inn as serious preparations got underway. Emma was already getting stressed in the kitchen, making life difficult for Chris Salt, Lisa and Jo. There was no school today as there was too much work to do. Christine Lucas was in charge of getting the inn ready, scrubbing out places that looked clean to start with. She had found several huge boxes of decorations in the cellar. As Lisa and Jo were busy in the kitchen, she'd recruited the Fernyhough boys, Ian and William to help. Adam and Brian were out hunting at the crack of dawn to see what they could find in the woods. Ian and Phil had taken a chainsaw and axe to harvest a Christmas tree under orders to find a 'full one, at least twelve feet high'. They'd have to carry it back to the inn. Jim and I were taking one of the Landrovers back to Clitheroe to seek anti-biotics for Mo. Contrary to my protocol, we were just taking the one vehicle but had left the route with Paul Fernyhough, who would follow in the other Landrover if we failed to return by 2.30, meeting at the castle at 3.00.

I still had little idea what I was looking for. We had asked around the group but our collective knowledge of drugs was pitiful. Brian thought his wife had used anti-biotics and the names tended to end in micin or mycin. That was all I had to go on but it was better than nothing. We took the direct route to Clitheroe and parked on the High Street where I had spotted a pharmacy. This was seriously wrecked, with cabinets smashed and medicine packets strewn all over the floor amidst the broken glass. At least there were no rats in there. There was barely anything left on the shelves to check and rummaging through the packets on the floor there was nothing that appeared remotely likely. Jim took his torch and checked out the storeroom at the back but this was similarly ransacked. The looters had taken a serious interest in this place. I supposed that, unlike us, they knew what drugs they were after.

I shined my torch underneath the counter and found 15 to 20 prescription packets marked up for collection. Though most of them were unintelligible, one for Mrs E. Hughes was marked Neomycin and one for Mr J. Humphries labelled Paromomycin. They had the sought-after suffix and had to be worth a try. I stuffed them both in my bag along with a stray pack of Paracetamol, which even I knew was a mild painkiller.

"Right. That'll do. Let's get out of here."

The rest of the shops in the street were of little interest and as we had plenty of time to spare, we decided to investigate a few more houses, splitting up to increase our coverage. Apart from the usual selection of tins, always useful, some dried food and the odd miscellaneous item, at my third house in one of the high-level kitchen cupboards were a couple boxes labelled 'Xmas' containing some fluffy Christmas hats and an opened box of Christmas crackers. I counted seven left and added them to my haul. Although it wasn't many, Emma had specifically requested crackers and they were the first I had seen.

Soon after a quick lunch we decided to head back to save Paul Fernyhough making an unnecessary trip and arrived back at the inn by 2.00. Paul was pleased not to have to follow us out but there was a real buzz of excitement about the place.

"Just take a look in the kitchen", said Paul.

We duly obliged and were greeted by the most amazing sight. Emma, her kitchen assistants and old Paul Naden surrounded one of the large island worktops on which was stretched out the most magnificent stag, glassy eyed and with a massive wound in the side of its head.

Adam was in the background beaming. "Not a bad shot eh? We got him shortly after dawn this morning coming out of the woods into a clearing. First shot, straight through the head. Took me and Brian nearly an hour to drag him to a track where we could fetch the Landrover. We're going to mount the antlers on the wall. All those Sunday mornings at the gun club weren't wasted."

Emma was looking pleased but rather flustered. "Paul's showing us how to do the skinning and filleting. It's going to take some work to get this meat ready for tomorrow. All the menus have to be changed."

In the lounge Ian and Phil were busy erecting a huge Christmas tree. They were positioning the trunk into a large cast iron frame which they had brought up from the cellar. At their side were boxes of decorations for the tree and assorted garlands and ornaments for the rooms. The place would be transformed. Poppy was taking a great interest in the tree and ran off with a branch trimming to chew at her leisure.

I sought out Christine Lucas and showed her the prescriptions expropriated from the pharmacy. Mo's arm had not improved and we both agreed it was worth trying the drugs. We chose the packet labelled for Mr J. Humphries on the grounds that the other could possibly be to address a female condition. The packet contained capsules and advised Mr Humphries to take them three times a day for seven days. We would give those a try, keep Mrs Hughes' dose in reserve and hope for the best.

*

That evening, after dinner, Jim and Chris Salt organised the group for the Christmas Eve party. Everybody was there, even little Anna, who had been allowed to stay up late. We used the main lounge and were allocated to five tables grouped around a roaring fire which had been built up into a spectacular blaze. At the other end of the lounge near the patio doors was the most magnificent Christmas tree.

The lads reckoned they had cut three feet off the top to make it fit and yet the fairy on the top was still touching the ceiling. The decorations were bold in gold and silver, though rather uniform in an institutional style. I wished then I'd brought our own decorations from home which had far more character having been acquired piecemeal over many years from holidays in Austria and speciality shops in places like Lyndhurst and Harrogate. Nevertheless, with the subdued lighting of the oil lamps on each table and the flickering flames from the fireplace reflecting on the decorations, the effect was magical. The rest of the room was decked out with garlands and tinsel at every available spot. We were divided into teams for a Christmas quiz, four or five to a table with family groups split up apart from Anna, who was allowed to sit with her mother. I was allocated to a table with Phil Lucas, Emma Fernyhough and Christine Salt. Together, we reckoned we could bridge the generational gap to tackle the general knowledge questions.

Best of all, on each table was a large jug of warm mulled wine with a generous added measure of brandy. An alternative mix of half wine, half orange squash and no brandy was available for the youngsters and I made sure that this included Jo. To follow the mulled wine, a tempting array of fine wines, bottled beers and spirits, as well as soft drinks, were arranged on the bar. It looked like a long night. Poppy was basking in front of the fire as I had worn her out with a long walk before dinner, then fed her a generous bowl of scraps. Somehow, a sleeping dog just added to the cosy festive atmosphere.

After four testing rounds of movies, pop music, sport and general knowledge, our team felt we were holding our own. Jim was quizmaster and kept it flowing in good humour. A short interval was called while Emma and her assistants disappeared into the kitchen and brought out trays of little snacks, arranging them on a buffet table at the side of the lounge. I wondered what they could produce without much in the way of fresh food but apart from the inevitable bowls of crisps, there appeared an imaginative selection of such tasty morsels as red salmon blinis, cubes of spam and pineapple chunks on cocktail sticks, pieces of sausage and silverskin onions on sticks or cubes of corned beef and pickle. Everybody tucked in with enthusiasm, even Poppy waking up to take an interest. Although the mulled wine was delicious, I decided some ale was required to wash down the food and selected a couple bottles of Tim Taylor's Landlord to share with Phil. The girls stuck to the mulled wine which appeared to be bringing quite a glow to their cheeks.

Further rounds on history, science, literature and celebrities followed. I hoped my contributions on the first three made up for my total ignorance on the last. Chris Salt managed to fill the knowledge gap. When we had finished we passed our answer papers to the next table for marking while Jim gave the answers to a chorus of cheers and groans. Our team came a creditable second while the winners, Adam, John, Christine Lucas and Lisa were punching the air. The whole thing was very competitive, fuelled by the flow of alcohol.

The music that followed was a pleasant surprise. The CD collection that Jim had located had clearly belonged to someone of my generation, being confined almost entirely to the 1970s : David Bowie, Elton John, Stevie Wonder, Queen, Eagles, Fleetwood Mac. A lot of it was compilations of hits and it went down very well, even with the younger members of the group. To be honest, by this time I had moved on to the Glenfarclas and was past caring. All in all, a jolly good evening.

25 December

I woke to bright sunshine illuminating patterns of frost on my bedroom window. Realising it must be late, I grabbed for my watch on the bedside table.

"Ten to nine! Jesus!"

I don't think I had ever woken up so late. I had turned in around midnight somewhat under the influence, well, rather a lot actually. I didn't make a habit of drinking to excess but it had been a special occasion and a very successful evening.

I decided that I needed to get going and promptly stood up only to realise I was still unbalanced and fell back on the bed. I was now conscious of a throbbing pain in my head and over-enthusiastic heartbeat. It was years since I had had such a hangover.

"A good wash and some food, that's the answer" I told myself.

Arriving in the kitchen, I found Jo busily writing up Christmas menus attempting copperplate writing.

"Merry Christmas, Jo," I said, giving her a kiss.

"Merry Christmas, Dad," she replied without enthusiasm.

"Are you okay? That was a good night, wasn't it. You and Lisa were throwing yourselves into it."

"I'm alright." She sounded very flat. It wasn't difficult to deduce the reason.

"I know what you're going through. It's not the same without Mum and Lucy; it never will be. We've just got to soldier on and make the best of things. Everybody here has lost people close to them. Now we all need to support each other and make the day special. Mum would have wanted you to do that. You shouldn't feel guilty at enjoying yourself. I'll introduce you to Alice later when Bill gets here. I think you'll like her."

"Okay. I'd better get on with these menus. We've got loads of jobs this morning."

The kitchen was already a hive of activity which was too

much for my head. I helped myself to a large mug of black coffee from the pot bubbling on one of the stoves and took it through to the lounge, fending off a very excited Poppy. I was planning to take her for a good run before lunch and John had offered to accompany me with his gun.

The coffee helped and I offered to take my turn at bringing in the water. This was one of our daily rituals. Down to the river, two buckets with two gallons in each, five trips to unload 20 gallons into the water tank. That usually sufficed for the day. I figured a little exercise in the cold morning air might help to clear my head. At Emma's request, I also retrieved two bottles of milk from the river. She had decanted the milk that Bill had supplied into screwtop wine bottles, which were completely immersed in the river, lodged between large stones and remained beautifully cold.

Returning for breakfast, Emma offered the Christmas special : porridge made with milk and a dollop of honey (it was usually made with water), a luxury fry-up of bacon, scrambled egg, mushrooms, tomatoes and beans, followed by toast and marmalade. It was all washed down with a glass of Bucks Fizz. Wonderful.

I had arranged to meet John Salt at ten for our walk with Poppy which left me five minutes to check on Mo. He had breakfasted early, taken his third dose of what we hoped was antibiotics and had the dressing on his arm removed. Chris Lucas decided a fresh dressing was not required as it would be better to give it some air. It still looked pretty angry and a gruesome mix of blacks and yellows around the puncture marks and jagged tear. Mo said it was sensitive rather than painful and was trusting that it was on the mend. Chris had told him it may take two or three days to get rid of the infection, so he couldn't expect miracles. I hoped that we had got away with it this time but it just demonstrated again our exposure to danger in the absence of any real medical expertise. At some point there was no doubt that we would experience worse than a dog bite.

Poppy was delighted to see her collar and lead and ran up to me quivering in excitement. There were only two things that enticed Poppy from the fire: food and walks in that order of priority. She also made a fuss of John when he joined us and patted her head. Poppy treated everybody as a long lost friend and it was easy to see why she had become a firm favourite at the inn. I took a whistle for retrieval and a handful of dog biscuits in my pocket and we set off up the lane towards Dunsop Bridge, John with a rifle slung over his shoulder. We soon let Poppy off the lead and she raced ahead to investigate the smells, stopping after a while to turn round and see where we were. If she went out of sight, I would whistle her back and knew she would respond quickly to secure a treat.

After comparing notes over our hangovers and the magnificent full breakfast, I enquired after the state of John's family, explaining Jo's reaction to facing Christmas without her mum and sister.

"I know what you mean. I think everybody's feeling much the same. Helen feels really bad about her folks as we couldn't find out what happened to them. After all the communications went down, we held out at home for several days, then we called at their place in Chesterfield but it was empty and cold, no note or anything and no sign of them. Obviously we feared the worst but it's terrible not knowing. They might have joined up with some others somewhere but I felt they would have returned home to leave us a note. We always had them over for Christmas, so Helen feels it today. My folks died some years back but my brother was working in Italy. When it started getting bad, he said he was trying to book a flight home but that was the last we heard. Helen's sister lived in London and we had no news from her either. Chris didn't have a regular boyfriend but she's lost all her friends from Uni. It was only when we met up with the Fernyhoughs that we heard this rumour about a survivor group in Manchester. It would have been a disaster otherwise."

"Yeah. It's worked well, hasn't it. I thought there might be more trouble, a bunch of strangers cooped up together, but everybody's just got on with it. Do you think it's a long term solution?"

"I'd give it a couple years and see where we are. We're a bit 'hand to mouth' at the moment, aren't we. If we can make a go of the farm so we've got fresh veg and dairy, a more regular supply of meat than we can shoot in the woods, set up some electricity and better security, we should be more or less self-sufficient within a year or so. I think we can survive here indefinitely but whether that's a 'long term solution' depends on what you're trying to achieve."

"Do you suppose there are many groups like ours?" I wondered. "I see so few signs of life when we're out foraging."

"It's hard to say, isn't it. Only a tiny percentage have survived the virus but there must be people who have hidden themselves away and avoided contact. Look at Bill you just came across."

"That's probably true, though Bill and Alice caught the flu and survived, like me and Jo. I think we passed on a degree of immunity."

"I do wonder whether there's something more organised that we don't know about" suggested John.

"What are you thinking of? Government? Military?"

"Well, either or both. When things were falling apart and martial law was applied with Cobra meetings every day, it must have been obvious that the status quo was unsustainable. I cannot believe that the powers that be didn't have contingency plans for the survival of the Establishment. They've had plans since at least the 60s to survive a nuclear holocaust. This is the same sort of thing. What about the Royal Family, for example? Do you seriously think they were left to their own devices?"

"I see your point," I said, "but it all happened so fast didn't it. If there was something organised, wouldn't we have seen some evidence by now, perhaps some military vehicles combing the area looking for survivors?"

"It's only been two months. They might allow say six months to make sure all traces of the virus have gone, then emerge to pick up the threads. Or maybe they are looking but we're too isolated to be found. Or maybe there are so few survivors out there, they don't think there's any point."

We continued our speculations as we left the road and followed a track alongside the river Hodder, Poppy racing ahead to investigate, disappearing into undergrowth with only the white tip of her tail visible. We arrived at a small farmhouse called Burholme and decided to turn back as I was keen to receive Bill and Alice. I felt this was my personal responsibility as I had found them, or perhaps it was more accurate to say that Bill had found me.

We returned shortly before eleven and gave Poppy a quick rub-down before releasing her into the inn to seek food. Within ten minutes Bill and Alice rolled up in the Range Rover, bearing more eggs and milk.

"Oh, you'll be popular. I had the best breakfast in over two months this morning, thanks to your supplies. Merry Christmas to you."

"And you. I couldn't imagine you lot managing without milk. I don't know what we'd do without our Mavis."

Virtually everybody was around the lounge or the kitchen now and everywhere looked so festive with the decorations and the Christmas tree, which now had a pile of gold and silver parcels beneath, and roaring fires. I introduced Bill and Alice to all the group and Bill managed to greet them all without any swearing. He was clearly on his best behaviour. Poppy decided that she should be the centre of attention and Alice was immediately smitten. I steered Alice towards Lisa and Jo, who were doing jobs in the kitchen and she immediately relaxed being with girls of her own age, offering to help out.

"That's very kind of you love," said Chris Salt. "Lisa and Jo will show you what to do. We've got a seating plan for lunch, there's that many of us. I've not put you with your dad, is that okay, only you'll have a better chat with the youngsters."

"That's fine thanks" said Alice, looking quite relieved to be let off the leash.

"Now then Bill. We've had to butcher this huge stag that Adam contrived to shoot. We can't possibly manage all of it, so we're hoping you'll take some home. I hear you've got a freezer running."

"Oh, very nice. I'll not say no, duck."

"No, it's venison. We've got some duck as well though." I think it was a joke.

We left Alice to the kitchen frivolity and withdrew to the lounge with a pot of coffee, joined by Brian and Paul Naden. Bill and Paul soon started comparing notes on their farming experience. The kitchen activity began to spread into the lounge with tables being laid very professionally complete with expensive looking crystal glasses and linen napkins. On each table was a stiff card menu handwritten in best copperplate style, which I recognised as Jo's efforts. I had a sneak preview and was totally amazed at the contents. It looked like this:

THE INN AT WHITEWELL

CHRISTMAS DAY LUNCH

****

Champagne reception with canapés

****

Slice of Pheasant Breast with Five Bean Salad

****

Cream of Mushroom Soup with fresh rolls

****

*Roast Venison, Yorkshire pudding, Roast Potatoes, vegetables
and cranberry sauce*

****

Christmas pudding with Brandy Sauce

****

*Mince Pies
Fresh coffee, mints and a selection of liquors*

The feast was to be accompanied by Mouton Cadet or Chablis. You had to take your hat off to Emma and her team. I knew she would do us proud but this was way beyond my expectations. Considering the facilities available and lack of fresh produce, it was nothing short of miraculous. The five bean salad, soup and vegetables had to be out of tins and clearly Bill's milk had been put to good use in the Yorkshire Pudding and the brandy sauce but roast potatoes? Perhaps they had taken fat from the stag. I couldn't wait to taste them. The pheasant would no doubt have been the main course until Adam's subsequent hunting success. I recognised some items from recent foraging, like the cranberry sauce and the mints.

We were all to assemble around the Christmas tree at 12.30 for the champagne and canapés. In the meantime Paul gave Bill a tour of the estate with particular emphasis on the Piggeries and our plans for developing the farm. Meanwhile Brian and I discussed tactics. We agreed to leave our approach until after lunch, by which time in addition to enjoying a sumptuous feast and a few drinks, Bill would hopefully have witnessed a transformation in Alice's demeanour which would convince him of the merits of joining us.

At 12.30 prompt we were all admiring the Christmas tree and enjoying the cosy ambience in the lounge with the log fire crackling when the 'kitchen staff' emerged with half a dozen bottles of best champagne, chilled all morning in the river and a couple trays of tempting looking canapés to an enthusiastic round of applause. Brian, John and I were charged with opening the first three bottles and there followed a race to fire the first cork, narrowly won by John, as all three corks fired across the room and bounced off the walls. That set Poppy off barking in pursuit of the corks. She carried one guiltily to the fireplace to settle down and chew it to pieces. In fact I'm sure she was eating some of it but I had long since ceased to be amazed at the items consumed by that dog.

Brian called a toast and there was much chinking of glasses, 'Merry Christmases' and general good humour. The youngsters participated apart from Anna who had some lemonade which she pretended was champagne. Jo was under instruction to restrict her intake to a single glass, after which she would have Coca Cola with the lunch. She was used to having a small glass of champagne at Christmas and birthdays.

Christine Lucas then distributed the presents, gold-wrapped for the girls and silver for the lads, each with a sticky label attached bearing our names. The presents were simple items collected on our foraging trips, chocolates, cosmetic sets, whisky miniatures and the like but it all added to the occasion. The champagne flowed freely and the well-received canapés soon disappeared. An easy, relaxed atmosphere had been established and everybody seemed happy in each other's company. Alice was sticking largely with Lisa and Jo, though I noticed young William Fernyhough was taking a keen interest. Jim and Chris Salt were getting on well too, but nothing new there.

We were given a seating plan for lunch. Lisa, Jo, Alice and Anna were seated with Chris Salt. Jo told me that William Fernyhough had been offered a seat at their table but felt he was too old to be with "the kids". Had he seen Alice first I suspect he may have changed his mind. In truth, he would have been embarrassed in being the only male. The Salts, Curtises and Fernyhoughs were split up in the interests of integration and appeared to be quite happy with the arrangement. Having been advised that he was "not a great mixer", Chris Lucas had placed Bill with me, Brian and Paul Naden, the gender mix complemented by Helen Salt. We were clearly the "oldies" table.

The "kids table" had the Christmas crackers, donning their paper hats and insisting on reading out the riddles. Anna was getting seriously excited, such that Chris Lucas was giving her some warning looks from the next table, all to no avail. Jo and Lisa then disappeared for waitress duties to be joined by the Fernyhough boys, each taking responsibility for one of the four tables. Emma and Chris Salt were in the kitchen serving out, then re-joined their tables for the start of each course, quickly disappearing again whilst the youngsters cleared the tables in a smooth and well-planned operation. There was just enough time between each course to relax and enjoy the excellent wines. We started with the Chablis to accompany the pheasant breast, leaving the Mouton Cadet for the main course. Bill restricted himself to a taste of each, mindful of the journey home.

The food surpassed expectations. The pheasant was moist and succulent, perfectly complemented by the five bean salad. Even the tinned mushroom soup had been enhanced with some subtle flavouring to give it something approaching a home-made taste and the freshly-baked rolls were a real treat. There was a short hiatus before the main course arrived to a round of applause. Although the venison had been butchered and cooked within 24 hours, it nevertheless retained a strong, distinctive flavour, perfectly complemented by the cranberry sauce. The roast potatoes were indeed cooked in venison fat and were to die for. I think we were all feeling rather full by the time the Christmas puddings emerged. The waiters carried them in on plates with little brandy flames flickering on the top, which produced a resounding cheer. We served ourselves and each table had a little jug of brandy sauce and it certainly wasn't short on brandy. Emma knew this was too rich for Anna's taste and brought her a bowl of tinned fruit salad.

We eventually struggled to our feet and ordered the cooks and waiters to relax while the rest of us cleared the tables and restored the kitchen. We also exempted Paul Naden on ground of age, Bill and Alice as guests and Mo in view of his injury. It still left nine of us to pitch in and if the preparation and serving of the meal was like a military campaign, the clearing up was more akin to organised chaos. Brian did his best to keep order but was fighting a lost cause against the general level of inebriation and high spirits. We got it done eventually with just a couple breakages and finally emerged with several pots of coffee and a large box of Bendicks Bittermints. We retired to the easy chairs to drink several coffees enhanced by a choice of over a dozen liquors and spirits lined up on the bar. I stuck to my favourite Glenfarclas, which I had never previously wasted in coffee, but I have to say it was rather good.

By this time it was well after three and Bill was beginning to make noises about "getting back to the animals". Alice had been cornered by young William and they seemed to be getting on very well. This was even better than expected. I hadn't banked on a love interest though it was hardly surprising as she was a very pretty girl and without Lisa's rough edges. It was time for Brian and me to make our move. I kicked off.

"It's been great having you and Alice here as guests. Have you had a good time then?"

"Aye. It's bin a right good do. I'm well stuffed. It's bin good to see the lass letting her hair down. Not seen 'er laugh so much since all the trouble kicked off. We can't replace 'er mum but it's bin like a family do."

"I'm glad you enjoyed it. I was thinking the same myself.

This is our new family now. If you can stay a bit longer, we'll be doing charades, then I've set up a Christmas treasure hunt. I spent most of yesterday afternoon setting up the clues. The others have got some games organised as well."

"No, no. Thanks like but I'll have to get back. It'll be quiet with just me and Alice but we're used to that."

Brian saw the chance to come in. "You know, Bill, it doesn't have to be like that. It would be fantastic if you could move in with us. You could help get the farm started. Old Paul needs a rest and the others are keen but need guidance. There's no substitute for experience. You'd be doing us a huge favour."

"I can see you need some help like but I already got a farm to run. It gives us everything me and Alice need. I reckon we'll stay as we are."

"Are you sure Alice has everything she needs," said Brian. "I know you look after her and are devoted to her wellbeing but do you not think she needs company of her own age, needs to chat to other girls, perhaps some attention from boys. You can see how she's come alive today, come out of her shell. She could join our little school group with Christine and gain a well-rounded development of skills and knowledge. If her mother were still alive, would she not want that for her?"

The last point hit Bill hard and I could sense his hackles rise.

"You don't need to lecture me on that. You might have all yer education and such but I can run a farm, provide for my lass and keep her safe. That's what I promised her mum on her death bed and I don't need you to tell me what she'd think."

"Okay Bill. You're quite right. I'm well out of order. I wasn't meaning to criticise or assume an insight into your wife's views. You've done a fantastic job with Alice but there's an opportunity here to take things further. I'm sorry if I've offended you."

"Alright then. I'll speak to Alice and see what she wants. I'll not make any promises but I'll think about it."

"Fair enough. That's all we can ask."

CHAPTER ELEVEN

ABDUCTION

Three Months Later

28 March

It started out as quite a routine day in late March. The regular foraging team of me, Mo, Ian and Phil had taken out the van and a Landrover to explore in the Settle and Giggleswick area, whilst Adam and John had accompanied us in the other Landrover as far as Gisburn Forest where they intended to spend the day hunting. We were to meet up on the way back and travel together on the return to Whitewell. Little did we suspect that the day would end in disaster.

Our community at the inn was thriving. We were now twenty with the addition of Bill and Alice. It had taken a couple weeks to persuade Bill to leave Horse Hey Farm and he did so with considerable reluctance. He had first toyed with the idea of dropping off Alice each day at the inn to join Christine's little school and to carry on supplying us with milk and eggs but eventually he surrendered to the inevitable and agreed to join us on condition that he brought all his livestock, which was more than welcome, and some favourite pieces of furniture together with quite a few boxes of personal effects. We kitted out Bill in his own bedroom, complete with open fire and four poster bed. Alice agreed to share with Christine as Jo and Lisa were already paired up in another room. The pigs, goats, geese and hens we managed to transport in the van but we had to acquire a horse box from a neighbouring farm to move Mavis. They all coped well with the move and were accommodated in extensive enclosures with indoor facilities for the pigs and a milking area set up in the Piggeries. We left room for a lot more livestock, in particular the sheep. Following old Paul's advice, we had identified a small flock of sheep, most of which had survived what turned out to be a mercifully mild winter and were now clearly in lamb. We reckoned they'd be lambing in the next couple weeks and we were checking them daily. As soon as the lambs were born we were planning to round up a couple dozen ewes with lambs to start our flock.

Mavis was in calf as well. Bill said she had been serviced by a bull the previous August and should deliver in late May, ensuring a continued supply of milk. We would then need to address how to get her serviced again. We had ploughed up a large area of land behind the inn and planted a variety of crops. The old orangery was now also given over to intense horticulture. We had planned to address most of our needs, such that foraging for food would soon become a thing of the past. We hadn't bothered with fruit trees as they would take too long to reach maturity but had noted the location of a number of apple, pear and plum trees in neighbouring villages. Soft fruit bushes like blackberries, raspberries, strawberries and others had been transplanted into the orangery.

The inn itself had been made more comfortable with the installation of generators providing lighting, power to the kitchen for the fridges and freezers, even TVs to play old DVDs. Adam had managed to produce hot running water, which was the greatest luxury of all. However we were still making the daily trip to the river to obtain the water in buckets and now needed far more water as people were using the showers regularly. Adam's next project was to install pumps and piping to refill the inn's water tanks directly from the river. The original idea of electrified security fencing had not yet got off the ground and may have been too ambitious and unnecessary in any event. We had erected strong wire-mesh fencing to a height of five feet which was perfectly adequate to protect the livestock from any dogs or foxes.

The school was developing nicely. Jo, Lisa and Alice all enjoyed their lessons with Christine, especially the English Literature and we had ransacked the library at Clitheroe to provide sufficient material. We all contributed what we could to the educational process and supplemented the academic work with practical experience of all aspects of housekeeping, property maintenance and horticulture. Anna continued to receive a good grounding in literacy and numeracy from Christine and the other girls.

Jo had her thirteenth birthday two weeks earlier. I had been dreading it, knowing how she would feel the loss of her mother and sister. Other people made a fuss and we wrapped some parcels and Emma made a lovely cake. Jo put on a brave face but her low mood was clear to see. I considered the possibility of taking Jo back to Saltersford Hall to see the graves but felt the risk was too great, though we would return one day. Fortunately, Jo's low moods never lasted long as she enjoyed the company of Lisa and Alice, not to mention the attention-seeking Poppy. Having a dog had been a great benefit to Jo.

Mo made a full recovery from his infected wound. It had taken a few days for the anti-biotics to kick in and he continued to take them for a week as per the prescription. We kept the other prescription, hopefully also antibiotics, in reserve in case it was needed but remarkably, nobody else had fallen seriously ill. For twenty people to survive for four months with only one significant medical problem was quite incredible and extremely fortuitous given our pitiful resources. We could not expect this to continue indefinitely and improving our medical knowledge, equipment and drugs had to be one of our priorities.

All in all, we were feeling pretty pleased with ourselves and the progress made in developing our little self-sufficient community.

*

It was around 4.30 pm when we left Settle after a good day's foraging and survey of resources, particularly the local farms. We hadn't encountered any other survivors but we were used to that and didn't expect it any more. Nevertheless, we were constantly on the alert for smoke and it was agreed that any signs of human habitation would be investigated, though with care. We were expected back around 6.00 pm but had arranged to meet up with Adam and John at the village of Tosside on the edge of Gisburn Forest at 5.00. They could need some help retrieving their spoils, depending on what they had bagged. One thing for sure, they never came back empty handed and it was our main source of fresh meat until we could build up the farm stock. As we approached the village we could see them at the side of the road, propping themselves up against the Landrover, enjoying the last of the evening sunshine.

"How'd you get on lads," I shouted through the van window as we pulled up alongside.

"Not bad," replied Adam . "Four rabbits, six pheasants and a couple of hares we bagged out on the moor. We missed the main prize though, a huge stag in the depths of the forest. I had him in my sights but something spooked him before I could get a shot away. We were downwind and quiet as mice. I'm sure he didn't know we were there. We're coming back tomorrow to see if we can track him down. I fancy a nice bit of venison."

"Okay. Well if you're all loaded up, we can head back to the inn." The sun had gone down but a warm glow remained in the sky. I was nevertheless surprised to see no lights at the inn. Since we set up the generators, it usually resembled Blackpool illuminations. We parked all three vehicles at the front and blew the horn in case they hadn't heard our approach. The front doors were always locked from the inside and we never took keys when we were out and about. Still no lights switched on or doors opened.

"Are they all having a nap or what?" said Adam. Let's go round to the patio."

It was when we reached the back of the inn we realised something was amiss. The patio door was smashed and hanging open.

"Shit. This looks bad. Get the guns out of the car," ordered Adam. Mo, Phil and John ran back to the vehicles to fetch the weapons whilst I, Adam and Ian peered into the lounge to assess the situation. The first thing I saw was a bloody heap on the carpet just six feet or so inside the door, which was all that remained of Poppy.

"Oh Christ. The poor little thing. What bastards have done this? What have they done with everybody?" I moved forward to touch Poppy. She was cold and stiff with glassy eyes. "She's been dead a while. Whoever's been in is long gone."

It was at that point we heard hammering and shouting, calling our names.

"It's coming from the cellar," said John. "They must be locked in."

We all ran to the door only to find it locked and without the key. Mo spotted the key lying on the floor about ten feet up the hall. "Here it is. They must have thrown it there to stop them pushing it out of the lock to get it under the door."

As we opened the door the others emerged, all clearly distressed. Helen threw herself into John's arms in floods of tears. "Oh John. They've taken Chris. I couldn't do anything."

Anna ran up to Phil. "Daddy! Mummy went with them. I want her back."

As the rest emerged up the steps, my heart sank. There was

Brian, with a huge red weal across his forehead, Paul, Emma and William Fernyhough, Jim and finally Bill, silent but with a face like thunder. No sign of Jo, Lisa or Alice.

"They've taken the girls as well?" I asked.

The others nodded solemnly.

"I'm going after them," I said, turning away.

"I'm with you," said Bill. "Anybody that's messed with my Alice is dead. Let's get the guns."

"Tom! Bill! Just a minute. Don't be fools. They've been gone hours and could be anywhere by now." It was Brian, wincing as he fingered his forehead. "We need to think this through and plan a strategy. It's no good driving off aimlessly." He was right of course but my heart was pumping so fast I couldn't think. I was close to blind panic. My little Jo, after all we had been through. I promised at Sue's grave that I would look after her and now this.

"Alright," I agreed. "I want to know everything that's happened. Every little detail."

We all sat in the kitchen and Jim started brewing some tea. Brian held cloths filled with ice against his forehead but looked like he was on the point of passing out. Helen was shaking like a leaf, clearly in shock. With careful questioning, Adam managed to extract the full story whilst I jotted down every material detail. This is what emerged.

Helen had seen them first, or at least two of them, at around eleven o'clock. She heard a vehicle pulling up at the front of the inn and thought we must have returned for something but was then surprised by a knock at the door. She knew that we would sound our horns but it still didn't occur to her that it could be strangers, not having had visitors at the door in our four months occupation. Opening the door she found two men in their twenties, one of average height with lots of tattoos and a short, stocky fellow. They said they were passing up the valley and saw the smoke from the inn. They felt they should make contact and also asked if they could refill their water containers. A large black four-wheel drive vehicle was parked at the front of the inn pointing north towards Dunsop Bridge as though they had travelled up the valley from the south. Helen couldn't remember anything of the number plate or anything else distinctive about the vehicle. It occurred to Helen afterwards that if they had travelled alongside the river, they'd had plenty of opportunity to get water, but she hadn't thought twice at the time. They seemed quite friendly and pleased to find people, so she invited them in for a cup of tea and slice of cake. Emma, Helen, Chris Lucas and Jim had entertained them in the kitchen. The other men were working in the Piggeries or out on the farm, whilst Chris Salt was holding class with the girls. Poppy made friends with them immediately of course.

The fellow with tattoos identified himself as Dale and spoke with a strong Manchester accent and the shorter man was referred to as Geordie, with an accent to match. They had appeared to be very interested in our community and how we had set ourselves up at the inn, asking lots of questions about our numbers and how we managed to defend ourselves. They had ascertained that six of the men were out hunting and foraging, with others working on the farm. Emma had started to be concerned at the amount of information they were sharing, whereas all the visitors had said was that the two of them were travelling alone.

Emma explained the Brian was the group's leader and would like the meet them. She would send Jim to find him and the others but Dale and Geordie then said they had to be on their way and left fairly quickly. When Brian and the others arrived they had driven off. Brian was not pleased and felt they should have been summoned as soon as the two men had arrived. The fact that they just happened to be passing on such a remote country lane going nowhere significant, that they needed water when they were next to a river, and the extent of their questioning on the size and state of our group, were all rather suspicious.

Nearly two hours later, all hell broke loose. It was shortly after one and everyone was in the kitchen having lunch when they heard a loud smashing sound from the lounge as the patio doors were forced. Several men, including the two seen earlier, ran through the inn firing guns indiscriminately. Brian had made a dash for a gun but was clubbed on the head with a pistol by a tall black fellow, who they later heard the others call "Leroy". Dale grabbed Anna and pressed a pistol against the side of her head informing them that any more nonsense and he would take pleasure in putting a bullet in her brain. He sounded as though he meant it. This made Poppy furious. She had already been barking at the commotion but now was showing her teeth and snapping at Dale, then backing off and barking some more. Dale said "shut the fuck up" and put two bullets in her from close range, killing her instantly. He and Leroy sniggered afterwards and informed them that Anna would be next. A fourth man, quieter than the others and with spectacles, had also appeared. He hadn't spoken and the others had not referred to him by name. They had spread out and were pointing guns at them from all directions. They had no choice but to surrender. On Dale's instructions, Leroy and Geordie proceeded to separate Chris Salt, Chris Lucas, Jo , Lisa and Alice from the others while the "quiet man" kept his pistol trained on them. The others were herded into the cellar, locked in and heard the key being removed. Before entering the cellar Jim caught a glimpse though the front lounge window of a white van parked in front of the inn. On the side was something like a cartoon character of a man on a ladder and a business name which was several initials followed by "roofers".

Once they were in the cellar, Jim and Paul Fernyhough pressed their ears to the door to hear what the men were saying. The sound was very muffled but Paul was pretty sure one of them had queried whether they had enough diesel in the van to get back to the lake. Paul was questioned repeatedly but felt that he heard "lake" rather than "lakes". Jim wasn't sure either way.

That was it, the sum total of our intelligence. That we would mount a search party was not in doubt but we talked around the options before coming up with a strategy. What did we know for sure?

There was at least four of them but could well be others in the van or other vehicles or most likely at a base where they were taking the girls. They were well armed, callous and appeared to be experienced at this sort of operation, suggesting this was not an isolated event. The intention of their attack had clearly been the abduction of young women. It seemed odd that they had included Jo who was only thirteen. It was not as if she was advanced for her age and her figure had not yet started to fill out. If this was purely for lust, they must be catering for the appetite of a paedophile or was there a more long-term objective of collecting females of reproductive age? That might suggest a larger organised group. Was this gang one of a number? If there was a significant group of abducted women, whether for sexual gratification or some sort of breeding colony, they must expect to be pursued and will have organised robust defences. It was very likely that we would have to face more than our four thugs if we were to recover our loved ones. We would need to be well organised, well-armed and determined to succeed. This could take considerable time.

Two pieces of intelligence were critical. Jim's description of the van sounded fairly unique and should enable us to know when we had found our quarry, assuming they didn't just dump the van and use another. Paul's overhearing of lake or lakes would form the focus of our search. If it was indeed 'lake', it could of course be any lake in the country but it seemed unlikely that they would be hunting outside normal daily travel, say 100 miles each way. We would presumably be looking for a substantial property on the banks of a lake. On the other hand, if it was 'lakes' that was mentioned, this would surely be short for the Lake District but the property could be anywhere within that region, not necessarily on the shore of a lake. In either case, the largest concentration of lakes within range would be the Lake District and that seemed the best place to start a search.

The search party was selected quite easily. The four fathers of the missing girls, namely Bill, John, Phil and me were not to be denied. Adam offered his services as firearms expert and Jim was very keen to be included. We felt that six men in three vehicles would give us the strength and flexibility required, including the van to carry supplies and, if necessary, as emergency sleeping accommodation, Bill's Range Rover and one of the Landrovers. That would only leave one working vehicle at the inn but Paul and Mo could find replacements. In their haste to get away the raiders had not located our store of diesel in the Piggeries, which left sufficient to fill each vehicle and load a spare jerry can of diesel into each, ensuring that we wouldn't have to waste time finding fuel. We loaded a couple camping gaz stoves, spare gas canisters, some pans and plenty of tinned soups, meat, fish and fruit. Emma and Helen immediately set to making bread and cakes for us to take and we calculated sufficient rations for two weeks but would probably supplement our supplies with what we came across. We each packed clothes for at least two weeks, sleeping bags and extra blankets.

Firearms were an issue. The raiders had taken what they had spotted and most of the guns were not well hidden as they needed to be readily accessible, not that that proved to be any advantage. Adam and John had taken a couple of rifles out hunting and we had taken four handguns whilst we were foraging. Bill's shotgun had been locked in his Range Rover. Apart from that, Brian had a handgun in his room and two others were stored in the cellar along with the ammunition. In total we had lost two rifles and two handguns but it could have been worse. We agreed that Adam would take his rifle, Bill his shotgun and the other four would take handguns. That would leave three handguns for defence at the inn while we were away. We had all been trained in the use of handguns and rifles, though I had to admit I was more comfortable with the former. Being right-handed but with a weak right eye, I had never managed to fire the rifle with any accuracy but holding a handgun in front of me with both hands, I was quite effective over short distances. The weapon I used was described as semi-automatic with a little magazine of ammunition to clip on which meant it didn't need frequent re-loading.

We had sufficient roadmaps for one in each vehicle, though we had no OS maps covering the Lake District and would need to acquire some in one of the towns. It was difficult to be precise about a search strategy until we got there and assessed the situation. There was one lake close to home which needed to be checked out first, Stocks Reservoir next to Gisburn Forest, not strictly a lake but possibly referred to as such. According to the OS map there were a few country houses in the vicinity. After that there were no lakes between Whitewell and the Lake District. We would start with Windermere as the most southern lake, probably split up and cover the whole of the shoreline. We were aware of the huge number of large properties around Windermere but would rely upon spotting smoke or lights. However, any searching at night would risk giving ourselves away as the vehicle headlights would be visible for miles. One thing for sure was that any hope of a successful rescue would depend on arriving undetected. We decided to stick to daylight searches as far as possible. If there was no result at Windermere, we would move on to the next lake and so on until every lake had been covered. If we still drew a blank we would have to re-assess our strategy. After two weeks at least one of the vehicles would return to Whitewell to liaise with the others.

It seemed a reasonable plan and we busied ourselves preparing the supplies for a departure at 7.30 am the next day. An hour or so later I was collecting supplies from the kitchen when I heard the most ear-splitting screeching noise coming from the cellar and went to investigate. I found Bill with his shotgun fixed in a vice sawing off the end of the barrel. When he noticed my presence he simply remarked: "Well, I'm not shooting fucking pheasants, am I? This'll put a fucking hole straight through 'em. And I tell you what, anybody that's messed with my Alice is getting both fucking barrels!"

CHAPTER TWELVE

THE SEARCH PARTY

29 March

We were washed, breakfasted, packed up and on the road at 7.30 prompt. I don't think any of us had managed much sleep the previous night and were just eager to be doing something. There were no high spirits, rather a mood of grim determination not to return to Whitewell without the girls. There was also an undercurrent of anger and desire for vengeance, a general expectation that the expedition would end in considerable violence. I felt Bill was more than ready to vent his aggression and John gave the impression of being able to look after himself but the rest of us were clearly not men of violence. I didn't know how I would cope with such a situation. Although I had developed a level of competence with a handgun, I had fired it only at targets, not people, let alone people that were likely to fire back. But this was what the world had become, a world in which the strongest prevailed, law enforcement now part of history and the only moral code was derived from the individual's conscience. Nothing in my experience had prepared me for this and I didn't know how I would cope but I had to try for Jo's sake.

The cold and misty start to the day did nothing to lift the spirits. We all set off together for Slaidburn where we would split up to explore the Stocks Reservoir area. None of us anticipated success so close to home but it would be illogical to explore the Lake District before checking out somewhere just fifteen miles away. I drove the Citroen Dispatch accompanied by Jim, Bill took his Range Rover with Phil and John the Landrover with Adam. We stopped at the crossroads in the centre of Slaidburn to go our separate ways as arranged the previous evening.

Jim and I were to take the van on the track due north taking in Wood House Gate and Hollins House. Bill and Phil would take the rough track north-east to Hammerton Hall and onto Back House on the banks of the reservoir, while John and Adam would continue on the B6478 east towards Long Preston before turning north at Stephen Moor, over the causeway and into Gisburn Forest. We split up at 8.15 agreeing to regroup in Slaidburn at 10.00. Any signs of life were to be reported back but not investigated without backup.

Jim and I found the track easily enough. It was heading straight across the moors to the west of the reservoir and forest, marked to High Bentham. As we drove I confided to Jim my fears over whether I could cope with a shoot-out.

"I think we're all in the same boat, Tom. I'd never handled a gun in my life until we started our sessions with John and Adam. The thought of killing somebody doesn't seem real but I tell you what, I'll do it if I have to. This is a nasty bunch we're dealing with. They thought nothing of shooting your dog and holding a gun to little Anna's head. They're the lowest of the low and I hate to think of the girls in their clutches. Anyway, it might not come to that. If we find out where they're being held without being spotted, we might be able to take them by surprise or even sneak them out."

I don't think he was convincing himself, let alone me. It wouldn't be that easy. What if we didn't find them at all? We could spend months, even years scouring the country. I wasn't usually so negative in my outlook but my level of anxiety was totally debilitating.

Reaching Wood House Gate after a mile or so, it looked deserted, no smoke, no lights or vehicles. We drove straight past and were then in an elevated position to look down across the reservoir to our right. A few small buildings below the dam at the base of the reservoir looked to be part of the water works but no houses were visible anywhere. The only properties shown on the OS map that were near the banks of the reservoir were Black House, which Bill would be checking, and Hollins House but neither were visible. No smoke was showing in any direction though it was still a dank, misty day which wouldn't make it easy to distinguish smoke.

After a further couple miles we reached a rough track which according to the map would take us to Hollins House. The track was full of pot holes, stones and puddles which meant moving very slowly in the van, not ideal for the terrain, but we slowly mounted the brow of the hill and as it curved to the right and dropped down towards the reservoir we could see Hollins House in front of us and stopped a couple hundred yards short to observe. I was conscious that if we could see the house, any occupants could probably see us and a van descending down the hill would be pretty conspicuous. I felt we needed to be more discreet in our reconnaissance but we really just wanted to get this done and head for the Lake District. Again there was no smoke or vehicles so we decided to drive up to the house but detected no obvious signs of life. An open-top truck was parked at the back of the house but nothing else.

"Come on, there's nothing here. Let's try further up the track", I suggested. We bounced our way back up to the main track and, and as we had time to spare, continued northwards for a few miles but were now moving away from the reservoir. There were tracks to a couple farms but no smoke visible. We decided to give up and return to Slaidburn.

We were the first back and after twenty minutes or so were joined by Bill and Phil. Shortly before ten John and Adam turned up. "Nothing" was the consensus. Off to the Lakes for some serious searching. It was a little frustrating that we had already lost nearly two hours but we had to stick to a systematic approach. We had already agreed the previous evening to commence our search at Lake Windermere and gradually move north, taking in the lakes to the immediate east and west as we went, leaving the most westerly lakes like Ennerdale and Wastwater that needed to be approached from the coast until last. We decided firstly to call in at Kendal on route to pick up some supplies.

*

Kendal was every bit as devastated as the towns around Manchester. We parked on the edge of the centre as the High Street was a mass of debris from looted shops and burnt out cars. Living in the peace and tranquillity of the Lake District appeared to have made little difference to the local yobs' propensity to wreak destruction once law and order had broken down. Not wanting to waste too much time in Kendal, we simply concentrated on High Street shops selling cameras and optical equipment, of which there must certainly be at least one. We walked up the steep incline of the main shopping street, three on each side, quickly checking out each shop. So many of the shop fronts were burnt out and shelves stripped that it was difficult to discern what they had been selling and whilst most of the shops had relatively narrow frontage but were deep, very little light permeated beyond the first ten feet. Phil spotted some ripped packaging on the floor of one which appeared to relate to some specialist photographic equipment, which merited further investigation. Phil, Jim and I entered with our torches and surveyed the empty shelves and piles of rubbish on the floor. They did appear to have been selling cameras amongst other items and at the far end of the store we found the entrance to a storeroom or possibly an office. It was locked with a stout mortice lock and no sign of a key. This we regarded as optimistic as any stock would remain undisturbed. We each tried kicking the door around the area of the lock but with the surrounding debris, it was impossible to get much of a run-up and we couldn't produce enough force to smash the lock. Phil took a few steps and launched himself feet first into the centre of the door producing a splintering of wood but still no movement on the lock.

"The door's strongest at the edges," observed Phil. "I think we might be able to open up the middle."

We continued kicking and hammering at the door with limited results until Bill appeared to check why we were making so much noise. "We're trying to get into the storeroom but we can't shift this bloody mortice lock."

"Aye. Stand back lad", said Bill levelling his shotgun. He fired off one barrel, an ear-splitting noise reverberating around the confined space. When the dust settled, what was left of the door, which wasn't much, was swinging freely. Our torches revealed piles of cases inside and we entered to investigate. After twenty minutes or so we found what we were looking for, a case of Praktica binoculars. There were eight pairs in the case. We unpacked three, one for each sub-team and were away. Now we were equipped for distant surveillance. Finding the OS maps was relatively easy at WH Smiths on the High Street.

Next stop Windermere.

*

At Windermere we split up once again. Jim and I were taking the main lakeside A592 south to Newby Bridge, then up the western bank of the lake as far as the ferry crossing to Bowness, then moving towards Hawkshead via Far Sawrey and Near Sawrey, taking in a circuit of Esthwaite Water. Bill and Phil would explore the Windermere/Bowness area and the north-east of the lake. John and Adam would drive straight to Ambleside at the north of the lake, then explore the north-west corner. It was already approaching two and we agreed to meet up in the public car park at Hawkshead by 4.30. As usual we were looking for smoke or any other signs of life and would watch from a distance, hopefully undetected. If anybody failed to make the rendezvous by 5.00, the others would set off to search for them. Nobody was to approach any survivors before we had pooled our intelligence. It seemed a good plan. If we could eliminate the whole of the Windermere area on day one, that would constitute good progress. At that rate we could cover all the lakes within a week. Even so, the prospect of Jo in the clutches of thugs for up to a week filled me with dread. There was an argument for taking it in turns to search for lights through the night but we had decided the risk of detection was too great. Our only chance of this ending well was to retain the element of surprise.

Jim and I set off south through Bowness on the main lakeside road, driving slowly with the windows half open on the theory that we might smell smoke rather than see it. We had an intermittent view of the lake through the trees to our right whilst to the left the ground rose steeply and was mainly forested. The only lakeside properties were on the main road and once we left Bowness they were few and far between. We passed a couple hotels, including the extensive Beech Hill Hotel but detected no signs of life and through breaks in the trees we could see across to the western bank of Windermere but it was still rather gloomy and misty, not the best weather to be looking for smoke.

Arriving at Newby Bridge at the most southern point of the lake, having spotted nothing of interest, we decided to take a small detour to the village of Staveley-in-Cartmel, less than a mile off our route, but apart from a couple parked cars it turned out to be another eerily deserted village. It felt like we were looking for a needle in a haystack and I worried that our search relied totally on one half overheard remark. We had barely started but I couldn't help feeling defeatist. Joining the main A590, we then almost immediately turned right again over a narrow stone bridge at the White Swan Hotel, following the track to Lakeside and another large deserted hotel, then the narrow road pulled away from the edge of the lake and wound its way through the eastern extreme of Grizedale Forest. We passed occasional houses, Graythwaite Old Hall and Graythwaite Hall but still nothing. The road then forked and we took the right, dropping steeply to the edge of the lake, passing a farm and a couple more houses before reaching the B5285 marked left to Far Sawrey, Near Sawrey and Hawkshead. Before following this, we turned right to reach the ferry terminal for the crossing to Bowness. The terminal was nothing more than a road running down to the water but it afforded an excellent view of the lake in all directions. We stopped for a break and took it in turns to train the binoculars along the banks. Neither of us spotted any smoke though the north and south extremities of the lake were lost in the mist.

"I think we can give up on Windermere Jim. Let's head on to Hawkshead. We're going to be early at this rate, so we've got plenty of time to explore en route. Surely there's somebody alive somewhere!"

We soon reached Far Sawrey, yet another deserted village and climbed the brow of the hill to see Near Sawrey laid out beneath us. I stopped the van suddenly as we both exclaimed together "smoke!" We had been looking for so long without result that the sight of smoke came as a total shock and we could see immediately that this came not from one but from several properties. Gathering my thoughts, I realised that the van being near the brow of the hill would be conspicuous and the only vehicle on the road. I backed it up below the brow and parked at the side. Now it was only visible from Far Sawrey.

"Right. Come on Jim, on foot. Bring the binoculars."

Walking back up to the brow of the hill, we edged behind

a low dry stone wall at the side of the road until we had a good vantage point and settled down to observe the village. We were still several hundred yards away and confident that we would not be seen as long as another vehicle didn't approach from Far Sawrey but even then the sound would allow us more than sufficient time to move to the other side of the wall. The van would attract attention but there was nowhere to hide it. Using the binoculars we could see clearly that the smoke was rising from three adjacent cottages in a row of four or five on a small lane rising to the right out of the centre of the village. They were typical old Lake District whitewashed stone and slate cottages. Nowhere else in the village was showing any sign of life and it was clearly significant to find three inhabited properties together. I wondered whether the cottages had been knocked through to form one large property but would all the chimneys be in use? Outside the small front gardens was a wide area before the lane narrowed as it disappeared up the hill and this contained several vehicles but whether these were still in use or simply abandoned, it was impossible to say. They weren't parked right in front of the cottage gates but that wouldn't be conclusive. There was certainly no roofer's van to be seen. Even with the binoculars it was impossible to see anything through the cottage windows and as there was no activity outside, we would have to get closer to continue our surveillance and maybe get a view of the back of the cottages.

We began to make our way down the hill using the dry stone wall as cover which meant walking in a permanent crouch. We were approximately half way down, perhaps a hundred yards away, when a large four-wheel drive vehicle emerged round the bend on the road from Hawkshead at the opposite end of the village. We were just about to nip over the wall when the car, possibly a Range Rover, turned left and parked up in front of the cottages. I had the binoculars and trained them on the car. A thick set man, average height with white hair emerged from the driver's side and a taller, apparently younger man followed from the passenger side carrying two rifles. The white haired man opened the back and two dogs bounded out barking, a black Labrador and a cocker or springer spaniel. He used keys to open the front door of the middle cottage of the three emitting smoke and went in with the dogs. The tall man took in the rifles, then returned to the car and collected a bulging sack. I could see him waving towards the front window of the first cottage, then he too disappeared inside.

"What do you reckon Jim? Hunting expedition?"

"Definitely. Looks like they've done pretty well by the size of that sack."

"I can't think these people have any connection with the thugs we're after. They like dogs for one thing. We could do with talking to them, see what they know."

"Agreed," said Jim, "but we said we wouldn't approach anybody until we'd reported back. They might be jumpy with those rifles, you know."

"Okay. You're right. We'll meet up with the others and suggest coming back here. Some local intelligence could be invaluable. If we are going to stay unobserved, we'll have to back-track through the forest and approach Esthwaite Water from the other side."

Having studied the OS map, I knew there were a couple large, secluded properties on the west bank of the lake which needed to be checked, though I was sure that the occupants of these cottages would be aware of any activity so close to home. In any event, we had plenty of time before the agreed rendezvous in Hawkshead, so we turned round the van and retraced our route to where we had branched right in the forest just past Graythwaite Hall. This time we headed due north to the southern extremity of Esthwaite Water and followed the track along the western bank, opposite Near Sawrey. We passed alongside both Esthwaite Hall and Esthwaite Lodge but both appeared to be deserted and arrived at Hawkshead twenty minutes early, the first to reach the car park.

Bill's Range Rover was the next to turn up.

"Nothing doing in Bowness/Windermere or anywhere en route to here," reported Phil, looking a little deflated. We began to fill them in on our experience in Near Sawrey but were only half way through the tale when Adam and John's Landrover pulled in.

"We found something," said Adam. "We drew a blank in Ambleside but at the edge of the town we had a view across the river to the hill beyond and thought we caught some smoke mixed in with the mist. We followed the track around the bottom of the hill and were pretty sure the smoke was coming from where the OS map shows as Brow Head Farm. We couldn't get a view of the farm buildings from the road and the only point of access would be up the farm drive which would have given us away. It's not really on the lake and I'd be very doubtful it's what we're looking for but it needs checking out."

Jim and I repeated and finished our account of Near Sawrey. We all agreed that from what Jim and I had observed, these were clearly not the kidnappers and could be approached for information. As it was just ten minutes down the road, this was worth checking out immediately.

"We'll still need to tackle this carefully," suggested Adam. "They have guns and dogs. If we scare them we could still end up with a dangerous situation."

We decided that the least threatening and most straight-forward approach would be for me to go alone and unarmed, simply knocking on the door of the cottage occupied by the men and dogs. The others and all the vehicles could stay out of sight until I had made an introduction. If I didn't return in say fifteen minutes, the others could follow to investigate. We set off immediately and in less than ten minutes reached the edge of the village and parked up. I walked the last 200 yards along the main road confident that our vehicles would not have been heard and turned left up the lane to the row of cottages. There were no lights showing as it was not yet dusk but all three cottages continued to emit smoke. As I approached the garden gate for the middle cottage, I glimpsed an elderly lady observing me from the first cottage. The gate opened with a squeak and I strode confidently to the door though I was starting to feel a little nervous. What if they'd had some bad experiences and were in the habit of shooting first and asking questions later or releasing the dogs? It was too late to reconsider. I gave a loud rap with the cast iron door knocker in the shape of a wolf. As expected, this was followed by excited barking from the two dogs and an exclamation.

"Who's the hell that? Get the gun Andy!"

I heard some scrabbling about inside, a key turning in the lock and, as the door opened, a rifle pointed at my chest. It was the younger man I had seen through the binoculars. The older fellow was holding the dogs who were eager to get out but didn't look too threatening. The older man spoke.

"Who are you? What d'ya want?"

I held my hands up in a submissive gesture. "Sorry for the intrusion. I didn't mean to alarm you. We were just passing through, looking for some missing people and we saw your smoke. We were hoping we might be able to talk to you. I'm Tom Morton, by the way."

The old fellow looked suspicious.

"Who's we? Where are the others? If this is some sort of trick, we're not afraid to use these guns."

"I'm sure you're not. There are six of us and we're travelling in three vehicles parked at the edge of the village. I came on my own as we didn't want to alarm you. If it's okay, I'll collect the others and introduce them."

"Don't trust him Dad. It could be a trick," said the younger man.

"I can assure you we don't mean any harm. We only want to talk. Our wives and daughters have been abducted and we think they're being held in the Lake District. We're desperate for any information. We had to bring guns but we'll leave them in the cars."

The older fellow was thinking about it, still apparently unconvinced.

"I'll tell you what we'll do. We'll walk you back to your cars and we'll take it from there."

He put the dogs in a back room and picked up another rifle. We walked back down the road, the younger man with his rifle poked into my back, the older man hanging back five yards or so, looking to the sides with his rifle at the ready. I wasn't sure this was the outcome we were seeking but we would have to play by their rules. One could hardly blame them for being suspicious.

As we approached the cars I could see the alarm in the faces of my colleagues as Bill and Adam grabbed for their guns.

"Tell them to get out and leave the guns inside," ordered the older man.

"Its okay lads," I shouted. "They're just worried about the guns. Come on out and leave the guns." I breathed a sigh of relief as Adam emerged and beckoned to the others. It was a tense situation but I was convinced we were not in danger as long as nobody did anything hasty. Faced with six armed men it was only natural that they felt threatened.

As they all left the cars and locked the guns inside, the white-haired man took charge. "Alright. Now we're all walking back to the cottage and you'll have a chance to explain yourselves. I'm responsible for the people in there and I'm not prepared to put them in danger. If anybody tries anything, we're not afraid to use these guns."

We marched back to the cottage, the young man still holding his gun to my back and the white-haired man bringing up the rear, covering the others. Bill looked distinctly aggrieved but

Adam assured our captors that there would be no violence. As we passed the first cottage I could now see two elderly ladies peering out of the front window.

We entered the men's cottage to much barking from the back room and were directed into the kitchen. On instruction, the younger man fetched some extra chairs from another room and we all sat down, the white haired man sitting at the door with his gun on his knee. He introduced himself.

"Right then. I'm Harry Knox and this is my lad Andy. Introduce yourselves and let's hear your story. Then we'll decide what to do with you. What's all this about abductions?"

We all introduced ourselves and Adam took the lead in explaining our set-up at the inn, the encounter with the thugs and our mission to track down our women folk. His reasonable and persuasive tone gradually won over Harry and Andy, the atmosphere becoming more relaxed. Harry parked his gun in the corner, shook hands with Adam and even apologised for his initial response.

"You see, we've got women folk of our own and me and Andy are here to protect them. We can't just let people in with guns."

We assured Harry that it wasn't a problem and that his stance had been entirely sensible. The dogs were making a terrible noise in the back, scrabbling at the door. Harry sent Andy to let them out.

"They won't hurt. They just don't like to be left out."

As Andy released them, the two dogs shot into the kitchen barking excitedly. The Labrador ran round and round the confined space, bumping into the chairs while the spaniel approached submissively. I ruffled his ears and he immediately rolled onto his back with his legs in the air. Then the Labrador came to be stroked as well, recognising a dog-friendly person. Harry laughed. "That's Jet and the spaniel's Jarvis. We take them hunting but they're too bloody soft really. They've been brought up as family pets."

Harry suggested that the "old girls", as he called them, would want to meet us and were no doubt wondering what was going on. He sent Andy to fetch them. "Then give Amelia a knock, will you."

A few minutes later the two ladies I had seen through the cottage window arrived all of a fluster. One was a little older and introduced herself as Meg Turner.

"Oh my goodness, how exciting, guests for high tea. Its months since we've had company. Oh I do hope Harry didn't frighten you with his gun. You will stay for tea, won't you? It's just sandwiches but with wholemeal bread, freshly baked this morning and some scones and jam, no cream I'm afraid. We'd better put some more scones on, Cynthia. There'll be twelve of us for tea, how lovely."

After what we'd been through, it was quite surreal, like a holiday in the Lakes, tea and scones in a whitewashed cottage, it was hard to believe.

The slightly younger lady was introduced as Cynthia Potter.

"No relation to Beatrix, you know," she said with a giggle. "She used to live just round the corner you know. We used to get coaches of Japanese coming to visit, didn't we Meg?"

This pair seemed ideally suited and I was already looking forward to high tea.

Another lady then entered the now rather crowded cottage with a young girl in tow. "Amelia Kirkpatrick. Pleased to meet you all." Amelia looked about thirty and introduced the child as the ten year old Kate Gibbs. This completed the entourage. Given the composition of the group, it was easy to see why Harry had been so cautious.

*

An hour or so later we were all seated in Meg's cottage enjoying a sumptuous Lake District high tea. A selection of fresh chicken, tinned red salmon and corned beef sandwiches on fresh crusty wholemeal bread, followed by huge fruit scones with butter and strawberry jam. The scones were still warm from the oven. The tea was served with fresh milk in delicate china cups. Meg explained that before the flu she used to serve afternoon teas in the front garden, which was especially popular with the Japanese tourists.

"You wouldn't expect it, would you dear? They just couldn't get enough of Beatrix Potter. I've taken so many photographs of them in front of my cottage, we must be famous in Japan!"

We enquired as to their source of fresh milk and butter, having seen chickens at the back of the cottages but certainly no cow.

"Oh, that comes from old Bert's farm," said Meg.

"It's the only farm still operating round here. Harry and Andy take him some game from the forest and he keeps us going for milk, butter and cheese. Poor old Bert, he's turned 70 you know and he's keeping the place running on his own but I think it's too much for him. He had two strapping lads but they're dead now and old Carol too. It's very sad, you know." Adam asked for the location of Bert's farm and was pretty sure it was the same place where he had observed smoke earlier.

"We might have a word with Bert tomorrow."

"You better not turn up unannounced," said Harry. "He'll take a pot shot at you. I'm taking him a pheasant tomorrow. You can come along if you like."

"Thanks Harry. I might take you up on that."

Hearing our story in detail, the ladies were quite appalled.

"I don't think they'd be from round here," offered Cynthia. "Sounds like city folk to me. Fancy just shooting a dog for no reason, that's simply dreadful."

"I'll tell you one thing for sure," said Harry. "They're not holed up in Grizedale Forest. We've covered every inch of it. You might be better trying the northern lakes like Ullswater or Derwentwater,"

"We have in mind to check every lake in the Lake District, one by one," said Adam. "We don't intend to give up until we've explore every possibility."

"I ain't giving up 'til I'm in bloody grave," added Bill. "I'm not leaving my Alice with those bastards. Pardon the language, like."

Nobody could recollect seeing a roofer's van as described by Jim. Indeed, apart from old Bert, we were the first people they had met for several months and during the course of the evening we pieced together how this disparate group had ended up together. Meg was the only survivor from Near Sawrey, having contracted the virus but pulled through.

"It laid me low for a while but it takes a lot to finish me off. I'm a tough old bird."

She had lived in the same cottage for over twenty years, alone for the last five since her husband died. Although nearly 70, she had turned to serving afternoon teas for the tourists and, keeping her own hens, reckoned the fresh free-range eggs contributed to the appeal of her renowned home-made cakes. She had two adult daughters with families living in Leeds and Leicester, who had avoided the virus before the phones went down, since when she had heard nothing. She retained some hope that some of her five grandchildren may be cared for somewhere but realistically felt her daughters would long since have travelled to Near Sawrey if they were still alive.

"I was a bit depressed for a while but you've just got to get on with it, haven't you, whatever life throws at you."

Cynthia was the sole survivor from Far Sawrey and already knew Meg as they had attended the same church. She lost her husband to the flu but had no children and had moved in with Meg to support each other but still looked after her cottage in Far Sawrey and assured us that it was "absolutely spotless". The old girls had met Harry and Andy whilst looking for supplies in Ambleside. Harry and Andy had been in business together as plumbers and both lost their wives to the flu as well as Harry's daughter who had still been living at home. They and the dogs had taken over the cottage next to Meg for mutual benefit. Harry and Andy supplied fresh meat from the forest and fish from the lake whilst Meg and Cynthia cooked for them and did their laundry. The old girls felt a lot safer having a couple men around.

Amelia had been an artist in Hawkshead living with her female partner who was taken by the flu. She had found young Kate foraging for food in a neighbour's house, having cycled from her home in Coniston. She was the sole survivor from her family and had gladly taken up the offer from Amelia to move in. They had subsequently travelled through Near Sawrey and met Meg and Cynthia whilst the men were out hunting, and the group became six. They had tried to persuade old Bert to join them but he wasn't for leaving his farm, so they visited at least twice a week to exchange goods. None of them were aware of any similar groups but they rarely ventured beyond the west of Lake Windermere. One wondered how many informal groupings had been thrown together through circumstance up and down the country as opposed to our own more structured and long-term plans at Whitewell. In the short-term it was all about security and obtaining a regular source of food though it was hard to see much future for such small groups. Meg and Cynthia's needs would be met but the others would wish to find partners and poor Kate would be very isolated as the only child. We enquired gently whether they may wish to join us in Whitewell at some point but they all expressed a firm desire to stay as they were. We didn't press the issue as we had other priorities, having made little real progress in our search other than eliminating the Windermere area, which was of some value.

As it was now dark outside, the Near Sawrey group suggested that we should stay the night before resuming our search and we needed little persuading.

"Its game casserole for supper!" declared Meg.

30 March

We spent a very comfortable night at Near Sawrey, two of us in each of the cottages, but were up with the dawn eager to resume our quest. First we took up Meg's invitation to a special Lake District breakfast of thick porridge followed by pancakes with hot maple syrup. Delicious.

Having made our plans the previous evening, we took our leave of Meg, Cynthia, Amelia and Kate with a firm promise to call again in better times. It was arranged that Harry and Andy would escort Adam and John to call on farmer Bert at Brow Head Farm. They would then check out Rydal Water and Grasmere. Jim and I were to tackle Coniston Water and Elterwater, while Bill and Phil were to make another circuit of Windermere in case we had missed anything. Same rules as before: look for signs of life, observe and report back without making contact and, if possible, undetected. We would re group at Ambleside between 3.30 and 4.00 pm.

As Jim and I headed back towards Hawkshead in the Citroen, the sun was just clearing the horizon on the far side of Windermere. It looked like a decent day which would make it easier to spot smoke at a distance. However, it concerned me again that perhaps we were placing too much reliance on observing smoke. What if our chums had set themselves up with generators to power electric heating and cooking. I voiced my concerns to Jim but he considered it to be unlikely.

"I mean, you can't rule it out but it you're in a big property with open fires, it seems obvious to use them and there's plenty of wood to be found. If they're relying on a generator for everything it would need to be a big one rather than a little portable, which would not be easy to install and they'd need a constant supply of diesel."

"That's true," I conceded, "but if they're scouring the countryside abducting young women, it's very unlikely our group was the first to be attacked. They must expect to be pursued, so what makes them confident they can avoid detection. Smoke is such an obvious giveaway. If they're not generating smoke, we could have already passed them and not realised."

"If they were scouting around Windermere, I reckon Harry and Andy would have come across them by now, or maybe spotted that distinctive van," suggested Jim.

"It's distinctive to us because you've seen it. They wouldn't have taken any notice."

"Fair enough but I still don't think they're around here. The sooner we move on the better."

We passed through Hawkshead and branched off west towards Coniston. At least we were now in new territory. As we climbed up the ridge we had a good view of Grizedale Forest stretched out to the left.

"You know, our friends back there have got a great spot for resourcing food, haven't they, all this forest and the lakes for fishing," observed Jim.

"Yes, you're right, they won't starve. They've got quite a good set up there for the present. You have to wonder though what will become of Kate as the youngster. If we keep in touch with them, maybe we can offer her a better future at some point. In the long-term we need larger communities to be genuinely self-sufficient. But first of all, we need to get our girls back."

Before we reached the town of Coniston, we arrived at the northern tip of the lake and turned left down the track which hugs the eastern shore. There were very few large houses on that side but the track afforded an excellent view across the lake such that any smoke in the vicinity should be easily visible. Initially we passed a few significant properties in Tent Lodge, How Head, Bank Ground, Thurston and Brantwood but none showed any sign of activity. The track then moved to the water's edge, hemmed in by a steeply wooded bank and leaving no room for properties. Each time we reached a gap in the trees we parked up and trained the binoculars across the opposite shore looking for any smoke, vehicles or movement of any kind but all was deathly still. On one such break we were startled by a rabbit scuttling out of the forest at speed. The reason was soon apparent as a large Lurcher dog raced in hot pursuit. The rabbit kept changing direction to avoid the dog but was no match for the speed of the lurcher. As he closed on the rabbit he whipped it into the air, caught it again and shook it violently until the rabbit lay still. The lurcher appeared about to enjoy it's meal when several other dogs emerged from the forest barking madly. An Alsatian reached them first, pursued by a Doberman, or possibly a thin Rottweiler, and some sort of terrier. They all went for the rabbit but quickly turned to attacking each other in a vicious frenzy. The terrier and lurcher seem to come off the worst whilst the Alsatian and Doberman reached some form of standoff before the Alsatian picked up the rabbit and retreated back into the forest.

It was quite an eye-opener for us. We had both witnessed dogs fighting before but these were really going for it, clearly driven by hunger. The forest no longer seemed such an attractive source of food. Harry had mentioned that the dogs had become quite a problem in the forest and he had been forced to shoot several to warn them off. They had at first encountered escaped farm stock in the outskirts of the forest, which had been easy pickings but such sightings were becoming rare, which Harry had attributed to the dog packs. The dogs were certainly at the top of the food chain and Harry had envisaged hunting the dogs simply to preserve the rest of the wildlife. One wondered how hungry the dogs needed to become before they in turn would hunt people for food, though on current evidence they would have thin pickings.

The dogs disappeared as quickly as they had appeared and all was quiet again. The shocking episode had got us thinking.

"I suppose it was inevitable really," I suggested. "From all indications, the dogs were not affected by the flu virus and so many are running wild, they must massively outnumber the surviving people. Once the remaining farm stock had died, escaped or been attacked by dogs, they were bound to retreat to the forests. Being descended from wolves, it's their natural environment and there's nothing to prey on them. Most of these dogs were probably family pets but the most aggressive pack leaders were probably farm dogs or even guard dogs. Within a few years most of the dogs will have been born in the wild and behave accordingly."

"Well, if it's a question of survival and we're in competition with the dogs, we'll have to hunt them down and clear the forests," said Jim.

"Perhaps, but that might not be so easy if there are so many dogs and so few people. I think it reinforces the long-term plan of living in farming communities rather than relying on hunting. It's obviously a more efficient way of providing food anyway, especially if the numbers in the community are increasing."

"Then maybe we just surrender the forests to the dogs until we're well established. God, it's like stepping back in time, isn't it."

"That's effectively what we've done," I said. "The things we're relying on at the moment, like this van and finding enough diesel to put in it, it'll all be gone within a couple of generations. We're going to have to model our communities on a sustainable technology, probably at the level of the seventeenth or early eighteenth century, before the Industrial Revolution. Even to do that we'll need to re-discover the old skills of the blacksmith, the miller, the baker, pre-mechanised farming techniques. It's going to be a massive challenge. Our little project at Whitewell is just the start."

Jim was noticeably quiet for a while. I don't think he'd thought things through to that extent and was somewhat daunted by the prospect.

We completed our circuit of Coniston Water without result and headed back northwards to Elterwater. There were no properties actually on the banks of the lake but as we had time to spare, we checked out the village of Elterwater and Chapel Stile up the valley above it. Still no signs of life. We decided to head towards the appointed meeting place in front of the church in Ambleside, arriving almost an hour early.

Bill and Phil were next to arrive, reporting a similarly unproductive day. Lastly, Adam and John parked up in the Landrover. They had had an interesting conversation with Bert at the farm but he had no useful intelligence with regard to any possible locations for our quarry, any sightings of the gang or their vehicles, or any other known survivors to contact. In total, we had drawn a complete blank and we were all quite convinced that we were looking in the wrong place. We were all a little downhearted to feel that we'd wasted a day whilst our loved ones were surrendered to their fate.

After a very brief conference we were all agreed to set off immediately for the northern lakes and that Ullswater seemed a good bet. It was one of the largest lakes with plenty of waterfront property and wasn't readily accessible from the current location, which could explain why the gang had not apparently sought victims at Windermere. From the Preston area the obvious route to Ullswater was straight up the M6 to Penrith, by-passing the Windermere area. It was possible that the gang didn't operate locally, fearing pursuit, but used the motorway to reach further flung locations and to disappear quickly without trace. It seemed a reasonable theory.

The quickest route to Ullswater was over the Kirkstone Pass to join the A592 north to reach Patterdale at the southern tip of the lake. That was our objective for the day and we set off in convoy. Navigating the pass was rather more testing for the Citroen than the other vehicles but she made it and less than an hour after leaving Ambleside, we arrived at Patterdale. We had a couple hours of daylight left which would enable us to explore Patterdale and Glenridding at the south of the lake and possibly find somewhere to spend the night more comfortable than the back of the van.

We parked up in the centre of Patterdale and proceeded together on foot. It seemed quiet as usual and we were ready to write it off as yet another deserted village when an extraordinary sound filled the air. We stared at each other in astonishment. "It can't be," said Adam.

"It bloody is," said Bill. "They're singing a hymn. It's coming from that church down the road. Well I'll be buggered!"

CHAPTER THIRTEEN

PEOPLE OF THE LAKES

We ran the hundred yards to the source of the singing, a lovely little Lake District church with a clock tower and slate roof, and approached through the small graveyard. A sign announced that this was St Patrick's Church with the Reverend M. Watson. We opened the door and filed in as the singing abruptly ceased and astonished heads turned to face us. There were at least fifteen assembled in the pews, of all ages from a young girl to a very old lady. Facing this small congregation was a white-haired vicar complete in clerical vestments. He alone remained composed and seemed unsurprised at our arrival. He smiled and addressed us.

"Greetings brethren. You are most welcome to join us. Please take a pew."

In the circumstances it seemed impolite to do otherwise and we all sat at the first empty pew.

The reverend continued the service. "We thank you Lord for delivering us from the great pestilence. We thank you for choosing us to do your work. We thank you for protecting us and providing our needs. We thank you for guiding these friends to our door. We are the servants of our most merciful Lord. Amen"

All the congregation responded: "Amen".

The service appeared to be concluded as people began to stand and turned to look at us. The vicar walked down the aisle to our pew where we remained seated.

"Good evening gentlemen. It's wonderful to see you. I'm the Reverend Mark Watson and this is my little flock. I hope you will join us. Have you travelled far?"

We each introduced ourselves and briefly explained our quest. The Reverend was visibly shocked at the mention of abductions and invited us back to their "hostel", as he called it, to discuss how they may help us.

We followed the congregation as they filed up the road before arriving at Patterdale Youth Hostel which they had made into their temporary refuge. Others in the group began to introduce themselves. Rose Tierney, a woman in her late thirties was accompanied by her 12 year old daughter, Sonya. All the others appeared to be alone, including Jamie Ferguson, a jovial fellow of around 50, Winston Barnes, a portly black gentleman of similar age, Emily Gibbons, a somewhat frail lady in her eighties, Richard Preston, a tall, imposing fellow in his thirties, Claire Potts, a friendly young lady in her twenties who also introduced the youngest member of the group, Sophie Higgins, a six year old orphan. There were others whose names I didn't catch as they all milled around and busied themselves preparing some tea. We were then invited to sit at long benches and tables in the kitchen/dining area whilst the lady who had identified herself as Rose Tierney instructed her daughter to serve scones and jam. We gratefully accepted and whilst we ate, surrounded by the rest of his "flock", the Reverend began to tell their story.

"It must seem strange to you to encounter our little congregation singing hymns and enjoying a traditional Lake District afternoon tea in the midst of a ravaged world." That was an understatement but after meeting the old girls at Near Sawrey, we were getting used to the idea.

"I've tended to the ministry here at St Patrick's for over ten years now, although sad to say our numbers have been dropping off for some time. The pestilence arrived at Patterdale a little later than in the big cities and we had seen such terrible sights on the television. Once it came, it spread throughout the village within a few days and nobody was spared. I too was struck down and took to my bed, for how long I do not know, but when I regained my senses I discovered my dead wife and was overcome with grief. As I moved through the village all our neighbours, friends and loyal members of my congregation were all dead until I found I was the sole survivor and felt useless and impotent but God came to me in the night and spoke to me. He told me he had chosen me to do his work. I and others of his selection were to rebuild a better world, to turn our backs on the old ways and devote ourselves to the worship of the Lord. I set about burying the dead and recorded their details in the church register, 142 all told. It took me over a month to dig the graves but every member of the village received a proper Christian burial. I cut wood to build fires and lived on the food in the villagers' houses. God directed me to a farm a mile or so up the road and I returned with some animals to start afresh, a milking cow, a couple pigs, a dozen hens and so on. God selected others to join my flock. Rose and Sonya were the first, the only survivors from the neighbouring village of Glenridding, then Jamie the innkeeper from Dockray, Richard the police sergeant from Pooley Bridge. We then travelled afield to spread the Lord's message and most of the people you see are from Penrith and outlying villages. As our numbers increased we moved into the youth hostel so we could support each other and pool our skills. We will eventually repopulate the village and live as one, united in the worship of God. Our community will be modelled on the Amish settlements in the USA. We will use our hands and traditional tools and skills to survive. There will be no return to the science and technology that fed mankind's vanity, nor the alcohol, tobacco and drugs that polluted his mind and body. We hope you can share our faith in the Lord and bring your families to join our community."

It was quite a speech and one couldn't help being impressed

by the vicar's industry in digging 142 graves on his own. His objective of building a self-sufficient community based on traditional skills and husbandry was not so far removed from our own at Whitewell. We too expected to outgrow the hotel at some point. He had simply imposed a hefty dollop of religion on top. Despite my absence of religion, I had always admired the Amish way of life and it was a worthwhile model for our current circumstances. However there was something about the vicar's certainties which I found disturbing and as for talking to God, it wasn't clear whether this was simply an expression of his faith or rather schizophrenic tendencies. It was quite possible he was simply a fruitcake. However, he appeared to have a loyal following and had been very successful in persuading others to join. It would be interesting to gauge to what extent the others shared his religious convictions or were simply seeking safety in numbers. It was also unclear how strictly his disapproval of technology was being applied. There appeared to be no electricity, so possibly the absence of a generator was a decision of principle. On the other hand I could see several calor gas stoves in the kitchen area. Did that not count as technology? I had also seen several vehicles parked outside the hostel and these must surely be in use if they had travelled to the Penrith area to search for survivors. How was this squared with the vicar's philosophy? There were questions to be answered but, to be fair, anything that worked in this post-apocalyptic world had to be applauded.

Under the vicar's leadership, the whole group were most hospitable and keen that we should stay with them for as long as we needed. We readily agreed to use the hostel as a base for our search of the northern lakes. If that proved to be fruitless, we would probably need to move on again as the western lakes would need to be approached from the coast but first we could at least make a comprehensive search of Ullswater, Haweswater, Thirlmere, Derwentwater, Bassenthwaite Lake, Buttermere and Crummock Water which could take two or three days. If we drew a blank again, it could result in some questioning of our strategy. The western lakes like Wast Water and Ennerdale Water would not provide ready access to the road network and it would seem most unlikely that any group based there would be operating in the Preston area. One couldn't help a sense of foreboding that weeks of searching may yield nothing and that our girls were surrendered to a dreadful fate.

In accepting the group's kind hospitality, we insisted that we should make ourselves useful and my role was to join Winston Barnes at the back of the hostel in a spot of log-splitting. The only heating in the hostel appeared to be open fires and although the weather was reasonably mild, it was still necessary to stoke up the fire after dark. It was already dusk and we took a couple oil lamps outside to a small car park at the rear of the hostel with various outbuildings. A van with a trailer was parked in the corner, the trailer piled up with branches, whilst stacked up against the hostel wall was a heap of logs and smaller pieces of branches. A tree stump was surrounded by sawdust and next to it a couple heavy axes and a bowsaw were left on the ground. The work required was fairly self-explanatory. "Me and Richard got this lot from the woods this morning," explained Winston. "We go two or three times a week, pick up dead stuff where we can, any broken branches when we've had high winds in the night, otherwise we saw 'em off with the bow-saw. It's hard work, like. I suggested looking for a petrol-driven chainsaw – bound to be one in the village somewhere or at the farms – but his lordship wasn't having that."

"We'll live by the fruits of our own labour," he said, imitating the reverend's voice and rolling his eyes. It was the first sign of disrespect I had seen.

"I must admit, I was a little curious as to this anti-technology policy," I confided. "I mean I can understand the reference to the Amish philosophy and, leaving the religion on one side, there is undoubtedly some merit in basing a community on a long-term sustainable basis. After all, the petrol won't last forever and we won't be able to keep machines running forever without spare parts and engineering know-how. However, you're using a van and a trailer to pick up the wood and I noticed you're using calor gas stoves. Surely that's still technology? Where so you draw the line?"

"Well, what his lordship says is we're in a transition and we can use the old technology short-term while we build our sustainable community, as he calls it. We're supposed to set ourselves up with horses and carts for transport, horse-drawn ploughs and the like for the farming and we've got to put in a wood-burning stove for heating and cooking. We got these calor gas stoves from the caravan park up the road. Anyway, once we're set up with sustainable stuff, we're going to dump all the technology like cars and tractors and stuff. He wouldn't let me have a chainsaw because we've already got axes and hand-saws, so I do as I'm told."

"I suppose there's some logic to that," I conceded. "In fifty years time, any communities that have survived will be using traditional crafts. We've just taken the view that while we've got the means to make our lives a bit easier, we might as well take advantage. We're planning to grow crops and breed animals but at the moment we're still doing a lot of foraging and that would be impossible without motor vehicles. Installing generators has made a huge difference as well, just being able to refrigerate food, for example."

"Aye, I'm with you pal. Just do what you need to survive and use what you've got, but his lordship's got it into his head that it's sinful. He thinks mankind got above itself and had to be taught a lesson by God. I don't know. I keep me head down, to be honest. If I have to say a few prayers and chop a few logs to live here, then I'll do it. He don't know everything that goes on, anyhow, like that nice drop of Aberlour at the back of my wardrobe. It'd be a shame to waste it."

"I don't blame you for that one, Winston. A drop of quality Scotch in moderation isn't going to damage your soul."

As we talked, we worked our way through the branches. A lot of it we could break with our hands or prop them against the wall and break them by kicking. The thicker stuff we attacked with the bow saw, cutting twelve inch sections, then splitting them with the axe. We made good progress between us and after an hour more than half the trailer load had been removed.

"So how did you come to join this little congregation then Winston?"

"Ah well, there's a tale. I work on the railways, see, least I did, engine driver, over twenty years. We came up from Birmingham about six years ago, the wife and me, and got a house in Penrith. That's where I was based like and went all over on inter-city trains, up to Edinburgh, Glasgow, Newcastle, down to Leeds, Manchester, London. Anyway, I did my best to keep going when that flu was spreading and all the drivers were crying off sick. As luck would have it, I'd taken a train down to Euston but everything was falling apart and there were no trains back up North. I found a bed and breakfast place for the night and thought I'd report for duty at Euston in the morning, even though I was supposed to be at Penrith. Anyway, next day the bloody station was closed, big sign up, no trains 'til further notice, telephone number and website for further info, sort of thing. Well I tried ringing but I couldn't get any answer from the wife and the mobile had no signal. By this time I was feeling rough myself and thought "Christ, I'm getting this bloody flu". It was getting pretty hairy around London by then, looting and riots and the like. I went back to the bed and breakfast for another night before I collapsed in the street. Then I was really taken bad, didn't get out of my room for three days or more and when I made my way out, all groggy like, found the old girl what ran the place dead in her armchair. It was chaos by then. No trains, buses or taxis. All the phones were down and no TV or radio. There were dead bodies everywhere, in cars, in the street, what a mess. I thought "right, I'm getting home". I dragged a dead bloke out of the nearest car, checked there was plenty petrol and set off for Penrith. It took me over two hours just to get out of London, all bloody day to get home. I'd never seen anything like it. Anyway, cut a long story short, when I got back I found the missus in bed, cold as stone. Neighbours were dead. I couldn't contact my daughter, what lives in Wales.

"I didn't know what to do. The power was off, so I had no heating and the weather was perishing. I couldn't stay there, so I just went into the centre of Penrith to see what I could find. The place was deserted and virtually wrecked but as I was looking around for food I bumped into Richard. He was a police sergeant based in Penrith but lived in Pooley Bridge at the top of Ullswater. He'd also lost his wife but recovered from the flu. Anyway, he was quite well set up with plenty of food, water from the lake and open fires to keep the place warm. He offered to let me stay, so I jumped at the chance. He helped me bury Jill in the garden – that's my wife like – and I took what I needed from home and moved to Pooley Bridge. It was about a week later we were exploring around Glenridding and Patterdale and found this set up. The Reverend, Rose and Sonya and Jamie were already here and we fancied the idea of a project to set up a self-sufficient group. The others have joined since, mainly from the Penrith area. That's it, my story, we've all got them."

I responded with my own survivor tale, the move to Saltersford Hall, encountering the survivor group in Manchester, the death of Sue and Lucy, our set up at Whitewell, the attack and abductions and our search efforts to date. For his part, Winston was pretty confident that no large group was based on the banks of Ullswater and had never seen the roofer's van described. I could tell from his manner that he had little confidence in the success of our mission but I assured him that I would find my daughter however long it took.

We had converted all the wood into useable fuel and moved it into the shed to keep dry, filling one basket to take into the hostel. Re-joining the others, we were just in time for dinner which was centred around freshly caught fish from the lake, Jamie Ferguson having taken a boat out earlier in the day. The food was washed down with water. Although I felt like asking the Reverend to have another word with his God to convert the water to wine, I thought better of it. We were grateful guests and wouldn't be staying for long. I felt sorry for the others though. I had already heard what Winston thought of the temperance arrangements and, as an innkeeper, I couldn't imagine that Jamie was too impressed. Maybe he also kept a bottle or two in his wardrobe. As a group of survivors together why should they accept that the Reverend Mark Watson should lay down all the rules? Some good quality alcohol in moderation was a great compensation for the many things of which we were now deprived. If the group continued to grow, I could imagine some challenge to the Reverend's authority.

After dinner we all sat around the fire drinking tea and coffee and exchanging survival stories. One of the most harrowing accounts was from Claire Potts, a 27 year old nurse from Penrith Hospital. She had worked throughout the pandemic and witnessed the gradual collapse of the health services. They had not been equipped for dealing with contagion and only had rudimentary protection – face masks, gloves etc – none of the protective suits that we saw on the isolation wards on TV in the early stages of the epidemic.

Nevertheless, people had turned up in their droves expecting help and served only to infect others and as the doctors and nursing staff became infected the hospital ground to a halt. Claire was one of the last to succumb and stayed in the hospital but with virtually no assistance. By the time she had recovered, and she was only aware of three survivors, the hospital had effectively been abandoned and Penrith had descended into chaos. She had no close family to hand and had shared a flat in Penrith with another girl – anything to escape hospital accommodation – but on her return there was no trace of her friend, no note or anything. It was Claire who had discovered six-year-old Sophie Higgins trying without much success to find food in a Tesco supermarket. Poor Sophie had recovered from the flu only to find her mother, father and two younger brothers all dead in the house. It had taken her a long time to come out of her shell but she was beginning to adjust to life at the hostel and was very attached to Claire.

After talking to everybody at the hostel we still had no leads on our missing girls. The only lake with which most of them were familiar was Ullswater and nobody was aware of any likely hideouts for our gang, nor had anybody seen a roofer's van with the sign of a man climbing a ladder. The good reverend promised to lead prayers for the success of our quest and the safety of our womenfolk. In any event we were grateful for the food and rooms for the night as we made our plans to continue the search.

31 March

We woke to driving rain hammering against the hostel windows but completed our preparations quickly in order to resume our search. The plan was once again to split into three vehicles to cover as much territory as possible, although this exposed us to risk of mishap. We had a copy of the OS map in each vehicle and exchanged our planned routes. We paired off as before with Jim and myself in the van, Bill and Phil in the Range Rover and John and Adam in the Landrover. Bill and Phil were to explore every settlement and building on the west bank of Ullswater from Patterdale to Pooley Bridge. Jim and I were to drive straight to Pooley Bridge, then cut across to Askham and south to Haweswater Reservoir. From the map, there was very little to check there, just one hotel and the odd farm, which shouldn't take long. We would then double back to Pooley Bridge and take the east bank of Ullswater. John and Adam were to head north to the A66 then south to Thirlmere, circle the lake and retrace their steps. Our objective was to meet up again at Pooley Bridge by 4.00pm at the latest. If anybody failed to show by 4.30 we would go looking by the same agreed route. In the event of a breakdown or accident, our first recourse would be to find another useable vehicle but if that proved to be impossible, we would await rescue. Contrary to our previous policy, we agreed to investigate any signs of life unless it appeared that we may have located our quarry, in which case we would attempt to observe from a distance and report our findings at the meeting point. It was a little more risky but necessary to move on more quickly, for example a small isolated cottage showing smoke was hardly likely to house our gang and captives but speaking to the survivors could provide useful intelligence.

Our journey to Pooley Bridge was uneventful but mercifully without any obstructions on the road. We then peeled off from the B5320 to take a hill track round the edge of the lake to Askham. A quick circuit of the village revealed no signs of life and we headed on south through Helton and Bampton to the dam at the bottom of Hayeswater Reservoir. Looking across to the western bank there were no roads or tracks of any type, just a very steep valley wall up to the crags above. A small road ran the length of the eastern bank and from the map we could see that a small hotel half way down was the only building. It was worth checking out. As we approached we found two buildings together but no smoke, no vehicles, no discernible activity. The first building had been a mountain rescue post and the hotel was adjoined. Parking the van in front of the hotel we tried the front door which surprisingly opened. Inside, the reception area was basically undisturbed but there was a dreadful damp, musty smell with something even more noxious in the background. "That's disgusting," said Jim. "I reckon there's some rotten bodies in here, probably rat droppings as well."

We decided against looking any further and made our way back to the van, continuing to the top of the reservoir and turned round, there being nothing else of note. Back at the dam we found the expected track marked to Naddle Farm. The farm buildings were visible nestling in the side of the hill about a couple hundred yards up a dirt track. We bounced up in the van, trying to avoid the worst of the potholes and thinking we'd be better off with another Landrover. There were no signs of habitation at the farm and no livestock. It had almost certainly been a sheep farm and a few old vehicles were rusting away at the back. Time to move on.

Before leaving the environs of the reservoir, we decided to check on Thornthwaite Hall, not exactly lakeside but clearly large enough to accommodate a substantial group. The hall could be seen from the road back to Bampton and we approached via a long straight driveway. There were several substantial chimney stacks but none emitted any smoke and we felt it was safe to drive to the front of the hall. This time the door was locked and we circled the hall peering through the windows but all appeared to be deserted. All the doors we tried were locked and all the windows were intact. It occurred to me that if nobody had been here before there could be some useful supplies to be had but we were not on a foraging expedition and may need the time for what we find at Ullswater. Once again we agreed to move on and retraced our route back to Pooley Bridge.

Consulting the OS map again, we confirmed that, in contrast to the deserted Haweswater, there was a wealth of settlements on the east bank of Ullswater which would take a long time to survey. There would be insufficient time to enter properties without a pressing reason but we could at least drive up to each house, check for vehicles and any signs of recent activity. Initially we were confined to the lakeside road and a few tracks up to the farms and caravan sites. Taking in Eusemere, Elderback, Park Foot, Waterside House, Cross Dormant, Seat Farm, Thwaitehill and Crook-a-dyke, all without result, we passed another mountain rescue post beneath the cliffs of Swarth Fell and a small hotel at Howtown, all deserted, as we left the bank of the lake behind to climb a steep track over a saddle between two peaks. As we dropped down the other side and approached a farm at a split in the road we finally observed smoke for the first time that day.

It was a little late to be discreet. We were only fifty yards from the farmhouse which was right next to the road. Furthermore the van moving over the steep pass in second gear must have been quite noisy and attracted the attention of the farm dogs, two border collies barking excitedly at the farm gate. We stopped at the gate next to a sign that announced "Hallinbank House Farm" but decided against joining the dogs for the moment until we collected our thoughts. Whoever was responsible for the smoke billowing from the farmhouse chimney must have heard the commotion. Sure enough, within a couple minutes a burley fellow emerged from the side of the farmhouse, looked about mid-forties, complete with an old cap, bulky jacket and corduroy trousers tucked into green wellington boots. He was also carrying a shotgun but thankfully the barrel was pointed at the ground. He stood there and eyed us suspiciously, then slowly moved forwards. I thought it would be better to get out of the van and show that we were not a threat. That set the dogs barking even more but they didn't move beyond the gate. Jim joined me outside, leaving our guns in the van as the farmer reached the gate.

"Meg, Fern, get back, quiet!"

The dogs cowered behind him, quivering.

"What you doing here in the back of beyond then eh?"

He had a rough manner to him but did not appear to be

aggressive. "Hello. I'm Tom Morton. This is Jim Clarke. We've been searching for survivors around the lake. We'd like to have a quick chat with you, if that's okay."

"Well, you best come in then, hadn't ya. You're the first people I've seen in months. It's Sam Mellor, just me and the dogs now."

We shook hands and moved towards the farmhouse, the dogs now sniffing around our ankles. To be frank, it was a bit of a mess inside but the old farmhouse kitchen was as warm as toast with a large wood-burning stove in the middle. "Don't mind the mess like, I've not cleared up yet. It's not quite as slick as when Kathy was in charge. She and the boys are buried out back."

It was the one shared experience of survivors: burying your loved ones, or in the case of the vicar of St Patrick's, a whole village. There was nothing like it to reinforce the sense of grief.

"I can offer you coffee. It'll have to be black though. I've run out of tinned and powdered milk."

"Black's good," we agreed.

"So, what do you get up to here, on your own?" I enquired.

Well, I've still got to look after my sheep, haven't I. All them, on side of hill, their all mine, over 60 ewes. We'll be lambing over the next couple weeks, should be well over 100. That's going to keep us busy, ain't it Meg? We've never had to do lambing without Kathy. She were great with 'em, she were."

"But what on earth are you going to do with a hundred lambs?" I had to ask.

"Well, we won't starve, will we? I reckon me and the dogs will eat at least one a month. We got chickens out back as well and sometimes I do a bit of fishing, if I got time, but everything else has been out of tins. Mind you, I'm not short."

He opened some cupboards and every one was stacked to the top with tins.

"I go once a week to Penrith, pick a different street each time and work my way through. I usually fill the boot, much more than we're getting through but you don't know how long it's got to last, do you?"

It looked like several years' stock and he was undoubtedly well provided for. The main things he was missing were dairy produce and bread. We filled him in on the Patterdale group, which unsurprisingly was news to him.

"Patterdale! Why that's just over the tops there at the head of that valley." He said, pointing to the back of the farmhouse. We suggested that they would welcome a new recruit, especially somebody with some farming knowledge.

"I dunno, we're alright here, me and the dogs. I wouldn't want to leave the sheep and then there's Kathy and the lads out back. Still, I'll drive round sometime and say hello. I could take 'em a lamb."

"I'm sure that would be appreciated. I dare say they would sort you out with some fresh bread, butter, cheese and the like. Give you a chance to balance your diet," I suggested. "We'll tell them to expect you, shall we?"

"Aye. Do that."

We explained the circumstances of the abduction and what we were seeking. Sam was quite taken aback.

"Christ! What bastards! Well, if they come sniffing around here, I'll give 'em both barrels. I hope you find 'em and give 'em a good hiding." As usual, there was no intelligence to work on. Sam hadn't spotted any large properties in use and hadn't seen any vehicles on the move for two or three months. The van with the roofer's logo meant nothing to him.

We thanked Sam for the coffee and made a move. Although we were not expecting to find anything, we checked out the head of the valley, actually two valleys running up from the farm, Bannerdale and Boardale. We passed a few deserted properties and also took a track down to the lakeside at Sandwick, also abandoned. It was time to head back to Pooley Bridge.

Jim and I were the first to the rendezvous point, the old ferry terminal at Pooley Bridge. Shortly after 4.00 Bill and Phil arrived after their search of the west bank of Ullswater.

"Bloody hell!" complained Phil. "We've done every property on the lake and every road and track leading off it. Not a sausage! The vicar's hoovered up every survivor from Ullswater."

"No quite" said Jim and filled them in our encounter with Sam Mellor.

"No nearer finding the girls though," said Bill, "unless the others have found owt at Thirlmere. Must have seen summat of interest to make 'em last back."

4.30 passed and no sign of John and Adam. "They've either spotted something interesting or they've broken down," I suggested. "Nothing else would make them late. We'll give them another 15 minutes, then set off to find them."

4.45 and still no Landrover. "Okay, let's go. Jim and I will lead. Back down the lake, then cut across to the A66. Watch the verges carefully in case they've come off the road."

In Adam's absence, it was up to me to take charge. However, we had no sooner re-joined the main road, half a mile beyond the ferry pier, when we spotted Adam's Landrover heading up the lake at a fair old pace. They flashed their lights as they saw us and we stopped at the side of the road.

"Sorry we missed the rendezvous," said Adam. "We really thought we'd found them but it turned out to be another group of survivors. We'll tell you all about it when we get back. How about you, anything?"

"Just a farmer and a couple sheepdogs," I said.

"Not a bloody sausage all day" said Phil, somewhat disappointed that he and Bill were the only ones not to encounter survivors.

We returned to the hostel to be bombarded with questions

from the Patterdale group. Only the vicar hung back with a sympathetic smile as though he already knew the result of our search. One could almost describe his demeanour as smug but perhaps I was being too sensitive or frustrated at the day's passing without success. In any event I was more concerned to hear John and Adam's story of their encounter. John took up the tale.

"It started off quite routinely. We found nothing of note on the way to Thirlmere and decided to take the little track first on the western bank as we'd get a better view of the lake than from the main road. Anyway, we'd only gone a mile or so when we spotted smoke rising out of the trees on the other side. We consulted the OS map and decided it had to be coming from Dalehead Hall but we couldn't see it because it was surrounded by trees. So we thought, substantial property, secluded, probably quite secure, right on the bank of the lake and clearly occupied. We thought we'd found what we were looking for. We drove slowly down the track opposite the hall trying to get a view, then we had to get out and scramble through the trees and undergrowth until eventually we found a spot directly across from where the hall's gardens ran down to the lakeside in a narrow clearing in the trees. That gave us the only possible view of the hall and we watched with our binoculars for a while. The smoke was clearly coming from the hall's chimney stack but the garden was empty and it was impossible to see anything through the windows because of the direction of the light. We were on the wrong side of the hall to spot any vehicles. There was nothing for it but to drive round to the other side of the lake."

By this time John had his audience riveted, hanging on to every word.

"So we drove on round to the southern tip of the lake and joined the main A591 and headed north on the eastern bank, though because the land fell away towards the lake the ridge at the side of the road pretty much obscured our view. After a few miles the road veered away from the lakeside and we could see down towards the northern end of the lake but once again a copse hid the hall from view. We passed the drive entrance which couldn't be more than 300 yards from the hall, hoping our approach had not been heard and carried on a short distance on the main road until we finally gained an open view of the front of the hall. We parked the Landrover out of view and found a spot where we could observe with the binoculars. We were much closer now and with the light behind us, although it was cloudy, we had a clear view. Several vehicles were visible at the front and side of the hall, a plain white van and a couple of four-wheel drives but nothing with the roofer's logo described by Jim. After half an hour or so, a couple men emerged from the side of the hall and began messing with the van. It was difficult to tell through the binoculars but they appeared to be middle-aged, not the young thugs that carried out the attack on Whitewell and neither of them was black. We were starting to go cool on the idea that we had found our quarry and were discussing tactics on how we might approach them when suddenly the two men jumped into the van and started her up. We scrambled back to the Landrover knowing it would only be minutes before they reached the main road. There was no time to drive off and we were parked less than 200 yards from the entrance.

If they turned left to head north, they couldn't fail to see us. Sure enough, they turned left, gathered pace then immediately slowed as they spotted the Landrover, bringing the van up behind it. The decision on making contact had been taken out of our hands. We got out of the Landrover to greet them but they certainly spotted the binoculars thrown onto the back seat and approached us with some suspicion. We told them we had been passing and stopped when we saw the smoke from their chimneys but didn't explain why we had stopped 200 yards past the entrance and had binoculars to hand. They clearly deduced that we'd been spying on them but nevertheless expressed their surprise and pleasure to meet survivors and invited us back to the hall. They came in with us and either their intended trip was not urgent or they didn't trust us and wanted to maintain safety in numbers.

Our arrival caused some commotion and others came rushing out until we were all gathered in the entrance hall, the two of us and eight of them. The two we had met had introduced themselves as Rob and Kevin, both well into their forties. An older man called Clive appeared to act with some authority and did most of the talking. There were two teenaged girls, Chloe and Alice, a younger mixed-race boy called Ali and two middle-aged ladies, Lesley and Lynne. Of course they wanted to know everything about us and offered us coffee and homemade biscuits – chocolate chip cookies – delicious! Well, by this time Adam and I were pretty convinced that this was not the group we were looking for, so Adam levelled with them and explained the reason for our Lake District tour. When they heard of our loss they expressed their sympathies and understood the covert nature of our approach. They were totally appalled at the attack on Whitewell and Chloe and Alice in particular were quite frightened at the prospect of roaming gangs abducting young ladies. They had seen no evidence of any such activity, although none of them had travelled extensively since the epidemic hit. None of them were related and they all had their own survival tales and loss of loved ones but they all hailed from the Keswick area. A few had known each other previously, Chloe and Alice attending the same school, but basically they had got together and then searched for a suitable property to use, settling on the hall, much as our group had moved out of Manchester to Whitwell, except that they had stayed fairly local. They still used Keswick for all their foraging.

We told them that if we found nothing today we'd be moving on to Bassenthwaite and Derwent Water tomorrow but they weren't very optimistic that we'd find anything. They know those lakes well and have searched exhaustively for survivors. That's how some of them got together but they said if anybody was generating smoke or moving around on the roads, they'd have spotted them long ago, so we might have a wasted trip. None of them had seen the roofer's van with the ladder on the side. The one person they did mention was an old fellow known as Merlin, presumably not his real name but he's got a white beard, he's rather eccentric and keeps loads of cats. He used to run a caravan and camping site at Castlerigg, just outside Keswick. He still lives in one of the caravans apparently. Clive's known him for years and when he found he was still living there – I think they went looking for calor gas heaters – he tried to persuade him to join them at Thirlmere, cats and all, but Merlin wouldn't have it. Clive drops in every now and them to check on him. He said Merlin knows everything there is to know about Keswick and Derwent Water and suggested it would be worth talking to him. That's about it really. They're a nice bunch and we enjoyed a good lunch with them, sharing experiences, but at the end of the day we're not any further forward."

"Well, in a way we are," added Adam. "Every lake that we clear from our search narrows down the options. I think we'll seek out old Merlin first thing tomorrow to see if he can give us any pointers."

We agreed to set off at first light to maximise the search time. Four days and no result.

1 April

It was four days since Jo was taken and I was worried sick. It was difficult to sleep, despite a clandestine nightcap of Aberlour with Winston. What if we were on a fool's errand? There wasn't much to go on after all. A mumbled remark heard through a door? If they weren't on the banks of a lake we could be searching for a needle in a haystack. As for the van, how clearly had Jim seen this? The more I asked him, the vaguer his recollection became. In any event, they may well have dumped a vehicle so conspicuous. Our search relied very heavily on spotting a smoking chimney but what if they were deliberately avoiding the generation of smoke. They must be wary of pursuit and the need to avoid detection, choosing to use calor gas or paraffin for their fuel. Their vehicles could be hidden in a garage. We may have already driven past them and not realised. Perhaps my first instinct of setting off immediately in pursuit would have been more effective. We had lost so much time. We had mixed with a lot of survivors but none have been able to assist us. I felt I'd let Jo down and anything could have happened to her. I'd failed in my first duty as a father to protect my daughter. Why had I taken her to Whitewell in the first place? We could have stayed in the Goyt Valley and tended Sue and Lucy's graves. What a fucking mess! These thoughts turned over and over in my mind. I tried to introduce some logical and positive arguments but was overwhelmed with a tide of negativity.

I was up well before dawn and relieved when the others were ready for the off. Jim must have seen the fatigue in my face and offered to drive, which I gratefully accepted. Talking to Jim in the van I felt more positive but at night-time I just couldn't escape the negative thoughts. I had barely slept for five nights and felt my systems were shutting down. I didn't know how long I could carry on like this without some positive development to cling to.

*

It took us less than an hour to reach Castlerigg, a small group of houses half a mile up a track off the A591 just to the east of Keswick. We found the entrance to the caravan park and stopped to confer, deciding that Adam and I would talk to

Merlin while Bill and Phil would make a circuit of Derwent Water in the Range Rover and Jim would pair up with John taking the Landrover round Bassenthwaite Lake. No other survivors were to be approached at this stage and we would all regroup at Castlerigg in two hours to discuss findings. I was still feeling pretty shattered and welcomed the chance to get off the road for a while.

We left the van at the entrance and walked into the park which contained only three caravans. The trade had obviously been based on holiday-makers towing their own caravans and paying site fees. We were still wondering whether it was a little early, barely 8.00 am, to be disturbing Merlin when the door opened on the nearest caravan and a small man with shoulder- length snow white hair and a matching beard emerged to greet us.

"Good morning gentlemen! First customers of the day! Come to think of it, first customers of the year. Things are looking up! Hee, hee, hee!

Adam responded first. "Morning. You must be Merlin? Clive from Dalehead Hall suggested we come to see you. You might be able to help us."

"Ah, Clive was it, my good friend. Well, come on in then gentlemen, join me in some breakfast. Let's see if I can help you. I must tell you though, I don't do magic spells, despite the name. Hee, hee!"

He seemed a jovial fellow and took our arrival out of the blue completely in his stride. One had to wonder whether he retained a firm grip on reality. Looking him over, it was very difficult to assess his age but I reckoned he was over 70.

"85 last month! Me and the girls had a little party."

It seemed his powers extended to mind-reading. "I'm sorry. I didn't mean to stare but you're right, I was wondering. You don't look a day over 70."

His "girls" were all over the caravan. He began to introduce them.

"The black and white one on the bench seat, that's Tabatha. Next to her is Socks. The two tabbies on the table, those are Phyllis and Fergy, though blessed if I can remember which is which. That tortoiseshell on the back window ledge is Pippa, the fluffy ginger one is Marmalade and these under my feet are Roberta, Whiskers and Sooty. The rest of them must be out hunting, they're always bringing stuff back, mice, voles, birds, all sorts."

"The rest of them! How many have you got?" I asked.

"Fifteen at the last count, I think."

The cats were clearly a major part of Merlin's life and good luck to him. We declined the breakfast, having eaten at the hostel, but agreed to a coffee.

"It's only instant, is that alright?"

"That'll be fine Merlin. Very kind" said Adam diplomatically. Anything to counteract the smell of the cats which was overwhelming.

"Now don't mind me while I prepare my breakfast. It's scrambled eggs today. Mind you, it was scrambled eggs yesterday and it'll be scrambled eggs tomorrow. I've got a dozen chickens you see and it's a lot of eggs for one person."

Eventually Merlin's old kettle on his calor gas stove began to whistle and he opened several cupboards before locating the jar of coffee. Our jaws dropped at the sight of the stacks of cat food filling each cupboard. He read our minds again. "I don't want to run short, do I".

We assumed he had a separate store of human food and were relieved when another cupboard revealed a paltry selection of bits and pieces including a tin of Marvel. He spooned the Tesco own-brand coffee into three rather grubby looking mugs and invited us to help ourselves to powdered milk, which was covered with cat's hairs. I couldn't think why Merlin would choose a supermarket own-brand coffee when he had all the kitchens in Keswick to choose from but I didn't like to ask.

We pretended to enjoy our coffee while we broached the purpose of our visit. Adam and I took it in turns to explain, for what seemed like the tenth time, the background of our set up at Whitewell, the details of the abduction, our search party and the various encounters with survivors groups in the Lake District, finishing with Dalehead Hall. For all our previous accounts the reactions had been those of shock and sympathy but there was none of that from Merlin. He just nodded as though it was an entirely normal and expected occurrence, interspersing "I see" and "hmm" at strategic points but nevertheless he listened intently and one could see him weighing up the issues in his mind.

When we had finished our account and Merlin had finished his scrambled eggs, he was quiet for a while, then addressed us with purpose. "So what you're looking for is a substantial property on a lake where a number of people could be held prisoner. Do you know, I just might be able to help you there."

These were the words we had longed to hear. We remained silent while Merlin said his piece. "You see, I was born in Keswick, spent my whole life here. I know every house, every track, every blade of grass around Derwent Water. This is my lake. There were very few people left after the flu struck and most of them went to join Clive down at Thirlmere, though why they want to settle there I don't know. This is a far better lake. Anyway, every building around Derwent Water has been abandoned, take my word for it, but twice in the last month when I've been on the west side of Keswick just after dark near the lakeside, I've heard a motor running. I'd swear it's a boat on the lake. Now I ask myself, why would anybody want to take a boat onto the lake after dark? It was too late for fishing and anyway, the motor would frighten off the fish. There's no point taking a boat to cross the lake – it's easier to drive round. But what if somebody was living on one of the islands? What if they waited until after dark so they're not seen? You follow me?"

We both nodded allowing him to continue. "Well, if you're looking for a big property where you can keep prisoners, what better than an island? There's only one candidate. You see, St Herbert's Island, that's just trees, nowhere to live there. Lord's Island, there's an old manor house but that's been ruined for God knows how long. But Derwent Isle has a big property in good repair. That would make an ideal base. That's what you're looking for if you ask me."

He ended triumphantly as though the mystery was solved.

Adam and I looked at each other and raised our eyebrows. This was a theory not to be dismissed. "That's really interesting, Merlin," said Adam. "When did you last hear this motor?"

"Now then, it was about five or six days ago, can't tell you exactly. One day's much like another now."

Adam turned to me. "That could be the day of the abduction, transferring prisoners to the island. It makes sense."

"If you've been at the lakeside at night, have you seen any lights?" I asked. "Or any smoke during the day?"

"Definitely no smoke, I couldn't have missed that, but you'd have a job to see any lights. That house is surrounded by trees. That's what I say, it's the perfect hideaway."

"Can you tell us everything you know about the island and the house?" asked Adam.

"Well, I went there once, quite a few years back. There were people living there but some of the time the public could visit. I think it was National Trust but I wouldn't swear to it. I know it's been used since the old days. At one time it was connected with Fountains Abbey until Cromwell's dissolution of the monasteries. Then it was used by German miners in the time of Queen Elizabeth. The house came a lot later but still over 200 years ago. It was known then as Vicar's Island."

"So what's on the island exactly," prompted Adam.

"It's mainly woods. There's a jetty and a small boathouse on the west of the island, then a track that winds through the trees up to the house. As I recall there's a small clearing north of the house, lawns and the like leading down to the lake but you wouldn't see that from Keswick or the roads round the lake. If you get me a map, I'll show you what I mean."

I popped out to the van and found the correct OS map, returned to Merlin's caravan and opened it up at Keswick.

"Right" said Merlin, "you can't make much of the island on here, it's very small, but that clearing I'm talking about, it would face this wooded area that juts out into the lake south-west of Keswick – see where it says Nichal End? If you take the path through those woods to the lakeside, you should be able to get a view of the house."

"That's brilliant" said Adam. "So if you've looked round this house, how big is it?"

"Oh it's a good size, six or seven bedrooms at least, three storeys. As I recall, it was quite plush in there, beautiful fireplaces, chandeliers and lots of old portraits on the wall."

"So where would you most likely take a boat from, if you wanted to get to the island?" I asked.

"Oh that's easy. You'd go from the marina at Portinscale, just west of Keswick, see?" He pointed out the location on the map. "That serves the whole lake."

After some more general chat, we thanked Merlin for his help and took our leave. As soon as we left the caravan, Adam turned to me.

"What do you think?"

"We've got to go for it, haven't we? It's the best lead we've had, in fact the only lead. If he definitely heard boats, they've got to be going to the island."

"I agree. Subject to anything the others have found, we'll need to find that viewing spot and observe the house, also check out that marina. We might be getting somewhere here."

*

The others returned within twenty minutes of each other but had nothing to report. We gave them the bare bones of Merlin's intelligence which created a buzz. We were all of one mind : we were not leaving without setting foot on Derwent Isle. After studying the OS map we worked out a route to get close to the island. Adam and I lead the way with the other two vehicles following, into the centre of Keswick, doubling back on the lakeside road then forking right on a track towards Friar's Crag. We immediately saw the island to the right of us, less than 200 yards away. As Merlin had indicated, nothing was visible but trees. The house was completely hidden and there was certainly no smoke rising above the island. We turned round, back up the track until we spotted the path on the left leading towards the woods. Parking up, three of us took binoculars and three took guns as we made our way into the woods. It was only a short distance to the edge of the lake and we were now due north of the island. We could see the clearing that Merlin mentioned but were not lined up to see through to the house. We would have to work our way around the shore. This was tricky without a path but after sixty yards or so the house came into view. I was carrying one set of binoculars and immediately trained them on the house.

It was indeed substantial, three storeys high including dormer windows on the roof space, several tall chimney stacks but no smoke, and what looked like an extension on the right side, single storey but with a terrace above and some sort of Italianate style structure on top. We appeared to be looking at the rear of the property. There were no people or vehicles visible. We would just have to watch and wait. We found some logs to sit on and made ourselves comfortable, taking it in turns with the binoculars. As we had an unobstructed view of the house, in theory we would be visible from the rear windows but felt we were fairly inconspicuous in the edge of the woods. They would have to be training their binoculars on the woods to have any chance of seeing us. It was approaching midday and if it were sunny we would be looking directly into the sun but for the present it was cloudy and the sun showed no sign of breaking through, so there seemed little risk of any reflective flash from the binoculars.

An hour passed. Still no activity in the clearing, no people emerging onto the terrace and no smoke from the chimneys. We were beginning to doubt Merlin's theory. Perhaps he was mistaken in what he had heard. Maybe it wasn't a boat motor at all. It could even have been stags bellowing in the woods, although admittedly it was well past the rutting season. Perhaps some very noisy birds? This place just looked deserted. Adam proposed that he and I should check out the boat situation at the marina while the others kept watch and I welcomed the opportunity to stretch my legs.

We tracked back through the woods to the cars and took the Landrover. Back into Keswick and out west in the direction of Cockermouth until we reached the turning to Portinscale and headed back down towards the lake through an area of housing estates. Approaching the lake, a sea of boat masts came into view, though as we came close we could see that many of the boats were lying on their side in the water and lots showed severe damage. They must have been knocked about by winter storms. We drove up towards the jetties and a large open car park. There were still a dozen or so vehicles parked up. And then it hit us. Next to one of the jetties was parked a white van with signage on the side: JAB Roofers with a man climbing a ladder.

After all the searching, we couldn't believe it.

"Yes!" exclaimed Adam. "We've found the buggers at last. Good old Merlin. He was right after all"

We looked at each other in elation for several seconds before Adam added what we were both thinking. "How the hell are we going to get them off that island?"

CHAPTER FOURTEEN

THE BATTLE OF DERWENT ISLE

"We'll have to wait until dark before we set foot on the island," said Adam. "They may have lookouts or spot us anyway from the windows".

"Agreed," I said. "It should be pitch dark by ten though it looks like it's going to be a clear night, so we may have some moonlight. It's not full, is it?"

"No, it's less than half," said John. "Ideal really. A full moon would be too bright but we need something to see where we're going."

It was a conference of war in the marina car park. We were eager to get to the island now we were sure of our objective but needed to get our strategy in place.

"We need silence, so that means rowing boats," added Adam. "Say three boats, two in each?"

"Sounds good but we need room for the girls," said Jim.

"Presumably all the boats they've been using must be moored on the island. If we manage to free the girls, we should also be able to take the boats, don't you think?"

"I would think so," mused Adam. "It seems extremely unlikely that we'll be able to sneak them out. We have to anticipate confrontation. If we've got the better of them, then we can take the boats".

"The one thing we've got going for us is the element of

surprise," I suggested. "They've got the perfect hideaway, on an island, almost completely hidden from the shore, no smoke, which is clearly deliberate on their part, and how would they think anyone knew to pursue them there? It could make them complacent in protecting the house. If we can reach the house undetected, we've got a big advantage."

"Well, looking at the map, it should be easily possible to row from here to the jetty without being seen from the house unless they've mounted a lookout on the other side of the island."

"I can't see that," I said. "They think they're safe. It's still worth ensuring we're invisible. Dark jackets for sure. What about blacking up our faces, commando style?"

We took stock of our clothes. We all wore dark trousers and most of the jackets were black, brown and navy blue but Jim's had yellow edges which could reflect the moonlight. Some of the shirts were light but that was okay, we would keep the jackets fastened.

"What about getting tooled up?" asked Bill. "We're okay for guns but we need stuff for forcing windows or smashing our way in.

"We've plenty of time before ten," said Adam. "If we check out some of these garages in that estate we drove through, I'm sure we'll find what we need, maybe a darker jacket for Jim as well."

We spent the next few hours trying all the garage doors in the vicinity of the marina. Most of them were locked but sufficient were not to meet our needs and we were soon equipped with a variety of both sharp and blunt instruments suitable for breaking and entering or for use as auxiliary weapons. Some of the garages had connecting doors to the houses and we managed to secure a dark anorak with a hood for Jim as well as some dark woolly hats. With a bit of mud on our faces, we'd pass for an SAS troop. Well, maybe not.

We finished up most of our supplies as we weren't sure

when we would next eat and still needed to kill time. Speaking of killing, the conversation whilst we ate in the back of the van turned to how we might approach the fighting.

"This isn't about retribution," warned Adam. "All that matters is rescuing the girls as efficiently as possible, hopefully without casualties. If we need to defend ourselves, then we use our weapons."

That drew a snort from Bill. "That's all nice and polite like but these are hard-nosed villains and we have to be as ruthless as they are. I say if you get chance to take one out, do it and make sure he don't get up again. They've had our girls for a week now. God knows what they've bin through. Now it's payback time and I didn't bring this shotgun not to use bugger!"

"I think you're both right," said John. "All that matters is getting the girls back but having gone to the trouble they have, I can't see them giving them up lightly. We don't want a war but I'm sure people are going to get killed or wounded tonight and better them than us."

"This is where the element of surprise comes in, isn't it," I suggested. "If we can make a sneak attack and catch them cold, there may not need to be any killing. But if we try blasting our way in, there'll be carnage on both sides."

"Nah, go in 'ard before they know what's hit 'em." Bill was warming to his theme.

"Well let's just get to the house first as quietly as possible," said Adam. "Once we've got the lie of the land, we can assess tactics but we have to be prepared to adapt to circumstances."

I was experiencing considerate disquiet by this time. If this turns out to be some type of bloodbath, how would I cope? I had never been a violent man and had only recently fired a gun, just at static targets. My anger at Jo's abduction had not abated and my fear only increased as each day passed, but to start killing people? I just wasn't sure I could do it. I was far more likely to fall victim myself. I couldn't help feeling that Bill was probably right and the sense of dread was sapping my spirit. This day would not end well.

*

It was 10.00 pm prompt when we set off from the marina in three rowing boats with room for four in each boat, leaving space for the girls if we had to make our escape in the same way. The night was clear and the crescent moon gave a little light but it was still extremely dark. We were now all clad in dark coats, hoods or hats and had smeared a little mud on our faces which felt decidedly uncomfortable but rendered us near invisible. Taking care to use the oars quietly, we avoided any splashing and spoke only in whispers, satisfied that even if they had a lookout, we were sure to avoid detection. I was in the second boat with Jim. He did the rowing and as he had his back to the direction of travel relied on me for prompts. Phil was rowing Adam in the first boat and we kept about twenty yards apart, following them down the western shore for about a mile before turning across the lake to approach the island. In the gloom it was difficult to distinguish the wooded shore of the island from the eastern shore of the lake but as we got closer it was just possible to make out the shape of the island. From where we were it just looked like a small clump of trees and one would not have thought these shielded a large property had we not viewed it from the clearing to the north. There was no doubt that without Merlin's information we would never have found this place.

As we approached, a small jetty came into view with an outline behind and to the side, presumably the boathouse surrounded by trees. Phil and Adam were at the jetty tieing up their boat as we arrived alongside. I climbed onto the jetty as quietly as I could to secure the boat as Jim shipped the oars. John and Bill did the same and we silently made our way to the boathouse. The door was unlocked, in fact, the lock no longer appeared to be serviceable. As we entered we were able to use our torches, being careful to keep them pointed down, and saw a decent looking motor boat, maybe twenty feet in length with a cabin below. The lettering on the side proudly proclaimed her to be the "Derwent Queen", a rather grandiose claim for a twenty footer but a small boat nevertheless. If we needed to make a quick exit, this was the way to do it.

"Keys?" whispered Adam.

A quick search of the boat and boathouse produced no keys, which was only to be expected especially if the boathouse couldn't be locked. They couldn't be too concerned about uninvited guests or surely they could have replaced the lock or at least put a large padlock on the outside.

"If we can't use the boat, we may need to disable her," I whispered.

"Okay, but not yet," replied Adam. "We don't want any noise."

We switched off the torches and emerged from the boathouse, gently pushing the door closed. A track at the side curved away into the woods, obviously leading to the house but we couldn't afford to take that route. At this stage it was better to stick together and Adam led the way through the trees on the opposite side of the boathouse. As we left the shore and entered the woods we lost even the dim light of the moon and in the pitch black we had to feel our way, taking care not to break any branches. We moved in a tight crocodile each touching the person in front. It couldn't have been more than a hundred yards from the jetty to the house but without a proper path it seemed to take for ever and several times I had twigs snapped back into my face.

Gradually the trees thinned and the outline of the house emerged against the night sky. We were to the west of the house less than twenty yards from the extension with the sun terrace on top which we had seen from the shore through the binoculars. The lights were on in several rooms at the front of the house and this was a strong and consistent light which indicated electricity rather than candles or oil lamps. They clearly had a generator which explained the absence of smoke. The rooms that were lit were on the side of the house that could not be seen from the shore. It was clear that they had thought through their situation with a view to avoiding detection and had gone to some lengths. They would certainly not expect any night-time visitors on the island. We had a quick conference by whispering and agreed to stay together where we were under cover of the trees, watch the house and make our move once all the lights were off. We had a very good chance of catching them cold.

It was already approaching 11.00 pm and I hoped we wouldn't have too long to wait. Luckily the weather was reasonably warm for early April though the clear sky meant the temperature was falling and we only had cold water to drink. We didn't have long to wait. By 11.30 the last of the lights was extinguished and we agreed to give it 30 minutes before moving in. The easiest point of access appeared to be some French doors at the conservatory on the sun terrace. There were some drainpipes running down from the terrace which was no more than ten feet above the ground. The younger members of our party, namely Phil and Jim were confident they could shin up the drainpipes in a matter of seconds, mount the balustrade and reach the French doors quietly. We assumed they would have to force the lock and they had a heavy wheel brace acquired that afternoon which should do the job. Once inside, they would signal to us with their torches and we would follow. To say I had butterflies at this point would be an understatement.

Midnight and the house remained quiet. Phil and Jim ran softly to the house, took one drainpipe each and climbed without difficulty, pulled themselves over the low balustrade and reached the French doors. So far, so good. We could just make out their shapes in front of the doors but it was too dark to distinguish any detail. We assumed they were applying some force to the lock but it seemed to be taking a while. Then we heard an almighty crack like a rifle shot.

"Jesus! That's loud enough to wake the dead," hissed Bill.

The shapes had disappeared. They had to be in. We were awaiting their signal when the sound of dogs barking came from the house. Hell! We hadn't planned on dogs. A light came on in one of the upstairs rooms, then another. We had certainly lost the element of surprise. The next shock was gunfire, at least four shots.

"Shit! This is a disaster," said John. "What are we going to do?"

"Let's just go in the front, shooting," proposed Bill. "I can have that door off in one shot."

"Okay. Two in the front, two round the back. Create as much noise and confusion as possible," said Adam. "Let them think they're under a mass attack."

We were about to move when the front door opened and two men emerged. Two large black shapes shot past them. One of the men shouted "find them Bruce! Go Olly." They were barking aggressively, noses to the ground, dashing this way and that. They looked like Dobermans.

"Quick", hissed Adam, "back to the boathouse, same way we came before they pick up our scent."

We scrambled back, keeping well away from the house and trying to avoid making any noise. The men appeared to be moving around the outside of the house but they were soon out of sight. The dogs could be anywhere but from their barking they didn't appear to be getting any closer. In a matter of minutes we could see the boathouse and jetty.

"Into the boathouse," called Adam. Shoot at anything that comes in."

We reached the jetty and John was on the point of pulling open the door to the boathouse when the first of the dogs emerged from the woods and raced towards us, snarling manically. These were fighting dogs alright. The dog was no more than six feet away when Bill opened fire with instant results, the dog simply destroyed, a mess of blood, bone and hair. As we bundled into the boathouse the second dog shot inside after us before anybody could react and flew at Adam who instinctively put up his arm to fend it off. The dog sank in its teeth and was ripping at Adam's hand and wrist. In desperation, I reached behind me and pulled from a shelf some sort of heavy wrench, bringing it down sharply onto the top of the dog's head. I could sense the dog's skull caving in and it dropped to the floor, quivering. Immediately, a sound of running announced the arrival of one of the men who appeared on the jetty, firing indiscriminately into the boathouse. There was no way he could see anything but his silhouette was dimly visible against the night sky. John raised his gun in both hands and fired a single shot, the man falling backwards onto the jetty just as the second man showed up. John fired again but missed. The second man had seen enough and ran back in the direction of the house but the first man lay still on the jetty. Bill took one look at him, said "dead", dragged him to the edge and dropped him into the lake, adding "one man and two dogs down, should give us a better chance".

I switched on my torch to examine Adam's wound. It was pretty nasty with big flaps of skin hanging loose and blood dripping, a lot of damage for the few seconds that the dog had hold. Most of the damage was to his hand with just a few teeth marks on his wrist. If the dog had torn at his wrist as it had the hand, it could have ripped an artery. I tied a handkerchief round Adam's hand and sealed it with some duct tape in the boathouse at least to stem the bleeding. Adam was putting a brave face on it but I could see he was in considerable pain.

"It's my gun hand," said Adam. "I'm useless with my left."

This wasn't good. Adam was disabled and both Phil and Jim either shot or captive. The second man would have returned to the house and alerted the others, the element of surprise gone.

On the other hand, they were one man down and the dogs were out of the way but we didn't know how many they were. Our plan had not been too successful. Maybe Bill's all-out assault would have worked better. Now we had Phil and Jim to rescue in addition to the girls and only Bill and John capable and competent in handling a firearm.

We headed back towards the house, straight up the track this time. There seemed little point creeping through the woods when they knew we were coming. We discussed tactics as we walked.

"We can't take 'em by surprise but we can move fast," said Bill. "I can take the door out with the shotgun and we can all storm in, fan out and shoot everybody in sight."

"What if they have automatic weapons with somebody guarding the front door? They could take down the lot of us in seconds." John was not impressed with the full frontal plan. "Let's at least check round the back for the easiest attack route."

"I agree," said Adam. "If need be, we'll go in from two directions. We're a bit short-handed admittedly but I'll shoot left-handed. I might not hit anything, just don't get in my way." By this stage I was shaking at the prospect of a gunfight. I couldn't see myself being much use. Just clubbing that dog had nearly turned my stomach. I was not cut out for violence.

As we approached the house we moved to the right of the path under cover of the trees and worked our way to the side. Suddenly the whole of the house exterior was bathed in light from powerful lamps mounted just below the roof. It wasn't clear whether we'd set these off by activating motion detectors or somebody inside had just switched them on. The next shock was the opening of the front door and two men emerging holding two of the girls, Alice and Lisa.

"Right, games up! Show yourselves, we know you're there." After a short pause, "you've got five seconds before we start cutting your girls."

"We ducked back round the side of the house out of view.

"There's only two of them," said John. "We can rush them." A moment's indecision was interrupted by a scream from one of the girls.

Adam stepped forward into the light. "Okay, okay. Leave them alone. We're coming."

John and I followed but Bill hung back and started creeping round to the back of the house.

"Throw your guns on the floor and get over here," ordered the man. He looked like he could have been the second man of our confrontation at the jetty, same height and build. We threw down our guns and as we approached I could see blood running down Lisa's chin. She was crying and both girls looked absolutely terrified. The men had what looked like hunting knives pressed against the girls' necks and beckoned for us to enter the house. The man who had been doing the talking had tattoos on his hands and neck. The second man was a tall black fellow. They fitted the descriptions of Dale and Leroy, two of the attackers at Whitewell. Two more men faced us in the entrance hall, both pointing handguns at us. One was slightly older than the others, maybe early thirties and wearing spectacles. Was this the "quiet man"?

He spoke to the fourth man, a big athletic looking fellow. "Joe, get the guns and lock up. Leroy, take the girls back upstairs."

"Right Vince."

"Let's have them in the dining room Dale, with the others." Tattooed man was Dale and Vince appeared to be in charge.

We were shepherded into a room on the right and greeted by the sight of Phil and Jim tied to chairs. At least they were still alive, though Jim was bleeding from a gash to the head.

"Do take a seat," said Vince with mock politeness. "The boss would like to talk to you."

So Vince wasn't in charge. That meant there were at least five of them and only Bill still free. We were not going to fight our way out of this.

As we sat we were re-joined by Leroy and Joe who positioned themselves with guns trained on us.

"Tie them up," said Vince, "and make it tight." They tied our hands behind the chairs with white flex and tight wasn't the word for it. It felt like the blood was cut off already. Adam grimaced as they tied his injured hand. In addition they bound our ankles to the chair legs with duct tape. We were going nowhere.

"Sorry lads," said Phil.

Dale took two steps over and punched Phil in the mouth, hard. "Shut it! You'll speak when you're spoken to." Phil blinked, shook his head and spat out a tooth and a lot of blood. Dale grinned. "That's just the start pal."

We sat in silence for maybe five minutes before a distinguished looking gentleman of perhaps sixty entered the room.

"Good evening, gentlemen, or good morning I should say," checking his watch. James Montgomery but everybody calls me Monty. I see my lads have been entertaining you. Most regrettably, yes. I'm not a violent man myself but needs must, we have to defend ourselves. You've put us to a lot of trouble this evening and I understand you've killed one of my best men as well as my dogs. Now we can't have that, can we?"

He sat down in front of us and poured himself a glass of water. He appeared to be totally composed, undisturbed by the violence. He addressed Dale. "Have we got everybody now? We can't afford any more interruptions, can we?"

"I think so, boss."

"Well, 'think so' isn't good enough, is it. Just pop out again and check round the house, there's a good fellow. Check the boathouse as well. Take Joe with you. If you find anybody, you have my blessing to shoot them. We have quite enough guests for one evening."

"Right boss. Come on Joe."

The two of them disappeared. Would they run into Bill? Where was he hiding? I had expected Bill to come blasting his way through the front door but surely not on his own. However, he would undoubtedly be incensed that anyone would hold a knife to Alice's throat.

Monty returned his attention to his captives.

"Alright, pleasantries aside. Who's in charge here?"

"That would be me," said Adam.

"And your name would be?"

"Adam Griffin."

"Right Adam Griffin. Let me tell you how this is going to work. I'm going to put some questions to you and you're going to answer them promptly and truthfully. If I even suspect you're holding out on me, we'll bring the girls down and the boys will do some more cutting. Have you got that?"

"There's no need for that. I'll answer your questions."

"Pleased to hear it. Now, is there anybody else on the island or following you to the island?"

"No, just the five of us. That's it." Adam was unhesitating and convincing. He wanted to give Bill a chance to remain undetected. I had a dread that Bill would come across Dale and Joe and let loose with his shotgun. I had no doubt that Monty would carry out his threat. Adam had taken a calculated gamble.

"Now I understand from your young colleagues here that some of our breeding assets came from your little nest near Preston, yes?"

"Correct. You've got six of our girls. That's all we want. We don't meant you any harm. If we can take our girls, we'll leave you in peace and not return."

"In peace? It's a bit late for that, isn't it? You invade our little island, attack our house and kill my man and dogs. You may have noticed you're all my captives. You're not really in a position to negotiate are you?"

"Okay, it's not gone well. We didn't intend to kill anybody but we had to stop the dogs attacking us and we shot your man in self-defence. He came at us, shooting."

"Self-defence? Who invited you here with your guns? You mount an attack on my house, however incompetent and claim self-defence. Sorry, I'm not having that."

Monty appeared to be losing a little of his cool. I was hoping that Adam wouldn't provoke him too much.

"Fair enough," conceded Adam. "We have attacked you but we didn't intend any harm. We had to try and track down our girls. You must have known we would."

"That's just the point," said Monty. "How the hell did you track us down? We made sure we avoided any local contact. Our boys went straight to the M6, then past Carlisle to the north or past Lancaster to the south. Nobody knew we were on the island. We just struck lucky with your place. The lads were searching the Preston area and took a few wrong turns trying to cut across to the motorway, stumbled across Whitewell. Vince and the lads couldn't believe their luck when they chanced upon all those young ladies and most of the menfolk out for the day. You should have done a better job looking after them. We know we weren't followed so how did you turn up here? I need an answer."

"We didn't know where you were but somebody heard your boys discussing whether they had sufficient fuel to get back to the lake. We figured Lake District and we've been searching all the lakes for the last week."

"So how did you know we were on the island? You can't see anything from the shore."

"One of our lads clocked your builder's van and we eventually spotted it parked up in the marina outside Keswick. It didn't take a genius to work out why you would need a boat."

Monty rolled his eyes. "I told Dale to get rid of that van. What's wrong with a plain white one."

He seemed to be satisfied with Adam's explanation which conveniently left out Merlin's involvement.

"So nobody else knows you're here? That's useful." I didn't like where this was heading.

We heard Dale and Joe returning.

"Okay boss, there's nobody else."

Well done Bill. He was well hidden and didn't give himself away. He was biding his time although what could one man with a shotgun do against a heavily armed gang of five. Adam attempted a question of his own.

"So what's your plan for this place, to fill it with babies?"

"This is just the start, we won't be here long-term. We've got to rebuild, you must see that. There are so few people left, the entire population could die out. This is our first breeding centre and the island gives us security, or at least it did until your arrival. We'll expand the centres into a linked community, each centre having a few studs and up to ten breeding assets. Each girl will have produced at least six offspring and within fifteen years or so, the cycle starts again. The male offspring will be distributed between the centres as studs and the girls will start breeding. That way, we'll maintain a healthy gene pool. Within a couple generations it'll become self-sustaining. There's no alternative to using some compulsion to get it started, which is why I need these rough diamonds, but it'll soon become a normal way of life."

"You make kidnapping and rape sound quite acceptable," said Adam.

"I can understand your being bitter but you have to let go of the old social norms. This is a battle for survival now and we do what's necessary."

I couldn't stay quiet any longer. "Please tell me why you would take a thirteen year old girl?"

"Oh, that one. Would that be your daughter? Yes she was a bit young. My brief to the lads was mid-teens to mid-thirties and the younger the better but I think Dale took a bit of a fancy, didn't you?" Monty looked at Dale who remained stone–faced but Leroy goaded him.

"Dale likes virgins. They've got nothing to compare him with, what with having a small dick 'n all."

"Shut it, you black cunt! I was going to be nice to her and the fucking bitch gives me this." Dale pointed to a barely healed scar on his forehead.

"Alright lads, that's enough." Monty intervened. "I'm afraid your young daughter drowned almost as soon as she arrived. She must have panicked and took herself into the freezing waters late at night. We found her clothes in the bushes. I really am terribly sorry."

Nothing had prepared me for such a shock. I had assumed Jo was upstairs with the others. My mind was in turmoil and I couldn't find the words. My beautiful defenceless Jo. After all we had been through, to meet her end with a monster like Dale, it was unbearable. Eventually, I managed to get out : "How do you know she drowned? Did you find her body?"

"Don't delude yourself," said Monty with the appearance of genuine sympathy. That lake in March is barely above freezing. To go in there naked in the dark, well, it's suicide really. It's most regrettable but wasn't intended. We treat our girls well. They're our future. Dale has been reprimanded, I can assure you."

Reprimanded! If I hadn't been tied to the chair, I'd have torn him apart, callous bastard! I had never felt such rage, my blood was boiling. My heart was beating so fast, I thought I'd pass out. I strained at the flex around my wrists but there was no movement in them at all.

The conversation continued, mainly between Monty and Adam but I couldn't follow what was said. I was in a blind panic and all I could think of was what I would do to Dale, given the chance. Then I thought, what if she made it despite everything. Jo was a good swimmer. She got all her badges, sharks and whales and God knows what. She could be out there somewhere. She might even have found her way back to Whitewell. The others would know about the island then. This must have happened nearly a week ago. Maybe they were on their way? My mind was rambling. I just couldn't deal with it.

It finally registered that Monty was talking about what to do with us. Something about putting us off the island and various threats to us or the girls or both. The next thing I knew we were being released from the chairs, having our hands tied behind our backs and marched out of the front door with Dale and Leroy pointing guns at us. Once out of the house, Dale took charge again.

"Right. Down to the boathouse. Anybody gives me any trouble, I'll shoot the fucking lot of you, and don't think I won't."

It was the early hours of the morning and the night air was cold, which cleared my head a little. I could think clearly again but my rage towards Dale remained undiminished. We walked in silence, as instructed, down the winding track back to the jetty, Dale in front with a powerful torch and Leroy bringing up the rear. We were quite unsteady on our feet, our balance compromised by the position of our arms but we managed nevertheless. Any possibility of making a break for it into the trees was out of the question. The perilous nature of our situation had now dawned upon me. We were not being taken across to the marina. Monty knew we would simply find new weapons and a boat and return to the island. Monty meant to get rid of us and had chosen his worst thugs, Dale and Leroy to do the job. Why had they not shot us at the house? They must be intending to dump us in the lake. Would they do it at the jetty or take us out in the boat and throw us overboard?

When we reached the jetty Dale opened the door to the boathouse.

"Right. Everybody in the boat. We're taking you back to Portinscale."

They both had their guns ready and we were not in a position to argue. When we were all on board Dale stepped onto the deck.

"Get down in the cabin. You'll be more comfy in there," and to Leroy: "cast off. I'll start her up."

Leroy was untying the rope at the stern of the boat as we

were all filing down into the cabin. Suddenly a shape loomed up from the boxes and coats at the back of the boathouse and swung something heavy at Leroy's head before he could react. It hit with a sickening thud and Leroy crumpled without a sound. It was Bill! Dale left the controls and turned with his gun aimed at Bill. Instinctively, I took my chance, launching myself headfirst into his back. Dale fired his shot as he was falling and hit the wall of the boathouse. Bill stepped forward, grabbed his head and smashed it against the side of the boat. He lay still.

"That should even things up a bit, bastards!" said Bill with venom. "I thought you'd have to turn up here sooner or later. I had more chance of catching 'em 'ere than attacking the house on me own."

"Well done Bill," I said. "You saved our lives. We were heading for the bottom of the lake."

The others emerged from the cabin and Bill found a sharp knife to cut our bonds. It was such a relief to get some feeling back in my hands. We examined the thugs. Leroy's skull was caved in and death must have been instantaneous. Dale appeared to be relatively unharmed and was coming round.

"Shall I finish him off?" asked Bill.

"No. Tie him up tight and secure him to the boat" said Adam, "and gag him. We don't want him shouting for help."

John used our own bonds to tie Dale's wrists behind his back and put another round his neck and attached to the chrome rail at the stern of the boat. I searched for some rags and found one that was filthy and oil-soaked, stuffed the whole of the rag into Dale's mouth and sealed it with duct tape wound round his head several times.

"Come on," said Bill, clutching his trusty shotgun, "back to the house. This time I'll blow that fucking door off."

John and Phil took the handguns and the rest of us armed ourselves with heavy tools as clubs. When everybody had left the boat, I stepped back on board and faced Dale who was sitting on the deck with a mixture of fury and panic in his eyes.

"Take this one for Jo." I kicked him in the groin as hard as I could. Dale's face contorted in pain but he couldn't issue a sound. It felt so good I gave him another kick in the same place. "I'll see you later." I hadn't finished with Dale.

We ran back up the track towards the house. Adam agreed to Bill's demand to "blow that fucking door off." To be honest, it would have been fruitless trying to stop him, his blood was up. Adam, John and I would follow Bill through the front, though only John was armed with the handgun taken from Leroy. Jim and Phil were dispatched to shin up the drainpipes again and enter through the French doors. The gang had had no time to do anything with the smashed lock. This time the noise would be intentional as a diversion and Phil, who had Dale's handgun, was told to shoot on sight. We were not going in to negotiate. The anxiety I had previously experienced had completely dissipated. The news of Jo's fate had left me emotionally numb and I just didn't care anymore what happened to me. I wanted vengeance.

We gave Phil and Jim a few minutes start, heard them kick open the door, smashing glass in the process, soon followed by two shots. Adam nodded to Bill and we rushed the front door. Bill opened fire from about four feet and virtually destroyed the door in a splintering of wood, leaving it swinging open on one remaining hinge. We ran inside to find the huge figure of Joe emerging from the back, both hands on his gun in a military style stance. He let off several shots before we could react and I heard a grunt from Bill as he went down. John returned fire and caught Joe somewhere in the torso. Joe looked stunned and immobile for a moment but still clutched his gun until John followed up with a shot to the head. I checked on Bill who was now lying on the floor, bleeding profusely from his chest. It didn't look good. I grabbed a small cloth from a hall table, balled it up and pressed it onto Bill's wound. Meanwhile the sound of further gunshots came from somewhere in the house, followed by silence.

"Stay here," said John. "I'll check it out. If anybody gets past me, there's another shell in that shotgun."

I tried to make Bill comfortable but was conscious of fighting a losing battle. With no medical facilities he had no chance. If he could just see that Alice was okay before he died. I didn't have long to wait. Within a few minutes I heard voices, then Monty walked through with an air of calm resignation, Phil holding a gun at his back. You had to hand it to him, he wasn't one for panicking. John and Jim followed.

"Vince is dead. That's the lot", announced John.

"I underestimated you," said Monty. "Perhaps we should have shot you while we had the chance. So you had somebody else outside. Ah yes, I see," looking at the prostrate form of Bill. "Don't worry. They're quite alright. They're all in first floor bedrooms. You'll see the keys in the locks."

Jim and Phil ran upstairs. Goodness knows what the girls thought was going on. John and Adam took Monty into the dining room where we'd been held captive earlier. They would tie him up whilst we decided what to do with him. I stayed with Bill who was deteriorating fast. He seemed to have difficulty speaking. "I'm finished," he croaked. "Can you get my Alice?"

"She's coming Bill. You did it. You beat them."

"Aye, fucking showed 'em. Make sure you shoot that bastard."

We could hear a commotion upstairs, conversation and sobbing. Alice appeared at the head of the stairs. "Dad!" She ran down and threw her arms around him. She looked with horror at his blood-soaked clothes and his ashen face.

"We've got to do something!" she implored looking round at the rest of us.

"Hush child," whispered Bill between weak coughs which spattered blood over his chin. "Seeing you safe is all I wanted.

I'm done. Will you see that I'm buried at the old farm alongside your mum and Jack? I'll be content there."

"No Dad! We'll stop this bleeding. You'll be alright."

"No lass." Bill was trying to speak but was choking on his own blood which was now running from the corner of his mouth. Bill gave a big sigh and said no more.

Alice lay on him, heaving and sobbing until Jim stepped forward and gently eased her away. She was now covered in Bill's blood.

All were now gathered around, horrified at Bill's fate. Chris Salt was in John's arms, Chris Lucas with Phil. Lisa had a makeshift bandage under her chin where Dale had cut her. There were two other girls I hadn't seen before, who were introduced as Jane Robinson and Milly Cooper, both early twenties.

Now Lisa was crying. "Tom, I'm so sorry. I tried to look after Jo but that animal Dale took her outside. They said she drowned. Then he raped me instead. Is he dead?"

"No but we've got him tied up. The others are all dead apart from Monty."

"Just give me a knife. I'll see to Dale."

"No Lisa. You've been through enough. We'll sort out what to do with them"

We moved into the kitchen where Chris Salt made some tea and found us some cold food as we exchanged stories. All the girls had been raped with varying degrees of violence depending on their resistance, often with two men involved, one to hold down the victim and the other to finish the job. Alice had suffered her fate at the hands of Leroy, Chris Salt with Joe and Chris Lucas with Vince. Jane and Milly had been captive for some time and had been raped by several of the gang. They had a system apparently and Monty kept a record of all the matings. They attempted to work out the girls' most fertile time of the month and each month they were scheduled to have a different partner. Milly was late that month and feared she may already be pregnant. Milly had been taken from her farm near Lancaster. Jane had been taken from a house in Carlisle when Dale had shot her father in front of her. In their competition for levels of depravity, Dale appeared to excel. Jim suggested bringing Dale up to the house but I told him to leave him until the morning. If he was cold and uncomfortable, that was just fine with me. I didn't know how we were going to resolve this with two of them left but Adam suggested discussing it in the morning after some sleep if that was possible. I was going to find some scotch.

2 April

I managed a few hours' sleep thanks to several glasses of scotch. Physically I was refreshed, having avoided the injuries suffered by some of the others. Jim's wound to his forehead and John's injury to his mouth did not appear to be too serious, once cleaned up, but Adam's hand was a mess. Chris Lucas had cleaned it quite well using neat gin but the wound was still open and bleeding where it had been torn by the dog. Chris thought it would have to be stitched but nobody could find any needle and thread, so that was deferred until we returned to Whitewell, which we were determined to do that day. We cleaned up Bill as best we could and wrapped him in a sheet for the journey home.

I felt sympathy for Alice, of course, having to witness her father's death and the others for everything they had gone through. I also felt relief that the rescue operation had been completed and that the others were reunited with their loved ones, and yet my feelings were strangely muted, almost disinterested. It was like I was operating on half power, firing on two cylinders. Conversation was difficult and I just felt detached. I cared about the others but I was only really there for Jo and since I had learned of her fate, the floor had dropped out of my world. Nothing else seemed important.

We busied ourselves with breakfast and Jim and Phil took guns to retrieve Dale from the boat. We checked on Monty who had clearly spent a most uncomfortable night tied to his chair and appeared to have wet himself.

Jim and Phil returned after twenty minutes and reported that Dale was dead.

"He must have choked on the gag," said Phil.

"I think he'd been dead for a while. We tipped him into the lake."

I wondered curiously whether these bodies we kept dumping off the jetty would re-surface after a while. There were three of them down there. It would look like a war zone but then dead bodies had become commonplace. What did I think about Dale's death? Guilt? I had pushed quite a large cloth into his mouth and my kicks may have aided the process. But no, there was no guilt. Vengeance for Jo? I would like to feel that but no, that wasn't there either, just emptiness. I really didn't care. Dale was a worthless piece of humanity who should never have survived the flu if there was any justice in the world, but his death wouldn't bring back Jo.

That just left Monty. What should we do with him? Adam proposed taking him back to Whitewell and holding a proper trial but the rest of us wanted this finished on the island. There was no point in putting forward evidence of his crimes. They were self-evident. We decided instead on a straightforward interrogation and an opportunity for Monty to put forward arguments in mitigation. Then we would need to make a difficult decision.

Adam lead the questioning: "Do you accept that you were the head of this gang and responsible for its actions?"

"I object to the use of the word 'gang'. We are not criminals. We were setting up a self-sustaining community to ensure people's long-term survival in a harsh new world. I accept an element of coercion was involved initially but that was for the greater good. But if you're asking whether I was in charge, yes, it was my project and I recruited the others that you have executed."

"The abductions at Whitewell and those at Lancaster and Carlisle were on your instructions?"

"Well, the lads were following the objectives I had laid down in bringing women of child-bearing age to the island but how they achieved this was left to them according to the circumstances they found."

"And that included the murder of Jane Robinson's father?"

"That was young Dale I believe. He's not the easiest to control, believe me. As I understand it, they were attacked by the young lady's father and had no choice."

"On the island you've overseen a programme of systematic rape of seven women and attempted rape of a thirteen year old girl which lead to her death and have personally raped two of the girls. Correct?"

"Firstly, I do not accept the term 'rape'. You are attempting to apply the laws of a dead civilisation which has no relevance to the new world. We were giving these girls an opportunity to join the start of a pioneering venture. They would have thanked us in time when their offspring thrived in a secure community. As for the thirteen year old, I accept that Dale was out of line but he was not acting on my instructions."

"You also caused the death of Bill Weston and the attempted murder of five other men."

"Absolutely not! If anybody is responsible for the death of that man, it is you sir. You launched a reckless and foolhardy attack on my island and killed five of my men. My god, that fellow blasted through my front door. My man was simply defending himself. If anybody should be on trial for murder, it is you. As for the rest of you, I could have had you shot but chose to put you off the island."

"Dump us in the lake, you mean."

"That's your assumption. I gave no such instructions."

"Alright, we've heard enough and have witnessed your actions. Do you have anything to add in mitigation?"

"No mitigation is required as I have always acted with the best intentions. Who gives you the authority to put me on trial without following any proper legal process? This is just a kangaroo court and you are clearly seeking to assuage your conscience in an act of judicial murder.

"We'll let the girls decide," said Adam. "We're charging this man with eight counts of kidnapping, the murder of Mr Robinson, manslaughter of Bill Weston, multiple counts of rape, assaults and wounding. How do you find him?"

"Guilty!" they all shouted.

"This is just obscene," spat Monty.

"You've had your chance, now keep quiet or you'll be gagged," ordered Adam. "Now, what are we going to do with him? Suggestions?"

"Shoot him!" shouted Alice. "He's the cause of all of it. He's evil!"

"I agree," said Jim. "I'll take him out back and finish it. Let's go home." Jim picked up one of the handguns.

"Now just a minute. Put the gun down, Jim." Adam intervened. "This isn't the Wild West. We'll talk this through and arrive at a consensus. If necessary we'll take a vote on it. What's your view Tom?"

"My gut instinct is that he deserves to die. His crimes are heinous. If we are trying to abide by our old judicial code, we had no death penalty but he would probably have received a whole life tariff, certainly thirty years, which would amount to the same thing. But what is the practical solution when we have no prisons? If we don't execute him we'll have to let him go free. That hardly seems just when he's caused the death of Jo and Bill and the suffering and emotional scars of our women.

If we leave him alive how can we be sure he will not find some more thugs and start again? The survivor groups we've met in the Lakes would all be vulnerable to attack, apart from our own community in Whitewell. The only alternative to execution I could suggest would be to maroon him on the island and take all the boats and guns, if we're prepared to take the risk of leaving him alive. Whatever we do won't bring back Jo and Bill. I'm content to leave others to decide."

John was invited to respond.

"There has to be an element of punishment. If we don't kill him, then leave him here but burn down the house. He'd most likely starve here or drown trying to escape. He doesn't look fit enough to swim to the shore. We could leave him to his fate."

There were no further suggestions and Adam put it to a show of hands. Alice, Jim, Jane, Milly and Lisa voted for execution. Adam, John and Chris Salt, Phil and Chris Lucas and I voted to maroon him. Six to five.

"No!" screamed Alice, pouncing on Jim's gun on the table. She started firing wildly at Monty, the first shot hitting the wall but the next three finding a home in his chest and stomach. She kept pulling the trigger but the gun was empty. She looked at Monty's lifeless form and collapsed in tears.

The rest of us were too shocked to say or do anything until Jim put his arm round and pulled her to him.

What an end to a bloody battle. I wished then that I had voted for execution. At least that would have spared Alice this trauma. She would have to live with this for the rest of her life.

*

Pulling things together, we packed up some food and water and carried Bill's body to the boat. We left Monty where he was, not being prepared to waste time on a burial or carrying him out to dump in the lake. Joe and Vince's bodies were also left where they fell. Presumably birds or rats would find them, if there were any rats on the island. We just wanted to be rid of the place. We found some car keys which we assumed would fit something parked at the marina and all squeezed into the Derwent Queen.

The keys belonged to the builders van. The back was virtually empty and we eased in Bill's body as delicately as we could. Jim offered to drive the van along with Alice, the rest of us fitting into the Citroen, Range Rover and Landrover easily enough.

On the sixth day of our search, we were finally heading for home, battered and exhausted. The journey back was very quiet. I think we were all numbed by the events of the last week. I slumped in the back of the Range Rover attempting to sleep, unsuccessfully, but at least it avoided conversation. I longed to be on my own with my thoughts.

*

A couple hours later, somewhere around 4.00 pm, we pulled up outside the inn at Whitewell. All the way back I had been sustained by the thought that maybe Jo had made it against all the odds. Maybe she had survived the freezing waters of a nightime lake at the end of March, swam naked to the shore, found shelter, food and clothes, perhaps a survivor to help her and somehow made it back to Whitewell where she was awaiting my return. She would dash from the inn to hug me and the tears would flow. I knew that this was absurd and yet I could but hope.

Paul Fernyhough was the first to see us. He was messing with the Landrover in front of the inn with the bonnet popped up when all four vehicles arrived in convoy with the horns blaring.

"Well I'll be dammed! Look who's here!" he shouted into the inn.

Helen Salt was next out, desperately seeking out Chris, closely followed by Mo and the Fernyhough boys. Emma then emerged holding little Anna's hand. Finally Brian and Paul Naden joined the throng.

No sign of Jo. I wasn't really disappointed . I had expected it. I knew she was gone. I had got used to the sense of emptiness and the joyful reunions around me just left me completely cold. Part of me almost resented their high spirits, which was nevertheless dampened somewhat by the absence of Jo and the discovery that the builder's van contained Bill's body.

We all drifted into the house and Brian put his hand on my shoulder.

"I'm sorry Tom. I know how you must be feeling."

"Thanks. I'd just like to be on my own for a bit." I walked away.

Emma busied herself bringing drinks and snacks from the kitchen, promising a feast for supper. I waited until everybody was in the lounge exchanging stories and entered the kitchen myself. I knew where Emma kept the medicines and first aid and stuff that we had salvaged from various pharmacies and found four packets of paracetamol. I put three packets in my pocket and went to my room. I took the bottle of Glenfarclas from my wardrobe and the whisky tumbler. It wasn't the cask strength stuff I had brought from home. That was long gone and I hadn't been able to source a replacement, though I'd searched far and wide. This was bog-standard 40% Glenfarclas but good nonetheless. I had about three quarters of a bottle and reckoned that would be enough. I sat in my chair with my feet on the bed, the bottle at my side and began to swallow the tablets. I had to crunch them as I had never overcome a phobia over swallowing whole tablets and the taste was unpleasant but compensated by a full glass of whisky. I refilled the glass and moved onto the second packet of twelve tablets. As I ate and drank my thoughts were with Sue, Lucy and particularly Jo. Since losing the others my whole purpose had been to protect Jo. I had failed miserably. It would have been a good time to believe in the afterlife but I couldn't overturn a lifetime of conviction. This was nothing to do with joining Sue, Lucy and Jo. This was just checking out. I had had my fill.

As the pills disappeared and bottle emptied, I could feel myself drifting off. That's the end of my story, a survivor no more. I just settled down to sleep. Peace at last.

CHAPTER FIFTEEN

JO'S STORY: CAPTIVITY

28 March

Jo was in class when the men arrived at the inn, discussing Hardy's "Far from the Madding Crowd" with Chris Salt and Lisa. They were so disappointed at lunchtime to have missed the visitors. It was the sole topic of conversation over lunch. The more Brian heard, the more concerned he became.

"I have to say, the whole thing sounds very odd. Two young men travelling alone who just happen to be passing on a lane to nowhere, asking for water, pumping you for information, then disappearing in a hurry. I wish you'd sent for me as soon as they arrived."

"I'm sorry Brian," said Emma, getting a little flustered. "It seemed alright at first and it was so unusual to have visitors after so long. I thought they'd stay and meet everybody but I must admit they did seem a bit shifty when I suggested that Jim would fetch the others, especially the one with all the tattoos. It was almost like he was trying too hard to be polite."

"No, it's my fault," said Jim. "I should have just slipped out and fetched you anyway. We just didn't think they'd make such a quick exit."

"But what were they after," mused Brian. "We haven't got anything they couldn't find elsewhere. Even so, I think when the others get back, we'll arrange a watch rota for tonight, maybe for a few nights. It wouldn't be difficult for people to break in here if they wanted. It's a great location in many ways but it has to be said, it's not the most secure."

Jo was still digesting this thought when right on cue she heard a terrifying smash from the lounge, a sound like splintering wood and glass. Everyone ran out of the kitchen and things seemed to happen so quickly. There seemed to be strange men everywhere and they were firing guns. The noise was horrendous. She threw herself to the floor behind a sofa. It was like a nightmare. As she peeked out from the side of the sofa she was horrified to see Brian lying on the floor at the feet of a tall black man. He was bleeding from a head wound. The man with tattoos was holding a gun to Anna's head as he bellowed "Right. That's enough. You can all stand over there," he said, pointing towards the bar, "or this one gets a bullet in the brain. I'm not fucking messing!"

Poppy was barking madly and snapping around the tattooed man's heels. She'd realised that little Anna was threatened. Jo tried to call her off but Poppy took no notice. The tattooed man took the gun away from Anna's head for an instant and with an irritated "Shut the fuck up!" shot Poppy twice. There was the tiniest whimper from the first shot then nothing.

"No! Poppy!" Jo exclaimed as tattooed man and tall black man exchanged sniggers. The hatred boiled inside Jo and she wanted to throw herself onto the tattooed man but Jim took her hand and brought her over to the bar. The men started separating them into two groups, supervised by the tattooed man. Chris Salt, Chris Lucas, Lisa and Alice were pushed onto one side. The black man was putting Jo with Brian, Jim and the others but tattooed man intervened. "No, we'll take her, Leroy."

"What? Too young, man."

"I said, put her with the other girls."

"Jesus, Dale, you perv. The boss won't like it you know."

"Fuck the boss. I'm taking her."

The man addressed as Leroy turned to a fourth man with spectacles who had not yet spoken. He nodded.

The girls were herded out of the front door of the inn to a white van parked outside. Leroy opened the back to reveal an empty space with a bit of sacking on the floor.

"Get in. Make yourselves comfortable. It could be a couple of hours."

A couple hours! Where were they taking them? Jo was beginning to panic. Would she ever see Dad again? What would they do to them? She had some idea from the short exchange she had heard between Dale and Leroy. However, her most immediate concern was that she had been about to visit the bathroom and she wasn't sure if she could last another two hours. It was too late to do anything about it. As soon as the girls were bundled into the van, the door was locked and within minutes they set off. There were no windows and no lights inside the van. At first they could see nothing but as their eyes adjusted to the dark, slightly ameliorated by sunlight around the edges of the door, they could just make out each other's shapes. They positioned themselves with their backs against the sides of the van, their legs interspersed in the centre like sardines in a tin. They had nothing to hold onto whilst they sensed from the momentum that the van was taking the bends in the road rather quickly but the cramped conditions helped them to support each other.

"Are they going to rape us?" asked Alice in a small voice.

"I'm pretty sure that's what they have in mind." Chris Lucas was grave. "Why else would they pick all the young girls, even Jo? That Dale with the tattoos is sick but I don't think Leroy is much better. Best not antagonise them until we can assess the situation. It sounds like their boss might not be happy with Dale. Perhaps we can exploit the situation."

"I'd kill myself rather than be raped by one of them," asserted Jo.

Alice nodded. "My dad will be off his head when he hears what happened. He's very protective of me. He'll kill them."

"Trouble is, he'll have to find us first," said Chris Lucas. "We could go an awful long way in two hours and they'll have no idea where to look."

"That won't stop my dad. He'll find them."

After half an hour of bends and jolts they settled into a steady rhythm of constant speed and no gear changes. Chris Salt was deep in thought, then addressed the others. "Have you noticed how smooth the ride is now? I think we're on an open clear road with no sharp turns. It has to be a motorway. I've been looking at the light seeping in at the cracks. I'm pretty sure the sun's at the back of the van. For early afternoon that means we must be heading north. I think we must be on the M6. It would've taken half an hour or so to reach it, wouldn't it. If we're going to travel for two hours, that could take us to Scotland."

"Well done Chris, I think you're right," said Chris Lucas. "It could be useful to know roughly where we're being taken. Can anybody see what time it is?"

Lisa was holding her wristwatch to the crack in the door. "I think that shows 2.15."

"The engine noise isn't that loud. It sounds comfortable doesn't it?" continued Chris. "A van like this can't be cruising at much more than 60 and we would have joined the motorway somewhere near Lancaster to head north. If we time it, we'll work out how far we've gone." It lifted spirits just a little to feel that they could respond to their situation and do something.

It was quite a while later before they sensed any change in speed, the gear changes and turns.

"We've left the motorway!" hissed Chris Lucas. "What time is it Lisa?"

Lisa held her watch to the door, squinting. "I think that's a couple minutes to three."

"Right. That's nearly 45 minutes at say 60 miles per hour. We must have covered something approaching 45 miles. North of Lancaster. Where would that take us to? God, I wish we had a map and a torch."

They were riding smoothly again, another major road. "We've changed direction!" announced Chris Salt. "See how much brighter the light is on the right side of the door, compared with the left. We're travelling west."

"We're a long way past Kendal," said Jo, summoning up a mental image of the road maps she knew so well. We must have left the motorway at Penrith, unless we were going fast enough to reach Carlisle. It's not Scotland. We're heading for the northern end of the Lake District."

"Excellent!" cried Chris Lucas. "Well done, girls." They could now sense that the van was not travelling quite as quickly and with the occasional gear change and labouring engine suggesting a hill climb but the general direction remained west. After half an hour or so the van dropped speed, changed gears repeatedly and took a number of turns.

"Wherever it is, I think we've got there." Chris Lucas requested another time check.

"3:25."

"OK, that's 25 minutes or so at perhaps 40 to 50 mph, say 20 miles west of Penrith. Any ideas Jo?"

"That has to be somewhere around Keswick, definitely."

The van stopped abruptly and the girls could hear muffled voiced from the front. Then the door was opened and light flooded in, blinding them temporarily after two hours of darkness.

"Right! Everybody out! We've not tied you up, so just behave yourselves." Dale gave the orders. "If anybody wants to make a run for it, I'll shoot you in the legs."

They gingerly stepped down from the van, stretching their stiff legs. They looked around to see a host of small boats and beyond, a large lake. They were in a car park at the water's edge. Jo could last no longer.

"I'm sorry but I have to go to the toilet." This seemed to amuse Leroy.

"You've got the whole car park luv. Just squat where you want."

Jo began to walk towards a shed at the edge of the car park. After twenty yards or so Dale barked "That's enough. You can do it there."

Jo was frozen, mortified. She couldn't pull down her jeans in the middle of the car park with four men watching. The other two had alighted from a large four-wheel drive vehicle. Chris Salt and Chris Lucas moved towards her to shield her from view. Jo was shaking but managed to pull down her jeans and pants and relieved herself for an embarrassingly long time to the sound of cheers from Dale and Leroy.

"Okay, show's over. There's your transport." Dale indicated a small motor boat moored at the end of a jetty. You lot, in the cabin." They filed in, Jo crying with embarrassment but nevertheless noting the name on the boat. "Derwent Queen." As she had thought, Derwent Water. At least they knew where they were.

The boat set off immediately, moving smoothly and quietly across the lake. They could see nothing from below deck but Jo whispered to the others "It is Keswick. We're on Derwent Water."

It seemed to be only a matter of minutes before they heard the engine being throttled back, men jumping out and tying up the boat. The door to the cabin opened and once more it was Dale issuing the orders.

"Everybody out. We're going to walk up this drive, nice and orderly like, to your holiday accommodation. Don't even think of making a bolt for it, you're on an island now."

Dale and Leroy took the lead, followed by the girls with the other two men bringing up the rear. The drive curved round to the right with thick woods on each side then as it curved again to the left they could see a rather impressive house rising up above them. As they approached the front door, it opened and a tall, strongly- built man greeted them.

"Alright lads? Five! You've hit the jackpot, eh?"

"Hi Joe," Dale replied. "Not bad eh? They were just waiting for us. Couldn't have bin easier."

Joe's eye settled on Jo. "She's a bit young, ain't she? Boss won't be pleased."

"I fucking told 'im". It was Leroy. "Fucking perv."

Dale gave them a smirk. "Well she's fucking 'ere now, ain't she. He's not going to send her back."

Once they were inside, Joe locked the door and pocketed the key. He indicated a downstairs bathroom. "You can get cleaned up in there. The boss will want to see you in twenty minutes. Just do as you're told and you'll be okay." Joe didn't appear to be quite as uncouth as Dale and Leroy.

*

Twenty minutes later they were assembled in a grand room with a large dining table, crystal chandeliers and old portraits on the walls.

A tall, rather distinguished looking man with white hair, possibly mid-sixties, entered the room.

"Good evening ladies. My name is James Montgomery but everybody calls me Monty. I must apologise for the inconvenience but I trust you've been well treated."

It clearly wasn't intended as a question but Chris Lucas jumped in.

"We most certainly have not been well treated by these foul apes. I don't know what disgusting little set up you've got here but if you think we're going along with this, you're sadly mistaken."

She was about to say more but Dale approached her with his fist raised. Monty raised his hand in conciliation.

"As you've just arrived I will allow that outburst to pass but you need to understand that we have rules here. Behave as we expect and you will be well treated. If not, we do have a punishment suite. Any further outbursts and I'm afraid you will become acquainted with our less congenial facilities." His icy tone was more menacing than any of Dale's and Leroy's profanities.

"Now, if you'll allow me to continue, I'll explain why you're here. This isn't a prison. I hope in time you will see this as your home. This country has been devastated by the new plague and it is very close to the point of no return. We do not know the position abroad but suspect it is very similar throughout the world. With tiny pockets of survivors producing the odd child there is a strong possibility that the entire human race will die out within a few generations. We have to organise ourselves to reproduce quickly from a mixed gene pool. This island project is but a start. We chose the island after much searching for seclusion and security. Nobody knows that we are here and we recruit our breeding stock outside the local area so that we are not pursued. I am sorry if you find the term "breeding stock" offensive but that is your purpose here. The men you have seen will provide the seed and all we ask is that each of you produces four offspring. The females will be retained for further breeding and the males will be farmed out to sister projects across the country. We will soon outgrow this island and move on to form larger self-sufficient communities and in so doing will help to ensure the survival of the species. In generations to come your names will be legend as they appear at the head of vast family trees.

"Your progress will be closely monitored and recorded from the dates of your periods and your matings. You will each be allocated a new mate each month during your most fertile week. The rest of the month you will be left alone. Once your pregnancy is confirmed you will be left alone until three months after the birth and then the cycle will continue but excluding the birth father. Ideally, you will produce four children from four different mates. Once that position has been achieved you will be free to leave the island and join one of our sister colonies when they are established. Any male children can accompany you. We aim to establish one new colony each two to three years until we have a network covering the country.

"Until then, I regret that you cannot leave the island but you will be very comfortable here, I assure you. We have electricity from our own generators, hot and cold running water, flushing toilets and plentiful food and drink. You will find an assortment of clothes and female necessities in your room and reasonable requests for additional items will be sourced wherever possible. All the bedrooms have TVs which will play CDs or DVDs which you can choose from our extensive collection. We also have a good library of books. You will be placed on a rota for domestic duties, cleaning, cooking and the like.

"Now, a warning on misbehaviour. Any failure to comply with allocated duties, any acts of violence towards the men caring for you, any attempts to escape the island will be punishable in the first instance by 24 hours in the punishment suite. You are unlikely to repeat the offence. I will leave you to settle in and meet your fellow guests. We will reconvene in here at 7.00 pm prompt for dinner. Thank you."

Monty then turned his attention to Jo. "How old are you, my dear?"

"Just thirteen sir."

"Oh dear." Monty gave a withering look in Dale's direction. "I'm sorry you are caught up in this. It is quite contrary to my express instructions. I am afraid we cannot let you go as that would jeopardise our security but I can assure you that you will not be scheduled to join the breeding programme until your fifteenth birthday. Please accept my apologies."

"Thank you sir."

That was a huge relief to Jo. Her fifteenth birthday seemed a long way away and she was absolutely determined that she would find an opportunity to escape long before then.

They were taken upstairs by Joe to two rooms allocated to them. Each of the rooms had three single beds and they were left to decide amongst themselves who slept where. Jo, Alice and Lisa asked to share, leaving the other room for the two Christines. Joe left them to sort themselves out but first unlocked a third room and called to the occupants.

"Jane, Milly, come on out and meet our new arrivals. Show them what's what, will you? You'll need to sort out bedding, nightclothes and a change of clothes. There should be plenty to go around. Let me know if you're missing anything." Big Joe seemed much more pleasant that the others, certainly better than Dale and Leroy.

Two young girls emerged, about twentyish with a mixture of relief and concern on their faces, introducing themselves as Jane Robinson, 19, from Carlisle and Milly Cooper, 22, from a farm near Lancaster . They were most surprised to see five new arrivals. Jane had been taken two weeks previously but Milly was into her sixth week. They seemed glad of the company but sorry that others were to share their fate. They had lots of questions for them which confirmed their impressions of the men.

"Vince and Joe are not too bad," said Milly. "Monty's creepy. He pretends to be a gentleman but he's hard underneath. The other three are thugs but Dale's the worst. You want to stay out of his way. I think he's got a screw loose. There's a really vicious streak to him, as though he likes people to suffer. Geordie's his mate. They've known each other for years. Dale and Leroy wind each other up but they're almost as bad as each other."

"It must be possible to escape," suggested Chris Lucas. "We're not tied up and there's no bars on the windows."

"Don't think we haven't thought about it but there are always some of them around during the day. All the outer doors are locked and they've never left keys where we can get them. We're allowed outside once a day but they're always with us. At night we're locked in our rooms. We can't even use the bathroom. If you're caught short, you have to use the pots under the bed. All the windows are locked as well."

Lisa was examining the window. "Even though it's locked, if we had something heavy enough we could smash the whole thing out. We could easily fit through there."

"Yeah but apart from the noise, look where you are. These are dormer windows, half way up the roof. You couldn't climb down from there. They'd be in here straightaway and even if you did get out, they'd be waiting for you outside. Then you'd be in the punishment suite." The look on Milly's face made clear that was to be avoided.

"So what is that exactly?" asked Chris Salt.

"It's a small room in the cellar, about ten feet square, no windows, no light, no heating, no toilet. They just leave you in there all day with a bottle of water, no food. I've been in there once when I tried to stab Dale with a kitchen knife. He had his hands all over me, the bastard. You really don't want to go there."

"So you get raped every month?" asked Alice.

"Yes. They've got a system. It's all organised. Monty records everything in his ledger. You get the same person five nights in a row. It was Joe for me last month and Vince last week. I've got three weeks off now. You had Geordie, didn't you Jane? If you don't submit to them, they come in pairs. One holds a knife to your throat and the other does the business. See?" Milly raised her head to show two jagged cuts under her chin. I told Jane to go with it. It's not worth fighting."

Jane had left Milly to answer our questions but then spoke quietly and dispassionately. "I'm biding my time. I'll submit to them, do what they want but everyday I'm waiting for a chance to hide a knife. They watch us when we have to work in the kitchen and search us when we leave, but one day they'll slip up and I'll get a knife and hide in under my bed. Then when it's Dale's turn to have me and he exposes himself, I'm going to stick it in his private parts, the evil bastard. When they took me, it was me and my dad in the house. We had no guns, no defence and there were three of them, Dale, Leroy and Geordie. My dad had gone for them but Leroy had knocked him to the floor. He couldn't save me but Dale just stood over him and shot him in the head. He was actually grinning when he did it, the sick bastard. I don't care what happens to me as long as I can get a knife into Dale."

They all decided to be on their best behaviour during dinner. Nobody fancied spending their first night in the cellar. Afterward, they were locked into their respective rooms and settled down for the night. Jo, Alice and Lisa changed into the pyjamas provided and were comfortable enough. A little pile of DVDs was stacked next to the television but none of them felt in the mood to watch films. They shared their thoughts on their predicament, their captors and outlandish schemes of escape. Alice remained convinced that her father would come for her and seek retribution. Jo and Lisa were not persuaded that this was possible. Jo had decided that she had to find a way to escape this hell.

29 March

The next day was surprisingly routine. After breakfast they were allocated their duties according to a rota drawn up by Vince, Jo paired with Jane for cleaning duties and they were pretty much left to get on with it. Jane warned Jo that they needed to be meticulous in the standard of cleaning as Monty would be furious if anything was discovered less than sparkling. She thought he must have some sort of phobia as everything in the house had to be cleaned each day and Jo had never seen such a well-stocked cleaning cupboard. Jane wasn't sure whether Monty's dissatisfaction would result in 24 hours in the punishment suite but it wasn't worth taking the chance. None of the men bothered them which was a great relief but although Jane was constantly on the lookout for any unattended knives that she could smuggle into her room, no opportunities presented themselves. Jo had noted that at dinner the previous evening and breakfast that morning only spoons and forks had been provided, even for the men. The only time knives were in use was in food preparation and that was closely supervised, probably to guard against adulteration of the food. Jane was convinced that the time would come and Jo had no doubt whatsoever that she was capable of carrying out her promise. Having seen the pleasure Dale derived from killing Poppy, Jo could understand the trauma Jane must have experienced from her abduction.

They spent most of the day cleaning and Jo was quite happy to keep busy rather than having time to dwell on her fate, having barely slept the previous night, such was her level of anxiety. At 2.00pm they were all allowed outside for an hour but were accompanied by Dale, Leroy and Geordie, all sporting guns. They were taking no chances. The girls were allowed the freedom of the island, provided they could be seen by the men, but were not permitted to enter the boathouse. All that was left was to walk around the exterior of the house, the grounds to the north of the house running down to the shore and the winding drive through the woods to the jetty. Jo was keen to discover what she could see on the mainland but was disappointed to find that the answer was very little. It was a cold and damp day with a low mist on the lake which had never properly lifted, such that visibility was poor. From the jetty they could see south down the length of the lake, though the far shore was lost in the mist. All they could see of the mainland in any direction was woodland and not a single building was spotted. Even from the cleared grounds behind the house looking north, only further woodland was visible. Jo knew that Keswick must be behind the woodland but nothing could be seen. Unfortunately, that meant nobody could see them. The men had chosen their location well. Jo knew that the others would come after them but couldn't see how they would ever find this place and didn't share Alice's expectation of rescue. No, they would have to manage their own escape. The only boat appeared to be the Derwent Queen, which must be in the boathouse. Unless there was a chance to steal the keys, the only way off the island was to build a raft or swim for it. She couldn't see any possibility of secretly building a raft, which left swimming. Jo tried to estimate the distance to the mainland. The shortest stretch appeared to be to the east, possibly 500 yards, and slightly further to the north. To the west and south was just open water. Five hundred yards represented about ten lengths of an Olympic pool, tough but not impossible. It would mean breaking out of the house in the night or giving the men the slip during the exercise period. She would have to discuss this with the others. The problem at present would be the temperature of the water. The lake would always be cold but in March, there was no chance, unless there were some wet suits tucked away in the house. Would it be possible to make a wetsuit? Jo didn't think so.

Running these thoughts through her mind made Jo feel a little more positive and during the rest of her cleaning duties she continued to turn over the possibilities. That evening, when they were locked into their rooms and changed into their pyjamas, Jo ran her ideas past Alice and Lisa.

"I think the boat's our best chance," said Lisa. "If we find out where they keep the keys, we might sneak down in the night. We could be away before they realise we've gone."

"We need to figure out how to get out of the room first," pointed out Alice. "Then we need to get out of the house, then open the boathouse, then start up the boat. That's four sets of keys. How can we get all those on the same day?"

She was right and the others realised it. They were quiet for a while, struggling to come up with a solution.

"Well, what about swimming for it?" piped up Jo. "It's no more than 500 yards at the shortest point. That's ten lengths of a pool."

"I can't swim," said Lisa. "I never went for lessons and when the school went swimming I used to bunk off."

"We'd still have the problem of getting out of the house," said Alice, "unless we could find the key to these window locks and get out onto the roof. Perhaps we could tie some sheets together?"

Lisa and Jo looked dubious.

"I think we'll be rescued." It was Alice. "I bet they're looking for us right now. My dad won't give up until he finds me."

"I'm sure they will be searching", said Jo, "but what chance have they got of finding this place? It's completely screened from the mainland by the woods, apart from the lawns behind the house but there are no buildings on the shore in that direction. They're not using the fires to make any smoke and those generators you can hardly hear. Nobody on the mainland would know there's a house here. And why would they look here anyway?"

Lisa put forward a different strategy. "When we get a turn in the kitchen, what about poisoning their food?"

Jo shook her head. "Milly said they've got that well covered. There's no poisonous stuff like cleaning materials kept in the kitchen, they're watched all the time and we all have to eat the same food. Even if we had some poison, we'd have to disguise it, maybe a spicy curry or something."

Their plans were interrupted by the sound of the key turning in the lock. Dale strode into the room, grabbed Jo by the arm and produced a hunting knife. He pressed the knife under her chin and Jo immediately felt a sharp pain and sensed the blood on her neck. "Come with me. I've got a job for ya." Dale stared menacingly at Lisa and Alice. "Any sound out of you two and you're in the punishment suite. Got it?"

Jo was barefoot and in her pyjamas. "Please can I just get dressed first?"

"Nah, you'll be fine as you are, lass."

He bundled her through the door, hanging on tightly to her arm but removed the knife from Jo's neck in order to lock the door. Jo thought of making a bolt for it but wasn't sure she could break loose and where could she run?

"What do you want with me?" She had a pretty good idea but spoke out of desperation.

"Quiet! One more word out of you and you'll feel my knife."

Dale dragged Jo downstairs to the front door and Jo was surprised to see the key in the lock. Had Dale prepared the way? He clearly intended to take her outside so they could not be heard. Should she shout for help? She was fairly sure the others would not allow Dale to take her. No, she decided to wait until she was outside, then make a run for it. He would have difficulty finding her in the dark, especially in the woods. As the door opened Jo was hit with a blast of cold night air. It was pitch black outside. She shivered violently.

"Alright. Grab this!" Dale picked an overcoat hanging on a stand next to the door and allowed Jo to pull it round her. As they left the house Dale kept a vice-like grip on Jo's wrist and pulled the door closed without pausing to lock it. Jo had lost her chance to run. With his free hand Dale had his knife at Jo's throat again. She was powerless to resist. Dale pushed her round to the side of the house and indicated the trees some ten yards clear. Perhaps she could reason with him.

"You're going to get into a lot of trouble, you know. Monty promised that I wouldn't be touched until I was fifteen."

"Monty? Oh yeah, I'm quaking! All he's good for is talking. I do all the fucking dirty work. He's nothing without me and he fucking knows it. He can't touch me."

She tried a different tack. "Please don't hurt me. I'm only thirteen. I've not had a boyfriend yet."

"Don't worry lass. I'll be nice and gentle with you if you're a good girl and do as you're told. You gotta lose it someday. Better with me than fucking Leroy. Those blacks have got pricks the size of cucumbers. He'd half kill ya."

As they moved into the trees Dale took the overcoat and threw it on the ground, pushing Jo onto her back and in the same movement, grabbed her pyjama bottoms by the ankles and ripped them off. Before she could realise what was happening, Dale was on top of her, pinning her down. Now she was in a blind panic, trying to kick and scratch but he was too strong for her.

"Just take it easy or I'll fucking cut ya."

He pulled out his knife again while he used his other hand to pin down Jo by her shoulder. This left her right arm free and she desperately scrabbled around in the undergrowth until her fingers closed on something cold and hard. She instinctively swung her fist towards Dale catching him full on the head.

"Oh fuck! Shit! What have you fucking done?"

He rolled off her continuing to curse. Jo didn't think twice. She sprang to her feet, evading Dale's swipe, and started running into the woods as fast as she could, ignoring the pain on her bare feet. All she had left was the pyjama top which was woefully inadequate protection against the bitterly cold night air and strong breeze. She could hear Dale struggling to his feet, cursing.

"You fucking bitch! Look what you've done. You've fucking had it now. You're in for some rough sex, then I'm gonna carve my name on your fucking buttocks. Nobody messes with Dale."

Jo had to put some distance between herself and Dale but where to run. The island was too small. If she could find somewhere to hide, he might give up and go inside to tend his injury. She had hit him really hard. It must be bad. She scrambled down towards the lake, trying not to make a noise, until she found some dense bushes and ducked down into the middle. Dale was walking now but still heading in Jo's direction keeping up a running commentary. "Where are ya, bitch? You've got nowhere to go. Ya might as well come out. I was only joshing. I'll not cut ya, but if I have to drag ya out, I will. Come on, just be a good girl. We'll soon be done and ya can get back into the warm."

He couldn't be more than five yards away and he started thrashing about in the bushes with his hunting knife. Jo was petrified, too frightened to move. The lake water was lapping against the shore just a few feet away. Then Jo made a decision. She would not surrender herself to Dale. She would take her chance in the lake. She crouched in the bushes and eased off the pyjama top, stepping gingerly towards the water, waiting for Dale to react. He hadn't seen her. This was her chance. She eased herself into the water, trying not to gasp with the freezing cold. She could feel her muscles seizing up immediately and knew she would not be able to swim. Nevertheless, she was completely immersed in the water and pushed away from the island. Her feet were off the ground. She was afloat and attempted some breaststrokes without breaking the surface of the water. She had moved from the shore and it was so dark she was now confident that she would not be seen. She could still hear Dale chuntering and cursing and slowly swam away from the sound. She would most likely drown but at least she was off the island.

CHAPTER SIXTEEN

JO'S STORY: ESCAPE

The cold was unbearable. Jo could hardly move her limbs to stay afloat and was having difficulty breathing. She was taking in short gasps of air and beginning to panic. She knew she had to relax and breathe regularly but couldn't force her body to respond while she was thrashing her arms and legs rapidly just to keep her head above water. Every part of her body felt numb and she knew she would drown within minutes if she couldn't control herself.

Jo forced herself to concentrate and suppress the urge to panic, slowing her movements to more regular and powerful strokes which gradually produced a near normal breathing rhythm, albeit interspersed with violent shivers. She was not about to sink but sensed she would be unable to keep it up for long. She toyed with the idea of swimming to a different part of the island but could still hear Dale cursing and thrashing about. No, she would swim to the mainland or die in the attempt. It was preferable to returning to the clutches of Dale. Jo continued to put distance between herself and Dale and thought she must be at least fifty yards out into the lake but had no idea of which direction. It was so dark. There was no moon that she could see and just the odd star through breaks in the clouds. She couldn't even see the outline of the island, let alone the mainland. Realising that without any point of reference, she could be swimming aimlessly for hours, not that she could possibly survive for that long in such temperatures, Jo just swam and swam, eager to use the exercise to generate some body warmth to counteract the debilitating cold.

After what seemed an age of floating and swimming she could still see nothing but could no longer hear any sounds from the island. Either Dale had given up looking or she had moved far enough to be out of earshot. But in which direction? She knew she needed to go east to the closest bank but had no idea which way was east and was wasting precious energy to little effect. She felt exhausted and needed to rest but was numb with the cold. It was just pointless. She may as well admit defeat. Why not just stop swimming and allow herself to slip under the water? It surely wouldn't take long and at least her ordeal would be over. Jo thought of her father who was surely looking for her and knew that since her mum and sister had died, she was all that was left for her father. He would be heartbroken.

"I'm sorry dad, I tried," she whispered.

It was time to surrender to the lake and finish her suffering. As she looked to the sky it seemed that something miraculous had happened. There was sufficient break in the clouds to reveal the distinctive shape of the Great Bear, or as she liked to call it the Plough. On many night time walks her father had pointed out the constellations and they had marvelled at Orion's Belt, the brightness of Sirius, the beauty of the Plaides but, most importantly, how to locate the North Star. Jo followed the line of the last two stars of the plough shape, projected it up and there, all on its own, was Polaris. Now she was excited, having the means to control her situation. She was still intensely cold and exhausted but no longer felt at the end of her tether. Turning to face the North Star, she then turned ninety degrees to the right. Now Jo knew she was facing east and she struck out with vigour, finding hidden reserves of energy.

"Yes! I can do this."

Now she was getting somewhere, swimming determinedly and even felt slightly less cold. She kept glancing up to the North Star, keeping it directly to her left. Although she could still see nothing and hear nothing, she knew she must be closing on the east shore of the lake. The island was long gone. Jo had estimated ten pool lengths, but it seemed to be taking an awful long time. Of course, she wasn't aware of her starting position before she spotted the North Star. She may have been closer to the west shore or she could have drifted south where the lake was wider. It may be necessary to swim a lot more than ten lengths. Jo was beginning to despair once more of ever finding the shore when she heard the hoot of an owl almost directly in front of her and not too far away.

"I must be near the trees."

She strained her eyes and was unsure whether she could see a dim outline of tree tops against the night sky. It may be her imagination but she had to be close and she needed to be. She couldn't take this much longer. Then she felt ground beneath her feet. Jo ran the last few steps out of the water and collapsed on the sandy scrub. She had to rest. Her limbs ached but she'd made it. If she'd had the energy, Jo would have punched the air.

Jo slowly raised herself to stand on wobbly legs, feeling even colder than she had in the water, the cruel night breeze whipping around her naked body. She used her hands to rub her arms and legs vigorously and this seemed to restore a little feeling but Jo knew she had to find shelter and clothes quickly. Her only chance was a lakeside lodge or something but would have to find a road first. Jo was unsure whether there would be something close to the lakeside but all she could see was an open space ahead and some woods to the right. She decided to head for the woods in case anybody from the island came in pursuit and was also very conscious of being naked even though there was nobody to see her. Perhaps the trees would give her a little shelter from the breeze. Her legs felt stiff, either from the cold or the effort of swimming for so long, but she managed a slow walk, hindered by the sharp stones underfoot.

Jo felt like sitting down and having a good cry but knew she had to find somewhere she could get warm and forced herself to carry on and ignore her cut feet. It was no easier walking through the woods until she found what appeared to be a path, possibly just an animal track, but at least it was taking her through the woods and she picked up the pace a little, generating a modicum of body heat to counter the external cold. After ten minutes or so the path turned sharply to the right and was now easier to follow. This must lead somewhere, she thought. Sure enough, after another five or ten minutes the path left the woods and joined a tarmac drive heading back down to the lake. Jo thought this had to lead to a property and followed its curved path towards the water. As she turned the bend she made out the outline of a roof against the night sky. Thank God! Whatever it was, she was going in. A sign on the gate announced "Stable Hills".

Jo needed to get inside quickly. She was chilled to the bone and still soaking wet, the breeze whipping across the surface of the lake. She didn't care whether this little lodge or cottage was full of decomposing bodies or rats, she had to get under cover, get herself dried and find some clothes. The front door was locked. Another door around the side was also locked. It would have to be a window. It was so dark it was impossible to see anything inside the lodge and ascertain how the windows were fastened or locked. Jo searched around the outside of the lodge looking for large stones and came across a few bricks. She didn't hesitate. It would make a noise but that couldn't be helped. She picked up a brick, drew back her arm and hurled it with all the force she could muster against the lowest window at the side of the lodge. In the cold and emptiness of the night the sound of shattered glass and splintered wood was shocking. Would that be heard back on the island? Surely not.

Jo reached carefully inside the broken window, avoiding the jagged shards of glass and found a handle half way up. Releasing this, the remnants of the window frame opened wide. Jo was relieved to find no locking mechanism in place. The window ledge was just above waist height and she would have no difficulty hoisting herself inside. First she used her hands to brush away the broken glass, conscious of the vulnerability of her nakedness. She placed her hands on the window shelf and sprung up onto her knees, then her feet, crouching in the empty space of the window. Jo eased herself down inside the lodge, stepping carefully onto a carpeted floor. She crouched down and felt with her hands for shards of glass, of which there were many, throwing them into the corner of the room. Her feet were already in a mess and she needed to avoid stepping on glass. Gradually she felt able to move from the window and closed what was left of it behind her. No point in advertising her presence. Jo was waiting for her eyes to adjust to the dark but there was simply insufficient light to see anything and she would have to move blind. She brushed against a sofa which suggested she was in a lounge. Crouching with her arms in front of her, she slowly moved around the room until she found a doorway. Passing through, she winced as her feet touched an even colder surface, probably floor tiles. More doors. She thought this must be an entrance hall. Through another door and more floor tiles. After the comparative relief of walking on carpet, it felt like her feet were burning. She would give anything to find a pair of fluffy slippers!

As she felt round the walls again, she found lots of cupboards, above and below and deduced she had entered the kitchen. Jo pulled open some drawers, just hoping she might find a torch but in the second drawer she found a small box with a rough edge. She shook it and heard the matches inside. Eagerly she took out a match and struck it. Nothing. The box felt damp. She struck another and another. No luck. On the sixth or seventh attempt, the match flared and the room came into view. She held it up to keep it burning and quickly found her bearings. A fitted kitchen, quite smart, small table and chairs, external door, meter cupboard. The match went out. She decided to plump for the meter cupboard as that's where they had always kept a torch at home. She lit another match at the fourth attempt, conscious that the matches would not last long at this rate. Jo opened the meter cupboard to discover a solitary torch. She prayed that there was some power left in the battery as she pushed the switch. It emitted a weak light but compared to the total darkness before, it was magnificent. Now she could search the lodge. She was careful to point the torch at the floor as some of the windows had to be visible from the lake, but now she could find her way around easily. One thing she was grateful for was the absence of rats.

Jo quickly found the stairs and ran up to find the bathroom, in search of a towel. The bathroom was very smelly but she found two things to cheer her up, a good –sized towel draped over a radiator and a towelling dressing gown hanging on the back of the door. Jo grabbed the towel and started rubbing herself vigorously, bringing a little sensation back to her body and once dry, she put on the gown. It was cold and possibly slightly damp but nevertheless gave her considerable comfort to cover her nakedness. She moved into one of the bedrooms. Twin beds with duvets, a large free-standing wardrobe and a chest of drawers. The wardrobe contained mainly dresses and jackets suitable for a smart but elderly lady. She tried the chest. Underwear, socks, jumpers. That would do to start. She chose the thickest pair of socks she could find, some knickers which were too big for her and a winter jumper. In the other bedroom – there were only two – she found some trousers which were much too big but by folding back the trouser leg by several inches and pulling a belt tight, they would do. What she couldn't locate was any footwear but Jo was pleased with her finds. Although it seemed just as cold in the lodge as it had outside, at least she was out of the wind, dry and clothed. It was an easy decision to stay there the night.

The torch was getting dimmer and would not last much longer. Jo felt her energy levels matched that of the torch. The desperate swimming and fighting the cold for so long had taken their toll. She was absolutely exhausted. Jo knew she should make a plan to evade capture the next day but first she just had to sleep. She felt inside the beds but, like everything else in the lodge, they felt cold and damp so she decided to lie on top of the duvet, wearing her newly acquired clothes, with another duvet on top and the dressing gown. It still felt cold and she lay there shivering for what seemed like ages until her body warmth, such as it was, contained under the covers, began to take effect and eventually she found sleep.

30 March

The next morning Jo woke to the sound of birdsong and bright sunshine streaming through the bedroom window. She felt surprisingly snug as the filling in a duvet sandwich and wonderfully refreshed following the night's exertions. She also felt extremely hungry and thirsty. It then dawned on her that the sun was already well above the horizon. She had no watch but thought it must be at least 10.00 am. Jo jumped off the bed with a start. She had to get going fast. If they were looking for her, a lakeside lodge was an obvious place and the broken window would be a giveaway. First she needed to look for food and water. She wasn't prepared to drink anything left in the pipes for the last five months but the lake would do as a last resort.

The contents of the kitchen cupboards was a sight to behold. Decaying packets with a layer of furry mould, chewed remains, possibly from mice though it appeared they had long since given up on the place, and very little else. Jo was only interested in tins or unopened bottles. After a full search of the kitchen, her total yield was a tin of pilchards, two tins of baked beans and a plastic bottle of mineral water. She drank half the water at one go. Finding a tin opener and a spoon, she decided to finish the pilchards and one tin of beans. Jo had never been keen on pilchards but these were absolutely delicious. The beans were in ring-pull tins and she thought it would be feasible to carry the second tin as emergency supplies along with the rest of the water, which could be topped up at a stream. In the absence of anything more suitable, she stuck with the clothes she had found the previous night.

A waterproof anorak was hanging on a peg next to the front door. The sleeves were about four inches too long but were easy enough to fold back. She also found a rucksack to put her things in, which included the torch, matches and some changes of underwear. What she really needed was suitable footwear. The only thing she could find was an ancient pair of battered hiking boots at the back door which looked to be far too big. She tried them on and found them to be at least three sizes too big. She would get blisters in no time. There being nothing else to try, she had to make the best of it. Jo unravelled balls of toilet paper and stuffed them into the toes. She then put on two pairs of the thickest socks she could find, with an extra pair for the rucksack, and laced them as tight as she could. They would stay on at any rate. Her feet felt huge but they were wedged into the boots, which may be enough to prevent blisters in addition to all the cuts acquired the previous night.

Finally, after leaving a farewell deposit in the toilet, Jo was ready to hit the road and feeling quite pleased with herself. The one thing she would have liked but couldn't find was a map. To head for home she knew she needed to head south and a touch to the east but had little idea where that would take her from Derwent Water. She wanted to avoid Keswick and the main roads or she would soon be found, feeling fortunate that she had not been discovered already. If they had taken out the boat at first light, they could have found the lodge some time ago.

Her only possible route from the lodge was back up the driveway which would presumably take her to the lakeside road. She would have to be careful there but should be able to hear any vehicle from a good distance, giving her time to hide. The wind had dropped and the only sound was that of the birds. She had to clump a little in her oversized boots but soon struck up a rhythm and reached the lakeside road in less than 15 minutes. Even without a map Jo could see that left would take her to Keswick and danger. Right meant due south along the lake. She chose right.

Jo struck up a good pace, notwithstanding her clumping oversized boots, and as she walked, thought she ought to have some sort of strategy. She knew they had travelled a considerable distance from Whitewell and that was on the main roads which she needed to avoid. It would take an awful long time to walk it cross-country and would be impossible to navigate without a map. Maybe once she reached a village she would be able to find a map and even if it was only a road map it would tell her where she was and the right direction to take. For the present, all she could do was use the position of the sun to head south or south-east until she found her bearings. Jo wanted to get away from Derwent Water as quickly as possible in case they were searching. They were surely bound to check the lakeside road and Jo decided to take the first track off the road that looked like it was going somewhere. She was thankful that it was a sunny day and from the height of the sun, thought it must be late morning, certainly after 11.00. It was a pity she hadn't got going a little earlier but at least she was rested and fed, feeling so much more positive than the previous night. Having made her escape, Jo was determined to make it back to Whitewell, however long it took, so they could rescue the others, imagining their astonishment at her survival.

The road was taking her through a wooded area, a little way in from the edge of the lake, when she thought she heard a faint sound in the distance, possibly a motor. She stopped and listened carefully. This time she was sure a car was coming from Keswick direction. It had to be them. There was a low dry stone wall along the side of the road, which she quickly scrambled over and ducked down, spying through the gaps between the stones, confident she would not be seen. In less than a minute the vehicle appeared, the same roofers van they had travelled in to Keswick, moving steadily down the road at no more than 25-30mph, checking the sides of the road. The glare of the sun on the windscreen obscured whoever was in the van but Jo felt sure Dale would be there. She wondered whether they had been to the lodge at Stable Hills and spotted the broken window. Had she left any tell-tale signs of her visit? Probably. Or maybe they were just doing a circuit of the lake. She could only hope they would assume she had drowned in the lake and even now she didn't know how she'd survived that night. The van passed by without slowing and she waited a further five minutes until she could no longer hear the engine before daring to scale the wall and re-joining the road. It was possible they would come back but she should get plenty of warning. Even so, she would feel a lot more comfortable when she was able to leave the road.

Half an hour later Jo had her chance, a steep track climbing up the side of the fell away from the lake, a sign indicating three miles to Watendlath. Jo had no idea where that was but it would do to start. At first the track was very steep but then levelled out, following the side of the lake but at a much higher level than the road. Beneath was a steeply wooded slope but above was the open fell and blue sky. With the effort of climbing up the track and the direct sun, Jo was getting very warm in her makeshift walking gear. She passed a driveway marked to Askness Farm but decided against searching for more supplies as she wanted to put some distance between herself and the lake. It would be quite possible for Dale to bring the van up the track, depending on the thoroughness of the search. The track then took her deep into the woods and she lost sight of the lake which made her feel safer. Jo wondered what the others would be thinking, especially Alice and Lisa. Would Dale admit to what had happened or make up some cover story? How could he explain being outside the house with Jo in the night? She hoped he would get into serious trouble but perhaps Monty was afraid to deal with him, or just tolerated his behaviour to get his dirty work done. She knew she had been lucky to survive and they would surely assume she had drowned. Jo imagined returning to a heroine's welcome at Whitewell and giving the men the information to rescue the girls. She was their only chance of being found and would not let them down.

As Jo progressed through the woods, the sound of rustling in the trees she assumed to be forest animals, perhaps rabbits or a fox. The noise increased and became more in the nature of panting and maybe even a little snarling. This had to be dogs and definitely plural, sounding agitated and quite close. Jo had never been afraid of dogs but was wary since her father's account of the winter night in the snow when Bill had saved the day. Were the dogs possibly following her scent and were they desperate enough to attack? Jo didn't wish to wait and find out, looking around for an escape but seeing nothing but trees in every direction. She wasn't going to risk staying on the track. Perhaps she could climb a tree? The dogs sounded closer now and Jo needed to make her move. Most of the trees were young firs with no substantial low branches. Then she spotted something like an oak about twenty yards further on. Some of the branches were only four or five feet off the ground. That would have to do and she started running towards it, as fast as her oversized boots would allow, just as the first dog emerged from the trees alongside her. A big one, maybe a Great Dane. It gave out one loud "woof" and loped towards her. It didn't appear to be over aggressive but she wasn't waiting to find out. She dashed to the oak just as three more dogs appeared, now barking and snarling, intent on reaching her. Jo threw herself at the lowest branch, wrapping her arms round it and swinging herself up in one movement. Now she was lying on the branch, maybe five feet from the ground and even the Great Dane couldn't reach her. The Dane was joined by a boxer, a lurcher and some sort of terrier, all scrabbling at the tree and barking fiercely. In their excitement the dogs were even snapping at each other. There was no way Jo was leaving the tree while these were around. She had no means of defending herself and the Dane would have her over in no time. She would just have to wait it out.

After ten minutes or so, the dogs stopped barking and snapping but showed no sign of moving away from the tree. Jo felt she had to move to a more comfortable position, gradually easing herself up and edging her back against the trunk, which was enough to set the dogs off again. She looked at the branches above, which did not appear to be too difficult to climb. It was unnerving adjusting to a standing position on her branch while the dogs were snapping just a few feet below and she knew if she lost her balance and slipped, she would not have a second chance to get back in the tree. Jo managed to squeeze between two thick branches and wedge herself in, resting her back against the trunk. Now she was in a stable position and eight or nine feet off the ground. If she kept still, surely the dogs would give up and find a rabbit or a squirrel to chase.

At least an hour later and the dogs were still there. They had settled and some may even have been asleep but Jo knew that would change quickly if she attempted to get down. As she was stuck there, Jo thought she may as well have her emergency tin of beans. She retrieved the tin from her rucksack and pulled off the lid. Unfortunately that reignited the dogs' interest as they smelled food but Jo ignored them, pulled out her spoon and enjoyed the beans. She threw the empty tin at the dogs out of spite more than anything, then settled again to wait it out. Jo could feel her limbs stiffening and her bottom was numb from sitting on the branch as she wondered how long she had to endure this ludicrous situation.

It was resolved in a most unexpected way as several gunshots rang out from further up the fell. It was some distance away but enough to spook the dogs as they scuttled away into the woods. Jo allowed another five minutes in case the dogs returned but hearing nothing, concluded it was safe to come down from the tree. She had to perform stretches to relieve the stiffness from being immobile but was greatly relieved to be on her feet again. She wasn't sure how long she'd been stuck in the tree but from the sun's position she deduced it was early afternoon. She also now knew that she was not alone on the fell. Somebody must be out hunting. Jo would have to be careful not to be mistaken for a deer.

She re-joined the track and resumed her walk moving up through the woods towards Watendlath, listening carefully for any vehicles, any further shots or any returning dogs. The episode had given her quite a shock to think what would have happened to her if she had fallen from the tree. The dogs must be seriously hungry but she had never viewed them in that way before. One thing for sure, she would have to find secure shelter well before dark. What if dogs had found her the previous night when she had emerged naked from the lake, exhausted and half frozen? Jo realised she would have to take precautions if she was going to make it back to Whitewell.

The track eventually emerged from the woods and was following up the course of a stream, gradually climbing the fell. Looking back from such an elevated position, Jo could see across much of Derwent Water. She could see one island in the middle of the lake but was fairly sure it was not where she'd been held captive. She wondered how the others were faring and felt that, however perilous, her own position was far preferable. Jo strode out now to make up for lost time and walked for the best part of an hour without incident until she saw a couple buildings ahead at the bottom of a small lake. That appeared to be the end of the road and had to be Watendlath. Jo had been expecting a village but this just looked like a farm and out-buildings. Furthermore, she could see smoke rising from the main farmhouse chimney but didn't know whether to be pleased or frightened. There may be people there who could help her. On the other hand, she may be in danger. Jo had assumed she would find some more abandoned homes that she could use for shelter and supplies and hadn't envisaged throwing herself on the mercy of strangers. Possibly these were the people hunting in the woods. She had to decide as there appeared to be nowhere else to go. She either took her chance here or back-tracked to Derwent Water where Dale could still be searching. She couldn't face going back. She would knock on the front door and hope for the best.

Jo took in the farmhouse as she approached. It looked rather rundown with lots of slates missing from the roof and part of the guttering hanging loose. The windows were so filthy as to be almost impenetrable and several panes were cracked. The house itself was surrounded by junk, including a rusty old truck. Nevertheless, the smoke indicated that somebody was living there. With some trepidation Jo knocked on the door.

"Ginny? Is that you? Where have you been?"

It was a woman's voice and fairly elderly, thought Jo. The sound of footsteps inside and the door opened. It hadn't been locked.

Jo was faced by a lady with grey hair, perhaps mid-fifties, rather unkempt. She would realise that it wasn't the Ginny she expected and Jo wondered how much she should explain.

"Well don't just stand there like a lemon, letting all the heat out. Get yourself in girl. Taking off like that, I didn't know where you were." Jo walked in, bemused. She had been mistaken for Ginny. Perhaps the lady had poor eyesight.

"Sorry. You don't understand. I'm Jo Morton. I was being held against my will but managed to escape. I have to get home and bring help to rescue the others."

"What! What nonsense! What are you talking about girl? You and your daft notions. If you father was alive, he'd knock some sense into you. Now get in the back and get those rabbits skinned. We'll have them in the pot tonight."

This was surreal. Was she demented? Jo decided that rather than persist, she would go along with it and see what came. At least she had somewhere to stay and a hot meal in prospect. She would have a chance to clean up, perhaps acquire some more suitable clothes and supplies to continue her journey. There might be some explaining to be done if and when the real Ginny turned up.

Jo found the kitchen and saw two dead rabbits lying on the farmhouse table. Apart from that the place was an absolute mess and filthy. She had the impression that the lady was living alone and maybe Ginny had left some time back. It appeared that her husband was dead and that perhaps explained the dilapidation of the property. A gun was propped against the back door. If she had shot these rabbits herself, there was clearly nothing wrong with her eyesight. Why had she taken Jo to be Ginny? The state of the place suggested her mind had gone and yet she was managing to survive on her own.

Jo set to with the rabbits, not having a clue what she was meant to do. Jo's experience of meat was confined to opening packs from the supermarket. She found the sharpest knife she could and began cutting at the skin but soon found that once she had made an incision, she could literally pull the skin off and it wasn't quite as difficult as she had imagined. Cleaning out the insides was stomach-churning and then she used her fingers to pull the meat off the bones. It took her close to an hour to complete both rabbits but she ended with a plateful of rabbit meat and was quite proud of herself. The lady popped in now and then to chide "Ginny" and complain about various matters. It seemed to Jo that if Ginny had gone missing for some time, her supposed return did not appear to have engendered much in the way of affection. Maybe that was why she left in the first place.

The meal was difficult. The casserole was delicious but conversation was strained or non-existent. There were awkward silences and what exchanges there were usually ended at cross purposes. Jo attempted to explain again her true position but nothing she said seemed to register. This lady was clearly living in her own world and her relationship with Ginny remained unclear.

Jo decided to make herself useful while she was there and after clearing away the dinner things, set to in cleaning and tidying the kitchen. In truth, the whole house was a mess but the kitchen was especially messy. The only available water came in buckets hauled from the stream that ran down from the lake, in reality a small tarn, and Jo made several trips, filling jugs and containers in the toilet and bathroom before the light failed. It took her the best part of two hours but eventually the kitchen was sparkling, everything put back in the cupboards, the surfaces and floor clean. She noticed that the cupboards were quite well stocked, at least with tins and jars, so the woman had enough about her to source supplies, presumably from Keswick. Yet when she entered the kitchen there was no acknowledgment of the transformation or even apparent recognition. Jo couldn't make her out.

Jo had located Ginny's room quite easily. The Johnny Depp calendar on the wall was a giveaway although it was still showing October. Had Ginny been gone that long? There being no light other than candles and no sensible conversation, Jo made herself as comfortable as possible in Ginny's room and settled down for the night. The mattress was very cold but there was plenty of bedding and Jo eventually warmed up, the exertions of the last two days ensuring a sound night's sleep.

31 March

Jo was woken by driving rain hammering against the bedroom window. The weather had taken a turn for the worst in typical Lake District style. She stretched her limbs, feeling refreshed from a good night's sleep, and wandered into the bathroom to wash. Although the water was cold she managed a thorough strip-wash and washed her hair, reviving herself with a vigorous rub-down with a scratchy towel. She felt human again for the first time since the abduction. She dumped the clothes in which she had travelled and found far more acceptable attire in Ginny's bedroom: jeans, a top, warm jumper and even a pair of trainers that fit.

Entering the kitchen to get some breakfast she was greeted by the lady of the house.

"What sort of time do you call this then? Sleeping to all hours! The goats need milking and eggs needs collecting. I suppose you'll leave it all to me as usual. And when are you going to tend to Merrylegs, she's your wretched horse! My God, if your dad was alive, your feet wouldn't touch the floor!"

Yes, good morning to you too and don't mention the spotless kitchen. Jo sighed. "Fine. I'll get the milk and eggs. I'll see Merrylegs after breakfast." Ginny must be a fan of "Black Beauty".

Jo left through the back door without waiting for any more abuse. She was forming a deep dislike for Ginny's mother but maybe it was the dementia talking. She had clearly lost it. Jo found three goats that required milking and a clean pail nearby that looked fit for purpose. Jo had experience of milking goats acquired on a farm holiday in Cornwall a few years back and the goats seemed quite content to be handled by her. Next she located the hen house and found a dozen or so freshly laid eggs, at least she assumed they were freshly laid but the way the place was being run, who knew? Before returning for breakfast she peeked inside the barn and found a horse tethered in a stall at the back. The straw in the stall was filthy and the place reeked. Merrylegs herself looked rather distressed, a dull coat of hair, very dirty and with a matted main and tail. She certainly needed "tending". Jo loved horses and looked forward to pampering Merrylegs after breakfast.

When she returned, the old lady had left the kitchen, much to Jo's relief, and she set about making a large omelette with three of the eggs she had found. The kitchen was equipped with a wood-burning cooker similar to the one at Saltersford Hall, which was easy for Jo to use and kept the kitchen very warm. After breakfast she thought it advisable to keep out of the old lady's way, preferring to acquaint herself with Merrylegs. Jo ran to the barn as the rain was coming down in waves. The horse acknowledged her arrival with a "harrumph" and Jo went to introduce herself. She stroked Merrylegs' nose while the horse pushed her head into Jo's chest, clearly glad of the company. Jo found a sack of oats and fed some to Merrylegs from her hand, the horse snorting in contentment though Jo noticed that at least she wasn't malnourished. She just needed a really good clean and probably some exercise. Jo located buckets, soap, cloths, brushes and combs along with a saddle and bridle. She fetched water and started to soap her down, working slowly and firmly, messaging Merrylegs, then rinsing her coat, drying her and brushing until her arms ached. The mane and tail took the longest and needed soaping and rinsing several times before Jo made any progress clearing the matted hair. Eventually she was able to force the comb through the hair with considerable tugging which Merrylegs tolerated stoically. Jo cleaned round her eyes with clean water and even lifted the hooves between her legs to clear the grit and small stones stuck inside the shoe. The shoes looked rather worn but there was nothing Jo could do about that. By the time she had finished, Jo and Merrylegs were firmly bonded and the horse's coat had a hint of shine to it. Jo decided that the horse was quite healthy and had just needed a good clean up.

It was approaching midday and the rain had eased to a drizzle. Jo was dying to take Merrylegs for a ride and she felt sure that the horse would enjoy it. She decided against asking Ginny's mother in case she was expected to repair the farmhouse roof next, saddling up Merrylegs expertly and leading her out of the barn. Merrylegs perked up noticeably to be out in the open and was quite content for Jo to pull herself into the saddle. They set off for a gentle walk around the tarn, occasionally breaking into a rising trot where the terrain was flat enough for easy riding. After three circuits of the tarn the rain returned with a vengeance and Jo decided to call it a day rather than risk Merrylegs catching a chill. She rubbed her down again and gave her another stiff brushing. Before leaving the barn, Jo cleaned out the stall and spread out a fresh bale of straw, refilled the water bucket and fed Merrylegs some more oats. She had made a firm friend.

Jo returned via the back of the farmhouse to see what was there. Once past the goat enclosure and the hen house, she reached what looked like a rather weather beaten garden with an old broken down shed and a greenhouse, the glass panels murky with mildew. Then something surprising caught her eye. Behind the greenhouse were two mounds of earth, one with a wooden cross and one with a large white stone at the head. There was something written on it. These were clearly graves and reminded Jo of the makeshift arrangements they had made for Mum and Lucy at Saltersford. She moved closer to read the inscription on the stone, carefully drawn in black paint.

VIRGINIA McLEAN
R.I.P

Of course! She should have realised. Ginny hadn't gone anywhere. She had died of the flu like everyone else. Her mum

351

must have suffered some sort of breakdown and refused to accept that her daughter was dead.

The wooden cross was very crudely made, just two rough pieces of wood nailed together and knocked into the ground, possibly straight at the time but now hanging at an angle. There was just a name etched onto the wood and inked in with what looked like felt tip pen. Only part of it was now legible but Jo could see enough to make out what once read:

WILLIAM McLEAN

No dates or words.

This must be Ginny's dad. Jo deduced that Ginny must have died first and her father prepared the gravestone before succumbing to the same fate. His widow must have constructed the makeshift cross. Now Jo felt more sympathy for Ginny's mother, just one more victim in a world of tragedies.

*

That afternoon, while the rain continued to sweep down the fells, Jo busied herself tidying the farmhouse and clearing out the accumulation of rubbish. A lot of muddles and old paperwork was stuffed into an old fashioned bookcase, which nevertheless actually contained a few dozen books, very old and dusty hardbacks. Many of them were children's classics like "The Secret Garden", "Wind in the Willows", "Alice's Adventures in Wonderland" and of course, "Black Beauty". Jo had read and loved them all. There were none of the more recent paperbacks that one might expect with a teenage daughter in the family. Of greatest interest to Jo, however, was an old copy of the local OS map. It was the only map she had discovered in the house but now she would be able to assess her position. She took the map to Ginny's bedroom and spread it open on the bed. She soon found

Watlendlath and could not have picked a more isolated spot if she had tried and, as she had already deduced, it was a complete dead end. Unless she wanted to return to Derwent Water, Jo's only option was to hike over the top of the fells. When she had been riding Merrylegs around the tarn, she had noticed a path from the side of the farmhouse which cut straight up the steep side of the fell. Following this on the map, she saw that once the path reached a high level, it turned to the south-east and was a little less severe until it cut down the other side of the fells to the southern end of Thirlmere. From there she could pick up the main road south to Grasmere. It would be tough but feasible in a day, especially if she was on horseback. Jo began to make her plan. She would pack everything she needed that night and sneak out at first light before Ginny's mother had risen. She was confident that Merrylegs would let her saddle her up without making a noise. She would have to lead the horse up the fell path, as it was far too steep to ride, but she was fairly sure she would not be seen from inside the house. Within twenty minutes she'd be out of sight. Once she reached Grasmere there would be plenty of places where she could shelter and plan the rest of her journey. She would have to find a roadmap somewhere to plan the best route to Whitewell. It was a good plan. Jo felt no guilt at the prospect of taking supplies, which would be replenished anyway, or of stealing the horse. She felt sure that she would have Ginny's blessing.

1 April

Jo had not slept well with the excitement of implementing her plan and the fear of oversleeping. Her rucksack was already packed with adequate supplies for two days. This time she had included a couple of sharp kitchen knives in case of further confrontations with wild dogs. She wasn't sure she had it in her to stab a dog but at least she didn't feel totally defenceless. She had no intention of spending another day stranded in a tree.

The rain had stopped in the early hours and as Jo peered out in the first dim light of the day, she could see that it was dry but misty. She pulled on a waterproof anorak from Ginny's wardrobe, crept out of her room and closed the door silently. As she passed the open door of the old lady's bedroom, she could hear regular breathing. So far, so good. Jo had no idea of the time. If Ginny had left a watch behind, Jo hadn't found it and she hadn't seen a clock in the house that was working. She and Ginny's mother had barely exchanged a word the previous evening. There had been no discussion of meal arrangements and Jo hadn't felt like asking. She had stayed in her room until the coast was clear, then helped herself to some tinned food and another omelette. She was glad to be leaving.

Jo exited quietly through the kitchen door and made her way to the barn. Merrylegs seemed surprised but pleased to see her. Jo calmed her and quickly but efficiently fitted her saddle and harness. As she led Merrylegs out of the barn, Jo was conscious of the noise of the horse's hooves on the farmyard before they reached the start of the path between the house and barn. If Ginny's mother had her bedroom window open, she would surely hear. What would Jo do if she came running out of the house? Jo thought she would leave Merrylegs and run up the path as fast as she could. It was so steep, there was no way she would be caught. Still there was no movement from the house and Jo began the long ascent, leading Merrylegs behind, quieter now on the soil of the path. They gained height very quickly but not without considerable effort, especially for Merrylegs, who stumbled a couple times. Only in the Lake District, thought Jo, would a path run straight up the side of a steep fell. Jo was used to walking holidays in Austria where any steep slope was tackled with a gradual ascent through a series of hairpin bends.

As they climbed Jo could no longer see the farmhouse and

knew her departure was undetected. She wondered whether her absence would even be noticed by such a peculiar woman. Above them it was very misty but Jo assumed this would be burnt off as the sun grew stronger. The path eventually turned to the right at the top of the steepest incline and followed the side of the fell. Now Jo felt able to mount Merrylegs and walk her slowly along the path. This was more like it. The path was not well worn and Jo supposed that in a year or so it would probably have disappeared as nature reasserted itself but it was straight and easy enough to follow. The only thing that concerned Jo was the mist which now enveloped them and rather than burning off, seemed to be thickening. She could only just see the path and nothing at all beyond twenty yards. If this became any thicker, they would have a serious problem.

Merrylegs plodded along and seemed to know the way. Jo wondered whether she had been up there before but thought it unlikely given the steep climb at the start. Jo had lost sight of any path and was reliant on Merrylegs finding her way. Jo decided to dismount and lead Merrylegs for a while so she could be sure they were following the right path. She knew from having studied the OS map that there was only one official path over the top of the fells. If anything, the mist was now even thicker and Jo was getting worried. She couldn't afford to get lost on the top of the fells and if they left the path there was little chance of reaching Thirlmere. Jo was alarmed to discover that she couldn't see any path whatsoever. She got down on her hands and knees and checked in each direction. Nothing. She cursed herself. What a fool! Why had she let Merrylegs walk on when she couldn't see the path?

Jo told herself not to panic. She would work this out. It was only a bit of mist. She took out the map and studied it carefully. Jo always felt more confident when she had a map to consult. She had only been riding for fifteen minutes or so, since climbing the ridge and could only have lost the path in the last few minutes.

She worked out roughly where this would place her on the map. The path would follow the contours along the side of the fell before climbing again, but nothing like as steeply as before, then reaching another mountain lake, Blea Tarn. That would be about two and half miles into the walk. If they had followed the path they should just about be starting the climb towards the tarn. If they had stayed at the same level, they must have drifted slightly to the right which would be due south rather than south-east. That would mean climbing to the left to find the path again. The problem was that Jo had turned round that many times, she no longer knew which way she was facing. Tricky! If she could see the sun, she'd have no problem but the mist was far too thick. This early in the day the sun would be almost due east. Jo stared into the mist in each direction. She could not be certain but thought the mist was slightly brighter to one side and reasoned that this must be east. She took a few steps towards the brightness and found she was climbing. Another glance at the map confirmed that if they were below the path, moving due east they were bound to cross it. If they continued to climb towards the brightness, they must come to the path. That was the theory anyway and Jo thought it was a good one.

Jo led Merrylegs up the slope as she carefully studied the ground in case she missed the path. It took longer than expected and they must have climbed a couple hundred feet until they reached the welcome sight of the rough path disappearing into the mist. Jo reasoned that they must have left the path at quite an angle to be so far off track and she needed to be more careful in the mist. That said, it had cleared a little and returned to around twenty yards visibility. It was good enough to mount Merrylegs once more and proceed at a leisurely pace. The path had levelled off and just to the right Jo could make out Blea Tarn before it began to climb once more to the top of the ridge. The mist was rising quickly now and Jo could just make out a row of glowering crags above her before the path pitched down to the left. This would be the start of the descent to Thirlmere. The worst was over now. Jo inwardly congratulated herself on navigating her way through the mist. Following her midnight swim under the stars, Jo felt she was developing excellent survival skills. Her dad would be proud of her. She wondered whether he would be waiting for her at Whitewell to hear her story or whether he was still out searching for them. She was confident now that she would make it back to the inn but her dad would surely not expect her to have escaped and returned under her own steam. What a tale she would have to tell him.

The path became steeper now as it dropped down towards a wooded area, which Jo had anticipated from her map but she was concerned that she may encounter more dogs. She had no alternative as this was the only route down from the fells. The hillside was very steep and dotted with crags which would make it extremely dangerous to attempt a diversion round the woods without a path, particularly for Merrylegs. As they entered the woods Jo listened carefully but could only hear birds. They encountered some wider, rutted tracks in the depth of the woods which must have taken vehicles in the past, possibly for logging. Jo knew she had to keep to the right and passed Harrop Tarn before emerging from the woods where the path cut steeply down towards the banks of Thirlmere. Jo had to dismount once more as the path was too steep to ride. Jo seemed to spend as much time leading Merrylegs as riding her but she was glad of the company.

They reached the lakeside road around the southern tip of Thirlmere and Jo rode Merrylegs again at a steady walk. She hadn't eaten since the previous evening and as it was at least mid-morning, Jo was getting very hungry but didn't want to stop where they could be seen. After a mile or so they approached a farmhouse and barn but beyond Jo could see the main A road leading south to Grasmere. This was the last chance for a quiet and safe break. As they approached, Jo began to notice that

Merrylegs was limping. The front leg on the right appeared to be giving her trouble. Perhaps she had picked up a stone in her shoe. Jo could see that the barn door was unfastened and walked Merrylegs inside to investigate the problem. There were no signs of life at the farmhouse so Jo felt it was a fairly safe assumption that it was empty. She could see now that Merrylegs was limping heavily but an inspection of all her hooves revealed no obvious problem. Jo had little knowledge of such matters. Although she had ridden for a number of years, she have never owned a horse. She supposed that it must be a muscle or a tendon which would need resting. Either Merrylegs was not used to the exercise or couldn't cope with the slope coming down from the fell. Jo realised that she would have to leave Merrylegs. She had to get home and couldn't afford to wait for however long it would take Merrylegs to recover. Jo realised then that it had been a mistake to take the horse. She could have managed the trek over the tops on foot.

"I'm sorry Merrylegs. What have I got you into?"

Jo considered the options. Across the road from the farm there was an extensive grassy area at the tip of the lake. She thought Merrylegs would be fine grazing there and if she wanted to be under cover she could go into the barn. She unfastened the saddle and lead Merrylegs down to the edge of the lake.

"I've got to leave you Merrylegs but I'll come back for you, I promise. We'll get a horsebox and take you back to the inn. You'll be happy there."

Jo noted that the farm was at Steel End. It would be easy enough to find again. After eating some of her supplies, Jo walked away towards the main road. At first Merrylegs began to follow but was clearly in pain and soon gave up the attempt. Jo hated leaving her but could see no alternative, even though she was terrified at the possibility of a dog attack.

As Jo reached the main road she consulted her map again, estimating another four miles to Grasmere. She would have to be careful as it was a very open road, wide and quite straight. She could see a long way in both directions which meant that she would be easily visible from a distance. She really needed somewhere to hide quickly if she heard any motor vehicles and couldn't risk being recaptured after what she had been through. She needn't have worried, however. The road was completely empty and in less than an hour and a half Jo reached the village of Grasmere. Despite the cuts and scratches on her feet, she had little problem walking now she had trainers that fit. Estimating that it must be around three in the afternoon, Jo considered whether to push on to Ambleside, another five miles or so, but she felt rather tired and needed to rest. She also needed to find somewhere suitable to spend the night. Jo had considered the options whilst walking and felt her best plan now was to look for a mountain bike and a road map to get her home.

The village was mainly stretched out along one road and Jo tried the doors to each home and garage as she passed. If necessary she would break in again but first she would try her luck. There had to be some unlocked properties in a place this size, though after the first ten houses she was beginning to wonder. Every house and every garage securely locked. Jo wondered how many bodies were behind those locked doors and what state they would be in after the best part of six months. The smell would be the giveaway when she opened the door. She tried the front doors, side doors, and back doors where accessible and even sheds if no padlock was visible. Still no luck.

At the eleventh house the front door was unlocked and although the air was musty and stale, there was no tell-tale smell of decay, nor any immediate scuttling of rats. This would do nicely. It was only a small house, part of a row near the middle of the village, and Jo began to explore. She was in a tiny entrance hall and the first door to the left took her into a sitting room. The first thing that struck Jo was how tidy and well-ordered was the room. It was almost as though the owners had just stepped out to buy a newspaper or to have a coffee at one of several nearby cafes. The only indication of the length of absence was a thin layer of dust on everything. There were holiday souvenirs on the mantelpiece and family photographs on a table. Jo thought it looked like an old person's house. She moved on to the back room which was a kitchen/diner with a small conservatory at the back. Again, everything was immaculate but dusty. As she entered the conservatory Jo gasped in shock at the sight of the patio outside. To one side was a wooden swing-seat which appeared to have blown over in the wind but in front of it lay two bodies, or rather virtual skeletons. They were on their backs but their faces were horrifying. The eyes had gone, as had the noses, lips and most of the skin and flesh. Jo had seen a number of dead bodies but these were the worst. She imagined this was the elderly couple that had lived in the house, possibly realising the end was near and choosing to die in their beloved garden. The garden was like the house, immaculate but suffering the ravages of winter. Next to the patio were walled flower beds full of yellow daffodils. As she surveyed the tragic scene a large black crow landed on one of the bodies and began to peck. Jo had to turn away, feeling queasy. There were blinds at the conservatory windows and Jo pulled them all shut. She decided she could spent the night there as long as she couldn't see the bodies.

Jo investigated the kitchen cupboards next to see if there was anything she could use. In the cupboard beneath the oven she was excited to find a little camping gaz just like the one they'd had at home. She turned on the gas and heared a strong hiss. Excellent! She could make coffee or maybe find a tin of something that could be warmed up. Cheered by the prospect of warm food and drink she searched for tins. The best she could find was a tin of minestrone soup and a tin of chopped tomatoes. She still had a tin of baked beans in her rucksack and thought if she put all three together in a pan and the camping gaz lasted long enough, she would have a warm nutritious meal. She left it all on the worktop ready to cook. Other finds were instant coffee and a half full tin of shortbread. This was going to be fine.

Preparing for the night Jo sought light and heat. It didn't take long to find candles dotted around the house, some in holders and some stuck on to saucers. The old couple had clearly survived beyond the power failures. The sitting room had an open fireplace filled with ashes. To the side was a cute little set of implements, a small brush, shovel and tongs on hooks. On the other side was a newspaper and some kindling. What she couldn't see was any coal or logs or any container to put them in. Jo hoped she wouldn't need to go to the back of the house but set to cleaning out the grate and laying the fire with matches at the ready. She just needed to find fuel. In any event she wouldn't light the fire until after dark or any of the candles until all the curtains were closed. It was still a risk but Jo was determined to be comfortable that night.

Having established basecamp, Jo decided to carry on searching the village while there was maybe a couple hours of daylight left. Her remaining objectives were a mountain bike, roadmap, fuel for the fire and some more water. She thought she would be better concentrating on garages. Finding the fuel was easy enough. Just another couple houses along the road Jo found a stack of logs at the side of the house. She made a couple trips carrying an armful of logs and dumped them in the entrance hall. Next she tried virtually every unlocked garage and in the third one she entered were two mountain bikes, which appeared to be in decent condition. They were both full-sized bikes but when she tried them, one was much too high for her, the other maybe an inch or two too high but she felt that would be manageable once she got started. She pumped up the tyres which were a little soft and sprayed all the moving parts with some WD40 that she found on the shelf. The wheels span freely, the brakes were sharp and the handlebars moved easily. She had found her transport though she still lacked a roadmap to plan the route. She knew she'd have to start through Ambleside and Windermere. Perhaps she could find something en route.

At the end of the village Jo reached a bridge which spanned a river flowing down into the lake of Grasmere. Scrambling down to the river, she washed out her two water bottles and refilled them. The water was crystal clear. Time to get settled in at the house. Jo rode her bike back through the village. She was a little wobbly at first but soon found her balance. She could reach the pedals but had to let the bike tip to one side in order to touch the ground. She would manage.

Back at the house and it was beginning to go dark. It had taken Jo longer than she anticipated to find what she needed. It had been a good decision to stay at Grasmere rather than press on to Ambleside. In any event, now that she had a working bike, she would cover the distance much more quickly. Jo went round the house closing every blind and curtain available, then lit sufficient candles in the living room and kitchen to see what she was doing. Next she lit the fire which caught quickly and threw on three of the logs. She would soon have a blaze to take the chill off the place. She emptied her tins into the largest saucepan and lit the camping gaz. It seemed an awful lot of food for one person but Jo was absolutely famished, having not eaten a great deal that day, yet having expended a great deal of energy.

It took quite a long time and a lot of stirring to warm up the soup, if that was still an appropriate description, but by the time it was ready and Jo retired into the sitting room with a steaming bowl on a tray, the fire was roaring. Jo sat on the sofa in front of the fire to enjoy her meal. With the flickering flames and the candles, it was so warm and cosy in the little sitting room, it reminded Jo of the wonderful lounge at Saltersford Hall with the oak panelling. Jo would spend the night in that room, making up a bed on the sofa. After a second large bowl of soup Jo was feeling rather full and decided to leave the rest in the pan for breakfast, hoping that the camping gaz would not expire. She tried one finger of the shortbread. It was not as crisp as it once would have been but was quite acceptable. She would save the rest for the journey home after transferring the contents of the tin into some food bags she found in the kitchen. Jo was planning to keep down the weight of her rucksack and the shortbread would be ideal.

Jo had to borrow a toothbrush from a beaker in the bathroom in order to brush her teeth, trying not to think of the bodies outside, but felt better for it. She used a little more of her water for a quick wash but decided to sleep in the same clothes in front of the fire. There would be time to get cleaned up when she got home. Jo thought she would nod off having a little read and went in search of books. There was a bookcase in one of the bedrooms which seemed a little odd but Jo supposed the sitting room was too small and cramped with the existing furniture. Most of the books were not to Jo's taste, historical romances and spy stories but she settled for Lorna Doone. Of greater interest however was an AA handbook with roadmaps in the back. It was too difficult to find a route by candlelight but Jo could make her plans in the morning. She banked up the fire once more and settled down to read. Whether it was the reading material, the warmth of the fire or Jo's exhaustion, she managed only a few pages before blowing out the candles and snuggling down under a duvet on the sofa. She hoped fervently that Merrylegs would be asleep in the barn and not troubled by any dog packs.

2 April

Up with the dawn and a quick wash, Jo wasted no time before warming up her leftover baked bean/minestrone soup to provide her with fuel for the journey ahead. She opened the curtains and blinds to inspect the weather: a little uncertain but at least it wasn't raining and Jo was glad of that. She had

had an excellent night's sleep in front of the fire and felt well refreshed. While she finished her breakfast Jo consulted the AA map. It was a small scale but sufficient to work out a route. She would avoid the M6 motorway for fear of being spotted but, other than that, plumped for the most direct route, A5074 to take her south of Windermere, a short stretch on the A590, then south on the A6 all the way to Lancaster. There she would have to pick up the cross-country lane over the Forest of Bowland to Dunsop Bridge and turn off to Whitewell for the last few miles. The only difficult piece of navigation would be finding the lane to the moors out of Lancaster, especially as it didn't even merit a road number but she would face that when she got there. Just getting to Lancaster would be huge progress. She tried to measure the distance involved and came up with around 70 miles, a hard day's cycling to be sure but she felt up to it. If she allowed a couple hours for food, toilet breaks and rests, she would be on the road for the best part of nine hours. The sun was just showing itself which indicated perhaps 9.00 am. If she kept to the route Jo could be in Whitewell by 6.00pm, comfortably before dark. She imagined the astonished looks on their faces when she arrived at the inn.

She would travel light. Her only supplies were a bottle of water, a tin of tuna and the shortbread but after a good breakfast, that would suffice. Packing a kitchen knife in case of any problems with dogs and a torch, Jo would wear the anorak to start but there would be room in the rucksack if she became too warm. She was relieved not to walking and excited at the prospect of finishing the day safely home at Whitewell.

Jo set off at a steady pace through the village without pushing too hard, aiming to maintain the same pace throughout the day. She was out of the village in a matter of minutes, re-joining the main A591 south towards Windermere, past the lakes of Grasmere and Rydal Water and soon approaching Ambleside. Pleased at the speed of her progress, so much more effective than walking with the cool morning breeze in her hair pleasantly refreshing, Jo thought how much time she could have saved if she had headed straight to Keswick after escaping from the island and taking a bike from there but she had been terrified of running into Dale and his chums. They must have long since given up on her by now and assumed she had drowned in the lake. In fact, she thought back, it was a miracle that she hadn't and resolved that she would never again swim at night time.

There were the usual sights of destruction and abandoned vehicles in Ambleside but it was easy for Jo to navigate her way through on the bike. She kept going without dropping her pace and followed the north-west shore of Windermere with its lakeside houses and hotels set high above the lake. She knew this stretch well from family holidays. Where the main road left the lake to cut across to Kendal, Jo turned off to follow the lakeside road through the villages of Windermere and Bowness before cutting across on the A5074, climbing up initially to Winster. The cycling was more difficult away from the lake with some fairly steep hills but Jo kept going, using the gears to good effect. She was determined not to get off and push, so she could maintain her rhythm. The scenery was beautiful as the road pitched and turned and took her through typical Lakeland villages, uplifting Jo's spirits. She could suspend belief for a while and think she was on holiday. Jo had always been the keenest cyclist in the family but occasionally they had all rented bikes for the day, usually on designated tracks like dismantled railways. The Tissington Trail near her home in Buxton had been a personal favourite. Sometimes they had attempted more adventurous routes in places like the New Forest in the early summer, delighting in the sight of new-born foals. It made her sad again to think that family outings were in the past. Maybe in the summer she would be able to get out with Lisa and Alice. She hoped they were okay. It suddenly occurred to her that Dale might take it out on her friends in revenge for her escape and the wound she had inflicted on him. If only she had hit him even harder while she had the chance.

These were the thoughts that ran through her mind as she moved steadily through the countryside until the road dropped down again and joined a big dual carriageway. She knew this was the A590 from the south of the lakes to the M6 motorway but only followed it for a couple miles before turning south on the A6, marked towards Milnthorpe. This road would take her all the way to Lancaster. It was still well before midday and Jo felt she was making good time and well on schedule for her six o'clock target. Once she had passed through Milnthorpe, Jo decided she could do with a rest and some refreshment, stopping at the village of Beetham and taking a side road off the A6 so she would be less conspicuous. She propped her bike against a garden wall and realised how stiff her legs and bottom felt, performing some stretches so her muscles wouldn't seize up and sat down gratefully on her anorak as the ground was a little damp, with her back resting against the wall. Until she had stopped, Jo had not realised how much the cycling had taken out of her. She hoped she hadn't been over-ambitious in attempting 70 miles in a day. It was the hills that made it so demanding, particularly cutting across from Windermere. Jo knew she would face a much longer stretch across the high moors from Lancaster to Whitewell. She wasn't particularly hungry however and restricted herself to a few fingers of shortbread to pump up her sugar levels. She allowed herself thirty minutes rest before stiffly mounting her bike once more and re-joining the A6.

Once Jo began cycling again the stiffness relented and she regained her usual rhythm, eating up the miles to Carnforth, the next town of any size. She rode straight through, oblivious now to the scenes of devastation. Even the occasional body lying at the side of the road had no impact as she cycled steadily through the town and on to Bolton-le-Sands, where she registered the views across the expanse of Morecombe Bay until she approached the city of Lancaster. She had another look at the map but it was such a small scale that it was impossible to discern any detail. She would stick to the A6 and follow the through route until she found her lane over the moors. It was a straight run through the outskirts and Jo kept going until she crossed the River Lune on the Skerton Bridge. Reaching a T junction the signs indicated right for the city centre. It wasn't clear whether she was still on the A6 but she would head for the centre until she knew where she was. The sign said Parliament Street but without a town plan that meant nothing to Jo who had never visited Lancaster. Next she came to a cross-roads and went straight over, then a fork where again she plumped for straight on as she knew she was still heading south. This took her onto North Road then Great John Street. The main shopping area appeared to be to her right and the streets were in a mess whereas she was on a wide road for through traffic and she thought she'd stick with it. Jo could see the top of a large dome ahead after the next crossroads and when she reached it, realised that this was Lancaster Town Hall. She cycled around the front of the hall until, with a cry of triumph, she spotted a large town plan mounted on a display board. Now she would be able to make some sense of it. Studying the plan, it was easy enough to spot her location and in the bottom right corner was a lane marked to Lancaster Leisure Park and the Trough of Bowland. That had to be her route.

Jo quickly deduced that she needed to take a left down Nelson Street, cross the canal, along East Road, then turn right down Wyredale Road past Williamson Park and the next left would be her road to the moors. It was imprinted on Jo's memory and she set off with confidence. When she reached Williamson Park, she saw lots of benches around a memorial and thought this would be a good opportunity to rest and refuel before tackling the moors as it had to be early afternoon. The park was a peaceful escape, unharmed by riots and thankfully free of bodies. Sitting in front of the Ashton Memorial, Jo consumed her tuna and half of the remaining shortbreads, enjoying the rest. Getting through Lancaster had not delayed her greatly and she felt she was still roughly on schedule but did not under-estimate the effort required to cross the moors.

After 30 minutes rest she set off once again and was very quickly out of the city, there being little development on her route. Another few hundred yards and Jo's lane passed underneath the eerily quiet M6 motorway. Now she knew she was on the right route. At first the climb was gentle, then progressively steeper, past Brow Top and on up to the top of the moors. Jo was puffing and her legs were aching but she managed to keep cycling. She had incredible views from the top, yet there wasn't a building to be seen for miles around, just open moorland with Lancaster in the distance behind her and beyond was Morecombe Bay. She could even see some of the peaks from the Lake District and was proud of the distance she had covered, at least two-thirds of the journey, maybe nearer three-quarters. The route was up and down now, which was exhilarating to freewheel down the hills but equally frustrating to lose the height gained with such pain and effort.

As Jo crossed the high moors, passing the hamlets of Lee and Marshaw, the weather began to take a turn for the worst, a persistent drizzle driving into her face and the wind had picked up. She still managed steady progress until she reached a long and progressively steep incline which caused her to work her way up through the gears until the pedals were rotating to little effect and she was forced to dismount for the first time. Jo began to push the bike up towards the summit, feeling weak with exhaustion. She couldn't take much more of this and stopped at the top for some water and to finish the rest of her shortbread. She wasn't hungry but felt the sugar might recharge her batteries. Jo was determined to have her next meal at the inn. The lane ahead dropped steeply through a virtual gorge with precipitous sides. At least she could rest her legs for a while and freewheel, picking up speed quickly and as the lane levelled off Jo shot through the hamlet of Sykes in a blur. She knew that Dunsop Bridge would be next which would put her in familiar territory. Then disaster struck.

She was still moving at a fast pace as she left Sykes and the rain was blowing into her face. She failed to notice that the tarmac surface of the lane had been broken up by the winter frosts leaving potholes and deep ruts. Her front wheel dropped a good six inches in to a hole and jammed. Jo completely left the bike, sailed through the air, bounced once on the lane and ended up head-first in a muddy ditch. At first she was so shocked, she didn't realise what had happened. There was no pain as such but she was half immersed in thick peaty mud. She had to spit to clear her mouth and could taste the peat. She wiped the mud from her eyes and nose, slowly composed herself and attempted to escape the ditch. The bike was lying across the lane, twisted out of shape with the front wheel wrecked and would take her no further. She would have to walk. Jo carefully checked herself over. Her right knee was out of her jeans and badly grazed, the blood beginning to ooze down her leg. That must have been where she hit the road. The palm of her left hand was also grazed and full of grit mingling with the blood. She must have put out her hand instinctively as she fell. Otherwise, apart from her head and shoulders being caked in mud, she seemed to be alright. Jo struggled to her feet but as soon as she put her weight on her right foot, the pain was excruciating. It wasn't her knee, it was the ankle. Now she was beginning to register the pain and realised she was in a fix. She couldn't ride and she couldn't walk. The chance of anybody finding her there was pretty remote.

Jo sat at the side of the ditch for a while, trying to think what to do. She couldn't stay there, that was for sure. If a pack of dogs came across her, she wouldn't stand a chance. She could shelter in one of the properties back up the road at Sykes but then what? There may not be any salvageable food. The ankle was not going to mend itself anytime soon and she still needed to get to Whitewell. She would just be postponing the problem. Jo took out her map to work out exactly where she was. It was maybe two to three miles to Dunsop Bridge and another three to Whitewell. In normal circumstances she could walk it in a couple hours but with the ankle, she would need to crawl. At least there was plenty daylight left. She estimated that it was around 4.00 pm and shouldn't be dark before 7.00, maybe earlier if the weather worsened. She might still do it if she could take the weight off her right foot. If she could find a really stout stick that she could use as a crutch, she might manage five or six miles. She looked around but there was nothing suitable. She had no alternative but to crawl back to Sykes and find something, a distance of maybe 150 yards. She would give it a go.

Jo tried hobbling along, putting most of the weight on her left but had to give up after a couple steps. She then tried crawling on her hands and knees but that aggravated her ankle just as much. Finally she resorted to sitting on the road and using her left foot to push herself backwards. The pain was just tolerable and she slowly edged herself back towards Sykes. By the time she reached the first of three houses, she was exhausted again and sat on the ground looking for anything useful. She just needed something to lean on so she could stand upright, perhaps a length of wood from a broken fence or maybe she could find a prop of some sort in a shed. Nothing useful presented itself at the first house. Jo resumed her bottom-shuffle to the second property where she could see a shed behind the house. She pushed herself along the side of the building until she spotted a yard brush propped up outside the side door. That might work, she thought. Jo eased herself upright leaning against the wall, turned the brush upside down and tucked the brush head under her armpit. It was sturdy enough and took her weight. She tried taking a step, using the brush as a crutch. It was a few inches too long for the purpose which meant propping it a couple feet to the side but it certainly took the pressure off her ankle. However, the stiff bristles cut into her armpit. The anorak provided some protection but Jo knew it would be unbearable after a hundred yards, let alone five or six miles. Then she had an idea. She didn't really need her rucksack any more. Pushing the torch into her pocket and the kitchen knife into her belt, Jo could carry the water bottle in her left hand even though it was badly grazed. That left her an empty rucksack which she wound round the brush head, positioning most of the material on the bottom. She tried walking with it again. It was uncomfortable, but tolerable. With frequent rests, she thought she could do it.

Not wishing to lose any more time as the evening gloom was closing in, Jo set off immediately in the direction of Dunsop Bridge. She was on the move again, albeit slowly, and once she had established a rhythm, she soon got the hang of using the brush in place of her right leg. Little did she know that at that very moment, less than three miles away, a small convoy of vehicles on the main road from the north was making its way through Dunsop Bridge bringing the rest of the girls, and Bill's body, back to Whitewell.

Progress was slow and by the time Jo reached Dunsop Bridge the night was closing in. She had fallen twice, adding to her growing list of injuries by cracking her right elbow on the road surface. The problem was the rounded smooth top of the brush handle and having to push on it well out to her right which caused it to slip. The top of the handle was becoming rougher with use but the fear of falling again slowed her progress even more. Jo resisted the temptation to rest at Dunsop Bridge as she was worried about the failing light and knew it would take her another couple hours at least to hobble through to Whitewell, by which time it would be pitch black. There was no moon because of the cloud cover and the rain was getting heavier, washing mud from her matted hair into her eyes. However, it wasn't the pain and discomfort that troubled her. She had grown used to that. It was the prospect of dogs hunting after dark. She hadn't heard or seen any dogs on her journey that day but didn't fancy her chances of defending herself with a kitchen knife when she couldn't even stand up. Jo was also getting hungry and wished she had brought more food. She also finished the last of her water and discarded the bottle. Although she was following the river beside the road to Whitewell and could have refilled the bottle, Jo considered it unwise to attempt to clamber down the bank with her injuries as she may have been unable to climb back up. In any event, ditching the water released her left hand to hold the torch which would at least warn her of further potholes. She had had enough falls for one day.

Jo followed the twists of the road, hoping at every bend to see the lights of the inn but it was further than she expected. At least she knew she was on the right road and it would be impossible to miss the inn. The rain was coming down in waves now and the mud from her hair was getting everywhere, just to complete her misery. The only light came from the small weak torch and as if to confirm the arrival of night, she could hear a pair of owls calling to each other. The whole of her right shoulder was now numb with the repeated effort of pushing on the brush. She was cold, wet, exhausted and with pain throughout her body, the only thing keeping her going the knowledge that salvation was somewhere around the corner. What a journey she had had since escaping from the island, what an adventure to relate to the others over a hot meal. One day she could tell her grandchildren and she imagined their faces and questions.

Just as she was lost in her thoughts and least expected it, Jo turned a corner and saw the sight she was waiting for, the lights of the inn, no more than 100 yards away. Her spirits lifted and she redoubled her efforts. Four days after leaving the island, she was home at last! As she approached the inn her torch picked out the vehicles parked outside and she froze in horror. Dale's van! It couldn't be, not here. Surely they hadn't come all the way back here to recapture her. What had happened to the others at the inn? Were they all captive again? Her heart sank. Jo didn't know what to do. She was all in. she couldn't go any further but she couldn't surrender to that odious Dale. She still had the kitchen knife. Maybe she could stab him but he wouldn't be alone. He would have Leroy and Geordie with him, perhaps Joe as well. After all she'd been through, this was just the last straw. Jo wanted to sit down and cry.

She at least had the presence of mind to switch off the torch and hoped it hadn't been spotted. Giving the front of the inn a wide berth, Jo made her way round to the side, thinking she could perhaps peek in at the patio doors to see what was happening. She could probably reach the Piggeries unobserved but doubted that there would be any food there. She was in a quandary. Jo hobbled round to the side of the patio trying not to make a sound, easing the brush quietly against the stone flags. She could hear voices coming from inside the inn, in fact quite an animated conversation, which was puzzling again. Jo tried to peek inside just as an arm was raised in the action of pulling the curtains across. Another shock. It was Lisa! How could she be here? At the same time, Lisa saw Jo and recoiled in surprise, then stared in astonishment until her face lit up. She hurriedly unlocked the door and swung it open.

"Jo? It can't be. Is it you? It's impossible!"

Then she realised that it was indeed possible and threw her arms round Jo. Others behind her came running to the door.

"My God! Look at you. Jesus, what have you been through. We all thought you were dead. Have you walked all the way back?"

Jo eventually found her voice.

"I don't understand. I left you on the island. But Dale's van? I thought they'd come back."

"No. We were rescued. There was a big fight. Dale's dead. They're all dead. We used the van for Bill's body."

"Bill's body? Oh no, poor Alice! What about my dad?"

"He's okay. He's up in his room, I think. He'll be all the better for seeing you. They told us you'd drowned."

Well I nearly did. It's a long story but I want to see Dad first. Can you help me? I can't walk on this ankle."

There was quite a commotion by this time, a mixture of elation at the sight of Jo alive, concern at the state of her and curiosity as to how she managed to get home. Jo's head was spinning as they carried her inside. "How could they rescue you? How did they know where you were?" she asked Lisa.

"That's also a long story. I'm sure your dad will be delighted to fill you in. I can't wait to see his face. I'm surprised he hasn't heard the noise. Perhaps he's taking a nap."

Jim and Phil carried Jo upstairs and knocked on Tom's door. No response.

"Hey Tom. Look who's come to see you!" bellowed Jim. Still no response.

Jim opened the door and peeked inside. Tom was slumped in his chair, his head to one side and his arms hanging limply. An empty glass was on the table next to an equally empty whisky bottle. An opened packet of pills lay on the table with another discarded on the floor.

"I don't like the look of this," said Jim. Phil stepped past, grabbed Tom by the shoulders and shook him hard. Still no response.

"Jesus. He's taken a bloody overdose."

Jo hobbled in, using the door for support.

"Dad, dad! It's me, Jo! I've come back! Wake up!"

Jim dashed back to the head of the stairs and shouted for Chris Lucas. Within seconds, it seemed, she was there, surveying the scene with concern. She held Tom's wrist.

"Well, there's a pulse. We're not too late. What's he taken?"

She picked up the empty packets.

"Is this all of it? These are all painkillers. It looks like he's taken a lot but he won't top himself with these. I think it's the whisky that's knocked him out. I hope that bottle wasn't full. I suggest dipping his head in a bucket of cold water. That might provoke a response."

Phil ran to the bathroom and brought back the bucket of water kept for flushing the toilet. They all manoeuvred Tom so they could position his head over the bucket and pushed it in, spilling water all over the floor.

Now Jo's panic over the sight of the medicine packages was replaced by a fear that her dad would be drowned.

After a worrying delay of no more than a couple seconds, Tom lurched back, coughing and spluttering. He gazed around him confused with his eyes unfocused until they rested on Jo.

"What? Jo? What's going on? Am I dead?"

"Dad! Are you alright? I got back. I escaped from the island. It's taken days to get here."

Jo was crying, her concern turned to relief. Tom was still confused but threw his arms round his muddy battered daughter.

"Jo! My God! I don't believe it. I thought you were dead, I'd failed you. I couldn't take it."

Now Tom was crying more than Jo. The others decided to withdraw quietly and leave them to it.

PART THREE

CHAPTER SEVENTEEN

NEW CARTMEL

Twelve Years Later

The big day had arrived at last after months of eager anticipation and weeks of preparation, our ten year anniversary festival. There had been considerable debate over how much resource we could afford to deploy on the event as we are essentially a subsistence settlement with little to spare but after all, ten years was an important milestone and we were all justly proud of what we had achieved since settling at Cartmel. The settlement now is unrecognisable from our first efforts and we think we have something that will stand the test of time.

My key role on the day was to entertain Sajid Mehta, the deputy leader of Ripley Settlement in North Yorkshire as part of the exchange visit. We value the exchanges very highly and this was our first visit from Ripley. Brian was looking after the Ripley leader and the others of the six person exchange had been farmed out to appropriate personnel. As Deputy Chairman of New Cartmel Council it fell to me to receive Sajid. I should say joint Deputy Chairman as Adam also holds that title but his engineering skills are in such demand that Adam spends little time on administrative duties, other than attending the monthly meetings. I am quite happy to take on the bulk of the work as it seems to fit better with my role as librarian, part-time teacher and historian. I am simply grateful that we are able to allocate some resource beyond the day to day necessities of putting food on the table and keeping the settlement running. I have actually taken on quite a lot of Brian's role as Chairman, given his frequent bouts of ill-health. He has done exceptionally well to lead the settlement for ten years but lately he's been finding it to be a strain.

I thought it appropriate to show Sajid our library facilities in the first instance as it's a major part of my function in the community and I am very proud of what we have achieved.

"So, this is my empire Sajid. I suspect some of them view this as my personal vanity project but I like to think it will make a long term contribution to the success of our community."

"Oh I'm sure it will Tom. I'm quite envious of your facility here. We inherited a small library at the castle, old literary classics and lots of rather obscure stuff but hardly anything after the nineteenth century. I can see this is properly organised."

Sajid's community are based at Ripley Castle but they are looking to expand into the village and hoping to pick up ideas from us. I started our library soon after we moved to Cartmel and it turned into quite a big project. We housed it in the old Priory C of E school, expanding their teaching materials into a fully-fledged academic, technical and recreational library by taking over two classrooms, the school being far larger than we would require for many years.

"As you can see Sajid, we have a pretty comprehensive coverage of English literature, everything from Chaucer and Shakespeare to contemporary classics from the likes of Ian McEwan and Sebastian Faulks, even the Harry Potter series. We think we've got something for every taste. Most of it was sourced at Waterstones. You could probably do the same in Harrogate. That's your nearest town is it?"

Sajid nodded in agreement.

"We're also proud of our English history section, everything from the Romans to the Cold War. These are mainly for use in the school of course. Very few of the adults dip into these, more's the pity. English Literature and history form the core of our academic teaching but we also see it as a way of preserving our culture. Practical skills take priority of course but unless we can maintain our culture, we are at risk of descending into a new Dark Age within a few generations."

"I couldn't agree more Tom. We've just confined ourselves to survival skills at Ripley but I would be very keen to move into these areas. So, you run the school as well, do you?"

"Good Lord, no. My work at the library and for the Council takes up most of my time. I'll introduce you to Christine Salt shortly. She heads the school and teaches English and English Literature. I just come in for some of the history lessons for the Middle and Senior School. It's split into four you see but our age structure is such that most of the children are in the crèche and the Junior School. We have 39 on the school roll but only six are in the senior school, that's 12 to 15 years, and four are in the middle school, which is 8 to 11. We have ten in the junior division, that's 4 to 7, but 19 in the crèche from six months to three years. So at the moment it's mainly early years stuff where I don't get involved. The older ones I take for history through from 1066 to the present. We expect the school to expand quite rapidly. At present we have 14 breeding mothers and we encourage them to have a minimum of four children each, more if they wish. Assuming two girls apiece, our breeding population, which we take as 16 to 40, should double with every generation, so the school age population increases exponentially. We've made population projections for the next 50 years, though the mortality is difficult to estimate. Our entire population at present is 69, with only 30 adults, which requires an extremely productive workforce to make any progress. This is why the children enter the crèche at six months to economise on child care. The mothers have all got essential day jobs."

"I see. I'd like to sit down with you and work through your

population projections before I go, if that's okay. Our settlement has grown through people joining us but our birth rate is nothing like yours and we haven't made such long-term plans. We have nearly 50 but we can accommodate these quite easily in the castle which is very secure. Taking on the rest of the village, which is basically rows of old cottages, this requires a lot of planning."

"No problem, Sajid. We've recruited outsiders as well as we've come across them, a lot in isolated farms. We even had a small group turning up at the gate in the early days but not in the last four or five years. Our future growth will depend on our plans which will inevitably produce a very young age structure. We're really designing the settlement for an optimum size of 250 but subsequent generations may decide to revise that upwards."

I took Sajid into the next room where I introduced Milly, my assistant, who was sorting and cataloguing the recent additions to the technical library.

"Officially Milly is still an apprentice but we expect to upgrade her to librarian shortly. You see, we regulate all our trades and professions to maintain the necessary skill base. The head of each trade is designated a master and every master is required to have at least one apprentice. When they are fully competent they become a qualified tradesperson in their chosen field and with sufficient experience, can become a master in turn. We have masters in engineering, property maintenance, baking, brewing, horticulture, animal husbandry, blacksmith, tailoring, hairdressing, you name it. Some of them are not full-time roles. All the children in the senior school are allocated apprenticeships as well as receiving tuition in other crafts. We try to give them a range of skills but at least one specialism, so we have flexibility to move people around if need be."

What I didn't divulge to Sajid was that Milly was taken on as a rehabilitation project after a period of severe depression. Unfortunately, her problems started with her incarceration at

Derwent Isle. She had been taken six weeks before the Whitewell girls and for the first month was the sole prisoner. A couple months after we got her back to Whitewell, her pregnancy was confirmed and she worked out that Vince, Monty's second in command, was the father. Milly was distraught and made a couple unsuccessful attempts to abort the child. Six months later Milly had a baby daughter and most of us thought she had reconciled herself to the situation as she was a lovely healthy baby. After two weeks Milly had still not decided on a name which should perhaps have alerted us to what was going on in her mind. A few days later we woke to find Milly cradling her soaking wet and very dead baby. She had drowned her in the river. There were no tears or hysterics, just a quiet satisfaction. Milly had never been the same since. She faced every situation with total apathy and was distant even from the girls of her own age. We've given her routine tasks to perform that don't require a great deal of training and she does them but without enthusiasm. She's 34 now and quite an attractive woman but despite lots of encouragement from the other women, she has spurned any male approaches. Since she has joined the library, I've been able to delegate many tasks and given her some responsibility. There are occasional signs that she may be finally emerging from the dark place created by Monty's misguided experiment.

The other real victim of Derwent Isle was Alice, which troubled me greatly. I felt responsible for recruiting Bill and Alice to the Whitewell group yet Bill ended up dead and Alice permanently damaged. I don't know if it was the witnessing of her father's shooting and watching him die or her manic execution of Monty which damaged her the most, possibly a combination of the two. Nobody blamed poor Alice for killing Monty even though we had decided against doing so, and everybody rallied round to support her. She didn't become depressed in the way that Milly did and she continued to function outwardly in a normal way, marrying William Fernyhough and now with three children at the school, working on the farm conscientiously tending the animals and maintaining a good family home. Yet there's a hard edge to her that undoubtedly derives from her experience on Derwent Isle. She was a lovely girl in her teens, quiet but always friendly and with a good word for everyone. Since Derwent Isle she has acquired a toughness and independence, bordering on sociopathic. Jo still sees her which is inevitable in such a small, closed community, but they are no longer close friends.

As for Jo, she bore no mental scars from her experience. It seems an odd thing to say but I'm sure she enhanced her personal confidence and resilience through facing adversity. At first I was horrified when she related her adventures, particularly Dale's attack and how close she came to drowning in the lake but that was replaced by pride in the way Jo had thought through her problems and overcome them, even to the extent of navigating by the stars on the point of drowning in freezing waters. I always knew Jo had a practical approach, an ability to cope, but I would never have imagined she was so capable and resourceful. Jo's story has become part of the village folklore and I understand it will even feature in today's celebrations. If I had harboured any feelings of remorse at my part in Dale's death, they were certainly extinguished when I heard Jo's story. If anyone deserved to die at Derwent Isle, it was Dale. Jo was married three years ago to Mark Ecclestone who joined our settlement a couple years before. Last year they made me a grandfather with baby Lucy. Sue would be so proud. Lucy's eight months old and in the school crèche with several other babies of similar age but Jo spends most of her time with the horses at Pit Farm. That's where we keep the livestock and grow the more extensive crops. She works with most of the animals but specialises in breeding and training the horses. We think it's important to maintain a productive herd for the future as, although at present we continue to run an extensive fleet of vehicles, it's inevitable that at some point in the future the horses will take over for transport and pulling farm machinery. We're already having to economise on the use of fuel. Merrylegs is still with Jo, albeit rather elderly. She produced a couple foals soon after we started breeding at the farm but she's past it now and kept as Jo's pet really. Although Jo initially found it difficult leaving Lucy at the crèche, she loves her work at the farm and says she has the best job in the village. Jo's been accredited as a master in horse husbandry and is shortly due to take on an apprentice of her own. She's also booked in to contribute to the farming lessons for the seniors at the school. I am so proud that Jo has made a good life for herself and to think I would have missed it all had I succeeded in my bungled attempt to take my own life.

Anyway, I digress. Our little guided tour for Sajid continued with the technical library. These materials have been carefully sourced both from bookshops and academic libraries. We made several trips to Manchester, returning with van loads from the Universities and the Central Reference Library. We now have collections and manuals for every trade and profession in the village and they are used extensively for reference or education. It's all comprehensively catalogued and we're still adding to it as required when gaps in our resources are identified. I see this as our investment in the future of New Cartmel and, more than that, a way of salvaging something from the centuries of scientific research and technical development that would otherwise be lost. I believe it's quite possible that we now have one of the best working libraries in the country. Sajid was duly impressed, almost overwhelmed.

I showed Sajid the two working photocopiers used sparingly for educational purposes.

"My goodness. These facilities are impressive Tom. And where does the power come from?"

"Ah right. That's a good question but you're taking me out of my field there. If you want technicalities, you'll need to speak to Adam. He and his team have set it all up but I can tell you roughly how it's evolved. When we first set up in New Cartmel we used a lot of mobile generators and we still have one in the school as a backup but Adam found that was rather inefficient, so after a year or so one of our biggest projects was to install an industrial sized generator to supply the whole village. Adam had to install cabling and all sorts to distribute the power. That was okay for a couple of years but we were finding it increasingly difficult to obtain sufficient diesel to keep it going. We've long since raided all the local farms, which was the best source, but beyond that we think the bulk of the available fuel is still in the tanks of cars and lorries, particularly the former as people panic bought when the flu hit but didn't get a chance to use it. We still syphon petrol and diesel out of car fuel tanks but we can't afford the resource to be doing this constantly. If a car's been abandoned with the keys in the ignition, that's fine, but most of them are locked up on driveways, in garages or on the road. For the time it takes to break in to houses, locate car keys and syphon off whatever's left in the tank, it can take hours just to fill a couple jerry cans. We just don't have the manpower. We then decided to go for wind turbines and if you look out of the window here, that one supplies electricity to the school buildings. When you entered the village at the main gate in the security fencing, you must have noticed the watchtower just inside the corner of the compound. There are four of those, one at each corner of the village. Each has a large turbine on the top and Adam uses those to supply the electricity to the fencing. There's another one on the flour mill behind the bakery and one on the microbrewery near the centre of the village. I'll show you those later. The problem as I understand it is that the wind turbines don't produce a constant supply. If they produce too much, we don't have any way of storing it and if they don't produce enough, the main generator has to take over. It creates a tricky problem which has absorbed a huge amount of Adam's time. I suppose in the old days these things would be controlled by computers and

386

cut in and out automatically but ours apparently require a lot of monitoring and manual intervention. I know Adam is planning to erect more wind turbines, to economise further on the use of the generator. As I say, Adam will fill in your team on the technical specifications if you want to go down that road."

We had reached the school hall with a stage at one end and stacks of chairs around the sides.

"This is where we hold our council meetings, in fact any meetings required in the village. We can accommodate the whole village in here, man, woman and child, if need be. However we restrict our meetings to a minimum as people are too busy to give up their time."

I took Sajid to a small office at the corner of the hall.

"This is what I think of as the control centre, it used to be the school office and Chris Salt has a desk in here for the school admin but that's kept to a minimum. She's in class at the moment. The other desk is used by my son-in-law, Mark. He's the communications manager, operating the short-wave radio and editing the quarterly newsletter. He has contacts all-round the country now and quite a few abroad. Don't ask me how it works. I think it's something to do with crystals, like spies used to operate in the Second World War. I've saved you a copy of the latest newsletter to take back with you. There's a riveting piece from the Isle of Wight settlement where they're pretty sure that the royal family took refuge for a while before flying abroad. We've also got reports from France, Germany and Holland."

A map on the wall showed England, Scotland and Wales with every survivor settlement identified and isolated dots where individual farms were still operating. There was even a dot at Keswick for old Merlin. I'd been back to see him a couple times and he was delighted to hear of our rescue operation based on his intelligence. His cat community is thriving and I was even persuaded to take a few kittens back to keep down the vermin. They've become firm favourites at the village.

After popping into Chris's English lesson with the seniors and Jim Clarke's Maths lesson for the juniors, our tour of the school was complete and it was obvious that Sajid was greatly impressed.

"This is fantastic Tom! I'm so glad I came. Some of us are completely consumed with day to day survival but you're building a future here. There is so much we can learn. I was particularly asked to check out your security arrangements against external attack and internal control."

"Sure. Security's not really my area but I can show you what's in place and I do have an occasional role in the administration of justice. Let's step outside."

We moved into the school grounds and I pointed out the obvious which was a large watchtower, basically just a platform with a little roof over it, accessed by a twenty foot ladder.

"You see the school is at one corner of our security compound, so we sited a watchtower in the grounds. It's not guarded on a regular basis as we can't afford the manpower but in any emergency the four watchtowers can be manned in minutes, are supplied with rifles and can signal to each other. That gives us a complete view of the surrounding area and this tower communicates with the school where we have command and control, basically the same personnel that form the council. There were five roads leading into Cartmel when we arrived and one of our early projects was to block the two roads to the south, one to the east and one to the north-west with boulders which extend to any accessible land to the side of the roadblocks. The only point of access left is to the north-east where you will have arrived through the entrance gate next to the north-east watchtower. The fencing is heavy duty industrial quality, twelve feet high and electrified at night time. Pit Farm, where we keep all the livestock and the bulk crops, is outside the compound but we have five feet of electrified fencing around the farm. That's basically to keep the dogs out, though they still try."

"Do you have problems with the dogs?"

"God yeah! You'd better believe it. There are several vicious packs in the area and there seem to be more and more of them. They've established themselves at the top of the food chain and have taken over the woods. We used to come across them when we were hunting but they have no fear. At one time you could fire a shot and they'd all disperse but not anymore. We don't hunt these days as we farm all the livestock we need. We have deer, cattle, sheep, goats, pigs, rabbits, geese, ducks and chickens but we do still use the woods to cut fuel for the fires. We manage it carefully and can cut enough locally at Hesketh Wood, Cark Shaws or Park Wood. The dogs don't live there but they do come in to hunt. Our lads always make sure they're armed and we have a policy of shooting dogs on sight. Of course the farm attracts them and they're always trying to get at our stock. They managed to get in a couple times in the early days but we've improved the fencing since then."

"And what about internal control. This is something you're involved in?"

"Well again it comes down to the council. There are twelve of us and we take responsibility for keeping order, resolving disputes and enforcing a criminal code in serious cases, but they're few and far between. We don't attempt to impose lots of petty regulations. As long as people do their job and contribute to the community, we try to let them get on with it. We're not trying to run a prison camp. People get on pretty well as a rule but occasionally there's a dispute and three of us from the council will adjudicate when they put their case to us. They get an immediate decision which is final, no appeals. We get a few fights, perhaps if the lads have had a bit to drink, usually over a girl. Generally we give them a warning and smooth things over but if the same person offends repeatedly we have a scale of punishments, perhaps a period without alcohol or additional menial tasks. If a youngster is seriously out of line we will administer corporal punishment. It's usually only needed the once. Our ultimate sanction is exile but that's reserved for the most serious cases."

Sajid looked shocked. "So, has anybody been exiled?"

"Only once in ten years. One Stuart Grindey for a vicious rape. He was only twenty and the girl was sixteen. She was rather flirtatious and had transferred her affections elsewhere. He forced himself on her and when she fought back, he knocked her about quite badly. He had only been with us a couple years. The whole of the council was convened and we decided we had to make an example of him. We gave him a week's supplies and deposited him outside the gate. I've no idea what happened to him. That was four years ago but he's not turned up at any of the settlements we've contacted since. I know it sounds harsh for a first offence but it's the only sanction we've got for a serious crime. We can't afford to resource a prison and have somebody sitting there inactive. As I say, with only one occurrence in ten years, it's not really been an issue."

I took Sajid from the school grounds towards the village centre. Opposite the school was the village green, the only piece of uncultivated land within the compound. Everywhere else was given up to fruit and vegetables with extensive greenhouses.

"The greenhouses allow us to grow more exotic crops like peppers, cherries, oranges and lemons as well as the obvious tomatoes and salad stuff. They also enable us to extend the seasons for some of our crops. In the spring and summer we virtually live on salads. We have more than sufficient root crops for the winter and with the help of some bottling, we have fruit right through the year. There's hops and barley to supply the micro-brewery – you must taste the New Cartmel Bitter before you go – enough wheat to provide a year's supply of flour at the mill. We have a pretty healthy diet really. Our only sin is the bakery. Emma's cream cakes are to die for! There'll be plenty of those around tonight for the festival. The fresh cream comes from our own dairy at the farm. They make several types of cheese, butter of course, yoghurt, cream. There's also fresh eggs from the farm every day. There's not much we can't produce here."

"I believe the only thing we have at Ripley that you are missing is bee hives. We have several and produce excellent honey. We will prepare you a hive to take back on your return visit. We have spare protective suits as well. The honey can also be used as a substitute for sugar."

"That's great Sajid. We have a small crop of sugar beet but honey would be a luxury."

Much activity was underway on the village green, the main site for the celebrations. Various stalls were being erected for food and games, a large beer tent in the centre of the green and, the jewel in the crown, the spit for a hog roast. I wondered whether this may offend Sajid's sensitivities but he informed me that his cultural background was Hindu, not Muslim, though he no longer observed a religion.

"We need to be back here at four for the start of the festival. Brian's going to say a few words but he's promised to keep it brief."

I led Sajid along the Causeway with the hive of activity on the village green to our left and a field of vegetables and soft fruit bushes to our right. Behind and to the left of the field rose the majestic Cartmel Priory, largely redundant but still a beautiful focal point to our settlement. At the end of the Causeway we turned right towards the Priory, the streets lined with houses.

"As you can probably see, most of these houses are empty but we make sure they're weatherproof with a sound roof and windows as we will need them in the future. We live in family units to economise on fuel, so we're using about fifteen houses at present, mainly grouped around the central square which is just ahead. I'm widowed with no plans to re-marry so I share my house with my daughter Jo, son-in-law Mark and baby Lucy.

Because we've maintained all the properties in the centre of the village we can bring additional stock into use quite quickly as we expand. We'll never need to build new houses as we'll need only fifty to sixty houses for our planned optimum and some of the outlying properties that are surplus to requirements, we strip out for spare materials."

As we approached the Priory, we passed the bakery and brewery on the left.

"We'll just have a peek in here. This is where it's all happening today."

A sign above the building declared "Unsworth Bakehouse".

"The bakery and brewery were in use in the old Cartmel. We've not had to change much here. The flour mill is round the back there and we have a fruit processing room where they do the bottling and jam making. You must take some jars of our cherry jam, it's so good."

Emma was in charge in the bakery but she'd drafted in extra support for the day and four of them had been at it full pelt since dawn. A huge volume of bread rolls and cakes of every description filled the shelves. Sajid was invited to sample a cake and on my recommendation, accepted an egg custard, Emma's speciality. He was suitably impressed.

We entered the grounds of the Priory and were immediately faced with the old cemetery.

"There were no survivors from the old Cartmel, so we have no attachment to this part of the cemetery but we still keep it tidy out of respect. Some of the older children work in here at the weekends."

I pointed to a corner of the cemetery to the right with fresh flowers on the graves.

"That's the New Cartmel cemetery, all the burials from the last ten years. Most of them were in our first winter here. We lost nine people in the Second Wave."

This was the general term given to the return of the virus

three years after the first pandemic, though in strictness I suppose it would have been a further mutation. We think it was brought by a stranger who arrived but was taken ill the following day. By the time we appreciated the seriousness of the situation, it was too late and the virus spread like wildfire, infecting the entire village within a week. Those of us who contracted the original virus and survived suffered a severe bout of flu. Others who had been incredibly lucky to avoid the original virus had no resistance and were like sitting ducks. The whole of the Lucas family, Phil, Chris, and little Anna were wiped out in a matter of days, John and Helen Salt succumbed, as did old Paul Naden and Paul Fernyhough together with a couple of recent arrivals. It was a heavy blow but thankfully there had been no recurrence since. People believe that the viruses have finally died out but we subsequently took the precaution of not accepting any visitors or sending any of our people to other settlements unless they appear to be in perfect health. Those of us that survived have generally exhibited pretty robust health and that extended to the children born here. None of the traditional childhood diseases like measles, mumps, chicken pox and whooping cough have been seen and our experience appears to have been shared in all the other settlements we have visited. We do appear to have created a healthier stock, which is just as well given our poor medical facilities.

Medical care is our weakest area and the council is acutely aware of this key development need. We simply have no doctors or dentists and no remaining drugs. We were fortunate to recruit Claire Potts from the Patterdale settlement, who came with my old chum, Winston Barnes shortly after we were set up. Claire used to be a hospital nurse but now she does the lot. Any medical problems are referred to Claire; she's the village herbalist, physio, and midwife and has even been known to extract teeth, without any anaesthetic of course. She has done extremely well. I've even seen her re-insert a dislocated shoulder following an accident at the farm, which was most impressive. Claire has some help with the maternities from some of the older women and out of 25 or so births to date only one went badly wrong with the loss of mother and child. We've had a couple stillbirths and quite a few miscarriages but that's probably only to be expected.

Claire had no experience of dentistry whatsoever and was very brave to offer any service. In fact she didn't really offer. Adam had a huge abscess and was climbing the walls. He pleaded with her to try something and had to down a quarter of a bottle of brandy before surrendering himself to Claire's pliers. Credit to her, she managed to get the root out with a great bulbous abscess attached to it. Lots of rinsing with saltwater prevented any infection setting in. It provided a very good lesson to the children to look after their teeth. Fortunately, we have a pretty healthy diet apart from Emma's delicious cakes.

As lunchtime approached I delivered Sajid to Brian's house in The Square where a lunch was being prepared for the visiting party. Sajid thanked me for my guided tour and we promised to meet up again at the festival that evening.

*

The entire village was gathered at four on the green facing the temporary stage erected for the presentation. Brian stood before them and cleared his throat.

"Thank you everybody and welcome, especially our guests from Ripley. I must say, you picked an excellent time to visit. I'll keep this brief but I must say a few words to mark this auspicious occasion, ten years in New Cartmel. It gives me enormous pleasure to say that. There were times when it seemed unlikely, when we were a small group in Whitewell and our young women were abducted, when we lost many of our founder members in the Second Wave, but we've overcome every problem put in our path to establish a secure, productive and vibrant community which can now move from strength to strength. We have a critical mass, a healthy birth-rate, a first class school, a copious supply of healthy food throughout the year and some amazing engineering to provide for our comfort and security. This place is a fantastic success and that's down to the hard work and team ethos displayed by every one of you."

"We know of 31 similar settlements around the country and look forward to exchange visits from all of them in time, learning from each other. As we expand we'll spawn further settlements and will eventually be in a position to move on from subsistence economies to specialise and manufacture goods, trading with each other. Mankind came perilously close to extinction but we're on the way back and you can all be proud of your contribution. Our community is ten years old and going strong. Enjoy the rest of the day. You deserve it. Thank you all."

Brian beamed as he received a spontaneous round of applause, then people dispersed to enjoy the festivities. I helped Brian down from the stage as he had suddenly appeared to become unsteady.

"Well said, Brian. I couldn't agree more. Are you okay?"

"Yes, thanks Tom. I'll try some of this tempting food, then I think I'll have a little lie down and leave the youngsters to it. Can you make sure our friends from Ripley enjoy themselves? I just don't have the energy anymore. I was hoping to see the year out as Chairman but I really don't think I'm up to it. Do you think you could step up for the rest of the year until the elections? You'll probably be unopposed anyway. I've mentioned it to Adam and he's happy to support you. I think he'd rather concentrate on his engineering projects and the more contact we have with other settlements, the more his skills will be in demand."

"Of course I will Brian. You deserve a rest. We can raise it at next week's meeting. Now if you'll excuse me, I think I'm due to perform in the archery competition."

Targets were set up on the other side of the drainage channel which ran across the middle of the green, such that the arrows were fired away from the various stalls and other activities where most of the people were gathered. There were two competitions, one for adults and one for children under sixteen. I felt special provision should be made for us over sixties but my suggestion fell on deaf ears. A selection of bows were available of different sizes, weights and tensions, all home-made from branches cut in the local woods and beautifully turned out. I spent some time selecting the most suitable bow and fired a couple practice arrows as I could tell this was a competition to be taken seriously. There were twenty adults in the event and we each released ten arrows for a score out of 100. My first arrow fell short of the target and the second sailed over the top before I found the range and scored a respectable 62. The best ten would go through to the final and I felt I was in with a shout.

While the competition proceeded I decided to try my skills at the penalty shoot-out. That looked easy enough and I was assured that I would not be required to take a turn in goal. We used the regular goalposts where the senior and middle children play football. The penalty spot was the regulation twelve yards from the goal but I hadn't appreciated that the goal was only three-quarter size which gave the goalkeeper an excellent chance of reaching the ball. I am ashamed to report that my efforts produced an embarrassing four out of ten. Even Jo managed five, much to her delight and I decided it was time to slink off to the beer tent for some refreshment.

My old mate Winston was serving the ale from a barrel resting on a trestle. "Oh Win, how ya doing? I'm ready for a pint of New Cartmel best bitter. Have one yourself, why don't you?"

"Aye Tom. Don't mind if I do. I'll nurse it like as I'm doing a two hour shift in here. Won't be any good if I'm flat on me back."

Sajid was passing the tent with the rest of the Ripley delegation and I called them in.

"I insist you try this brew, gents. It's simply the best, a wonderful bitter hoppy taste."

When Winston had served everyone, we drank a toast to the support between our communities. They all shared my appreciation of the beer; at least I'm fairly confident they were not merely being diplomatic.

I introduced Winston and explained the circumstances of our meeting. "There wasn't much call for train drivers in New Cartmel, so Winston divides his time between the brewery, bake-house and flour mill, as well as helping on the farm at harvest time, mind you, the whole village gets involved in that."

As the Ripley group moved on, Adam entered the tent so I felt obliged to stay for a second pint while we discussed his latest projects for the village. He was still looking to expand the number of wind turbines and hoping to install some solar panels to reduce even further our dependence on the diesel generators. His other pet project was to improve the water supply by connecting up with the original piping infrastructure instead of the current arrangement of pumping water from the river Eea to the village tanks. The problem was that he would need to increase massively the pumping capacity which would in turn consume more power. I wondered not for the first time how we would have managed without Adam's skills and know-how. He now headed a competent team of engineers which was a huge asset for the community. I mentioned Brian's intentions and Adam confirmed that he would be happy to continue as deputy if I assumed the role of council chairman but we both agreed that we wanted to bring in some young blood to reduce the council's age structure.

After two pints of the strong ale, I was beginning to feel the effect of drinking on an empty stomach as I had skipped lunch to leave room for the feast. Tempting smells were wafting across from the hog roast, so I decided to investigate whether it was ready. However, I no sooner emerged from the tent than Ian Fernyhough and his wife Lisa collared me to take my turn in the archery final. I had made the cut and the competition was really hotting up. This time I only managed to get two arrows on target, scoring a pathetic 13. Jim Clarke was the winner with an impressive 89 and I made a mental note: next time, finish the archery before the best bitter.

The hog roast was ready. Two of the lads were turning it on a huge spit over a roaring fire and the crackling looked well burnt. I was aware that Emma had had the pig in the largest oven in the bake-house for a number of hours to cook it through and they were using the open fire to finish it off and give it a charcoal taste. There was a pot of stuffing at the side and another of apple sauce, together with a massive sack of large bread buns. A small queue had developed and I took my turn. It was worth waiting for, the best hog roast I had tasted, by a distance. Sajid and the others from Ripley were tucking in and enjoying the hospitality. Wait until they taste Emma's sticky toffee pudding, I thought. That was in the very best traditions of old Cartmel and well worth preserving. There was a separate stall for the sticky toffee and a pan of custard if required. Another stall was serving beef burgers and sausages with a delicious smell of fried onions. Yet another food stall contained a magnificent selection of Emma's famous cakes. They had done us proud.

The children were enjoying the games stalls, old fairground favourites like hoopla, darts and knocking over towers of tins. Jo was busy supervising horse rides for the younger children while Mark was holding baby Lucy. I took my turn with Lucy while he sampled the food. While we circulated the school band struck up a tune which further added to the festive atmosphere.

At seven the main event commenced, the survival pageant. It was performed mainly by the older children, some of the teachers and one or two others. The intention was to act out our story from the beginning. The children had been making costumes and masks for weeks and the anticipation was intense. All other festival activities came to a halt as everybody gathered to watch, including Brian who had just returned. Chris Salt was producer and director, trying to keep calm in the midst of nervous and over-excited children. The first scene was quite chilling as one of the older children, dressed all in black with a skeleton mask represented Death and pursued the panic-stricken younger children. As he wrapped his large black cloak round them, they fell dead. The green was soon littered with bodies and a few weak survivors. A narrator linked the scenes as helpers wheeled on props and the children withdrew to a tent set up as their changing room. The highlight of the programme was the abduction of the girls from Whitewell, their incarceration on Derwent Isle and the efforts of the search party to locate them, followed by a mock battle. The violence was not too graphic in view of the children. Jo's escape and journey home was played largely for laughs as she suffered a series of misfortunes. Jo was played by twelve year old Charlotte Hannah, who was perfect in the role. Charlotte joined our community as a four year old with her mother Linda. She must have been conceived literally weeks before her father died in the epidemic and Linda only discovered she was pregnant after the world had fallen in around her. She had survived in a group of six at a farmhouse near Kendal where we came across them four years later. Charlotte was a very bright girl and jumped at the chance to play Jo. All the children knew the story and were constantly pressing Jo for recollections.

Charlotte acted out the fight with Dale, pretended to get undressed and enter the lake, feigning shock at the freezing water, peered confused at the sky to figure out the stars, tumbled around a mocked up house trying to find her way and hid up a tree pursued by dogs. The "dogs" were three of the youngest children in fluffy costumes. Merrylegs was played by one of her foals, Bella. Best of all was Charlotte careering around on a bicycle before falling off very convincingly and hobbling home supported by a brush.

The audience loved it, especially Jo who was in stitches holding baby Lucy. Jo then disappeared with Mark to settle Lucy down for the night, promising to return for the rest of the festivities.

As dusk fell the bonfire was lit, a huge pyramid of old furniture and kitchen units stripped out of the houses on the periphery of the village. The sparks flew into the air and the fire generated some welcome heat as the evening cooled. The bar tent was then doing a roaring trade. In addition to the New Cartmel Bitter, a fine selection of wines and spirits were on offer and jugs of home-made lemonade. The tent used as a changing room for the pageant became the disco tent with pop music blaring across the village. How Jo was intending to get Lucy to sleep was beyond me.

In the darkness the festive atmosphere was tremendous, the hog roast going strong and the drink flowing freely. It was the best evening in the ten years of New Cartmel.

*

So what does the future hold for New Cartmel? Will our self-sufficiency model stand the test of time? Will our community be large enough to be viable in the long-term? We have lauded our achievements over the last ten years and with some justification and when I think back to our family decision to find a base in the Goyt Valley, then to join the Whitewell group and finally to settle in New Cartmel, I couldn't imagine a more successful outcome. We are safe and secure in a relatively comfortable environment, well fed and with a good skills base perpetuated by an excellent school. These are fine achievements but we cannot pretend that we are truly self-sufficient. We are living in houses constructed in the old world. Our furniture, carpets and curtains were manufactured in the old factories. We replace broken roof tiles with those taken from empty houses. We make our own clothes but using cloth produced years ago in the old textile mills. We have not attempted to make shoes, still relying on ever more difficult foraging. Although we have horses and carts, our principal form of transport remains motor vehicles but for how long can we maintain them and source fuel to run them? Our medical facilities are almost non-existent.

To become truly self-sufficient will present challenges vastly greater than those tackled in the last ten years. This is not to criticise what we have achieved. It would be a nonsense not to take advantage of what we have but eventually there will be no remaining legacy from the old world. Foraging will be at an end as useful supplies are extinguished and the towns and cities return to nature. Our motor vehicles will rust away; our clothes and shoes will wear out. We will not starve, barring catastrophic crop failure or livestock disease, but our real age of self-sufficiency is yet to come and will require a new economic model.

The virus came close to extinguishing the human race. We have survived, just, and are clawing our way back, producing a new generation and equipping them with survival skills, but once the legacy of the old world is stripped away, how far back into history has mankind stepped. The pre-industrial age, clearly, but even in the medieval world internal and international trade generated development, specialisms and small-scale manufacturing. Beyond the odd jar of honey from Ripley or a sack of salt from Great Budworth, using the old Cheshire salt mines, we have nobody with which to trade. A network of self-sufficient communities is a recipe for very low living standards and minimal development. We've estimated the current population of Great Britain at 3000, almost certainly below the level of the Iron Age. From what we hear from abroad, this is not untypical.

Given the chance, we will grow the population, we will expand our communities, we will set up new communities but it will be many, many centuries before a national economy can be rebuilt with towns, factories, hospitals and the infrastructure for trade. We can enjoy our ten year festival and hopefully many more but the struggle for survival has only just begun.

meno
pause
zen

YOUR HOLISTIC ROADMAP TO
RELIEF IN 6 KEY AREAS, INCLUDING
FLUSHES, FATIGUE AND JOINT PAIN

Mahesh V Prabhu BSc